EXIT ADAM

Other Books by James Kilcullen include:

Final Pontiff

The Father of Troy

The Rape of the Rath & The West's Awake

EXIT ADAM

by

James Kilcullen

Literally Publishing Limited

Exit Adam
by
James Kilcullen

Published by James Kilcullen in conjunction with
Literally Publishing Limited
(www.literallypublishing.com)

ISBN 0-9554134-0-0
ISBN 978-0-9554134-0-7

Literally Publishing Limited
The Covert
Main Street
Claydon
Oxfordshire
OX17 1EU
United Kingdom

This book is dedicated to my children and grandchildren – and to all children – in the hope that they may have the opportunity of life.

Preface

It all seemed to go back to Kyoto, but the threat from global warming existed long before that. When the world's leading scientists, and many political leaders, assembled in Kyoto, Japan, in December 1997, Ron Bergin made a point of being there. A young, optimistic, recently appointed Professor of Science at Harvard University he was convinced concerted action would follow. That such a meeting could take place was confirmation in itself that the international community recognised the existence of a major threat and the need to deal with it.

The lead would have to come from the United States; they used more energy than any other country: quantified at one-quarter of the world's entire energy. At that time, 60 percent of US electricity was generated from coal. It was predicted that by 2020, the demand for electricity would increase threefold. Where was it going to come from if not fossil fuels? It was a daunting challenge.

One speaker appealed to the conference: "We know what we must do and it can only be done together – so let's get on with it."

It proved to be more complicated than that. Developing nations put it to the developed countries: "You caused this problem, you put these gases up there; we did not create the problem, so why should we take part in the solution?"

Kyoto was only saved from becoming a total failure by the late arrival of US Vice President, Al Gore, who addressed the delegates:

"The human consequences and economic costs of failing to act are unthinkable: more record floods, droughts, diseases, pests spreading to new areas, crop failure, famines, melting glaciers, stronger storms and rising seas. Our first step should be to set realistic and binding achievable limits. For our part, the US remains firmly committed to a strong, binding target that will reduce our emissions by 30 percent from what they would otherwise be; a commitment as strong as, or stronger than any we have heard here from any country. The imperative here is to do what we promise, rather than to promise what we cannot do."

An agreement was reached that let developing countries off the hook; in the US it required the approval of Congress. When Al Gore returned to Washington, the fossil fuel public relations people – Western Fuels Association Inc – strongly attacked the proposal.

One of its key members, Fred Palmer, commented:

"You can't live your life based on speculation. We know today that using fossil fuels is a good thing; it leads to greater economic growth and allows more people to live longer. CO_2 has been unfairly characterised as a pollutant. CO_2 is a benign gas required for life on Earth: it is not a pollutant. There are no State laws, no Congressional laws that give any agency the right to regulate the use of CO_2.

There is no basis, no mechanism anyone can point to, or look at, to say more CO_2 in the air is going to lead to catastrophic global warming as opposed to mild global warming. It's nothing to be concerned about at all."

One US president was followed by another. President George W Bush refused to sign the Kyoto Protocol – the Senate voted 95 to 0 to reject it. The US Administration shunned negotiations – held in Marrakech, in November 2001 – to revise Kyoto. According to the President, any future measures would have to be voluntary. He ordered the Environmental Protection Agency (EPA) to replace "global warming" with the less ominous "climate change" and issued a national energy policy that foresaw ever more drilling, refining and burning. Under the International Plan for Cleaner Energy, 2001, fossil fuel subsidies would be phased out, and finance for non-polluting energy sources would be increased world-wide. The US was the only country to oppose it.

In 2005 President George W Bush stated that Kyoto was unacceptable because it would cost American jobs. A few months afterwards, Hurricane Katrina – the most devastating to date – hit New Orleans, costing American lives, jobs and billions of dollars.

A US Republican Senator called global warming the "greatest single hoax ever perpetuated on the American people". A US Congressman – who received half a million dollars from the energy lobby for his election campaign – sent belligerent letters to Professor Michael Mann of the University of Virginia and two other scientists, accusing them of "methodological flaws and data errors" in their alarming studies of global warming, and demanding they provide lists of all financial support they received. Kyoto had become a political football.

Marty Hoffert – of New York University – summed up the dilemma:

"The world must stabilise greenhouse gases in the air, at the same time as it's planning to increase energy use by three or four times: the magnitude of the job is massive. If you confront the problem honestly, if you really look at the problem and say, what I want to do is stabilise the amount of carbon dioxide in the atmosphere at some level – twice the pre-industrial CO_2 level – it's almost impossible to do that, unless there's a truly massive transition in the global energy system: away from fossil fuels. That is the bitter pill at the bottom of all these discussions."

If Kyoto was accepted by all, and implemented, faithfully and in full, it would have been just one tiny step in the right direction. Climatologists were very unimpressed by what it could have achieved, but it would have been a start, it could have been built upon. Instead of the US achieving a seven percent reduction on its 1990 emissions, the increase by 2000 was 20 percent.

Henry Jacoby, of MIT – Massachusetts Institute of Technology – was equally concerned:

"It's not so distant; if I have a grandchild today, they will not be as old as I am until 2062. It's not that far away in terms of generations of people that are around. You can care about this issue because of people you know. I think this (global warming) is a very difficult problem and I wouldn't bet we can solve it. I think it is extremely, extremely difficult, but it's worth our effort to work really hard to try to find a way to solve it."

Earth Scientist, James Lovelock, commented:

"What I wish people were frightened about is the carbon dioxide waste. The world produces 25 gigatons every year; this volume of pure gas would cover the whole of the British Isles to a depth of 30 feet; now that is deadly waste. We're at war with the Earth; that's the greatest enemy we've ever known, and we're all of us in it.

Some time during this century, we will pass a threshold level of carbon dioxide in the atmosphere, which is somewhere in the region of 500 parts per million. When we pass that threshold, the system is then committed to change, and nothing we do after that will make the slightest difference. It will move, of its own accord, into a state much warmer – much hotter – than we've ever experienced."

A whole new, very destructive phenomenon was discovered, but only verified towards the end of the 20th Century. It would become known as "global dimming". In the 1950s, biologist Dr Gerard Stanhill, working on Israeli water irrigation schemes, measured the level of solar radiation, which determines how much water crops require. He repeated his measurements in the 1980s, and was astonished to find a reduction of 22 percent in sunlight. There was nothing wrong with the Sun; the problem had to be here on Earth. His findings were greeted with disbelief by world scientists, with good reason: the Earth was actually getting warmer.

In Germany, Dr Beate Liepert, of the Lamont-Doherty Earth Observatory, carried out similar tests over the Bavarian Alps, with similar results. Independently of each other, they researched solar radiation, temperature charts and meteorological statistics around the world. Their results were astonishing: between 1950 and the 1990s, solar energy had reduced by nine percent in Antarctica, ten percent in the US, 30 percent in Russia, and 16 percent in Britain.

In Australia, biologists Professor Graham Farquhar and Dr Michael Roderick, of the Australian National University, checked the pan evaporation rate, to see how much water needed to be added to a pan, to bring up the level to the point it was at on the previous morning. This procedure has been carried out by scientists for over 100 years all over the world, every day, using the same instruments. Results were evaluated over long periods. In the 1990s the ongoing fall in the evaporation rate was duly recorded. On a global scale, this fall matched the drop in sunlight.

Research carried out over a four-year period in the northern Maldive Islands, by Professor Veerabhadran Ramanathan, of the University of California, showed that in generating energy we put visible pollution – tiny particles of ash, soot, sulphur dioxide, nitrates, and other pollutants – into the atmosphere. This pollution lodges in the clouds, turns them into giant mirrors that reflect more light back into space, and prevents the heat of the Sun getting through.

After 9/11, in Madison, Dr David Travis of the University of Wisconsin had a unique, if unfortunate opportunity, to study the alteration in temperature when virtually all aircraft were grounded. During those three days he compiled figures from 48 American States – in the absence of vapour trails – seeking to establish the temperature range between high day and low night. During that time the temperature range rose by more than 1 degree Celsius: a huge increase in such a short period.

Global dimming is a killer: it causes respiratory diseases in humans and the haze over our cities. It alters rainfall patterns and probably caused the 1984 famine in Ethiopia. Dr Leon Rotstayn, of CSIRO Atmospheric Research, believes it's poised to strike again. Should it affect the Asian monsoon, billions of people will be at risk. We have to cut down or eliminate global dimming. Some progress has already been made by burning more cleanly, using scrubbers in power stations, catalytic converters in cars and low-sulphur fuels.

But there's a catch: in offsetting much of the rise in the Earth's temperature, global dimming has masked the rapid rise of carbon dioxide in the atmosphere. Dr Peter Cox – Hadley Centre, Meteorological Office – pointed out that scientists were projecting a 5-degree-Celsius increase in Earth's temperature by the year 2100: this has now been revised to 10 degrees.

"In the far north, a 10-degree warming might be enough to release a vast natural store of greenhouse gas – bigger than all the oil and coal resources of the planet. We would be in danger of destabilising substances called methane hydrates, which store a lot of methane at the bottom of the ocean in a kind of frozen form, and are known to be destabilised by warming. Should this happen (evidence first appeared in 2005 that the permafrost underneath the western Siberian peat-lands is thawing), 10,000 billion tons of methane – a greenhouse gas eight times stronger than carbon dioxide – would be released into the atmosphere. There would be no way back from there: the world would quickly spin out of control."

In 2005 there were a record 26 hurricanes in the Caribbean; beating the previous record of 21 in 1933. The ten warmest years on record have all occurred since 1994. Satellite images have revealed that – in the summer of 2005 – there was 20 percent less ice around the North Pole than 30 years previously. There are serious concerns about the long-term future of the polar bear.

An international meeting in Montreal towards the end of 2005 – hailed as a great success – ended with an agreement to keep talking. Subsequently, the major powers agreed to tackle the problem without eliminating the use of fossil fuels. One day – probably within the next 100 years – the world's stock of fossil fuels will be exhausted. The struggle for control of diminishing supplies has already started. Armageddon will come long before EE – Energy Exhaustion – day. The few who may survive will be living in caves.

It was a day like no other; a day on which – in a horrific manner – the sands of time were running out: it was the second Wednesday of July in the year 2040. The giant interstate rig powered its way west of Boston on the Mass Pike under the heat of the noonday sun. For many years it had made the trip once a week, delivering auto spares from DMD Inc. – Detroit Motor Distributors – to the Boston agents, and returning with new tyres. José Carvallo checked his cruise-speed control, lit another cigarette, turned up the music channel on his cab radio and tried not to think about the future. Eight years doing this run; he knew every mile of the road – not that the job bored him; he loved the controlled roar of the powerful engine beneath his feet that responded readily to his will. Well clear of Boston, the traffic was much lighter now.

This would be his last run. DMD was going out of business; the whole damn country was closing down. World Auto – which included GM, Ford, Mercedes, BMW, Toyota, Volkswagen and all the other major motor manufacturers – was still in Chapter 11 with no prospect of ever trading again. Why? Gas. With ever-increasing scarcity in oil supplies and the horrendous costs of finding new oil fields, the price of gas had forced a major fall-off in auto purchases. DMD had survived longer than most corporations because the demand for parts had held up well until now. Two wars had already been fought over oil finds in South Africa and Venezuela.

And it wasn't just gas: tyre manufacturers, steel and aluminium works, computer designers for the auto industry, electrical suppliers, upholsterers, windscreen manufacturers, most retail dealers and gas stations – gone. With millions unemployed, the ongoing effects rocketed through the economies: consumer spending down sharply, giving rise to even further unemployment. And all the time food prices just kept on rising. The experts still maintained more oil would be found, particularly under the Atlantic: it would require time and new technologies to bring it ashore – so they said. No-one believed them.

In the meantime, industry was demanding priority at the expense of domestic electricity users who, if lucky, could expect to have power for two or three hours a day. Major power failures were commonplace. There had been a 16-hour failure in the Boston region the previous week, with 50 people killed in the ensuing looting and rioting. There were no media reports; José learned about it in Boston. There had been similar riots in Detroit – and most probably in hundreds of other places – but no-one wanted to know. There was talk now about rationing energy.

Daytime Boston was like Chicago in the thirties: three heavily-armed gangs were fighting for control of the city; gun battles in the city streets were commonplace now. Despite the fact that all business premises were protected by armed guards, millions of dollars were stolen daily – mostly from the banks – and the number of fatalities kept rising. The police couldn't cope. The National Guard was deployed a few days earlier, and there was talk about bringing in the Marines.

He would not see Louisa Grossan again – the attractive little checker he had spent the night with. Big, powerfully built and very lean, he couldn't help it if women liked him; he was only 34, rugged-looking with swarthy features and smouldering blue eyes. He first met her two years earlier, shortly after she joined the company; finding her busily checking in his load, he remarked with a smile: 'Louisa, you got the cutest ass I've ever seen.'

His roving eyes lit up while he admired her very shapely figure, jet-black hair, fair complexion and the humorous – even mischievous – expression in her big brown eyes. Over her black jeans, she wore a white silk blouse that failed to conceal her firm thrusting breasts. She put down her calculator, stood before him, looked up into his eyes and smiled.

'And what are you going to do about it?'

He smiled at the memory. Christmas was coming early!

'Maybe we could have a pizza, or a curry, later – when you're finished here?'

She grinned up at him. 'Maybe we could have more; meet me over at Jake's Diner in Quincy at six.'

She didn't want to be seen leaving the job with him.

They met at Jake's and afterwards went to her tidy little apartment nearby. She was something else, couldn't get enough of it: he stayed that night and most Tuesday nights ever since. It was a marvellous lay-over. He was surprised to hear she was studying accountancy and expected to qualify as a CPA. She did take him to task once about his job.

'Are you going to spend the rest of your life driving a rig?'

'I love my job; I get to see the country and when I retire I'll set up an auto repair shop,' he pointed out. 'The pay is not so bad and it has its moments – like now when I get to be with you.'

He wondered if she entertained anyone else when he wasn't there, but didn't ask. He didn't tell her that when he was four years old, he used climb up on an old chair in their grotty little apartment in downtown Detroit to watch the gigantic rigs thundering past on the freeway below. He had promised himself that when he grew up, he would drive one of those mighty machines.

And he didn't tell her about Elvira Portman: five, or was it six years earlier, when he was seriously delayed by a bad accident up ahead, he decided to spend the night in the trailer caravan park at the Lake Side Roadhouse near Schenectady. He'd heard about it from Gomez, but had never been there. The large, sprawling single-storied diner, built of the finest pinewood, sat on high ground overlooking Lake Mohag – the finest trout-fishing lake in the area. There was a row of twin-roomed chalets on either side of the big diner. Parking the rig, he decided to have something to eat and watch telly, if there was any, before settling down for the night.

The diner was busy; he wasn't the only one getting off the Pike. He took a seat at the counter where three women were serving. Immediately, a very attractive-looking, full-figured woman, with deep brown eyes, approached and smiled.

'What can I get you?'

She had a very friendly smile and was quite a mixture, with beautiful tanned skin and frizzy brown hair. He learned later, her father was Jamaican Thai, her mother white American, but she was only sure about her mother. She was a rare blend of beauty, and apparently the boss here.

'Bacon, eggs and French fries, please.'

Food was still in good supply then.

'Anything to drink?'

'A beer.'

He dined slowly and, as the diner emptied, she came back to him.

'Haven't seen you here before?'

'I do Detroit Boston every week; usually spend Wednesday night at Luke's place.'

She smiled. 'You should spend it here. I'll fix you up with a nice chalet.'

Her clinging beige dress accentuated her perfect figure.

'You are one lovely lady.'

'Thank you. Please call me Elvira. I'll get you a key.'

She took the key to 202 – a very comfortable chalet at the far end of the complex – from a drawer under the counter. He would learn later that she lived in 201, which had a communicating door.

Handing him the key, she smiled. 'I'll come over to see if you're comfortable after a while, and I'll bring a bottle.' She looked at her watch. 'The electricity will be going off in about 20 minutes; we're down to eight hours a day now. The generator only operates here in the main building.'

He grinned as he rose. 'I guess we'll just have to get by in the dark.'

'That won't be a problem.'

It was a warm summer evening. Going to 202, a pinewood chalet overlooking the lake, he stripped and lay on the bed; he must have dozed off; the sound of the connecting door opening roused him. Elvira entered quietly, dressed in a pink negligee, carrying a bottle of Jack Daniels. Getting up, he stood before her. The negligee seemed to drop away of its own accord; before him, in the half-light, stood this lovely, tanned, nude figure of a goddess. She put aside the bottle, moved closer, stroked his lean hard body and looked up into his eyes. He took her in his arms. Later, much later, he poured two glasses of whiskey. They shared a cigarette, sipped the whiskey and basked – for a few moments – in the light of a passing moonbeam.

He was in awe. 'Elvira, you are so beautiful.'

She smiled. 'I like a man who knows how to tango. You are my dream man, so big, strong and gentle. I knew it the minute you walked into the diner.'

She noticed he was still randy and began to stroke him again.

'I also like a man who wants more.'

It was the first of many wonderful nights; they became friends as well as lovers.

Five years earlier, she told him, she came to work there for Mark Portman. Although nearly twice her age – she was only 28 – he asked her to marry him; she accepted and was loyal and faithful to him. The older of two sons, Mark, left home at 17 to work on the building sites in Boston. His father operated a successful boat hire business on the lake. Having saved his money, Mark returned and bought the roadhouse, constructed new chalets, extended the trailer park and built up a very good business. A big man with craggy features and a raucous sense of humour, he was very popular in the area. His younger brother, Reggie, inherited the boat hire business from their father. He was jealous of his successful older brother, and, as time went by, there was little contact between them. She was devastated when Mark died suddenly.

Being, as she said herself of "no race and every race" she was brought up by her single, alcoholic mother who died – from an overdose – when she was 12. Four years in care toughened her; she learned to stand up for herself. She loved her unfortunate mother, but she wasn't going to end up like her.

But she was worried. Reggie Portman was challenging his brother's will in the courts. She never had any time for the ill-tempered, mean-faced younger brother who always ignored her. He maintained she exercised undue influence over her husband: in fact, she had no idea he had even made a will. Her lawyer told her not to worry, but she did just the same. Her brother-in-law had influence in the area, and she would be appearing before a white judge. Having failed to intimidate her, he had finally put the case down for hearing.

***

Turning off the Pike, José took the road to Forest Springs up in the hills. It would soon be time for his midday break. He loved this part of the country when its fields were green and tall birch trees decorated the hills above the town. That was years ago, now everything was burned a dark shade of brown.

Time to ring home. He dialled his wife's work number and was put through to her.

'Maria, my love, how are you?'

She sounded angry. 'We had more riots here last night. What are you going to do for work?'

'I'll get a job as a security man: all the big stores are employing armed guards.'

'I don't like it. Several people were shot last night.'

'We have to live. How are the kids?'

'They're fine. I'm keeping them in at night.'

'Talk to you tomorrow.' He hung up.

Old and worn out before his time, his father, Pablo, worked as an office cleaner, but he didn't complain; life was better here than back in the old country. His mother, Annie, worked in a laundry and helped out at home in her spare time. When he married Maria, a very shapely brunette, with hazel eyes – manager of a local fashion outlet – it seemed right that his parents should live with them, and besides, Pablo helped out with the rent.

On Friday nights he usually watched TV, or took Pablo for a drink in the Latino boozer nearby, while Maria tidied up the apartment for the weekend. Their teenage children Antonio (15) and Ella (12) had their own friends. He tried to see as much of them as he could at weekends. From now on he would see them every day. Antonio, tall and lean, was already a noted basketball player and planned to turn professional when he left college; Ella wanted to be a nurse. Maria lost all interest in sex after Ella was born.

When José left school, he got a job as a trainee mechanic in the city's biggest commercial motor works – MCC – owned by Manuel Cortes, a rough diamond who built the business up from an old shed on a disused site. José liked the work, quickly learned to diagnose engine problems by computer and carry out speedy and efficient repairs. Manuel doubled his wages at the end of year one. But he wasn't satisfied: he wanted to become a full-time driver, and enrolled for an advanced driver's course.

He smiled to himself when he thought about it now. His driving instructor was Rosa Largas, a very sexy dark-haired Cuban, with blue eyes and a comfortably rounded well-endowed figure, ten years his senior and currently between husbands. Learning to drive the big rigs wasn't a problem; sitting beside Rosa was. He couldn't but be randy, when close to her. In his daydreams, he visualised himself fondling her ample breasts, tearing off her clothes and making violent love to her. Such are daydreams! Cheerful and outgoing, she usually dressed in a tight fitting yellow or white top, over blue jeans, and was in the habit of touching his hand on the steering column, or placing it gently on his knee. And the whiff of her seductive perfume!

One day, she directed him to a large trailer park where he spent an hour practising reversing the rig – easily the most difficult manoeuvre to master. It was a very hot day in June. Satisfied he had done well, he asked if he could drive back to the depot.

'No,' she smiled sweetly, 'my apartment is nearby. Let's go and have a cool drink first.'

He locked the cab, and walked with her through two narrow streets to a modern, high-rise apartment block. They entered, and took the elevator to the top floor, a tidy three-roomed apartment, tastefully furnished. His heart began to beat a little faster.

'José, help yourself to a beer from the cold box while I change into something cool.'

'Thanks, Rosa.'

She disappeared into the bedroom. He took out a can of beer, opened it and gulped down a mouthful, wondering what happens now. Moments later, she called out from the room.

'José, bring me a beer.'

'Sure.'

Taking a can out of the cold box, he walked towards the room. As he pushed in the door, his eyes opened wide; he couldn't believe what he was seeing! She was standing facing him, smiling seductively in a see-through negligee.

'You've been wanting it for long enough.'

He undressed quickly; she moved closer, her negligee slipped off her shoulders. He put his arms around her and she pulled him towards the bed.

'My goodness, you have a big Tom,' she murmured.

If there's a heaven, this must be it, he thought. She wrapped her legs around him and moaned with delight; all his daydreams were coming true. It was only the beginning: three hours later, they showered, dressed and returned the rig to the depot. It became a regular weekly date until he graduated and moved on to work for a trucking company. He heard afterwards, she'd married again and gone to live in Chicago. For him, that first day was the one he remembered most; it was the day he came of age; it was the day he learned he had a big Tom.

Taking out his cell phone again, he punched in Elvira's number.

'Lake Side Roadhouse,' she sounded bored.

'Elvira, my love.'

Her voice softened immediately.

'José, am I glad to hear from you. What time will you be here?'

'About six. I got some candles and a few batteries. Everything OK?'

'It will be when you get here. I'll have a tasty meal ready for you.'

That would be very welcome. Every Thursday morning, she handed him a bag full of potatoes, carrots, onions and apples, to take home with him. Grown locally, they were still in good supply.

'See you, my love.' He rang off.

He really liked Elvira: it wasn't just the sex, although that was great too. On fine evenings, they sometimes walked or sat by the lake and talked. She was interested in him as a man, not just a shag, and let him know he was the only man in her life. He hadn't told her yet that this was his last run. He would have to find some way of visiting her from time to time.

Approaching the town, he saw the familiar sign "Forest Springs – Pop 1,023". In his eight years calling here, the population, apparently, hadn't changed. Reducing speed, he eased the rig quietly down the long, wide – typical small town American – Main Street with its loud, multi-coloured shops and offices. A little, white wooden church with a bell tower was set well back behind the car park.

He headed for Pedro's Diner at the far end. The town appeared to be unusually quiet. A few small cars were parked along the sidewalk: "BCs" they called them – baby cars. He couldn't remember when he last saw an SUV on the highway; there were reports some time back of people shooting at them. The odd Mercedes or BMW that he saw from time to time carried armed guards.

Pulling into the parking area, he was pleased to see the diner was still operating. In Boston and Detroit diners were disappearing like flies in the fall. Getting down from the cab, he was hit by a blast of hot air. Checking, to be sure he had locked up securely and put on the alarm, he headed for the diner. Even in a small town like this you can't be too careful.

The diner was half full. He took a seat at the counter beside a flabby-looking older man who ignored his greeting. A radio blared loud music. The attractive blonde behind the counter didn't return his smile. Anne was usually very friendly; in fact, she came on to him a few times. When she leaned forward to pour coffee, she showed off her two most attractive assets. He didn't really fancy her.

'What will it be?' she demanded tersely.

'The usual, Anne.'

'What's that?'

'Hamburger, eggs, French fries and coffee.'

'We have only eggs and French fries,' she snapped.

'Whatever.'

She must have had a bad night. As she approached the kitchen hatch, he looked around him. There was an air of tension; diners ate in silence; the man beside him never spoke. Pedro, the chef and owner – usually very affable – made some sarcastic remark to Anne. He filled a glass of water while he waited. It was eerie – he wouldn't hang around here.

Anne put his dish before him without comment. He tucked in with little relish; his thoughts were still on Elvira. Close as they were, he didn't tell her about Louisa. It was best not to; she mightn't take kindly to him shacking up with a white woman. Louisa was different: with her it was strictly physical. She was really scared now, having witnessed an armed robbery – in which five people died – the previous day. He always made a point of showering before he left Boston on the return journey; it was uncanny how women can always pick up the scent of another woman. Friday mornings, he showered too, although he didn't think Maria would notice.

Just as he was finishing, the man beside him accidentally spilled some coffee on the man sitting next to him. The offended one – a lightly built young man in a dirty black tee-shirt – pulled out a gun and blew the man's brains out. Blood splattered into José's coffee and on to his clean white tee-shirt. The victim fell off the stool. Anne leaned over the counter and plunged a carving knife into the shooter's chest. José sat there, stunned: staring blankly at his bloody coffee, unable to take it in. Bloody hell, things like this only happen on TV.

It was like some kind of weird signal, the cataclysmic bursting of a dam: suddenly, everyone was attacking the one nearest to them, with knives, forks, anything they could lay their hands on; some produced guns and started shooting wildly. Anne attacked Pedro through the hatch; he leaned forward and plunged a long carving knife into her chest. No-one screamed in anger or pain; they uttered low, animal-like grunting sounds.

All José knew, was that he had to get the hell out of there, and fast. Everything appeared to be happening in slow motion. He turned to leave; a wild-looking white woman came at him with a knife; he grabbed her wrist and lashed out with his fist. She collapsed in a heap. A man jumped on his back; he threw him off, and, as he hit the floor, lashed out viciously with his boot. Instinct took over; terror galvanised him.

He climbed over two bodies before he made it to the door. Dashing into the open, he raced for his cab. Shots rang out behind him; he could feel bullets whizzing past his head; crying, screaming and gasping, he pulled the keys out of his pocket; his hands were shaking so badly he dropped them on the ground. When he stooped down to retrieve them, two bullets hit the door of the rig.

Somehow, he managed to get the door opened, and started to climb up into the cab. He felt a sharp sting in his left leg, just above the ankle. He screamed in agony. He was shot, but he had to keep going. Falling into the cab, he pulled the door shut behind him and tried to put the key in the ignition. He had to hold his right hand steady with his left. Looking down, he watched in horror while the gunman approached, eyes glazed over, shooting wildly; then, he was shot down by another madman, who appeared in front of the rig and started shooting at him.

José gunned the engine into life; a bullet crashed through the windscreen just missing his head. Putting the engine in gear, he didn't hesitate; the rig leaped forward and ran down his assailant. Despite the agonising pain in his leg, he screamed in triumphant hysteria as he pulled out on to the highway. They were still pouring out of the diner in an orgy of mass slaughter.

Then, he saw it wasn't just the diner; it was the same everywhere. On the sidewalk, a young attractive-looking woman pulled a baby out of her wheeler, and started to strangle her; an older woman approached her from behind, split her head open with a small axe, and then axed the baby. It was horrific; there was blood everywhere. A man ran through the baby killer with a screwdriver; two women tackled him with knives; when he collapsed, they went for one another.

José could hear the sound of shots coming from all sides now; he couldn't reach under his seat to get his own gun. A youngish man ran into the centre of the road and started firing at him. José put his foot down and drove straight over him. Shops and houses were burning; cars were crashing into one another, exploding in flames; people with clothes on fire were attacking one another with knives and hammers. As he reached the end of Main Street, an old grey Chevy was driven straight at him; it was kill, or be killed: he drove straight over it.

Screaming in agony, he tried to use his handkerchief as a tourniquet, but it wasn't very successful; a pool of blood was forming on the floor. A motorcycle cop rode up quickly from behind, firing as he drew level with the cab; José pulled on the wheel; his attacker and his cycle disappeared under the trailer.

He was leaving a scene from hell where he was forced to kill five or six human beings; he'd lost count. His mind kept telling him this can't be real, it's a nightmare; but it was real.

He was bawling like a child. As he headed towards the Mass Pike, he adjusted the tourniquet as best he could. He was beginning to feel weak, but he had to keep going. Eventually – after what seemed like an eternity – the giant rig lurched on to the Mass Pike. The pool of blood under his feet was getting bigger; he was beginning to feel sick, and knew he had to get to a doctor. Alerted by the sound of a police siren, he looked in his rear view mirror: a state police patrol car was signalling him to stop. His first instinct was to stop and reverse over it. They weren't shooting. Too weak to think straight, he pulled over and stopped.

The police car pulled in behind. One of the cops came forward. He didn't appear to be threatening. When he came level with the cab, saw the bullet holes in the door, and the front of the rig covered in blood, he pulled his gun. José unwound the window.

Seeing the gun, he screamed. 'Please, don't shoot.'

The cop, a youngish stern-looking man, stood back.

'Climb down, slowly now; keep your hands in sight.'

José opened the door and started to descend. Half way down, he muttered 'Forest Springs,' collapsed and knew no more.

***

Feeling old, tired and depressed, Professor Ronald Bergin waited to board the European Airways flight at Zurich airport. Seventy-four, and in failing health, his once trim figure was now flabby, his hair grey and complexion sallow: there was little fire left in his steel-blue eyes. Dressed in a light-grey suit, with a white shirt and maroon tie, he looked much better than he felt. Scheduled to fly to Las Vegas, en route to his home in the desert, he received an urgent phone call from Governor Carney asking him to come directly to Boston.

His best efforts had failed: the clever spin-doctors and their political masters had done a good job. "Ron Bergin, a brilliant scientist, climatologist and environmental expert, sure, but an alarmist. You know how it is with some of those academic guys; author of a few books on global warming, he's come to believe his own fiction. He's got a bee in his bonnet and just won't let go; we've got our own experts: they know better."

Only now, they were also saying. “He’s been at it for the past 40 years and we’re still here.”

He picked up a copy of the previous day’s *Herald Tribune*. Most of the front page was devoted to another rise in the price of oil: for the first time in history the price of a barrel of crude exceeded 1,000 dollars, sending shock waves around the world and precipitating a fall of 20 percent in world stock markets. Analysts rushed to soothe investors’ nerves, pointing out an expected early return to 750 dollars a barrel.

The Middle-Eastern repressive military dictator, Hassan Hussein – ruler of Iraq, Iran, Kuwait and Saudi Arabia – was merely flexing his muscles. In 2030, Iran’s 50-year-old dictator took advantage of serious civil commotion in Iraq – instigated by his supporters – to extend his rule there. He bided his time and played off China and America against one another, while rapidly expanding his own armed forces. Taking advantage of the bitterly contested US election in ‘36, he annexed the other oil-producing countries before anyone could move against him. Sitting on two-thirds of the world’s rapidly depleting oil, he abolished OPEC and consolidated the marketing of all Middle East oil through ARAMCO.

A very clever man, he met increasing demand for oil with reduced supplies. He always promised to increase supplies – even did so temporarily – before reverting to his old ways. Delegations from the major powers rushed to Teheran to plead for increased production. He greeted them most affably, made his usual promises and sent them away happy.

America’s main source of oil – Alaska – was being depleted so quickly it would run dry within another ten years. In desperation, it invaded and took over the oil wells of Venezuela – ignoring international outcry. There was no way America could invade the Middle East: China would not allow it. Hussein would just have to be removed; two CIA-inspired assassination attempts had failed. He blamed America and quickly dealt with the subordinate groomed to replace him.

Hassan wanted two things: to humiliate America, and to greatly increase his shareholdings in some of the world’s biggest companies. Increasing the price of oil gradually, would cause sufficient economic instability to – effectively – give him world dominance; but it would have to be finely balanced to avoid a major economic collapse.

The myopic dictator did not see the other players out there, plotting and planning world dominance for themselves; Ron did. For nearly 20 years, his secret information-gathering centre near Lugano received details of all kinds of human activities throughout the world. Through his network of hired-out robots, many in highly sensitive areas, he had been receiving information that governments would kill for – if only they knew the extent of the operation. He did not pass on any information to the US, where he had been persona non grata at the White House for many years, or to any other government: the US would not believe anything not uncovered by their own CIA anyway.

Before he left CosmosRX – his secret underground data centre near Lugano – Ron had spent hours examining reports received by his colleagues. He had known for many years that the world's biggest and fastest growing economy, China, had a massive energy problem: oil. They invested enormous sums in hydroelectricity – to little avail. Increasing hurricanes – and pollution caused by flooding – clogged up the dams with sludge and forced the closure of thousands of generators. Their coal mines would be exhausted within the next 20 years.

The Chinese Government made a momentous decision, in order to prevent a massive downturn in their living standards. If they couldn't buy enough oil, they would just have to take it. It was obvious to them that Hassan was playing games. Some oil was received from Russia, India, South Africa and Malaysia, but not nearly enough. With their own growing economies – and falling reserves – these countries had already had to seriously reduce their exports.

Some years earlier, China had sent a small team of specially-trained commandos to the oil-producing countries in the Middle East. They infiltrated the many local dissident organisations, supplied money and weapons and quietly made plans to remove the existing regime. In the meantime, the Chinese fleet was enlarged and ten aircraft carriers added. A motorised army of 50 divisions was mobilised at Koran near the border with Afghanistan.

Ron had now received the final details. In two weeks – with the tacit approval of India and Russia – Afghanistan would be invaded without warning. China would announce it was doing so to wipe out the poppy growers who were flooding the world with heroin. In a massive invasion, they would destroy the poppy fields, and move their fighters and bombers to airports in the western provinces. Missile silos in western China, already on full alert, would only be activated if necessary. At the same time, their mighty fleet, with 150,000 troops on board, would sail into the Indian Ocean as part of a naval exercise!

Now, several things would happen together: the dissidents in the Middle East would move to eliminate Hassan and take over the capital cities, the army in Afghanistan would advance quickly through the mountains into Iran, paratroopers would be dropped in the environs of major cities and oil installations, and the fleet would sail into the Gulf with all haste and start deploying troops. There was no way America could take them on unless they used their nuclear arsenal.

There was considerable resentment in certain sections of the American elite at the election – in '36 – of America's first black President, Elmer Harten. A Republican, he was now running for re-election against a very charismatic Democrat – Latino candidate, Pedro Rodregas. Following the abolition of the Mexican border, Latinos now made up 40 percent of the US population.

General Roderick Edward Jackson, Chairman of the Joint Chiefs in Washington, was particularly incensed at the very idea of a black President, and that he was likely to be followed by a Latino. A handsome, popular, military leader – at 53 – the General masterminded the invasion and occupation of Cuba, Venezuela and Panama. An all-American hero, he was talked about as a future presidential candidate. He was astute enough to know the days of white presidents were over.

Supported by some of America's wealthy businessmen, he decided to act to restore the dominance of white America. This could only be achieved by a military dictatorship. The other Joint Chiefs were on side, as well as most of the General Staff. The few who refused to join this conspiracy suffered unfortunate accidents.

With the Army behind him, it would be a simple task: deploy a small force of Marines around the White House, eliminate the President and the members of both Houses of Congress, declare an emergency, and move troops into the major cities to keep order. It would be a popular revolt. The people were thoroughly fed up with the present inept administration. The General needed an excuse: he would probably opt for the emergency caused by the oil crisis to justify his action.

On page six of the *Tribune*, Ron finally found a short, well-written, carefully-worded report on the Forest Springs disaster. Described as a serious outbreak of typhoid, possibly caused by terrorism, it played down the number of casualties. He knew it was neither typhoid nor terrorism, he also knew what it was: that knowledge only further increased his dismay.

Taking his seat in the near-empty first class compartment, he swallowed two pills and chased them with a glass of water. His two bodyguards sat quietly three rows behind him. He declined the stewardess's offer of champagne with a polite smile. She apologised for the in-flight service: despite her best efforts she could only get a few sandwiches and chocolate, but she had plenty of coffee. Before leaving Lugano, he was handed a food parcel for the journey.

A very attractive-looking, tan-coloured Euro-Asian, she seemed anxious to talk.

'It has taken me a long time to get used to the fact that our captain and first officer are robots.'

Supplied by his organisation.

'But they are highly trained?'

'Oh, yes, thank goodness. Two weeks ago, approaching Manchester, we found ourselves flying blind when a ferocious electric storm knocked out our control computer in Croydon. The captain took over, diverted to Dublin and landed safely 40 minutes later. I feel a lot safer now.' She paused as a bell sounded. 'I'd better take my seat for take off.'

When the giant aircraft reached cruising speed, the captain welcomed them aboard. "Because of precipitation along our route we will be flying at 60,000 feet. Sit back and enjoy the flight."

As flight EA64 flew north of Inverness, Ron's thoughts were interrupted.

"Ladies and gentlemen, this is the captain speaking. Due to a major electrical blackout in the north-eastern States, we are diverting to Montreal; the grid managers hope to restore supply within 12 hours. I apologise for the inconvenience caused."

Another power breakdown: looters would appear, as if from nowhere, to take whatever they could carry, burn what they couldn't, and fight pitched battles with the National Guard. Last time there were more than 300 casualties – many of them innocent residents. Fortunately, Sandi was at their home in the desert, near Las Vegas. Long predicted – long ignored: increasing demand for electricity – near static supply. As he had pointed out many times: electricity was the Achilles' heel of modern civilisation.

The captain's voice interrupted his thoughts.

"Charleston, South Carolina has just been hit by another hurricane, which the Met people describe as the most devastating one ever recorded. It is hoped, that by the time it reaches Washington DC, it will have eased to a tropical storm. Make yourselves comfortable, we will get you to Boston Worcester as quickly as possible."

The hostess served coffee; he declined the offer of a sandwich preferring to have one of his own. With little to do, she stayed to talk.

'This must be our tenth major blackout this year. We got caught up in the really bad one in Hong Kong in January; it was horrific; people trapped in the subways, traffic chaos; the airport had to close. We were on the 15th floor of the Skyway Hotel. The staff spent hours releasing people trapped in the elevators; many collapsed and several old people died. Worst of all, was the looters – they were like animals. The police started shooting them, and some returned fire. We heard afterwards that there were hundreds of casualties. I've never been so frightened in my life.'

'How long did it last?' he inquired.

'Twenty-six hours. I shudder to think what would have happened if it went on for another day.'

She paused. 'Can I get you a coffee, sir?'

'Just a glass of water, please.'

She lowered her voice. 'The captain told me there's another hurricane – an even bigger one – filling south of Cuba.'

He smiled reassuringly. There was no point in telling her this was only the beginning. She resumed her duties. He sat back and pondered: how did the people of this world with all their intelligence, knowledge, sophistication and technology fail to prevent this headlong rush towards oblivion?

***

In his first book entitled *Our Sacred Trust* Ron outlined the rapid rise of carbon dioxide (CO_2) in the atmosphere since the beginning of the industrial revolution: one-third more than pre-Industrial Revolution levels, more than for 55 million years; enough to melt all of the ice on the planet and submerge many of its greatest cities.

An ice-free Arctic Ocean would reflect back out to space significantly less of the incoming solar radiation, thereby having the potential to enhance the very global warming that had created the problem in the first place. When the Greenland ice cap goes, sea levels will rise by about 20 feet. When Antarctica melts – the land-based most southerly continent, with millions of years of ice and snow – sea levels will rise by 250 feet or more.

During the 20th Century the Earth's temperature rose by 0.6 degrees Celsius; an increase of 1 or perhaps 1.5 degrees during the 21st Century would cause problems, but should be sustainable. It now appeared to be heading for at least 5 or 6 degrees: that would be catastrophic. Alternative sources of energy must be found, and quickly.

Finally, he pleaded with all world governments, to take urgent action, to manage this problem while there was still time.

***

Ronald Joseph Bergin was born in Orange County, California in 1966, the only child of Joseph and Nancy Bergin. The family lived in a modern, comfortable two-storied house overlooking Dana Point. His father was District Attorney, before being appointed to the Appellate Court in Los Angeles. Much older than his wife, Joseph was very reserved, and deeply committed to his career. Nancy Bergin was a tall attractive, no nonsense blonde, with deep blue eyes. A computer software designer, she trained in Silicon Valley before starting her own business.

A close-knit family, Nancy was the outgoing, chatty one; she was also the boss, and didn't spoil her son. Every year they travelled abroad on vacation. By the time Ron was 16 years old, they had visited some of the most interesting places in the world, including the Great Wall of China. Such a massive and unique structure, built at the cost of thousands of lives, and yet, it didn't keep out the enemy. At home, Joseph and two of his friends sailed regularly out around the Catalinas. Ron joined them occasionally, but quickly realised that bouncing around in the ocean wasn't for him; he took up golf.

He didn't always agree with his father's views. The post-Vietnam War era was a very divisive time in America, and Joseph firmly believed that America should never have become involved. It ended in ignominious defeat and – in total – cost more than four million lives, 58,000 of which were Americans. That defeat should have enhanced the spread of Communism: it didn't; it had no effect whatsoever on world history then or since. Years later, he would come to realise that his father was right. America hadn't learned anything from that debacle.

As he progressed through school he became interested in science, physics and climatology; he registered as a science student at Berkeley University, and sailed through his exams without any difficulty, much to the joy of his proud parents. He was devastated when his father died suddenly, shortly before he graduated – just as they were becoming really close. He missed his company, reassuring presence and encouragement.

Mother smiled bravely through a very difficult Graduation Day, and afterwards immersed herself in her work; he went on to do his masters, and was appointed one of the science lecturers at Harvard, where he subsequently became Professor. Although flattered regularly by some of his female students, he made a point of not getting involved. He saw too much of that in Berkeley; it only served to increase the divorce rate.

His ban didn't include tutors. When Anika Hepper, recently arrived from Sweden, was appointed History lecturer, he fell deeply in love with her – a tall shapely blonde, with fair skin and deep blue eyes, she was a real beauty. He invited her to dinner, she accepted. He couldn't believe his luck! Two weeks later, she moved into his bachelor apartment in Cambridge. Their lovemaking was perfect, although he suspected she was more experienced than he. They ate in all the best restaurants, did the rounds of the theatres, and flew out to Los Angeles and Hawaii for long weekend breaks. He asked her to marry him; she accepted, but deferred it for the present; perhaps they should visit with her family in Sweden? Certainly, but not yet.

Two months later, he was astonished when she told him she had accepted a job as a model, and was leaving the university. She moved out and soon became the hottest property on the East Coast. Hurt as he was, he watched with bemusement while she married one of the latest young Hollywood studs. It was the first of many. He realised, ruefully that he had been in love with a dream, but never regretted it.

When doing his masters, he chose for his thesis a study of global warming. At that time, there were occasional references to the problem – mostly by the scientific community – but very little interest otherwise. The USSR had disintegrated, the Berlin Wall was down, the US was now the sole superpower in the world and future peace prospects looked bright: it would be a short lived illusion.

He was alarmed to find clear evidence that global warming presented a real and increasing threat; the nations of the world would have to take determined action to prevent disaster. Forty years earlier, insurance companies had moved to exclude payment for water damage caused solely by rising ocean levels: a shrewd decision. His high hopes for Kyoto were dashed by his own government's absolute refusal to sign up to the Protocol.

While on vacation in Vienna, he met Sandi Fellini, a 22-year-old languages lecturer who was touring Europe with her mother. He fell deeply in love with this attractive, chatty vivacious little woman, with dark hair, big brown eyes and a soft melodious accent. It was a romance that would last for the rest of their lives. Although born and reared in Hartford, she always insisted she was Italian. They were married the following year and settled down in a rented bungalow in Cape Cod. On those rare occasions, when frustrated or angry – as happens to all lovers – Sandi lapsed into her native fishmonger's Italian. It was fantastic; she could go for ten minutes without drawing breath. Ron, recognising only an odd word, here and there, could only put up his hands and surrender. When she ran out of steam, she rushed into his arms and all was well. Her mother, astounded at such language, blamed their Italian chef, Luigi.

Ron became particularly fond of Sandi's parents, Ricardo and Sophia, who emigrated to the US from Venice when their restaurant was flooded for the third time. They settled in Hartford where they opened what was now the famous "Ricardo" restaurant. They visited regularly; Ricardo, a rotund affable little man, with only a few words of English, made himself understood by gesticulating and smiling agreeably. In his quieter moments, he pined for his native Italy and returned to Tuscany for a month every year to select his wines for the coming season.

On 12 July 2001, after four miscarriages, Sandi gave birth to their son, Augustus. The gynaecologist told her that was it: any further pregnancies would be too risky. Disappointed as they were, they were grateful to have a thriving healthy baby.

***

The horrific terrorist attacks of 11 September 2001 changed everything. Ron and Sandi – preoccupied as they were with little Gus who was only two months old – were absolutely appalled. As the years passed, and, at least some of the facts were slowly and painfully extracted from the Bush administration, it became clear that adequate advance warnings were received and ignored. On the day, the terrorists could have hijacked 20 planes just as easily. With the limited information available to him, Ron summed up the horrific events of that awful day: 3,000 people died in the worst security failure in US history: no-one (in the US) was held accountable; some actually received medals for their non-performance. Was it possible that US security was so arrogant, inept, or downright stupid? Unlikely. Why was such a clear warning – five weeks earlier – totally ignored? How specific does a warning have to be to require action? Unless…

In the rush to war no-one asked the obvious question: why were those people prepared to sacrifice themselves to kill Americans? It's easy to persuade the hungry or oppressed – who have nothing to live for – that they have something to die for. Sending armies chasing shadows, killing thousands of innocent civilians, served only to create further terrorists. The same funds applied to world poverty would have helped to cure the causes of terrorism.

Americans were encouraged by their leaders to become ever more paranoid.

Iraq became another Vietnam – the world became less safe.

And, all the time, a much more serious threat was ignored.

***

Ron was surprised that demographists – despite early warnings – failed to foresee the forthcoming population explosion. The world's population was increasing at an unprecedented rate, although birth rates in developed countries had actually fallen. Cures for Alzheimer's, multiple sclerosis, Parkinson's, diabetes and most forms of cancer, plus the use of embedded sensors to detect and monitor cardiac-related problems, had led to an enormous increase in life expectancy. A successful anti-Aids vaccination was now in use, gene therapy had eradicated a number of genetic diseases and stem cell replacement therapy opened up a whole new medical speciality – with amazing results.

In developed countries, the average life expectancy for males had increased to 106 and 115 for females. A UN worldwide census in 2014 showed that there were more than a billion people in robust good health – aged 120 or more. By 2020, 59 percent of the US population would be over 65 years old, 58 percent in Britain, 61 percent in France, 83 percent in Japan and 73 percent in Italy. With increasing prosperity, China was forced to abolish its one-child family law. This led to a rapid increase in young skilled workers and a dramatic increase in total population: solving one problem, but creating another. Most countries were forced to increase the retirement age – first to age 75, then to 85 – and reduce Social Security by half. There was uproar: some private pension funds had to liquidate, and abortion on demand was rendered illegal.

Increasing populations require more food. Greater storm intensity with resulting floods, drought and land loss were, inevitably, followed by widespread, increasing and recurring crop failures. A horrific possibility began to loom on the horizon: worldwide famine.

When the rising Atlantic Ocean inundated most of Cape Cod, Martha's Vineyard and Nantucket, Ron bought a colonial style house in Brookline and an old ranch house in the desert near Las Vegas. They relaxed, whenever possible, in the warm dry air of Nevada. It was so peaceful to sit and watch the ever-changing colours of the desert. There, he caught up on the hundreds of reports he had been collecting, and worked on drafts for his books, assembled his facts – sometimes by candlelight – and entered them in his laptop. He had his own wind propeller erected, thus enabling him to study the effects of this new source of power. Sandi used bottled gas for cooking.

It was while they were there, at Christmas that year, that they watched horrific reports of a massive earthquake that destroyed the city of Istanbul, with the loss of more than 100,000 lives. To Ron, it was a frightening lesson. Nature will not be mocked. It was only a foretaste of what was yet to come.

***

He flew to New Delhi, India to see for himself what conditions were like. A few days later he travelled to the big industrial centres at Mumbai, Bangalore, Hyderabad and Visakhapatnam. A rural country for thousands of years, it was rapidly becoming industrialised, and with 1.5 billion people, was now the second largest economy – after China – in the world. He visited the gigantic steel works, car manufacturing plants, and electricity generating stations: all run on coal.

It was now a country criss-crossed with modern motorways and super monorail trains. The days of the clapped out old trucks, cars, and bicycles held together by string were long gone; passengers no longer sat on the tops of trains; the modern car population numbered in excess of 900 million.

Depressed, he flew to Madras to meet with his former pupil, Sami Guptu, now Science Professor at the University of Madras. He was introduced to his lovely wife, Sete and their four beautiful children. They lived in a modern bungalow on high ground – south of the city – overlooking the Bay of Bengal. Sami, tall and handsome, with swarthy features and deep blue eyes, was clearly worried, but didn't say anything until they were alone.

'Our government won't listen to us when we warn them about fossil fuels. They say: "There is no other way; we have to feed our people and raise living standards." They are more concerned about the growing political unease.'

'What about your hydroelectric stations?'

'We've had to shut down another 200 in the past year.'

'Are they not worried about the increasing intensity of storms, flooding and drought?'

Sami frowned. 'Politicians make fine speeches. The glaciers in the Himalayas are retreating further every year, lowering water levels in the rivers running down into the sub-continent. This is going to affect hundreds of millions of our people. At the same time, we have massive flooding in southern India, worse than anything we've experienced before.'

'Nuclear energy?'

'Is a bad word in India. The people here are doing well at the moment. They don't understand the problems of fossil fuels, they don't want to know. We have some wind farms and solar energy, but they don't amount to much. Everyone wants to have a car, air-conditioning, electric cooker, fridge, freezer and television: you can't blame them.'

'I don't blame them, Sami. It's wonderful to see the progress your people are making, but if it's to continue, fossil fuel energies have to go.'

He paused. 'How are your electricity supplies meeting current demand?'

'Demand is running way ahead of supply; blackouts are becoming an everyday occurrence. There are now plans to introduce rationing.' He paused, becoming agitated. 'My main concern, Ron, is food supplies. I now grow vegetables in my little garden. Crop failures are increasing; I lie awake at night worrying about this; I fear for my children. It's the same in China; the end is coming and we can't do anything about it.'

***

Gus studied engineering and computer science at Boston College. With handsome features, taller than his mother, he had the same black hair and big, friendly brown eyes. His grandmother – who now lived with them – introduced him to the enormous, and apparently never-ending, potential of computers. He always said he learned more from granny Nancy than in college.

After he graduated, he became intrigued with the idea of computerised robots. He went to Japan and Germany – the world's leading manufacturers of robots at that time – to study their progress. He was unimpressed: big and clumsy, they could walk and talk, carry out specific tasks, but they were still machines.

He made contact with a firm in Leeds, England, which was fabricating flexible webs of plastic that included temperature and pressure sensors, suitable for use as robotic skin. The key to the technique was the use of new revolutionary transistors made from organic semiconductors. Satisfied this new compound would give his robots a real, flesh-like appearance, he arranged a supply contract.

Taking over an industrial facility in Brixton, South London, he employed six people and started a small manufacturing unit. But how could he give a robot a human face? Curiously, the eyes weren't a problem, he could use tiny cameras made to look like human eyes. He went to see a make-up artist working on a film at Elstree Studios, and found him very helpful. Jack Lawford was arty, comfortably built, with long black hair, grey eyes and lived alone in a small apartment in Putney. In his spare time he painted portraits. His work was highly regarded, although, as he said himself, he was no Constable. He liked the idea and agreed to come and work with Gus between films. In the meantime, he sent a photographer around the streets of London taking photos of the faces of men and women of all ages. He would just copy life as he saw it.

After nearly two years, they admired their prototype, a robot five feet six inches tall, with blue eyes, a mop of black hair and a somewhat serious expression. Dressed in a black tee-shirt, trousers and a pair of runners, he could carry out orders and speak in simple phrases.

'What will you call him?' Jack asked.

'Darius,' Gus responded.

'Why Darius?'

'I don't know – it's something I read in Greek mythology at school.'

Gus returned to Boston to consult his grandmother. In her eighties, she had slowed down, but was still working. She listened in silence while he outlined his ideas.

'You want to give a robot human intelligence?'

'That's exactly right.'

She pondered for a moment.

'I'm not sure that's even possible.'

'Could you do it?' he asked quietly.

'No, I certainly couldn't.' She paused. 'But I know someone who might be able to help you. She's a freelance consultant who's helped me on a number of occasions; she sometimes acts as an advisor to Microsoft.'

'Will you talk to her?'

'I will. She's a very busy lady. Don't be disappointed if she's not interested.'

***

Ron completed his lecture tour of Europe in Paris and returned to his home in the desert where he wrote his second book *The World Can Be Saved.*

He quoted from Green spokespersons: "Nuclear is not an option; hydroelectric energy is not an option; fossil fuels are not an option." Pressed to nominate some options, they fell back on renewable energies such as bio, wind farming and solar energy. Leading scientists agreed that wind farming and solar energy were only a partial solution: in the most favourable areas in the world the wind blows for 25 percent of the time, and the Sun shines for a maximum of 265 days a year.

Could energy requirements be met, if derived directly from unfossilised plant matter or "biomass" as it's called? It is a potential source of hydrogen for fuel cells and ethanol for motor fuel. Brazil had some success until the rainforests were destroyed. Completely replacing 1997's fossil-fuel consumption increasing every year by at least ten percent – with fuels derived from biomass would use up almost a quarter of the Earth's primary production. Mankind could have either hydrogen and ethanol – or food: not both. With falling crop yields and the continuing loss of arable land, he was satisfied that this wasn't a viable option.

He dealt with the hype and hubris about hydrogen fuel-cell road vehicles, which many maintained would eliminate greenhouse gas emissions caused by road vehicle users. Fine – except that natural gas is used to produce hydrogen gas, thus largely defeating the purpose, and, at the same time, encouraging even greater profligacy among the motoring public. It was made to sound very exciting but, in reality, it would only postpone the inevitable.

He finished by pleading that nuclear energy be given another chance. There had been no serious research since the 1970s; safer ways of using nuclear energy should now be investigated as a matter of urgency.

The book was well received, but he was bitterly attacked by all those he dared to criticise. At a very well-attended public lecture in New York he answered his critics.

'Ask them to explain why the Earth's oceans are seven feet higher now than in 2000. Why have we lost eight percent of the world's landmass? Why have thousands of towns and cities had to be abandoned? How do they explain the destruction of Venice? Why are ocean levels still rising?

Why are we building a new international airport at Newark West? I'll tell you why: despite the billions of dollars spent trying to save Kennedy airport it will have to be abandoned to the Atlantic Ocean next month.

Why have our checkerspot butterflies, lemmings, caribou, reindeer and snowy owls been wiped out? They could not survive in the rising Arctic temperatures.'

The fossil fuel PR people returned to the attack.

"Professor Bergin is rapidly becoming a nutcase. We have positive evidence that the widespread use of carbon trading has reduced global gas emissions to very acceptable limits. Our leading climatologists at the National Center for Atmospheric Research, in Boulder, Colorado, have confirmed this. They are using the most sophisticated computer models in the world, and their findings flatly contradict his wild, disastrous scenarios."

Ron had friends at the centre in Boulder who confirmed that the PR people were highly selective in their arguments. The computer model results were highly contradictory, some showing benign effects, others a forthcoming catastrophe. This only confirmed – if confirmation were necessary – the complexity of the problem. All this at a time when the centre was only beginning to come to grips with the separate threat presented by global dimming, and the manner in which it caused serious underestimation of global warming.

At a subsequent lecture in San Francisco, Ron outlined the up-to-date information and continued.

'Computers are fine, but it's what's happening on the ground that counts: the snows of Kilimanjaro, Africa's highest mountain – 19,000 feet – are long gone; the glaciers of Montana's Glacier National Park are fast disappearing; in Nenana, a small town just south-east of Fairbanks, Alaska, the spring thaw this year was 77 days earlier than in 1924.

Some endangered species have potential use in medical treatment. These include snails that may contain more medicines to treat human disease than any other group of organisms in the world, and hibernating bears that could hold the secrets to preventing and treating osteoporosis. There are about 500 species of cone snails and each one contains up to ten different poisons. They make more poisons than any other organism on this planet. Scientists have only studied five snails in any depth and already have found medications that have totally revolutionised medicine. One of these medications is a drug for the treatment of chronic pain: a drug 1,000 times more potent than morphine. It's a race against time. The tropical coral reefs, where these snails live, will not exist in five years' time.

Why? Because global warming is not just continuing: it's getting worse. Demand for fossil fuels was never greater. The oil orgy is increasing at such a rate – particularly in China, India, America, Russia and Brazil – that the world's oil supplies will be gone within 50 years. Not that it matters; we haven't got 50 years. Carbon trading has proved to be a façade, a smokescreen, a sure-fire invitation to creative accountancy.

It took the world's scientists more than 30 years to recognise the existence of global dimming, the threat it presents, and the manner in which it distorts the true level of global warming. Are there any other hazards out there that have not yet manifested themselves?'

***

Arriving at Heathrow on an overnight flight from San Francisco, Sally O'Halloran closed the door of her first class compartment, and changed from her comfortable casuals into a smart black business suit. Although she knew London quite well, she decided to take a taxi to Brixton. She wanted to meet Gus before checking into her hotel.

He was gobsmacked: could this tall, beautiful young woman with long blonde hair and laughing blue eyes possibly be a computer expert?

'I was expecting someone older,' he blurted out as he shook her hand.

She grinned. 'In this business, you're over the hill at 20.'

She liked this young American with big brown eyes and a friendly expression. He led the way to his office where they sat at his workbench. A few minutes later, Darius arrived with the coffee. Gus introduced him.

He shook her hand and spoke in grave tones. 'I am pleased to meet you.'

He left them.

Sally grinned. 'We'll have to do something with him for a start; he's far too serious.' She paused. 'Now, what have you got in mind?'

While she took notes, he outlined the problem.

'I have worked on some of the current generation of robots,' she said when he finished. 'You want robots with human intelligence?'

He nodded. 'Exactly. Can it be done?'

'I have played around with the idea but, so far, have rejected it on moral grounds.'

'I don't understand.'

'Let me tell you about the American Army experience. They contracted a well-known firm to design and build thousands of robots specially programmed for military purposes. This all happened at a secret base in New Mexico. It was a programming disaster: in the first exercise the robots cut loose, attacked one another and the personnel at the base. They regarded everyone as the enemy. The Army had to bring in a large tank force to destroy them. The contract was quietly scrapped.'

'So you think it shouldn't be done?'

'I've been thinking about this since Nancy rang me. How do you program your robots at present?'

'Each one carries a tiny computer with a holographic memory. It has almost infinite capacity, and is stored in a sealed steel box in the chest area.'

She nodded. 'That's standard now.'

'But you still feel it shouldn't be done?'

'If we give robots human intelligence, they might decide to take over the world. That wouldn't do; we would have to leave out negative emotions such as fear, anger, ambition and arrogance.'

'Will you do it?'

She smiled. 'I will certainly try. I don't think anything like this has been attempted before. Will you let me have copies of your input disks? This could take quite some time.'

He was thrilled.

'I'll have them ready by tomorrow. I've booked a room for you at the Savoy. How long will you be able to stay?'

She got up. 'Just a few days this time.'

***

When the giant Airbus took off from Heathrow and headed north, Sally sipped a coffee and decided not to watch a film for the present. She felt the break had done her good. It was two years now since the tragic death of her parents – she would never forget that awful time – and her subsequent divorce. Married to an up-and-coming, very handsome ambitious lawyer from San Francisco, she was devastated when she learned he didn't want children. She loved Tom Cranstan dearly, and at first, thought he was joking. He made it quite clear: he would divorce her if she became pregnant. It seemed to be the perfect marriage; the sex was great; they shared his luxury apartment overlooking the Bay area; enjoyed vacations together and pursued their careers independently. She agonised for months before finally deciding she could not stay in a childless marriage.

She was born and raised in Lettermore, on the northern shores of Galway Bay, overlooking the Atlantic Ocean. Her father, a local school teacher, purchased a computer for her when she was four. It was the beginning of an astonishing career: she could do anything with it and, within a year, was advising Microsoft on improvements they were delighted to pay for. Two years later – unaware of her age – they offered her a job in California.

She continued her schooling and working from home. When she was 12, Galway University agreed to enrol her in their Computer Science course; she completed the degree in one year. Microsoft immediately invited her to visit them in Seattle. They made quite a fuss, and introduced her to some of the leading software designers in the world. She took it all in her stride and agreed, with her father's consent, to come and work in a special design unit, in San Francisco when she was 18.

Leaving home so young was quite traumatic: she was very close to her parents, her mother in particular. They drove her to Galway International Airport for her flight to San Francisco. There, they hugged one another tearfully before she boarded her flight. She promised to come home for Christmas, a promise she duly kept.

It was quite a change from working in the peace and quiet of her home, to becoming a member of a large team, some of whom didn't welcome her presence. She rented a small apartment from a nice elderly lady in Chinatown, and took the trolley to work most days. There she met Amanda Jackson – eight years her senior – who took her under her wing. A blow in, like herself, not accepted by many of her colleagues, Amanda was a glamorous dark-haired little beauty, with big brown eyes and beautifully tanned skin. Her father was white American, her mother Thai, and her family still lived in Hua Hin in Thailand. Her seven sisters and two brothers were married with large families, and owned a number of little restaurants.

Amanda, although much in demand, showed no interest in men. She rented a luxury apartment on Nob Hill, when she came to the US two years earlier, and drove a sports BMW. A prodigy, like Sally, they enjoyed working together and regularly bounced ideas off one another. She introduced her to a driving instructor, and on completing her course and getting her licence, Sally bought a small BMW. Together, they drove through California at the weekends. It was on one of those trips that Sally found her dream home in Pebble Beach.

It was a fine, single-storied house in its own grounds, high above the winding road by the Pacific. Its original owner – completely paranoid about the likelihood of a nuclear war – had a reinforced concrete bunker built into the foundations. The location reminded Sally of her old home beside the Atlantic Ocean. She bought it – money wasn't a problem, she was earning at least five million a year – and, with Amanda's help, furnished it tastefully, when the decorators moved out. Finally, she installed a modern computer system with email and Internet access.

Amanda could see she wasn't really a city girl, and would be much happier working from her home, especially after her divorce. Sally's skills were such that she could command very high fees operating as an independent consultant. Her managers were very receptive, and offered her a substantial retainer to be available to them for special projects. She set up her little office in her home and travelled to the San Francisco office once a week. They talked on the phone all the time and Amanda was a frequent visitor.

Amanda decided to stay with the company where she was earning up to eight million dollars a year, while continuing to expand her substantial equity portfolio. If she ever left, she said she would return to Thailand and set up her own business there. Her father's family were prominent in business in New York, but would not welcome a visit from her. She didn't mind. After he graduated from Yale, her father visited Thailand, became fascinated by its lovely friendly people and took a job as a computer programmer. There, he met her mother – she was so beautiful – who worked in her father's little clothes shop in Hua Hin. Later, after they married, he became a Buddhist. Amanda, their first-born, enjoyed a very happy childhood. She spent a month every year with her entire family in Hua Hin.

A devout Catholic, Sally went to Mass regularly at St Joseph's little church at the edge of Chinatown. It was there she met Fr John Stobar, a tall, youngish, affable, strikingly handsome curate, who liked her company and often invited her for a coffee in one of the nearby cafés. Dressed in a light grey shirt over black slacks, he was like any other young man about town. She regarded him as a sincere friend, but it was a friendship that would cause her great anguish.

***

Professor Seb Bransky summoned Ron to his office; a former professor of economics, he was Harvard's first African-American President. Ron knew him slightly from staff meetings. In his early forties, Seb Bransky was small, thin, with large blue eyes and a somewhat stern expression. Sitting behind the old mahogany desk that adorned the President's office, he greeted him briskly, without rising.

'Professor Bergin, your contract expires at the end of term. It will not be renewed.'

He was stunned. 'May I inquire why?'

'You have become too political.'

'In what way?'

His impatience increased.

'All this nonsensical talk about global warming is giving the college a bad name in Washington.'

He left without another word.

There was uproar when the Boston Globe published the story. It was suggested that Professor Bransky would be asked to serve as Economics Secretary in President Daly's new administration – should he be re-elected: he wasn't. Six other universities immediately invited Ron to become a visiting professor. He accepted gladly.

The following week, he received a mysterious phone call from a lawyer in Munich. A very important, unnamed client wished to meet him urgently; all his expenses would be paid. Intrigued, he flew to Munich where he was met by a chauffeured limo that took him to a 16th-Century castle in Berchtesgaden. Standing outside the darkened old stone entrance – on this beautiful sunny day – he looked down on the peaceful green valleys far below, and gazed up, in admiration, at the surrounding tall blue peaks of Bavaria. Then he was escorted down a long hallway adorned with some of the world's most famous paintings. At the end, he was shown into a comfortable, book-lined, library. A very genteel, dark-haired old lady with deep brown eyes – once a great beauty – came forward to greet him. Wearing a simple, very elegant black dress, she took him by the hand and smiled.

'Professor, I'm so grateful you could take the time to visit me; I know you're a very busy man. Please, come and sit down. Anna will bring some refreshments shortly.'

He recognised her; famously a recluse, she was one of the world's greatest philanthropists.

'It's a great pleasure to meet you, madam.'

They sat on either side of a low glass-topped table. Anna served tea and scones and left them. Ron was still intrigued: why would one of the wealthiest women in the world wish to see him?

She finished her tea and smiled pleasantly. 'I'm so glad you came. May I call you Ron? I feel I know you, I've read your books many times.'

He smiled. 'Of course.'

'Ron,' she began, 'I have children, grandchildren and soon, perhaps, even great-grandchildren. I want them to have the opportunity of life.' She paused and looked at him very directly. 'Do you think that's possible?'

She had read his books; she had to know his thinking.

'It's possible, but, as things stand, it's not likely.'

She nodded soberly.

'Thank you, for being so frank with me. I want to help you if I can.'

'I appreciate that, but I don't think there is anything you can do.'

'Ron, if you had unlimited funds at your disposal, what would you do?'

It was an unexpected question. He thought about it for a moment.

'I would initiate a major research program into the use of nuclear energy.'

'Please do, I'll provide any funds you require. No, don't protest. I'll open an account in your name at my Zurich bank.'

'But this type of research is unbelievably expensive,' he protested.

She smiled. 'Please indulge a selfish old woman. I have friends who also want to help.'

'I don't know what to say to you, except a very sincere thanks.'

'No,' she protested, 'I thank you, and I know you will continue to do your best.'

He rose to leave.

'One further thing, Ron, you must not reveal my part in this to anyone.' She paused. 'You will come to see me again?'

'Of course.'

She walked with him to the front door where they shook hands. With a mischievous gleam in her eyes, she looked up at him.

'By the way, Ron, I've just cancelled our ten million dollars a year subvention to Harvard University.'

***

Sally faced the greatest challenge of her career in the peace and quiet of her home at Pebble Beach. Amanda visited whenever she could, but close as they were, she didn't tell her about her current project; it would have been highly unprofessional to do so. They sat out on the porch, sipped wine and chatted, talked about men and Amanda's secret lover. They still laughed at the circumstances in which Sally learned this most closely-guarded secret, but in her private moments she still had some reservations.

She studied all available up-to-date publications on the human genome, building blocks and genes, taking particular interest in the work of biologist Dr Alan Weeks and computer scientist Edwardo Silva, who had published papers on the world's most extensive set of data on the machinations of the neocortex – the part of the brain responsible for learning, memory, language and complex thought. This provided the raw material for the simulation, and enabled them to connect artificial nerve cells up in a way that mimicked nature. This they did by assigning electrical properties to them, telling them how to communicate and modify their connections with one another. They simulated the molecular structure of the brain and examined the gene expression on brain function. Some adjustments would be necessary to allow for the differences between the male and female brain. The main problem remained: how to eliminate negative emotions. Maybe it was insoluble, but some stubborn streak wouldn't let her give up, at least, not yet.

She studied the neocortical columns – cylindrical elements about a third of a millimetre in diameter and three millimetres long – each containing some 10,000 nerve cells. These columns, arranged side-by-side, make up the grey matter that has become the shorthand for human intelligence. She now had enough independent processors – for simulation purposes – to emulate an individual nerve cell in a column.

Could she now identify the nerve cells associated with fear, anger or hatred? If so, could she then delete those cells? She knew the cells would react to fearful stimuli whether real or imaginary. Optimistic now, she programmed and input a truly fearful scenario that would convince the cells they were under attack. Fifteen nerve cells flashed red: she identified and deleted them. She input the scenario again to confirm they were gone; they were still there. Very disappointed, she reassessed the entire program. Could it be that the nerve cells she deleted were controlled or linked by master cells? If so, how could she possibly identify and delete these master cells? Would it be safe to do so? She could throw the entire network into disarray.

Deciding to forget about it for a while, she flew to New York with Amanda, where they indulged themselves in a delightful shopping spree. She felt much better when she returned home, but was no nearer a solution. Then, one morning, standing watching the mighty waves dashing against the rocks below, it suddenly hit her. She raced back to the house and turned on her computer. It was the last throw of the dice: if this didn't work it couldn't be done. The emotions of fear, anger and hatred are closely associated. What if she devised a scenario that would stimulate all three, and deleted them together? With shaking hands she input the scenario; 46 nerve cells flashed red. She hit the delete button; they disappeared from her screen.

Now for the moment of truth: she input the scenario again and held her breath. There was no reaction. She leapt for joy. She'd done it. She couldn't believe it; she checked again.

She rang Gus. He was so excited.

‘When will you be over, Sally?’

‘In about a week, I need to carry out some more tests and tidy up the system.’

***

Arriving back in Brixton, she spent days inputting and checking Darius’s new software. Ron arrived the following week. Sally, having read his books, knew he was quite famous. While she believed his dire warnings, she thought – like most young people – that governments would act to avert this catastrophe. She found him friendly and charming, not unlike Gus; a genuine human being with none of the trappings one expects of the famous.

It was time for what Gus called a “road test”. The new, friendly, smiling Darius had never been out of the facility. Now, he would be required to travel across London alone, on a route worked out by Gus. He had studied a dozen maps and videos, and was given 50 pounds, but how would he cope with people and traffic? Could he pass unnoticed in a crowd? This was also Sally’s first major trial of her new computerised communication system that would enable Darius to send information to, and receive instructions, via the computer. Gus and Ron would track his progress and thoughts; she would shadow him.

She was apprehensive. Had she overlooked anything? Could there be some interaction in the nerve cells that she was unaware of? Normally, she wore a smart business suit to work. For this experiment, she put on a pair of black slacks under an old raincoat, and hid her long blonde hair under a tight fitting cap.

Darius walked confidently to the Tube station in Brixton, bought a daily ticket for the outer ring, found his way to the north-bound platform, boarded and took his seat, quietly observing his surroundings. Sally followed, making sure he didn’t see her. He got off at Piccadilly Circus, walked to Knightsbridge – crossing streets at pedestrian crossings only – and wandered through every department in Harrods where he priced a number of items. At the Victoria and Albert Museum, he bought a ticket and strolled around admiring the paintings and exhibits.

He walked to South Kensington, took the Tube to Heathrow, wandered through Terminals One and Two, and spent some time watching planes landing and taking off. Sally was thrilled everything was going so well. She rang Gus on her cell phone.

'How is the communication system working?'

'Perfectly, you're in Heathrow. He's reporting back on everything he sees. I'm now changing his schedule, telling him to return by a different route. How is he reacting to people?'

'He's relaxed and friendly – a perfect gentleman – looks like he's been doing this all his life.'

'Good, you're due back in two hours.'

Darius took the Heathrow express to Paddington. While leaving the station, a scruffy-looking thug set upon him with a knife. Sally held her breath: if Darius reacted aggressively, he could seriously injure, even kill, his attacker. There wasn't a policeman in sight. The thug held his knife to Darius's throat.

'Your money and quick about it, shithead,' he rasped.

Darius smiled at him. Sally was shaking; he didn't understand the threat. Darius gripped the thug's wrist. He screamed in agony and dropped the knife. Still smiling, Darius let go of his wrist. He didn't hang around. She gasped with relief. Darius strolled to a nearby bus stop and boarded a bus to Marble Arch. An hour later, he arrived back in Brixton.

Gus was thrilled, but Sally was in for a let-down. Darius smiled gleefully at her.

'You were behind me all the time.'

'How could you possibly know that, I stayed well back?'

'Darius see everything.'

'What about that thug that attacked you?'

He grinned. 'I not told to give him money.'

'You weren't angry or afraid?'

He looked puzzled. 'Angry or afraid?'

'Never mind.'

***

After a meal in a local restaurant, they returned to Gus's office to plan the future.

Ron began. 'You have achieved something very unique, Sally. I'm hoping you will come on board full-time.'

She hadn't thought that far ahead.

'I normally charge a fee, and leave the scene as soon as the job is completed.'

He shook his head. 'This is too big, too important, Sally. Half of this venture is yours. I think you should receive ten million dollars for your work to date, and a further ten million a year, plus half the profits when we've repaid our financial backers.'

She was surprised. 'I don't normally earn that much in a year.'

Gus chipped in. 'It's more than justified, please say yes Sally.'

She laughed. 'When you put it like that, how could I refuse?'

Ron smiled happily. 'I'm so pleased, Sally, I think we should now set up a company to make, program, and hire out robots for all kinds of activities. Now you've done it once, am I right in thinking you can design robots to manufacture robots?'

'Of course.'

'Can we have robots working all around the world and, at the same time, sending us vital information?'

'Yes.'

'Sally, I've been given a secret underground complex in southern Switzerland. We have the most sophisticated computers in the world in a warehouse in Lugano. Can you program robots to install and operate these computers?'

'Certainly, provided you have electricity.'

'We have our own independent supply.' He paused. 'I think we should now move this manufacturing unit to a factory near Lugano.'

'And bring my staff from here?' Gus asked.

'No Gus, you no longer need staff. We'll have five or six factories in different parts of the world. A robot sent to India –

or any other country – will have to look, and speak like a native.'

'Dad, shouldn't we patent Sally's program?'

'Absolutely not.'

'Sally,' Ron continued. 'Have you a copy of the program on your computer at home?'

'Yes, under my own secret password.'

'Right, now we're protected by secrecy. When the robots go on the market we won't have that protection. I think you should remove everything from your home as soon as possible.'

She agreed. 'Before I go back to the States, I'll set up the computer centre in Lugano, and program a special computer robot with all my knowledge, including the program.'

Ron continued. 'We need an administration centre. I have a friend in one of the big accountancy firms in Paris – he also acts for our financial backers – I can get him to handle the business aspects; setting up hire contracts, passing on orders to our manufacturing centres, making sure the charges are paid, that type of thing.'

Sally found the prospect of returning to Europe quite attractive. She could spend more time in Galway, and exchange visits with Amanda a few times a year.

***

When Ron returned to Boston, he rang his old friend, Alex Purtzel. The 36-year-old nuclear physicist – Professor of Science at MIT – was once Ron's star pupil at Harvard. They'd remained friends ever since. Alex was a frequent visitor to his home. The tall, handsome, quietly spoken Irishman, with deep blue eyes, was recognised as one of America's leading physicists. He was a perfectionist in everything he did; perhaps it was because he was born with a slightly deformed leg and always walked with a stick. They usually played golf together once a week, out in Newton; a formidable team, with Alex playing off scratch; his own handicap in double figures.

Alex's mother, Caroline, a lovely, softly spoken tall brunette, with bright hazel eyes, was a medical doctor in the town of Yeatstown, near Sligo city in north-west Ireland. She visited Alex frequently in Boston, and became very fond of Sandi and Ron. They all dined regularly together. Sandi took her shopping and showed her the sights. They visited Caroline's lovely seaside home in Yeatstown, and enjoyed many happy vacations there.

Sandi and Caroline had serious reservations about Alex's marriage to Linda La Plante, beautiful, socialite daughter of one of the wealthiest lawyers in the state – but they didn't expect it to end so quickly and abruptly. Alex never talked about it.

He got on with his work, moved out to a penthouse apartment in Cambridge, and bought a high-powered Mercedes sports car. In all the years he knew them, Ron never heard Caroline refer to her husband, or Alex to his father.

They met in the coffee bar at the Sheraton.

'How would you like to do some real research into nuclear energy?' Ron asked.

'I would love to: it's a question of funds.'

He smiled. 'I have friends who will provide all the funds you need. Would the MIT board provide the necessary facilities?'

'I've got a better idea. In my spare time I work with Professor Levensor in Chicago. He's got a small facility there. With sufficient funding we could really do things. I particularly want to work on nuclear fusion.'

'I thought breeder reactors were the answer?'

'Part of it, yes, but with fusion we can generate power using the energy released when two light atomic nuclei are brought together to make a heavier one: It's a process similar to the one that powers the Sun. It's efficient, so only small quantities of fuel are needed. Radioactive processes are relatively short-lived, and the waste products benign. The all-important thing: there are no carbon dioxide emissions. The principal fuel, a heavy isotope of hydrogen called deuterium is present in ordinary water, of which there is no shortage.'

'That's the answer then.'

'We still have to do a lot of research: we haven't yet solved the problem of increasing the size of the reactor, and ensuring its walls can cope with being bombarded by neutrons. We're currently working on the magnetic bottle problem.'

'But it can be done?'

'Of course Ron, with sufficient funds and a team of nuclear physicists.'

'We've got the funds. Let me have your manuals and we'll program as many robotic physicists as you need.'

'That will be fantastic. I'm really looking forward to this. I suppose you could also program robots to man the power stations.'

'Of course; now all we have to do is persuade the powers that this is our only hope of survival.'

***

Sally took a flight from Zurich to Galway, where she hired a car, drove out along the coast into Connemara and checked into the Atlantic Hotel in Lettermore. Afterwards, she walked along the beach, and stood looking out across the bay to the Aran Islands. As a child, she'd played here with her older sister, Rachael; built her sandcastles and ventured into the noisy waves dashing against the rocky shore, under the watchful eye of her patient mother. She loved this place.

It was nearly three years now, since she received a phone call from Rachael, telling her to come home immediately: her beloved mother and father had been killed, earlier that awful day, in a horrific car accident near Galway City. She was stunned. Only the previous evening she had had her weekly conference call with them. They were in great spirits, planning a day's shopping in Galway. They always spent the month of August with her in Pebble Beach. There, she introduced them to Amanda. They were so pleased she had such a genuine friend.

She showed them the sights of California: they did the tourist rounds of San Francisco; drove across the Golden Gate Bridge, toured the wineries in Napa Valley, visited a Hollywood studio and enjoyed a walking tour in old San Diego. She arranged golf for her father at the Pebble Beach course nearby, and took her mother for a day's shopping to the South Coast Plaza near Los Angeles. In the evenings, they sat outside the house, basked in the warm sun and gentle winds blowing in from the Pacific. Wonderful happy times; now they were gone.

She remembered little about the trip home. Amanda travelled with her. She would always be grateful to her. The neighbours, teachers, past and present pupils, couldn't have been more helpful. She just couldn't take it in. Seeing them laid out in the hospital mortuary was heartbreaking: it was her first experience of death. She put her arms around Rachael and her two lovely nieces; they clung to one another for support. She would never forget that awful feeling of loneliness and desolation, when she stood by the open grave in the little cemetery above the village, and watched their coffins being lowered into the earth.

The hotel was quiet. The holiday season hadn't started yet. She sat outside in the evening sun for a while. It was so good to be home, even for a few hours. She used to dream of having a holiday home here, where she could bring her children to visit their grandparents. Going to the bar, she ordered a coffee.

Afterwards, she rang Rachael. They chatted for a while; the girls and Joe were fine. She got the impression all was not well with her, but, despite gentle probing, she refused to be drawn. Growing up, they weren't really close. Being the youngest she was the spoiled brat; maybe Rachael resented that.

She rang Amanda on her cell phone. She was in Hong Kong on her way back from Hua Hin and promised to ring as soon as she got back to San Francisco. She was in such high spirits that Sally inquired. 'Have you got your secret lover with you?'

'Yes.'

'Did you bring him to Hua Hin?'

She laughed aloud. 'No, I met him here in Hong Kong. Do you want me to scandalise my parents?'

The following morning was dull and overcast. She walked along the narrow, winding road to the cemetery, knelt at the graveside and said a prayer. There is something very final about death: she so wanted to believe they would all be together again, one day, in a happier place. Eventually, she left, walked slowly back to the hotel and drove to Galway International Airport at Oranmore for her flight to San Francisco. She relaxed in her comfortable first class seat while the giant Airbus cruised towards Greenland at 60,000 feet. Her conversation with Amanda prompted her to remember again – not that she could ever forget – the life-changing incident that occurred the previous year, shortly before she finally gave up her apartment in Chinatown. Her recollection was as hazy as the oppressive air that enveloped the city that day, but she felt she could live with it now.

It was a Sunday. She slept late and attended the noon Mass said by Father John, as she called him. He preached a very well-thought-out homily on Christian love. Afterwards, when saying farewell to his parishioners, he suggested that they meet for a snack at a popular café in the Bay area. She readily agreed; his conversation was always stimulating. Finding a table for two, she watched families and tourists wandering around happily, some queuing for boat rides on the bay. Dressed casually, he joined her 20 minutes later.

He ordered a beef sandwich, while she settled for a ham salad. She chose a good chardonnay from Napa Valley, introduced to her by Amanda who was something of a wine connoisseur. She rarely drank wine, but it was Sunday, and everyone was relaxing. She insisted on taking the check. He told her about his upbringing in Houston, where his late father was a planning official who drank too much; his mother, a hospital staff nurse, had remarried and was now living in Philadelphia.

His younger sister, Jane, was married to a commodities broker in Chicago.

Afterwards, she could never recall who suggested he should walk back to her apartment with her. She was floating on air. The wine had gone to her head; he didn't appear to notice as he chatted on. She couldn't remember anything he said; she was too busy trying to behave normally. Parched with the thirst, she longed for a glass of water. An on-street vendor sold her a plastic bottle of cold mineral water that she gulped down gratefully.

Arriving at her apartment, still very hazy, she couldn't remember inviting him in, but she must have. Once inside, with the door closed, he took her in his arms, kissed her with sudden passion, while he held her firmly, but gently, against the wall. Taken by surprise, she responded, putting her arms around him, while one half of her brain screamed “This can’t be happening”, the other half responded “Yes, yes.”

Taking off his shirt and dropping his slacks and trunks, he continued kissing her deeply. It was like a dream to her: part of her mind screamed “Yes, yes,” while another part screamed “Stop, stop, I can’t have sex with a priest, it’s sacrilege.” But she made no effort to stop him. Breathing heavily, his heart pounding, he entered her. She held him, conscious of his hard lean body and scented aftershave. Now, all of her mind screamed “Yes, yes, yes.” She moaned happily as the fires of her passion reached a climax.

All was quiet now except for the thumping of his heart and her breathlessness. Her thoughts in total confusion, she pushed him away gently, pulled down her dress and went into the bedroom. When she returned, he was dressed, sipping a glass of water, looking quite pleased with himself.

‘You’re very beautiful, Sally.’

Her mind was a bit clearer now.

‘I think you should go.’ She couldn’t call him “Father John”.

He smiled. ‘I was hoping we could spend the evening together.’

‘No, I have work to do.’

Disappointed, he rose. ‘Can I ring you tomorrow?’

‘Yes.’

After he left, she took a long cold shower, put on a fresh dress, made coffee and sat in her favourite chair, sipping it slowly. Her mind was quite clear now – what had she done? She had sex with a nice man and it was wonderful. There was nothing wrong with that except that he was a priest: there was everything wrong with that. Her dear departed mother would have been horrified at the very idea.

It was all her fault. She was responsible for a priest breaking his sacred vows. It was sacrilege. Girls don’t invite priests to their apartments. Did she invite him? She couldn’t remember, but it was entirely her fault. She was an occasion of sin to him, although he didn’t appear at all upset afterwards. She would have to confess, but how could she tell a priest she had sex with another priest and took pleasure in it?

The following afternoon she dropped by Amanda's office. She needed to talk – her sin had grown overnight. Amanda, seeing she was upset, suggested she reserve one of the executive meeting rooms where they wouldn't be disturbed. Ordering two coffees, they took the elevator to the tenth floor. Sally outlined the previous day's events as best she could, conscious that Amanda never showed any interest in men and was probably a virgin.

When she finished, Amanda sipped her coffee and grinned.

'You mustn't take this so seriously, Sally: all priests have sex with women – except the gay ones – and it's clear your friend isn't gay – and it wasn't his first time.'

She was shocked. 'Amanda, you're a Buddhist, how would you know?'

'Because I have a secret lover, and he's a Roman Catholic priest.'

'But I thought?'

'I know: everyone around here thinks I'm a lesbian because I'm a very private woman, and don't spend my time hanging around clubs and bars. It keeps the randy 50-year-olds, with growing families, from pawing me.'

Her eyes opened wide in astonishment.

'But don't you think it's wrong to have a priest as a lover?'

'Of course not, Sally. As a Buddhist, I commit sin when I do something that hurts another creature. What we're doing doesn't hurt anyone. If I had sex with a married man: that would be a sin.'

Sally was bemused now; there was a whole world out there she knew nothing about.

'You enjoy having sex?'

'Sally, I love having sex with my Jack, as I call him, and we're good friends. When he arrives after hearing confessions, I'm first on the menu. Goodness knows what lurid stories he has to listen to: they sure make him randy! When I know he's coming – he usually rings first – I put on a kimono over a pair of pink knickers. It's a fad, I suppose; he likes to take off my knickers.'

'But some day you'll want to get married and have kids?'

'No, I won't: I have my parents, six sisters, two brothers, and so far, 15 nieces and nephews to support back home in Thailand. I've set them up in business, and all the children are getting a good education. Five of them are well on their way to becoming IT experts.'

'But what if your Jack has other women?'

She grinned. 'I'd know if he had. We have great sex, I satisfy his every need and he satisfies mine.' She paused. 'It's good to be able to share my secret.'

'What would you do if he wanted to leave the Church and marry you, or was moved to another parish?'

'Marriage doesn't arise. If he was moved far away, I'd get another priest.'

'Just like that?'

'Of course. Jack is my second; his predecessor – lovely man – was made a bishop and moved to another city.'

'But how do you do it – you're not even a Catholic?'

She grinned. 'It's really quite simple. I visit local churches, and observe the priests until I select one who is clearly in need of comforting – that's how I got Jack. I went to confess to him – not that I confessed anything. I told him I liked him, gave him my card and suggested he ring if he wished to meet me. I was in his arms three hours later.' She paused. 'But enough about me, what are you going to do about your man?'

'I can't see him again, Amanda.'

'Why not?'

'I could easily fall in love with him, and being an old fashioned Irish colleen, would want to marry him.'

'I know how you feel.' She paused and grinned. 'He sounds nice. I'll be looking for his phone number, if my Jack gets promoted.'

Arriving in San Francisco, she collected her car from the airport car park, unaware she was being followed. She drove down Route 1 to Monterey, arriving home as the evening sun sank into the Pacific. Entering, she found the house had been thoroughly ransacked, with drawers and their contents scattered all around the floor. There was no sign of break-in, and as far as she could see, nothing had been taken. Then it struck her – the computer. Going quickly to her office, she switched it on, checked her codes and anti-hacker protection. It was a system she designed herself. It appeared to be in order.

Feeling personally violated, she tidied up as best she could. There was no point in calling the police. She slept fitfully and, in the morning, drove into Carmel to stock up her freezer. It would take a week to wind up her affairs, and she would have to see Amanda before she left. She was surprised to find half-empty shelves in Mac's superstore. Meat was in short supply. She bought some coffee, flakes, a chicken breast, bread and milk – spending nearly 250 dollars. Food prices just kept on rising.

It was a hot, sunny calm day. She rang Tony Hess in Monterey, the estate agent who sold her the property, and asked him to put the house and contents on the market immediately. She would copy her computer records to disks, and wipe the hard disk before returning to Lugano. Tony promised to call out later.

After breakfast, she started to gather up her personal papers; she would take them with her. She watched the TV news; there was nothing of interest on it. Checking her email, she was surprised to find a message from Tom Cranstan: she hadn't heard from her ex-husband in nearly two years.

"Hi kid. I miss you. I think we made a mistake splitting up. Can we meet and talk? I'll drive down if it's OK with you? Love, Tom."

She read it three times, shaking her head slowly. If she'd got that message a month after they parted, she would have rushed back into his arms. It was too late now; she was a different person. She would reply later. Time zones always confused her; could Amanda be home yet? She dialled her cell phone number.

'Sally, it's great to hear from you; where are you?'

'I'm in Pebble Beach, where are you?'

'We're due to land in San Francisco in half an hour. I've had a wonderful vacation in Hua Hin with my family. Dad isn't well, but he's hanging in there.'

'What about your vacation in Hong Kong?'

She could hear her laughing.

'That was wonderful too. I'll come down to see you tomorrow.'

'I look forward to it – we have lots to talk about; is your secret lover with you?'

'You bet. I'll have to get you one.'

She rang off, smiling.

A knock on the door surprised her. Tony could hardly be out so soon. Opening it absently, she was pushed roughly into the hall by a tall grey-suited man, with florid features; a second man, younger, lean and mean-looking, followed.

The older one spoke calmly. 'Don't do anything stupid, and you'll be all right.'

'What do you want?' She tried to sound brave.

She heard the familiar sound of rumbling down below, a low-grade earthquake.

'Just give us your robot software and we'll be on our way.'

'Who are you?' She demanded.

'You don't need to know.' His voice hardened. 'Let's cut the crap, we've got a flight to catch.'

'All right, I'll copy it off the computer.'

She led the way to her office, sat down, switched on the computer and entered her access code. They stood on either side of her. Her nimble fingers moved so quickly over the keyboard they couldn't see what was happening until the screen flashed: "Deleted."

The older one grabbed her by the hair of her head and dragged her away from the keyboard.

'You bloody bitch,' he yelled, turning to his companion. 'See if you can get it back, George.'

The rumbling down below continued.

George fiddled around with the keyboard before shaking his head.

'No good, it's gone.'

The older one pulled out his gun and pointed it at her head.

'Get it back, or you're dead.'

Terrified, she tried to appear calm.

'It's gone. No-one can get it back now.'

'What are we going to do?' the one called George asked.

The older one made up his mind.

'We'll take this bitch back east: she either produces a copy, or she's dead.'

Frightened as she was, she knew she had bought some time. Opening the front door, they pushed her out ahead of them. When they stepped out they were grabbed and pushed roughly aside. Her rescuer stood between her and her captors; regaining their balance, they reached for their guns.

She gasped with relief.

'Darius, how did you get here?'

Her former captors fired at him. He smiled, grabbed their wrists and squeezed hard. They screamed in agony, dropping their guns.

Darius grinned. 'This time, I follow you, all the way from CosmosRX. What do I do with these two?'

'Let them go.'

Dusting himself off, and backing away, the older one screamed 'We'll be back.'

They departed quickly.

The rumbling below became louder.

Darius stood outside the house with her, and watched them drive away. The rumbling below suddenly erupted in a thunderous explosion: the earth shook violently beneath their feet and they couldn't retain their balance. Sally found herself sitting on the rapidly vibrating ground. The sea road collapsed ahead of the departing car, it turned over and disappeared into the ocean. The noise was deafening: thoroughly frightened, she put her hands over her ears. Parts of the roof collapsed, the windows shattered, her lovely car tumbled down the hill and exploded in flames, trees started falling all around them; her neighbour's house disintegrated. Darius, who was quite calm, put his arms around her and held her. This, she was sure, must be the end of the world. A crevice nearly two feet deep, opened up below them and ran down towards the ocean. Shivering uncontrollably, she began to feel disoriented. Like everyone in California, she had experienced earthquakes before, but nothing like this.

Finally, it stopped: the silence was eerie. She just sat there; dishevelled, trembling, unable to move. The sea appeared to be boiling.

'We can go inside now,' Darius remarked.

His calmness was reassuring.

'Will you see if my neighbours are all right?'

She didn't know them, but this wasn't a time to stand on ceremony.

The house was a complete mess. She didn't mind, they were alive and unharmed. The electrics were gone. She rooted around until she found her battery operated radio and tried to find a station still on air.

A voice broke into her thoughts.

"This is José Hernandez, coming to you from a chopper high above San Francisco. Hundreds of properties in the bay area and Chinatown are collapsing: fires are breaking out all over the place, gas mains are exploding, freeways are collapsing, thousands of people are assembling in open areas. The bridges are swaying wildly: cars, coaches and trucks are being abandoned, their occupants running frantically towards the bridge ends. The Earthquake Center says this may be the big one – it's 9.9 on the Richter scale.

Oh my God, this is awful: the suspension cables holding the Golden Gate Bridge have started to snap; I can hear the whiplash crackle as they thrash all around the bridge; hundreds of people are running for their lives. Come on, you can do it. Some of them are carrying small children; one woman has a little baby in her arms. Oh my Jesus, this is awful: the spans are collapsing; people are falling into the bay; no-one can do anything for them." There was a pause in the broadcast. When he resumed it was clear he was weeping.

"Those poor people; the children and little babies." (Pause.) "The Golden Gate Bridge is no more. Its two uprights are leaning towards one another at a grotesque angle."

Unable to take anymore, Sally switched off and walked outside into the open. She tried to focus on time, but couldn't. Amanda: had she arrived, was she all right? She tried to ring her on the cell phone – there was no reply. Darius returned a few minutes later.

'There's no-one in that house. What do we do now?'

'We have to find some way of getting out of here.'

Her cell phone rang. It was Ron.

'Are you all right, Sally? Is Darius with you?'

'Yes, we're fine.'

She didn't want to talk about her attackers, at least, not yet.

'There could still be aftershocks. Listen carefully, Sally. I'm in Las Vegas, it's chaotic here: the quake has split California in two; you are now on an island. In less than three hours a tidal wave is going to hit your coast; can you get to high ground?'

'No, my car is wrecked, and the roads are out. We heard about San Francisco.'

'The Bay Bridge collapsed a few minutes ago. Have you any shelter there?'

Her cell phone was running very low.

'Ron, we have an old concrete basement. My cell phone is running low. I'll get Darius to stay in contact with you through CosmosRX.'

'I'll get a chopper…' The line went dead.

Darius cleared the way to the basement entrance, lifted the steel trapdoor and walked down the stone steps. Finding her torch, she followed. It was a big room, covered with cobwebs. The air smelled stale and musty. He brushed aside the cobwebs. The only item of furniture was a dusty-looking old bed.

He was impressed. 'Looks like it was built as a fall-out shelter. We'll have to leave the trapdoor open for a while.'

'I'll get some candles, food, water and bedclothes.' She paused. 'We could be trapped in here for days.'

Going up, she picked her way gingerly through the debris, and stood outside the remains of her home. It was unreal: the Sun was still high in the sky, yet, in three hours or less?

Darius checked in with CosmosRX, and reported back to her in a matter-of-fact tone.

'Casualties are thought to be very high; frantic efforts are being made to evacuate as many as possible.'

'How bad will it be?' She asked quietly.

'Bill says it's expected to be 100 feet high when it hits the coast and will travel inland for ten kilometres before subsiding.'

With less than an hour to go, they went down the steps into the basement. Darius closed and sealed the hatch. She lit a candle, sat on the bed and wrapped a blanket around her. Was it fate that brought her to this place at this time, she asked herself? She tried to pray, but the words wouldn't come; she didn't go to church much after her brief affair with Fr John. Amanda? Was she all right? Had her flight been diverted? Her mind was in turmoil. She didn't want to die, not here, not now: she hadn't lived yet. She always hoped she would live a long life, marry the man of her dreams, bring up her children and see her grandchildren.

At first, the dull sounds seemed far away. Coming closer, they grew louder. Then, with a god-awful roar, like nothing she had ever heard before, it was on them. The basement shook violently, rocked in its foundations; she was sure it was going to be swept away, or come crashing in on top of them. Thrown to the floor, she screamed as the bed started to slide towards her. Darius grabbed and held it. Deafened, she covered her ears and cried out to God to save her. The horrendous banging and crashing above continued unabated. Water started to pour in through the ventilators.

Then, just as it seemed they were about to be swept away, the basement shook less violently, the noise slowly subsided and became more distant. Still shaking, she switched on her torch.

'We're alive, Darius, we're alive.' She screamed with relief, unaware she was screaming.

'I'll let CosmosRX know,' he remarked quietly. 'Then we'll let the water settle above, before we try to leave here.'

She found her radio, and switched it on. It was a different voice to the one she heard earlier.

"A devastating tidal wave has hit the West Coast, sweeping away everything in its path; it will inundate most of the new island within the next 20 minutes. Massive reserves are being rushed to Portland, Reno, Las Vegas and Phoenix. Thousands of choppers are standing by, waiting to commence rescue operations as soon as the water subsides. San Francisco, Los Angeles and San Diego are now part of what's called 'California Island'. Eleven miles of ocean separates the island from the mainland."

She switched off.

Darius went up the steps and tried the trapdoor. He couldn't move it. They were trapped. He reported to CosmosRX again. An hour later he turned to Sally.

'Ron is trying to hire a chopper in Las Vegas. It's very difficult, there's absolute bedlam there. He will come for us as soon as possible.'

While Darius tried the trapdoor again, Sally put on her radio.

"There has been widespread condemnation of the disgraceful savagery that took place at San Francisco International Airport: six E64 planes, sent in to fly people to safety, have not returned. Reports from survivors are still coming in. Thousands of passengers swept aside airport security and fought their way on to the aircraft. The planes were still on the ground when the tidal wave struck."

She switched off. Darius called to her.

'It's moving just a little.'

Water poured in, shafts of light penetrated the darkness. Getting one hand outside, he started to push aside the accumulated rubble and debris. She was grateful for his superhuman strength. Nearly two hours later, he succeeded in opening the trapdoor. They emerged into the open. It was nearly dark. Sally had lost track of time. They surveyed the surrounding countryside: it was a scene of utter desolation with flattened trees, dead fish, rubble and debris everywhere.

She began to shiver with the cold, suddenly realising her clothes were in tatters and she was drenched.

She looked around again.

'What's that in the middle of the golf course?'

It looked like a long building.

'It's a ship.' He paused, 'All choppers have been grounded until dawn.'

He didn't tell her there was a riot at the airport. Many people were shot and several choppers badly damaged. Martial law was declared in Las Vegas and many other cities. It could be days before they were rescued.

He took charge. 'Sally, we have to leave here now, find you some dry clothes, clean drinking water and shelter.'

He took her in his arms, made his way slowly through the piles of rubble, and eventually reached the wreck. It was on its side, dug nearly 20 feet into the earth. He moved slowly, called out a few times. There was no sign of life: the entire area was littered with body parts – hands, arms, legs, heads and torsos.

The bridge was now almost at ground level. Leaving her for a few moments, he climbed through the front window of the wheel-house, removed two bodies, and punched a hole through the superstructure to drain off the rest of the accumulated water. He carried her into the wheel-house and laid her on an oil skin coat he removed from one of the bodies.

'Rest here a while, Sally, while I go below.'

She nodded silently. Then it hit her – the awful stench. She recoiled, covering her mouth and nose with her hand.

By now, most of the water had drained off the ship. He crept along the sides of dark walkways until he found what he was looking for: sealed cabins with dry clothes, a case of brandy, still intact, and some chocolate. Very gently, he carried Sally below – she was semi-conscious now – and persuaded her to sip some brandy, removed her wet clothes, massaged her gently and wrapped her in dry blankets.

She came around after a while. 'Where are we, Darius?' she asked hazily.

'We're in the ship. Ron knows you're safe, he'll be here later.' He handed her another glass of brandy. 'Sip this, it will do you good.'

Afterwards, she fell into a deep sleep. He rooted around the captain's cabin until he found a small fridge with bottled mineral water.

Five hours later, the chopper circled above them and landed nearby. Ron helped Darius lift her aboard. The pilot pulled away quickly. Ron sat with his arm around her, urging her quietly to drink the brandy.

She tried to smile. 'If I drink anymore, I'll get drunk.'

She hadn't taken a drink since that Sunday.

'You do that.'

They flew directly to his home in the desert where Sandi was waiting for them. She took Sally in hand, drew a hot bath, provided a change of clothes and, after a light meal, put her to bed. But she couldn't rest until she scribbled out Amanda's full name and address and handed it to Ron.

'Please, Ron, Amanda is my dearest friend. Try to find her and bring her to safety.'

'Don't you worry now, we'll do everything possible.'

As time passed – unable to leave for Boston because the entire area was under martial law – they followed the progress of the biggest rescue operation in history. Sally recovered slowly, hoping and praying Amanda was safe. Plague was inevitable; island airports were quickly cleared and reopened; massive supplies of medicine, food and drinking water were flown in; more than 100,000 troops – inoculated against a range of diseases – were deployed; looters were shot on sight. Aid workers, rescue specialists, doctors, engineers, counsellors and carers flew in from all over the world. Throughout the island, thousands of bodies were buried every day in mass graves: the grim task of identifying the dead would continue for months, perhaps years; some would never be found or identified. To Sally's dismay, the casualty list kept growing. It included many of her friends and her ex-husband, Tom Cranstan. She mourned them all; there was no word of Amanda.

***

Ron's six secure factories were located in different parts of the world. The one near Lugano – with a highly programmed robot, called Caesar, in charge – was formerly a car manufacturing plant that had moved to Thailand. To ensure continuity of supply he bought the plastics company in Leeds. Gus purchased language disks from a London firm. Within three months, production figures – per unit – were exceeding 1,000 a week and rising. The demand from the US and Europe was incredible; they took as many as they could get. This was another way of increasing their workforce; a very lucrative one. The robots were highly efficient, worked 24 hours a day, required no food, little accommodation, didn't age and never went on strike. Anxious to get a worldwide spread, they reduced the hire charges to developing countries.

A number of organisations tried, unsuccessfully, to copy them. They then tried to buy the company; even resorted to trying to take some of the robots apart to find out how they worked. They were forced to give up when a number of leading programmers were blown to bits. Gus had added a self-destruct mechanism.

Governmental agencies deployed them in highly sensitive areas: specialised computer control of defence systems, nuclear missiles, submarines, weapons of mass destruction, internal and external security, including close personal protection for heads of states. When a large number of satellite space operatives died from a muscle wasting disease, they were replaced by specially programmed robots.

***

Back in CosmosRX, Sally recovered slowly from her ordeal. For a long time the nightmares continued. She dreamt of the earth-shattering deafening roar of the tidal wave, only to wake up shivering in a lather of perspiration. There was still no word of Amanda.

She now set about developing "Supremos" as she called them: robots programmed with all the knowledge known to man, who would act as advisers to the director of CosmosRX. She decided to name them after some of the great geniuses in history.

Gus was impressed. 'Have you talked to Caesar?'

'Yes, he doesn't see any problem.'

'And what names have you in mind?'

'Michelangelo, Leonardo da Vinci, Plato – that's as far as I've got so far.'

'Sounds exciting.'

She spent days with Caesar and his robot make-up artists, setting out her requirements. Michelangelo would have an air of quiet confidence; a portly little man, with an unruly head of grey hair, good features and a long, but well-trimmed, beard. She was delighted when he reported for duty. Dressed in a black frock coat, with a white shirt over black trousers, he looked like an elderly Italian nobleman, his blue eyes highly alert, his voice that of a much younger man. Sally smiled and shook his hand. 'You are very welcome. I'll call you Michael if you don't mind.'

'That will be fine,' he replied.

Caesar prepared to depart. 'I'll bring Leonardo in the morning.'

'Come, Michael; let me register your voice with the CosmosRX computer. It will then carry out your instructions to the letter. Then, I'll introduce you to your assistants Kubla, George and Abe, and show you the common room.'

It still seemed strange to her, that she could not offer him a coffee.

'Thank you, Sally. Then I'll check today's incoming data.'

With Leonardo da Vinci, Caesar had the advantage of being able to work from an old self-portrait. He was a big, broad-faced man, with a prominent nose, long grey hair, a white flowing beard, soft brown eyes: a younger, more agreeable Leonardo, with a pleasant voice and firm features. She shook hands with him and smiled.

'You are very welcome, Leonardo da Vinci. Let me introduce you to the others.'

'Thank you, Sally; please call me Leonardo. I would like to start work now.'

When Leonardo cleared his voice with the computer, Darius appeared beside her.

'When will Gus be back?'

'Sometime next week; he's in London visiting friends.'

Jack Lawford was working on a film, and planned to move to Lugano when it was finished.

Plato arrived two days later. He was very different to the others, tall and thin with deep blue eyes, a kindly academic expression, completely bald with a neatly-trimmed white beard: he looked and sounded like a college professor. It struck Sally he would perhaps look more authentic wearing a tunic and robe, but it had been agreed they would dress casually. Michael was persuaded to exchange his frock coat for a tee-shirt.

Plato bowed before her. 'Sally, I'm delighted to meet you. Can I start work now?'

'You're very welcome Plato. I'll introduce you to the others first.'

He was more polite than the others were.

Galileo was an imposing figure: heavily-built, with wide features, black hair, expressive – even questioning – big brown eyes, a neatly-trimmed greying beard: a dour, even glowering expression, that was belied by his pleasant friendly voice.

Sally was pleased they were well disposed towards one another – not a feature of their illustrious originals.

She asked Caesar to program a security chief for CosmosRX. He sent her a big, friendly young man that for obvious reasons she called "Hercules". Could she have a skilled medical doctor? Certainly, but he would have to spend some time working in a hospital; knowledge alone would not be sufficient. She contacted a friend in Barts in London who agreed to accept Dr Kenneth Addison for a period of six months. She gave him an educated English accent to go with such a respectable name.

***

Sally travelled to Clifden to see Rachael and her family. How quickly the years go by! Ciara and Siobhan were teenagers now. Joe and Rachael appeared to be very moody. She didn't intrude, but later wished she had. Why didn't they talk to her? She might have been able to help. The teenage gigglers – as she called them – were full of mischief. She took them into town, and bought them colourful summer dresses. Ciara looked like her own mother; she had the same pleasant, easy way with her. Siobhan, a bit more serious, took after her father. She promised to visit them again soon.

***

Still no word of Amanda, nearly nine months since that awful day. If she was alive she would have contacted her. Officially listed among the "missing, presumed dead", they succeeded in establishing that Amanda was on a flight that touched down at San Francisco airport 15 minutes before the quake. What cruel fate. She didn't want to admit it, even to herself, but, deep down she knew Amanda was dead. She would not hear again her cheerful voice or watch that playful smile illuminate her beautiful face. She knew what it was to be a woman, and play out the unselfish maternal role of her kind all down the ages, and yet, in this life, she chose to put the needs of others before her deepest desire to have children of her own. She never said so; she didn't need to.

If it had been possible, Sally would have returned to the Island to attend Tom Cranstan's funeral; she owed him that much, even though she remembered him now only as a dear friend from the distant past. There were heroes too. Fr John Stobar died trying to save others. She wept when she read the report in the Herald Tribune. She refused to meet John again after their frenetic lovemaking that Sunday – not because she didn't want to; she was afraid of falling in love with him. She cherished the memory and didn't care now whether it was a sin or not. Amanda, dear wise Amanda, had taught her so much. John was dedicated to his ministry; she couldn't interfere with that. Her feelings of guilt returned yet again. Why should she have survived when more than a million people, including her dearest friends, were lost?

She flew to Bangkok. Gus insisted that Darius accompany her. Fascinated by such lovely people, she toured the city, visited the Royal Palace and sat, for an hour, in the Buddhist Temple there. It was so peaceful. She had to meet Amanda's family; she owed it to her to make sure they were all right.

The following day they flew down to Hua Hin, a big, rambling friendly town on the Gulf and checked into the Royal Garden Hotel. Knowing her need for solitude Darius watched her unobtrusively from a distance. Everyone knew the Jackson family. She was directed to a very well-kept little house quite close to the Catholic church on the main street. There, she was greeted by a very lovely little Thai lady who put her hands together and bowed, then led the way to a comfortable air-conditioned, colourfully decorated room, and sat her in an armchair.

'Mrs Jackson?'

'Yes, Sally, isn't it? Thank you for coming.' She spoke perfect English.

'How could you know?'

She smiled, Amanda's smile. 'We have many of your photographs. Welcome, welcome – I'm so pleased you came.'

'I would have come sooner, but I kept hoping Amanda would be found alive.'

She nodded philosophically. 'I know. Our beloved Amanda has gone on to her next life; two weeks ago, my dear husband, Robert, joined her.'

'Oh, I'm so sorry to intrude on your mourning.'

'No, my child, we don't mourn them – we miss them – we celebrate their lives and hope they will have a good rebirth.' She got up. 'Let me get you some tea or orange juice.'

'Tea would be lovely, please.'

She fussed around, made a nice pot of tea and served it with homemade scones.

Afterwards, Sally began diplomatically.

'Can I help you and your family? Is there anything you need?'

She smiled. 'No, my child, Amanda left a lot of money in the bank here, but we don't need it.' She paused. 'I'm so happy and thankful to you for coming to see us. Amanda loved you like a younger sister. She told me so. I would like you to meet the rest of my family.'

'I'm looking forward to meeting them. I feel I know them already. Amanda talked about them all the time.'

***

Ron came to CosmosRX on one of his regular visits. They sat around the table in the conference room. Michael summed it up for them.

'The US Congress has approved funds to build 1,500 electricity generating stations that will be operated by coal: with the number of existing energy producers – nuclear and hydroelectric – going out of service, there will be very little increase in the supply of electricity.

Considering their contribution to fossil-free energy, worldwide, the problems with the dams are now crucial: China has 23,000 large dams, America 7,100, India 4,900 and Japan 2,879. We haven't up-to-date figures yet for the other regions.

The build-up of sludge behind the dams is rendering them ineffective: in China, 11,000 hydroelectric power stations have had to be taken out of service; in the US, 2,800, and those figures will rise dramatically in the next five years.'

He paused. 'Then we have the threat to the ozone layer. Despite the 1979 ban, large amounts of chemical compounds – fluorocarbons – are being released into the atmosphere. These include pesticides such as DDT, industrial chemicals such as polychlorinated biphenyls – PCBs – and a range of other substances including chlorofluorocarbon – CFC – aerosol propellants.'

'What's the overall effect?' Ron asked wearily.

'Fluorocarbons rise slowly into the Earth's atmosphere. There, they are broken up by the Sun's ultraviolet rays and release chlorine atoms: these atoms react with other chemical substances in the atmosphere and will gradually destroy the Earth's protective ozone layer. We will then be fully exposed to the Sun's ultraviolet rays.'

'Is it already too late?' Ron asked quietly.

'With all our technology it's very difficult to establish the Point of No Return – or PNR as we call it – with any accuracy. We believe we will now reach PNR in August, or early September 2040.'

He paused.

'Crop returns are continuing to fall sharply; the livestock population is half what it was five years ago. If these trends continue, we'll have worldwide famine by 2041, possibly earlier.'

***

Gus took the ferry into Lugano to visit Jack, who now had a comfortable penthouse apartment overlooking the lake. He had just finished work on a film in Ireland. They were looking forward to spending some time together. Sally promised to meet them later for dinner at Benito's restaurant.

He was grabbed by two thugs, when he walked off the ferry at the promenade, and pushed into the back of a big black Mercedes. Taken completely by surprise, he gasped for breath as the car took off.

'Take us to the robot factory,' rasped one with an American accent.

There were four of them in the car, including the driver. Those on either side of him now produced Uzis.

'What do you want?' he asked, but he already knew.

'The blueprints for your dummies.'

His best chance was to go along with it for the present. Caesar's guards would deal with them.

'Drive out towards the airport,' he directed.

Once clear of the city the car picked up speed. Four Americans, Gus thought – youngish, lean and fit – probably CIA special operations. When they approached the airport, he directed.

'Turn left here.'

Up ahead, the security gates at the entrance to the complex came into view. Two unarmed robots stood guard. The car stopped; the one beside him lowered the car window. One of the guards came forward, looked into the car and recognised Gus.

'Good morning, sir.'

'Open up,' he ordered. 'And tell Caesar it's an alert.'

The Uzi was prodded viciously into his ribs. The high steel gates swung open.

'One more stunt like that and it will be your last,' he rasped.

The car proceeded up a long internal road, and approached the purpose-built shed-type factory. Two tall steel doors opened, and a guard waved them in. Gus was quite determined they were not going to get the blueprints.

The Mercedes was driven into a large, open, loading bay. It was immediately surrounded by six armed robots. The Uzi was pushed against Gus's head.

'One false move out of you and I'll blow your fucking head off. Tell them to put down their weapons.'

Gus saw Caesar standing with his men.

'Caesar,' he called out, 'tell your men to lay down their arms.'

They did as instructed. The American eased his way out of the car, keeping the Uzi to his head. The others followed, moved away from the car and formed a circle around him.

'Tell that dummy to get the blueprints,' the American rasped.

Gus turned to him. 'You can put down your guns now and walk out of here free.'

He was looking for an opportunity to throw them off balance.

The American prodded him. 'Give the order now, or I'll blow your fucking head off.'

'Caesar,' he raised his voice, 'take them alive.'

At that instant, while the robots charged forward, he grabbed the Uzi and tried to wrest it from the big thug. While they grappled, the others opened fire on the advancing robots; hundreds of rounds penetrated their chests, but they kept coming. Gus was swung around, thrown to the ground. He tried to roll free. Steadying himself, the big thug opened fire. Gus felt sharp pains in his chest – and knew no more. Closing in on the thugs, the robots grabbed their arms; screaming in agony, they dropped their weapons.

Two robots rushed to where Gus's body lay in a pool of blood. They lifted him gently and laid him on a table nearby. Caesar examined him, looking for some sign of life: there was none.

Meanwhile, the four prisoners were held pinned by their upper arms.

'Release us immediately,' the big one ordered.

Caesar ignored him. He looked at his four guards.

'Exert maximum pressure,' he ordered calmly.

The guards began to squeeze. The prisoners screamed in agony and kicked out at their captors; the pressure continued until their upper arm bones shattered with loud crunching sounds.

'Who sent you?'

'Go to hell.'

'You will tell me everything before you die'

Going to his office he rang through to Michael for instructions.

Michael contacted Ron in London. Stunned and absolutely shattered, he decided to fly to Boston first to break the news to Sandi.

Michael wasn't looking forward to his next task. Sally knew immediately something was seriously wrong. She couldn't take it in at first: mechanically, she started to tidy her room. He stood there silently, then, bursting into tears, she rushed into his arms. He held her gently; Plato and Leonardo joined them and hugged her briefly. She suddenly realised they were grieving too.

'I must go to him.'

'No Sally, Ron ordered a full alert: no-one is to leave here until he arrives with Sandi.'

'Poor Ron, poor dear Sandi.' She began to cry again, then suddenly stopped.

'It's my fault: I should have insisted he take guards with him.'

Michael nodded sadly. 'So should I, but he wouldn't hear of it.'

'Ron and Sandi?'

'I've already provided them with round-the-clock security.'

'Where are they taking Gus?' she asked quietly.

'To a private clinic in Lugano.'

He didn't tell her that his body would be cremated, and his ashes interred in Boston.

'What about his murderers?'

'Caesar has already dealt with them.'

'I have to ring Jack Lawford.'

***

Ron and Sandi arrived the following morning, accompanied by Alex Purtzel. Sally put her arms around Sandi – she was absolutely shattered – and took her to the living room where Darius made coffee. Later, Ron introduced his friend, Alexander Purtzel.

Michael took Ron aside.

'I've organised everything as you instructed. The local police raided the factory just before dawn: they found it empty and unguarded.'

'You've heard from Caesar?'

'Yes, he and his people are now at their new factory.'

He paused. 'We would like to attend the funeral service. We loved Gus and will miss him greatly.'

'I know, Michael, Gus would like that.'

He blamed himself, he should have insisted on greater security.

Michael continued. 'They will stop at nothing to get their hands on the blueprints: we need to be prepared, Ron.'

It was the first time he addressed him by his Christian name.

'We will be, Michael, we will be. I want to talk to Caesar before we bring Gus home.'

Despite her own grief, Sally's heart went out to Sandi and Ron; to lose their only son, in such a manner, was more than any loving parents could be expected to bear. Sandi, concerned for Ron's health, comforted him as best she could. She wouldn't let him blame himself. Jack Lawford was inconsolable. Sally insisted that he travel to Boston with them. Mechanically, they went through the funeral service and cremation.

Alex, quietly and calmly, took charge of everything. Sally found him to be reserved, efficient and sincere; he was a tower of strength in those awful days. He made all the arrangements and hired an executive jet to fly them directly to Boston Worcester. When they flew out, two days later, Michael and his colleagues were there to say their final farewells to a dear friend.

After the interment, Sally took Jack to the airport and put him on a flight to London. He was so upset, she worried for him. Knowing he had a sister living in Golders Green, she got her phone number, rang her and asked her to look after him for a while. She promised to meet the flight.

***

Sally flew to Galway and travelled to Clifden to be with her family. She spent days wandering along the beaches in Roundstone, feeling empty, confused and alone. She loved Gus, a dear and true friend who was always there for her. She didn't want to go back to CosmosRX: it wouldn't be the same without him.

It was lovely to see Ciara and Siobhan again. They were so full of life. Ciara wanted to be a doctor: would she tell her what she had to do to get into Galway University? Of course, she would. Siobhan planned to take up teaching; she encouraged her too. Immersed in her own grief, she failed to notice how moody Rachael was.

Ron Bergin arrived the following week.

'Sally, I want you to come back to CosmosRX.'

'It wouldn't be the same now.'

He paused for a moment. 'I know, that's how I feel too, but we have to go on. That's what Gus would have wanted, and as you can see, looking around you here, things are getting worse.'

***

A month later, Ron was approached by two men in trench coats, as he walked through arrivals in the new Newark West Airport.

'You will come with us, sir.' One of them ordered.

'Who are you?' he demanded.

'CIA. The Director would like to talk to you. We have a plane waiting.'

'Where are you taking me?'

'To Langley, sir.'

He led the way towards private departures. Ron's guards followed but – with no signal from Ron – did not intervene. Later, a blacked-out Mercedes was driven into the underground car park at the CIA headquarters. Ron was escorted, in a private elevator, to the Director's office on the sixth floor. The man sitting behind the big oak desk didn't rise. A familiar figure from his many TV appearances, Herbert Adams waved Ron to a lounge chair opposite him and dismissed the agents with a nod. Suave-looking, with greying hair, and penetrating blue eyes, he stared briefly at his visitor.

'Mr Bergin, I really think I should hand you over to the police, and have you charged with murder.'

Ron returned his stare evenly.

'On what basis?' He asked.

'Come now, don't play games with me; we know what we're talking about here.' He paused. 'Maybe we can resolve this matter peacefully.'

'What matter?'

He frowned, clearly not getting the subservience to which he was accustomed.

'Professor, I want you to resume the supply of robots to us. We will take as many as you can supply. They will be trained as front-line marines, vitally necessary for the defence of America.'

He smiled grimly, shaking his head. 'That's not going to happen.'

He tried persuasion. 'There's been a misunderstanding: I don't know what happened in Switzerland and I don't want to know. I assumed we suffered casualties when our people didn't return, but that shouldn't upset our good trading relations.'

Ron was finding it hard to keep cool.

'No further robots will be supplied to this country.' He was emphatic.

Adams lowered his voice. 'I could make you disappear, and send in people to take over your operation.'

'You've already tried and failed.'

Ron took a slim packet out of his pocket, extracted a disk and put it on the desk.

'Before you watch the disk, let me tell you something: it's a record of your thugs in action. It also records their confessions, in which they confirm they were acting on your personal instructions.' He paused while Adams picked up the disk. 'Five hundred copies of that disk are lodged in safe places around the world; if anything untoward should happen to me, they will be made public immediately.'

Still unfazed, the Director rose. 'I'll be back in a few minutes.'

He wasn't quite so relaxed when he returned and sat behind his desk.

'I'm sure, Professor, that we can put all this behind us. We're talking about national security here.' He paused and continued earnestly. 'Wars in the future will be fought by highly-programmed robots. I want you to recall all your robots and send them to us. Name your price. We will then be able to regain our correct position as the world's only superpower.'

Ron rose. 'The man your thugs gunned down was my son.'

'Dammit man, I'm appealing to your patriotism.' He paused. 'You have no choice.'

Ron paused at the door. 'Now, you listen to me, you murdering bastard. If there is even an attempt to take our blueprints, I'll hand them over to the Chinese.'

He was escorted to the main entrance where he was met by his two bodyguards. Sally had moved 50 into the area – fully prepared to take Langley apart, if it became necessary.

***

The following year, Ron published his final book *Adapt or Die*. Bangladesh – a country with more than 100 million people – was now part of the Bay of Bengal: its entire population currently trying to make new lives for themselves in India. The Seychelles, Maldives, Andaman and Nicobar islands were gone. He included a recent account of the accelerating retreat of glaciers in the Himalayas, the Andes – where the city of Lima was facing evacuation due to water shortage – Alaska, Labrador and the Poles.

He incorporated an up-to-date report on the nuclear research program carried out by Alex and his team. It indicated the high level of safety that could be achieved by using nuclear fusion and breeder reactors by manning them with specially programmed robots. He spelled it out in stark terms:

"There are some risks attached to the use of nuclear energy; there are risks attached to every human activity; life itself is a risk. If it becomes a choice between nuclear energy and Armageddon, are we going to choose Armageddon?"

This time he named the chief culprits: China, America, India, Russia, Europe and Brazil – they would have to lead the way.

He addressed himself to all those who were making fortunes out of fossil fuels: "You may continue to amass great wealth; you may continue to mock nature; you may believe you can buy your way out of the forthcoming crisis: not this time."

He addressed parents: "Mothers and fathers look upon your beautiful, beloved little children. Their lives and yours will end in a horrific cataclysm unless you demand immediate and drastic action to save the Earth. We are all members of the human race: we sink or swim together; we adapt or we die."

Thousands of scientists around the world supported his views and demanded urgent action: parents' committees were formed in many areas; a small number of leading newspapers demanded an immediate response from world leaders. Hundreds of websites were set up seeking additional information from people all around the world.

Under the glare of the TV cameras, the Greens led their supporters down Pennsylvania Avenue to the White House. More than a million people participated, carrying their white placards with the letters "NNN" in red – "No Nuclear – Never".

The fossil fuel lobby launched a billion-dollar campaign describing Ron as a fantasist, a lunatic and a scaremonger, and paid a number of scientists to support their views. Ron was disgusted: the initial positive response to his book had become mired in such controversy that people didn't know who, or what, to believe. He was dismayed. He and his scientific colleagues had failed to overcome the deep-rooted and well-fed fear of anything to do with nuclear energy.

***

He was exhausted when they arrived – the following afternoon – at Boston Worcester International Airport. Logan was abandoned to the rising ocean 15 years earlier. He rang Alex Purtzel before being driven to Government Buildings. City streets were a mess after the previous night's looting. Fire-fighters were still trying to bring a number of fires under control; a big cleanup operation was getting underway; armed members of the National Guard maintained a high profile. Later, he learned that six deputies and 42 looters were shot dead in Boston alone.

A worried-looking Governor Carney greeted him affably and led the way to his private office. A youngish, handsome-looking, African-American – former Professor of Economics in Columbia – he was now in his second term in office. He sat behind a large mahogany desk. Ron slumped into a comfortable armchair

'Thank you, for coming, Professor. It's nothing but problems these days. We can't depend on the electricity supply from one hour to the next. As for the looting…' He shook his head despairingly. 'I'm sure you appreciate the necessity for absolute secrecy.'

Ron merely nodded.

'You've heard about the tragedy at Forest Springs?'

'Only what I read in the Herald; doesn't sound like typhoid or terrorism to me.'

'It's not; we had to say something. To be frank Professor, we don't know what the hell happened out there. What do you think?'

'How many casualties?'

'Nine hundred and eighty-three dead, most hacked to pieces – they're the lucky ones – with 225 badly injured: all raving lunatics. Most of them will die from their horrific injuries.'

He sighed. 'Have the autopsies been carried out?'

'They're still working on them. Dr Steve Simmons, pathologist in Boston General, is in charge: says he never saw anything like it.'

Ron rose. 'I'll need to talk to Dr Simmons, and visit the scene. I want Professor Purtzel to accompany me.' He paused. 'Any sane survivors?'

'One, he's in Boston General.'

'I'll need to see him too.'

'Certainly, sir.' He hesitated. 'You know what it is?'

'I'm afraid so.'

Carney rose. 'Colonel Matt Dempsey is in charge out there. He'll give you every assistance. The entire area is cordoned off.' He paused. 'You won't speak to the press?'

'Governor, I stopped speaking to the press a long time ago.'

***

Governor Carney's car collected them in the morning. They went first to see José Carvallo, who was being kept under guard in a private room at Boston General. The rig driver was still in a state of shock. How could something like this happen? How could normal people suddenly become raving lunatics? His leg was very painful, but healing well. He could see no reason why he shouldn't be allowed home; Ron could. He listened to the driver's account of the massacre. Was José a native of Forest Springs? No, he wasn't, but how was he going to get home? Had he made a full statement yet? No, he hadn't. They wouldn't even let him make a phone call. Ron suggested total amnesia would be his best bet.

'What's that, sir?'

'If you convince them that you can't remember what happened in Forest Springs, they will probably let you go home.'

José lowered his voice. 'Thank you, sir. Would you make two phone calls for me?'

'Certainly, write down the names and numbers. I'll just say you had an accident and will be in touch shortly.'

'Thank you, sir.'

Ron cautioned him. 'And when you do get out of here, keep quiet; don't talk to anyone, not even your family.'

'I'll do as you say, sir. Can I ask your name?'

'It's best you don't know.'

The elderly pathologist, Dr Steve Simmons, was worried and extremely angry. He showed them one of the victims, a young female with her head almost hacked off. All of the victims, except four, were suffering from brain enlargement. In plain language, their brains were fried. The other four were not natives of Forest Springs.

'Do you know what caused 1,200 people to become raving homicidal lunatics, Professor?' he asked as the cadaver was removed.

Ron nodded silently.

'On second thoughts,' the pathologist continued, 'Better not tell me, I've been served with a gagging order. I'm instructed to certify cause of death as complications of typhoid.'

'By whom?'

'The White House.'

Alex couldn't believe this, but remained silent.

Ron held out his hand. 'Thank you for being so helpful, doctor.'

'Can I ask you one question? Why did this happen in Forest Springs, and could it happen again?'

Ron smiled grimly. 'That's two questions, but I think it better that I do not answer either.'

'You do know the answers?'

He nodded silently.

***

Colonel Matt Dempsey – a big solid man with a strong southern accent – showed them around Forest Springs. It was a complete mess. Many buildings were still smouldering. Removing the bodies had not taken away the awful stench of death, and there were dark blood stains everywhere. Ron could now visualise José's frantic struggle to escape the slaughter. He didn't feel like delaying. The Colonel was curious.

'What happened here, sir? You can tell me. I'm covered by the Official Secrets Act.'

'I can't say yet, Colonel, but I suggest you set up your cordon five miles back from the town. This entire area should be out of bounds.'

They were silent on the way back to Boston. Alex didn't ask any questions; he knew Ron would be very discreet in the presence of the driver.

'Alex, I have to report back to Governor Carney. Sandi is due at Boston Worcester in about two hours. Would you mind meeting her and taking her home?'

'I'll be glad to.'

'I'll be out later. We need to talk.'

***

Ron liked the young Governor. He seemed genuine and was clearly worried by this disaster, but he would tell him only what he needed to know. After all, why bother? The cover-up was already in place.

Carney waited until the coffee was served.

'What happened out there, Professor?'

He decided to be vague.

'It's weather related.'

'Could this happen again?'

'It's not a question of "could" Governor, it's a question of "when". We're looking at the beginning of a process: next time, it could be New York or Washington.'

He was shocked. 'Are you sure?'

'Unfortunately, I am.'

'What can we do?'

'I'm not sure there's anything you can do at this late stage.'

He paused.

'Governor, is it true that there were food riots in Harlem and Miami during the past week?'

He became defensive.

'No, Professor, certainly not, we had some racial conflict, but everything is under control now.'

Another cover-up.

***

Governor Carney phoned the White House when Ron departed. The President wasn't available; he was put through to the Pentagon. He spoke with Secretary of State, Charles Howell, checking first to ensure he was on a secure line. He passed on Ron's findings.

Howell laughed.

'Bergin, I know him. He's been crying wolf for years. Global warming, my arse. Professor Landers tells me we have nothing to worry about. The planet is going through one of its odd phases.'

'But Mr Secretary, we have no other explanation for what happened in Forest Springs.'

'We'll look at it again after the election. Right now, I'm more concerned about the possibility of a stock market collapse.'

'What if there isn't time?'

Howell reacted angrily. 'Do you want to see a Latino Democrat in the White House come January?'

'No.'

'Then continue with the agreed cover-up.'

***

In a ball of fire, the evening Sun sank quietly towards the western horizon behind Mount Tacoma. Captain Diego Vilero completed his inspection of the perimeter of Fortress Tacoma, as it was known: America's most secret underground base and silo. No unauthorised person could get within 20 miles without being apprehended, or shot; thousands of highly-trained marines guarded the complex, armed with the most sophisticated weapons, including nuclear missiles.

The Captain entered the solid reinforced concrete, central control unit and walked briskly to the heavily-guarded security post leading to the elevators. He stared briefly at the staff members leaving for the evening, mostly scientists and computer operators. Satisfied he knew most of them by sight, he directed his attention to those entering with him. It would not be possible for unauthorised personnel to get past this point. In the unlikely event of an armed attack, steel shutters would automatically close, sealing off the area. Saluted by the officer in charge, Sergeant Steve Rogan, he allowed himself to be scanned before entering one of the elevators. It descended quickly for more than 2,000 feet.

When it stopped, he stepped out into an enormous, well-lit, open area and took a seat on the local, single-carriage electric railway. It ran for more than a mile through a maze of tunnels, stopping from time to time to drop off, or pick up people. As it cruised along, he noted that some of the scientists were still at work. Here, America's biological weapons of mass destruction were developed and stored.

In the centre of the silo, line after line of missiles sat on launch pads: they could be primed and launched in 45 minutes. Three layers of bomb and missile-proof ceilings would be opened, temporarily, for that purpose. This was America's most powerful, dangerous and secret arsenal. An official – who was never more than one minute away from the President – carried the little black box. The President alone knew the codes that would authorise a launch.

Captain Diego Vilero arrived at the computer control room at the very end of the complex. Six operators were still on duty. He nodded to them briefly, and sat before his own screen. First, he checked the security reports. As he expected, there were none. Then he input a few figures. Satisfied, he left, boarded the train and returned to the elevators.

He was perfectly calm. The crucial numbers in the President's black box no longer controlled America's weapons of mass destruction and he had no way of knowing they had been changed. Now, the only one with the vital numbers was Captain Diego Vilero.

***

On the 52nd floor of the East Building in Lower Manhattan, Alfredo Corteso, sitting in his lavishly furnished office, had good reason to be feeling elated. CEO and majority shareholder of NEB – North East Banking Inc – he was about to pull off the greatest coup of his life. All the pieces were in place; all he had to do now was put his plan in motion. He put up Tokyo, Hong Kong and London on screen. Tokyo and Hong Kong closed down 60 percent, London – still trading – was close to meltdown. Good; a sharp fall on Wall Street would suit his purpose.

He rang through to his secretary, Nan Evans. 'Evans,' he never used her first name, 'get me John Ellison immediately.'

'Yes, sir.'

Two minutes later, the middle-aged, handsome, very well-groomed Executive Vice President entered his boss's office.

'Ellison,' Alfredo addressed him briskly, 'I've got a job for you.'

By employing a WASP – white Anglo Saxon Protestant – as his Executive Vice President, he was making a very definite statement; by paying him so handsomely, he was ensuring that he could not go elsewhere, and he could treat him as harshly as he wished.

'Yes, sir.' He remained standing. He always called him 'sir' – to do otherwise would risk instant dismissal.

'The market opens in an hour. Talk to you friends on the street. Put out the word on WFB – Washington First Bank Inc – accounting irregularities; profits overstated; possible fraud; Federal investigation underway.'

'We don't have any such reports, sir.'

He grew impatient. 'Just do it, and keep me advised.'

'Yes, sir.' He departed.

Alfredo used his private line for his next call.

'Wadham, you know who this is?'

'Sir.'

'What's WFB quoted at?'

'$53.50.'

'Tokyo, Hong Kong and London are on the floor. Are we likely to follow?'

'Word is we won't, but I think we will. What about our own shares?'

'I'm not worried about them, I already hold 70 percent and I'm not selling. I agree with you, I think the street is set for a sharp fall, but it will be temporary. Buy our own shares if they fall below $30.' He paused. 'Now, the real business of the day. I'm expecting WFB shares to fall sharply: buy when they hit $20 or lower.'

'How many, sir?'

'As many as you can get.'

He continued. 'Charles Howell was on from the State Department. I said I would donate the same as last time – five million, wasn't it?'

'Yes, but I thought you were supporting Rodregas?'

'I am; give Howell five million, and Rodregas ten. Make sure he knows where it's coming from.'

'Sir.'

He rang off and sat back in his executive chair.

***

John Ellison was seething as he walked briskly through Nan Evans' office. 'Why do I put up with that arrogant Latino bastard?' he thought, and he knew the answer; money. Son of a successful New Jersey lawyer, he majored in Business Studies before joining a Wall Street firm. Ten years on the Street, and he'd failed to become a dealer; the money was good, but he was going nowhere fast. He married his secretary, Joan, and bought a house in Riverhead on Long Island, a nice sprawling residence near the beach, but a long way from the city. He couldn't afford to live any nearer, so he commuted daily. Joan went to work for a local lawyer. Their son, Philip, was now 15.

Then, five years ago, his luck changed, or so he thought: his application for the position of Executive Vice President in NEB was successful and he went to work for Alfredo Corteso. The money was so good he could afford to rent an apartment on Fifth Avenue and spend the week nights in town. Joan didn't object, she had her own friends in Riverhead where she joined the local country club. The only drawback: the bastard he worked for missed no opportunity to belittle him. He looked around for another job, but soon realised he would have to take a major cut in salary.

It was about this time he met Laurie Fields – an aspiring actress 20 years his junior – who was taking classes at the NYC School of Acting. Vivacious and full of life, she fascinated him. He fell in love with this beautiful blonde; she made no secret of her feelings, and moved in with him. Laurie was making great progress with her lessons and recently applied for a small part in a Broadway play. He looked after all the expenses. Marriage was very much in his mind, but he didn't want to rush matters: she was very independent-minded and seemed quite happy with their present arrangements.

He knew what Corteso was up to: such damming rumours would bring about the collapse of the WFB share price, exposing it to takeover. The market was very jittery anyway.

He put the word around, as ordered, but not before taking advantage of a favourite stunt on Wall Street: he sold a million shares himself – at $53.50. Some of the dealers, reacting to the rumours, got in on the act, and started selling too. The shares plummeted. When they hit $20, John ordered his broker to buy. His 30 million dollars profit helped to improve his temper. Satisfied, he headed for his local; he could now afford a few large Remy Martins.

***

Nan Evans left the building at 5.30 pm and took the subway to Queens where she shared a tiny apartment with her mother Bertha, father Zack, and her little daughter, Jo Anne. Small, very attractive, with jet black hair, and somewhat plump, she had beautifully tanned features and smiling brown eyes. Her parents emigrated from Jamaica 26 years earlier, when she was just two years old. Her father worked in a laundry until he sustained a back injury that left him, more or less, an invalid. He received some compensation, enough at the time to put her through secretarial school. Mother worked in Tampini's, a nearby, old-style Italian grocery, meat and vegetable shop.

Her first job was in the ticket office at the Port Authority. It didn't pay much, but for the first time, she was able to contribute towards the family overheads. Zack worked occasionally as a night watchman in the rag trade. It was while she was working in the Port Authority she met and fell in love with Simon Lascas, one of the drivers. He was first generation Cuban, lightly-built with dark hair and big blue eyes. She was ecstatic; he loved her dearly, at least, until she told him she was pregnant. Then he said he couldn't marry her because he already had a Cuban wife in Florida. Next she heard of him, he had transferred out to another depot.

Jo Anne was born seven months later, a beautiful tan baby girl. Her parents concealed their dismay, here was another mouth to feed, but they quickly fell for the little beauty and Zack minded her while Nan continued working. It was very difficult financially, but she was determined her little baby would want for nothing.

Then she had a stroke of luck: she got the job of secretary to the CEO of NEB on Wall Street. The money was good, now she could really do things for her family. As time went by, she came to the conclusion that she got the job because she was coloured. Mr Alfredo Corteso wanted everyone to believe he looked after his own. He was an extremely difficult man to work for. Very conscientious, she gave no cause for complaint: she needed the money and good jobs were hard to come by.

She had already made provision for Jo Anne's new school term, but her mother needed an operation for her hiatus hernia. She was suffering extreme discomfort, and could only eat puréed rice or potatoes. This couldn't be delayed much longer. It would cost at least 15,000 dollars. She would have to borrow from a local loan company.

Leaving the crowded subway she joined the long queue outside Tampini's, as she did every evening. Two armed guards stood at the entrance; only ten customers were let in at a time. Supplies of bread, milk and meat were strictly rationed; the limit per customer had been reduced again two days earlier. Prices were rising all the time. With electricity for four hours a day, if lucky, she couldn't run her refrigerator or cold box. Tampini's had a big electricity generator at the back. Despite the shortages, Mother usually managed to get them enough to eat. Things were so slow this evening she rang her mother on her cell phone. She sounded very frustrated.

'It's bedlam here, we didn't get our usual supplies today. Go on home, love, I'll bring whatever I can later.'

Tampini's had their own vegetable, fruit, and livestock farms near Norfolk, Virginia. Increased hurricane activity had destroyed most of their root crops. They were now moving to higher ground, but it would be months before production returned to normal, always assuming the weather didn't deteriorate further. A large quantity of fruit and vegetables was stolen six months earlier. Armed guards now patrolled the farms, travelled with trucks carrying stocks into the city and provided round-the-clock security at the shop.

Nan cooked by gas, although the supply was very unreliable. They suffered winter and summer; with no air-conditioning in the long hot summers, and no heating in the bitterly cold winters. They had to endure it; promises of improved power supplies never came to anything.

***

The youngest son of Mexican immigrants, Alfredo Corteso was born in a squalid little apartment in Harlem. His father worked in the subway, his mother as a housekeeper in a Sixth Avenue hotel. He wanted to make it big, command respect and live in a big house. A quick learner, in the evenings and on Saturdays he ran errands for a local butcher. Lightly built, he worked out in a local gym. The girls loved his smooth, swarthy features, long black hair and smouldering black eyes. He despised his parents for their lack of ambition.

He worked as a courier for the NEB bank before getting a job in the post-room, where he learned a lot about banking and some of the privileged, well-spoken, useless WASPs that graced the upper levels of the bank: how he hated the condescending bastards.

Somerton Johnston Ranford, Chairman and CEO at the NEB, was one of the few old timers left in the banking world. The bank was a sleeping giant with branches in Washington, Los Angles, Chicago and Boston. Old fashioned and conservative, it had accounts with State Departments, the City of New York and some leading stores.

Every morning, he personally delivered the Chairman's post. The CEO liked him, and when his old driver retired, offered him the job. He readily accepted. Severing all contact with his family, he moved out to the Ranford estate on the sound near Garden City, where he was provided with a luxury apartment over the spacious garage that housed three Mercedes and a Rolls Royce.

Tall oak trees and spacious lawns surrounded the old colonial-style mansion. The stables were skilfully concealed behind the trees. It was a magnificent home for a family of three: in addition to "Mr Ranford", as he called him, there was "Mrs Eleanor" who didn't like him, and their very attractive, dark-haired daughter, Vanessa, who rode out every morning wearing a very eye-catching pair of riding britches.

The staff numbered at least 20, including a quite beautiful, African-American cook, called Adi. She came on to him several times and was he tempted! He would have loved to, but he never let pleasure get in the way of business. It was Vanessa he wanted to impress; he could read the signs, despite the little affectations instilled at the finishing school in Paris. In the meantime, he didn't neglect Maria, a randy little Mex who worked in accounts.

He was always very polite, and a little distant with Vanessa. Clearly she was attracted. Occasionally, he collected her from parties in other large domains. She sat in the front of the car with him, and invariably criticised the wimps attending these boring affairs. He was sympathetic, but held back. No hurry.

One night, he collected the elder Ranfords and Vanessa after a society wedding in Albany. Little was said on the way home; clearly Vanessa didn't enjoy the wedding and was thoroughly fed up. He came to the conclusion that words had passed between mother and daughter.

When he stopped the car outside the main entrance, Vanessa announced 'I'm going for a walk in the gardens,' and stomped away before anyone could object.

He parked the Rolls in the garage and stood outside watching her in the distance. She turned, and stood there looking back at him. Dressed in a strapless pink gown, she looked very attractive in the half-light from the garage. He sensed she was willing him on. He began to walk, very slowly, towards her. As the gap closed, he could see she was breathing heavily. Then, she was in his arms, kissing him, hugging him, panting, 'Alfredo, Alfredo.'

He took his time – she was in the hands of an expert – and made sure they could not be seen from the house, before she ripped off his clothes, and he laid her, none too gently, on the grassy lawn. He took her to heights in ecstasy she didn't dream existed before that night. Afterwards, they lay there entwined in one another for a long time. Later, they went back to his apartment and continued their lovemaking. Laughing, as she concealed her grass stained dress, she borrowed his dressing gown, and crept back to her room. It was only the beginning; every night she slipped out of the house and joined him. Fortunately, his apartment was well away from the house. There was a kind of noisy desperation in her lovemaking. She regarded her life, up to now, as a failure, and wanted to achieve something special: she wanted to have a baby.

There was uproar, six months later, when she announced she was going to marry him: no way would her mother hear of her marrying a mere driver. Her father was much calmer, Vanessa was happy for the first time in years, and if Alfredo was her choice, it was all right with him. He decided to promote him to Executive Vice President at the bank, at which the other executives protested loudly and cold-shouldered him at every opportunity.

They were married in a private ceremony and spent the honeymoon in Europe.

The following spring, Somerton Ranford died suddenly, leaving most of his shares in the bank to Vanessa and ten percent to Alfredo. His mother-in-law was so disgusted she went to live with her sister in Toronto. It was payback time: elected CEO and Chairman, he promptly dismissed most of the executives and replaced them with young Latino Vice Presidents. Vanessa was more important now than ever. He spent much time keeping her happy, but didn't neglect his current mistress either.

Conscious of the growing importance of his own people in the US economy he set out to take advantage of the situation. New branches were opened in strategic areas, and Latino managers appointed to cater for this vital sector of the population. It was remarkably successful; in less than ten years, NEB became one of the largest banks in the country. But he wasn't satisfied: he wanted to have the largest bank in the world.

He grew tired of Vanessa, but she wasn't aware of it. If she was, or suspected his other activities, she didn't complain; he still satisfied her every need. Adi was a constant distraction, strutting her shapely figure before him at every opportunity.

One night, after Vanessa retired, he went down to the kitchen to get a drink. Adi was there and up for it. He took her on the kitchen table, and afterwards – several times – in her room.

The following morning Vanessa went out riding as usual; an hour later her horse returned alone. The groom found her body under a tree at the far end of the estate. Alfredo was distraught, in his own way he liked Vanessa. He was on tenterhooks until the family lawyer read out her will: with great relief, he learned she left him her entire estate, including her shareholding in the bank. He was now his own man, and mourned her for all of two days before he returned to Adi's bed.

The ringing phone brought him back to the present. It was Wadham.

'Sir.' He sounded excited.

'Yes.'

'WFB down to $15 and falling. I've got 80 percent for you.' He paused. 'That's the good news. There's uproar here, panic selling – the market is in freefall – it's worse than '29.'

Alfredo switched on his desk monitor.

'What about our own shares?'

'Down to $11. I bought 25 million.'

Good. That would increase his holding to 90 percent.

The bell rang – it was much too early to be the closing bell.

'Hold on, sir, something's happening.'

The camera focused on the President of the NYSE who looked devastated.

"President Harten has ordered that all US stock markets close immediately. There will be a seven-day cooling-off period before we reopen: all other world stock markets have also closed."

Alfredo was unconcerned – he had achieved his life's ambition.

Wadham was less optimistic.

'Today's panic will ruin thousands of investors; I'm just hearing that all credit card facilities have been suspended.' He paused. 'Sir, this will precipitate a run on the banks.'

'I'll ring the President. If it does, we'll have to close too.'

He rang off. He could relax now. Maybe he should get married again: a beautiful white heiress would be very suitable; he would need an heir one day. Installing a generator and large freezer room at his mansion in the hills above Albany had proved to be a good investment. Ten years earlier he had to abandon his home on the Sound when the entire area was inundated by the rising Atlantic. He had enough dry foods, frozen meat, fish and poultry to last a year, not to mention a well-stocked wine cellar. He deplored the rise in violent crime. He travelled everywhere now with two armed bodyguards and installed a highly sophisticated alarm system at his home, with round-the-clock armed security men.

***

Shih Huang Ti was quite pleased with the visit of Chou Yat-sen, the ambassador from President Yang Tao-Tzu in Beijing. It was a very amicable meeting, in the great hall of his palace, high up in the hills overlooking his capital, Harbin. The infighting among the rulers in Beijing – much of it over food scarcity and energy shortages – had enabled him to take over Manchuria, Mongolia, and more recently, Korea. Odd, that America didn't even object when he annexed Korea. They had been very helpful from the start, supplying all the military equipment he required.

China was now the biggest economy in the world, exporting 40 percent of the world's goods. Standards of living had increased dramatically, but the oil shortage was becoming critical.

Why did President Yang Tao-Tzu send his affable ambassador offering to recognise the new state of Manchuria in return for peace? Was it weakness? He thought not. He informed Chou Yat-sen that he had only the greatest respect and admiration for President Tao-Tzu and he harboured no hostile intentions towards the peaceful people of Greater China.

Yat-sen was here to buy time. President Yang Tao-Tzu had underestimated him. He had his own spies in the inner circles in Beijing. They had provided him with the details of the Middle East oil plans. If Yang Tao-Tzu moved first, it would be unpatriotic of him to invade Greater China. He would now have to move quickly, take Beijing and follow through with Yang's Middle East operation. It was an excellent plan: whoever controlled the Middle East, ruled the world.

With a massive, highly-trained, and well-equipped army, he was ready: the hour was at hand. General Lin Pang had already drawn up the plans to move south and take Mukden. Little resistance was expected. He would then advance directly on Beijing, where his supporters were waiting to lead a peaceful demonstration demanding the resignation of the present government. He was confident of a successful, bloodless revolution. Standing by the window, he looked out on the great valley of Hwang Ho, where his illustrious ancestor, the great Chin, once marshalled his forces to begin the conquest of the country that now bore his name.

The lightly built 42-year-old Shih Huang Ti looked like a Buddhist monk, with ascetic features, bright blue eyes and a long flowing white beard. Brought up as the expected one, he was always surrounded by faithful servants waiting to do his bidding. He never raised his voice and had that rare quality granted to few men: he knew his destiny, and he knew he would fulfil it.

General Lin Pang was shown into his presence. He bowed low before him.

'Illustrious Emperor, all is in readiness for the attack on Mukden.'

'Good. Tomorrow, we will move south.'

***

In the Oval Office in the White House, President Elmer Franklin Harten was angry. A tall, handsome, African-American, former Governor of Illinois, he served two terms in the Senate before being elected President. He wanted to be the first African-American president to serve two terms; right now, it didn't look good, hence the reason for his anger.

Immigration had brought about some remarkable changes in American society: the white vote was now down to 20 percent. They still controlled enormous wealth, but their days were numbered. In another 20 years, Latinos, African-Americans, Chinese, Irish, Arabs, Indians and Cubans would dominate American society. They no longer talked about the WASPs in New York: now it was the BULLs – the Bright Upper-class Loquacious Latinos.

The President glared at his Secretary of State.

'Charles, the fucking election is only five months away. Why are we still 12 points behind that bastard, Rodregas?'

Charles Howell, a Jamaican – former Professor of Economics at Yale – reacted calmly. Tall and of slight build, he looked like a college professor, and was not without political ambitions himself.

'This is only July, Mr President. It's early days yet. I've been preoccupied with the stock markets.'

It was his suggestion that the stock markets, and later, the banks, be closed temporarily, to allow people to come to their senses. He hadn't disposed of any of his own shares; he had every confidence things would return to normal as soon as trading resumed.

The President's mind was elsewhere.

'Never mind that, I want to know what we're going to do. I thought my speech on the economy would reverse the trend.'

'Mr President, the food supply situation is getting worse: we haven't had any grain from the Mid-West for the past three years; our beef stock is only 20 percent of what it should be. Argentina is refusing to continue beef supplies. Their ambassador says they haven't enough for themselves.'

'China?'

'They're having problems too. We have three ships coming home empty.'

He paused for a moment.

'We've got to keep things going until after the election. Then, I'll declare a state of emergency, put more resources into stock breeding, and utilising whatever arable land we've got left.'

'Mr President that may not be enough.'

'I know, dammit. If we have to, we'll invade Argentina – or any other country that refuses to supply us – and damn well take their beef and grain.'

He paused and scratched his chin.

'But that's not the real problem; what the hell are we going to do with this poll?'

'I think you're worrying unnecessarily, Mr President, the polls don't take account of our strategically placed "Angel" voters. They performed very well last time.'

'I know, but 12 points is a hell of a lead?'

'There's plenty of time, Mr President.'

He insisted on being so addressed at all times. Dressed in a grey pinstriped suit, with a white shirt and red Hermes tie, he never removed his jacket, not even in the informality of the Oval Office.

'Haven't we got anything on this bastard, Rodregas?'

‘We’ve done a forensic investigation, Mr President. He’s fond of the women, but that seems to be an advantage these days.’

The President stared at him briefly – this wasn’t a subject for discussion.

‘So why are we so far behind then?’

‘The problem, Mr President, is simple: the Democrats, crafty bastards that they are, have chosen a Latino candidate. You took that vote last time and I believe you will hold much of it this time, but it’s not going to be easy.’

‘We need a diversion. What’s happening in China?’

‘President Yang Tao-Tzu reckons he won’t be ready to march on Manchuria for another three months.’

‘What the hell is keeping him? Didn’t we send him all the armaments he asked for? I need him to move now.’

‘I’ll talk to our ambassador today. Mr President, how will a civil war in China help us?’

‘For a start, it will wreck their economy. They’ve been getting too damn big for their boots. I will demand an immediate cease-fire, and – with the possibility of a world war – declare an emergency. I might have to postpone the election.’

The Secretary of State frowned. ‘That never happened before, Mr President, not even during World War II.’

He smiled. ‘I’ve discussed the idea with General Jackson, Chairman of the Joint Chiefs: he’s all for it.’

He considered it. ‘Congress would kick up a stink, but you do have the power.’

‘We’ll wait and see how the polls react over the next month.’

‘Mr President, what do you make of the CIA report suggesting China seems to be stirring things up in the Middle East?’

‘They’re wasting their time: Adams assures me he has arranged to take out Hussein and replace him with someone we can rely on.’

The phone on the desk rang. The President picked it up, listened for a moment, thanked the caller and turned to his Secretary of State smiling broadly.

'I've got the bastard now.'

'What is it, Mr President?'

'Rodregas has just announced, at a press conference in Chicago, that he will give serious consideration to a nuclear energy initiative after the election. That will cost him at least ten million votes.'

'What do you propose to do, Mr President?'

'I will issue an immediate statement: under no circumstances will nuclear become an option for us.'

'But, Mr President, I thought you had already decided we have no choice but to initiate a massive nuclear program after the election?'

He smiled broadly. 'I have, but until then it's "No Nuclear – Never".'

A presidential assistant knocked politely and entered.

'Mr President, you're due at Andrews for your flight to Austin.'

'Are Mrs Harten and my son ready?'

'Yes, Mr President.'

'Where is Sarscoff?'

'He's on his way to Andrews right now, Mr President.'

Half way to the door, he turned.

'Charles, how about increasing Social Security back to its old figure?'

'We can't afford to do that, Mr President.'

He smiled. 'No, but we can promise to do it. Afterwards, we'll blame Congress. I'll talk to you later.'

'Bon voyage, Mr President.'

***

Ron sat down with Alex and Sandi in the living room of their comfortable Boston home. It was undamaged in the recent riots; mainly because two of his guards took care of would-be looters. He updated Alex on CosmosRX and its potential.

At the end, he sat back wearily.

'I have no right to ask you to take it over, Alex, but you're the only one I can trust.'

'Is it that bad, Ron?'

'It's worse: we'll hit the point of no return within the next two months.' He paused. 'We may not even have two months.'

He didn't want to spell it out in front of Sandi. He was envisaging mass slaughter, rampant disease, and appalling inhumanities, including cannibalism: once underway, there would be no stopping it.

'What will you do?' Alex asked quietly.

'I would like you to take Sandi to CosmosRX. You can protect her there.'

Sandi disagreed. 'No Ron, when that time comes, we'll go together.'

***

Special Agents, Alan Warner and Jack Hardy arrived in Austin on the noon flight from Chicago. Young, with clear-cut bronzed features, they were met by local agents, Pedro Delgado and Joss Bergman. Pedro led the way to his grey Chevy in the underground car park.

Pulling out on to the freeway, he drove towards town. Sitting beside him, Alan Warner extracted several sheets of typed pages and passed them around.

'This is the President's detailed itinerary.'

They studied it and then handed the papers back.

Joss Bergman spoke quietly. 'A black President visiting Texas. Is he mad?'

'Maybe he is.'

'Are all our agents in place?' Alan Warner asked.

Bergman replied. 'Yes.'

He paused, as they entered heavier traffic. 'Have any of our people been assigned to the President's personal guard?'

'Three or four, I believe. Are you expecting trouble, Joss?'

'No.'

'Good. As soon as the orders come through we'll eliminate the President.'

***

Alex took the late night flight to Zurich, where he transferred to a local flight and landed at Lugano just before noon. He was met by Darius who took him by taxi to a lake-side ferry. Boarding, Alex looked around at the badly burned mountains surrounding the lake. This used to be such a beautiful place. The journey to Capalago took 20 minutes. Leaving the ferry, they crossed the road, and entered a single carriage cogwheel train. The driver nodded to Darius. There were no other passengers. The train climbed steadily to the top of the 6,000-foot mountain peak. Alighting, Alex looked down on the lake far below. Darius led him to a large building that had once been a cafeteria. Ten guards watched, but made no effort to approach them.

Darius led the way through the cafeteria to a large elevator concealed behind steel doors. They entered, and it descended.

'CosmosRX is at a level below that of the lake,' Darius volunteered.

The elevator stopped eventually. When the doors opened, Alex was met by Sally and her Supremos.

'Welcome to CosmosRX, Alex.'

'It's good to see you again, Sally.'

'You have already met Michelangelo, Leonardo da Vinci, Plato, Hercules and Bill.'

They stepped forward, smiled and shook hands with him.

Sally continued. 'Now that you have arrived, I am formally advising everyone here, that on the instructions of Professor Bergin, you are now the Director of CosmosRX.'

He hadn't realised she was so beautiful.

'I would like to have a meeting as soon as possible, but first, I want to have a look around and see my quarters.'

'Of course.' She turned to the others. 'Shall we say, the conference room in an hour?'

Sally led the way through the well-lit facility.

'Originally, this was designed and built as a fallout shelter for the Swiss President and his family: the very big rooms, high ceilings and daylight simulation help to reduce the claustrophobic tendencies that are associated with living in an underground complex. When it outlived its usefulness, it lay idle for a number of years, before Professor Bergin and his friends purchased it.

It's on four levels: the top one is taken up entirely with the utilities, water, air, and electricity and food supplies. The second level has a very extensive library – unfortunately all of the books are in French, German or Italian – stocks of medical supplies, a gym, swimming pool, cinema, a music centre with large stocks of films and CDs and a private meditation room. Makes you wonder if it was worth it. The boredom level of being confined to such a restricted space for years, perhaps decades, must be pretty awful.

On this level we have a large operations room with the most sophisticated computers in the world. Michael and the others monitor all incoming data and outgoing orders, as well as working on survival programs. At the far end we have a fully equipped kitchen, my apartment and a changing room and lounge for our robots.'

'I see.'

'Now, I'll take you to your private office and apartment.'

She led the way to the elevator. They went down one level and walked out into a large, comfortable office and library, its walls decorated with some of the world's most famous paintings.

'Copies,' she smiled, walking across the room to double doors.

'This leads to your sitting room and bedroom with bathroom en suite.'

The sitting room was lavishly furnished with red carpeting, a luxurious suite, writing desk, recessed lighting and a computer/television. A large double bed and a somewhat old-fashioned mahogany suite dominated the bedroom. His case was there already.

As she prepared to leave, he asked quietly 'Can it be done? Can the Earth be saved?'

'Michael says it can, but there isn't much time.'

***

Sally returned to the operations level. Despite her worries, she found herself strangely attracted to this very handsome reserved new director with sad blue eyes – but this was no time for romance.

The conference room was plainly furnished with a round table in the centre. Five wall clocks showed the time in Zurich, London, New York, Hong Kong and Sydney. She sat beside Michael. Alex opened his briefcase and extracted a notebook. He noticed there were no files on the table.

'Let me say first,' he began, 'that I know very little about CosmosRX, so I'm going to have to rely on you to fill me in. I'm basically a nuclear physicist. Please call me "Alex". Now, I would like to hear about your plans to save the Earth.'

Michael began, in a very matter-of-fact tone.

'I will start with the most immediate problem: we have a global population of 12 billion on a planet that – in ideal conditions – can only support six billion. Current conditions are far from ideal.'

'What do you suggest we do with six billion people?' Alex asked.

'Eliminate them.'

He looked at Sally, who was clearly shocked.

'Why eliminate half our people?'

'Alex, mankind is faced with extinction from any one of three different sources: depletion of the ozone layer, global warming or famine.'

'Professor Bergin didn't highlight the famine risk in public?'

'No, he was afraid such a warning would lead to widespread panic.'

'And you think the answer is to eliminate half our population?'

'That's part of the solution. In addition, we have to initiate a massive crop growing and livestock breeding program in areas not normally subject to drought or flooding.'

'So the threat from the ozone layer and global warming now becomes secondary?'

'That's correct.'

Sally was appalled, she hadn't heard this before. She had read harrowing tales of the potato famine in Ireland – in 1845 –

when millions of her people died of starvation. The old people still talked about it; the silent ruins of derelict villages could still be seen in many parts of the countryside, sharp reminders of a horrific tragedy. Hundreds of thousands sailed for America, in what became known as "the coffin ships".

Alex felt sick.

Outside, the alarm bells started ringing. Sally jumped up anxiously.

'Something's happened.'

The others reacted calmly.

Alex rose. 'Let's go and see.'

She led the way to the operations centre, where the operators sat quietly in front of their screens.

Kubla remarked 'It's another Forest Springs.'

'Where?'

'Mexico City.'

'Population 39 million,' Michael added.

The pictures were horrific: it was slaughter on a massive scale. The screen went blank. Someone had pulled the plug, but not before these appalling scenes were flashed around the world. Later, they would learn that the Mexican Army, and units of the US Army from Fort Worth, were ordered – as an act of mercy – to wipe out the entire population.

Alex ordered curtly 'Let us resume our meeting.'

They returned to the conference room. Alex closed his eyes for a moment. It's unreal, he thought. I'm sick to my stomach, while here they are calmly discussing the elimination of half the human race.

Michael spoke quietly. 'Perhaps it's as well we cannot share your feelings.'

He could not avoid the ultimate question.

'What happens if I cannot persuade world governments to act in time?'

'You will have to decide the fate of mankind.'

'Has CosmosRX got the resources?'

'Yes,' Plato replied, 'if we act quickly.'

'And if I refuse to act, will you do it anyway?'

Michael replied. ‘No, only the Director of CosmosRX can make that decision: if the situation becomes irreversible, our role will be to bring about the final destruction of mankind with as little suffering as possible.’

***

By the time he’d showered and shaved, Darius arrived carrying a tray with his favourite coffee and rolls.

‘How do you know what I like?’

Darius smiled. ‘Mrs Bergin told me to look after you well.’

Alex poured the coffee. ‘What else do you do?’

‘Everything: cook, waiter, valet, driver and I’m available 24 hours a day.’

He paused. ‘I’m also Sally’s professional hairdresser.’

‘How did you get that job?’

‘Before we left London, I was sent on a course.’

‘I’m going to lie down for a while. Will you call me in an hour?’

***

Alex was fully determined – when they reassembled in the conference centre – that no way was this his decision. World leaders would just damn well have to act.

‘Sally and gentlemen, I’m going to see Prime Minister Cyril Ramsey of Great Britain, and President Elmer Harten of the US.’ He turned to Sally. ‘Have you made the arrangements?’

She consulted her notes. ‘Yes, PM Cyril Ramsey will see you at 11.00 pm tonight at the temporary Number 10 in Birmingham. The centre of London is under water; millions of people have been evacuated. It must be dreadful there now. President Harten is canvassing in Texas. I’ve talked with his campaign manager, John Sarscoff. He’s agreed to get you 15 minutes with the President at 10.30 am tomorrow at the Hilton Hotel in Fort Worth. I had to use Professor Bergin’s name to get the appointments. I think they’re a bit shell-shocked by what happened in Mexico City, particularly as they failed to keep it off television. That four-minute coverage is being shown repeatedly all around the world. Your flight leaves Zurich at 8.30 pm and onwards from Birmingham – Heathrow closed five years ago – to Fort Worth at 5.00 am local time.'

'And the opposition leaders?'

'They won't agree to meet you.'

He rose. 'I'll be back as quickly as I can. In the meantime, I want you to try to find some way of letting the population reduce through natural wastage.'

***

Prime Minister Cyril Ramsey, a seasoned, very worried politician in his early fifties, greeted Alex affably. Coffee served, he listened to what his guest had to say, but his mind appeared to be elsewhere. Alex wasn't very specific and didn't disclose the existence of CosmosRX. His message was blunt – immediate action if Armageddon was to be avoided.

The grey-haired stocky politician reacted calmly.

'Can you be more specific, Professor?'

'Fossil fuels have got to go. For a start, all vehicles will have to be removed from the roads of every country in the world.'

He sat back, relieved.

'I can't act alone; if I tried I would be swept out of office. This is a matter for the UN.' He changed tack. 'What do you think happened in Mexico City?'

'It's another Forest Springs, a direct radiation hit.'

'Forest Springs, wasn't that typhoid?'

'That's what they told you.'

'They're saying the slaughter in Mexico City was caused by terrorists using a new form of gas. I'll have to see UN Secretary General, Jonathan Felton. We need an international committee to tackle this problem.'

Alex was exasperated. 'Prime Minister, there isn't time. I beg you to act and act now.'

'I'll ring Jon Felton and see what he says.' He paused. 'You will need to have President Harten on side; they're the biggest polluters in the world.'

'I'm meeting the President at Fort Worth in the morning.'

He rose and shook hands.

'Our most immediate problem is the restoration of confidence in world markets. Where can I contact you, Professor?'

'I'll give you my cell phone number. I'm moving around a lot.'

On his way back to the airport, Alex was told by his taxi driver that martial law and curfew had been imposed in most British cities. Negotiations with the Irish Government, over food supplies, had broken down. He understood the Army was getting ready to invade the Republic.

***

President Elmer Harten was in a really foul mood. The Democratic candidate's lead in the polls had increased to 14 percent. He greeted Alex brusquely.

'I've already spoken with Prime Minister Ramsey; now what's this nonsense about the end of the world?'

Alex knew he was on a loser, but he had to try. Half way through his presentation the irate President stopped him.

'Professor Landers doesn't agree with you. I'm making a major speech on global warming in Dallas at lunchtime. My immediate concern is the financial crisis. Come November, when I'm back in the White House, I'll set up a committee to consider your concerns. We don't need to panic every time the climate becomes erratic, and for your information that Mexican City business was terrorism: the CIA has confirmed it.'

Alex wasn't going to let him off the hook that easily.

'And Forest Springs, Mr President?'

He became flustered. 'Typhoid, sad business. Thank you for coming. These matters are best left to those of us who know what we're doing.'

When Alex left, the President rang his Secretary of State.

'This bastard Bergin and his friends are becoming a damn nuisance, as if I haven't enough fucking problems. If they go public it could be embarrassing.'

'Leave it with me, Mr President. What's his friend's name?'

'Purtzel, another egghead.'

Returning to the airport, Alex rang Ron, and took a flight to Boston Worcester.

***

Ron and Sandi greeted him warmly. He could see that Ron wasn't well, but he brushed aside all talk about his health. They sat outside in the shade, sipped coffee and talked. Afterwards, there was a long silence. Eventually, Ron spoke, very quietly. 'Alex, you are the only one who can now save this planet.'

'The price is too damn high.'

'Yes, it is, if those greedy stupid bastards had listened 40 years ago, we wouldn't be where we are today.'

Sandi joined them. They were silent for a while. Then Alex spoke.

'I'm worried about you two. Will you come to CosmosRX and let me take care of you?'

It was Sandi who replied. 'No, Alex, my love, when the time comes we will both go together. I'm looking forward to seeing Gus again; it's a strange thing for a mother to say, but I'm glad he didn't live to see what we're seeing now.'

Alex looked at his watch.

'Going so soon?'

'I'm booked on a flight to Sligo. I want to see Mother before returning to CosmosRX.'

'I've ordered four of our security people to escort you safely to the airport. We've heard reports of riots in the city.'

They rose and hugged one another tearfully. Sandi thrust a small parcel of sandwiches into his reluctant hands. Ron walked slowly with him to the gate. They hugged again. Alex had tears in his eyes as he was escorted to the waiting car. Sandi waved from the front door.

While waiting to board at Boston Worcester, where many flights were being cancelled, he received a phone call from PM Ramsey. President Harten had reassured him that these matters would have his urgent attention after the election. Fortunately, his flight to Sligo took off on time.

***

Ron found his two bodyguards watching television.

'My good friends, I won't need you any longer. I want you to report in to CosmosRX; you will be assigned to other duties.'

'Are you sure you will be all right, sir?' Andrew asked as they prepared to depart.

'Yes, we'll be fine.'

At the front door, he shook hands with them and wished them well.

He was taking his pills, prior to going to bed when the phone rang. Sandi was already upstairs. He thought it might be Alex.

'Professor Bergin?'

'Yes.'

'Secretary of State, Charles Howell here. The President is returning to the White House, and would like to talk to you. I'll send a car to take you to the airport.'

'Don't bother, tell him, he's 40 years too late.'

The line went dead. He watched the late night news. There was no further reference to the Mexico City disaster – good media management. The death toll in the Charleston hurricane now exceeded 25,000, with widespread damage to property and much of the city under water. The Governor had ordered that the entire city be evacuated. The National Guard was called out to deal with race riots – no mention of food – in Harlem, Chicago and Pittsburgh. Forest fires on California Island were burning out of control. Another extreme hurricane was sweeping up the East Coast, likely to come ashore in Wilmington, South Carolina. Following unprecedented rainfall in central Europe the river Danube had burst its banks again, and Budapest, Prague and Vienna were being evacuated. There was no let up in the rainfall in eastern China; the situation was now worse than the great flood of the Yangtze River and its tributaries in 1998. Cracks were beginning to appear in the Three Gorges Dam: the Chinese Government had ordered the immediate evacuation of Shanghai. There were power failures all over the place. Landslides were widespread. In many parts of the world, communications had broken down: large areas were now isolated. He'd had enough. He switched off, so weak and tired; he just wanted to fall asleep and not wake up.

The front doorbell rang.

Damn. He turned off the alarm and opened the door. A youngish man in a smart grey suit stood before him.

'Professor Bergin?'

'Yes.'

'Is Professor Purtzel here?'

'No.'

'Can you tell me where I can find him?'

Ron was becoming wary now.

'I have no idea where he is.'

The man produced a .38 and fired two shots. Ron collapsed in the hallway. The shooter put away his gun and walked calmly to a waiting car. Hearing the commotion, Sandi dashed down the stairs.

'Ron, Ron, my poor Ron,' she screamed taking him in her arms.

Somehow, she managed to drag him into the living room; put him in a half-sitting up position against the armchair, closed his eyes and held him in her arms, sobbing quietly. Time passed, then suddenly it struck her. Oh, my God, Alex – they'll be after him too.

Getting up, she rooted around for Sally's number. Ron must have it in his pocket book. With trembling hands, she took the pocket book from his inside pocket and flicked through the pages. Got it. She picked up the phone – it was dead.

With her heart pounding, she raced up the stairs. Where did she put her cell phone? It should be in her handbag; it wasn't; the charger, it must be there. Scrambling down the stairs she tripped and fell, hurting her arm; she ignored the pain, and breathed a sight of relief when she found the cell phone on the charger.

She tapped in her message. "Sally, Ron shot. Save Alex. Farewell love. Sandi."

She sent it twice. Moments later she received a reply: "Will mind Alex. I'm sending help. Love, Sally."

Now she could relax. Going to the kitchen she took a little phial from the food press, filled a glass of water, extracted a pill and swallowed it with the water. She sat down beside Ron, put her arms around him and whispered 'I'm coming Ron and Gus, my loves.'

She was past suffering when, ten minutes later, six CosmosRX security men entered the house. The leader contacted Sally for instructions.

Fifteen minutes later, the entire north-east was hit by another massive power failure.

***

Alex Purtzel was 16 when he learned the exact circumstances of his birth. Born with a malformed left leg, he had a slight limp, and always walked with the aid of a stick. To him this was perfectly normal, he didn't know any differently until he commenced school, and had to endure some cruel and sarcastic remarks from a few of his fellow pupils. He became very sensitive about his leg, but refused to accept that he was, in any sense, deficient. Academically, he was quite brilliant and got on well with most of his classmates.

His mother, Caroline, a GP in Yeatstown, was only 25 when he was born. Yeatstown is a seaside village – five miles from Sligo city – where the Garavogue River meets the sea. They lived in a fine, modern two-storied house facing the sea, at the end of a cul-de-sac. With wide spacious lawns, it was surrounded by small trees, shrubs and colourful flowers. Caroline had a wooden three-level deck erected by the sea. Here, they sat for hours on long summer evenings, and admired the magnificent view of the mountains of Knocknarea on the other side of the estuary, with the rocky cairn on top, under which, it was reputed, Queen Maeve was buried. Away to the west, the Ox mountain range ran for as far as the eye could see.

He grew up with a love of nature, conscious of its extraordinary variety and ever-changing moods. The swallows came for the summer and returned to southern Africa for the winter. He listened for the occasional cuckoo that still ventured from its natural habitat in southern Portugal. The cycle of the tides fascinated him. He would sit for hours listening to the birds chirping all around him. Then, in the evening, the crows assembled in the nearby tall oak trees. Now, the cawing commenced in earnest, it seemed they were all at it: were they relating the day's events to one another? Eventually, the cawing subsided, very slowly, and the silence of the night reigned. Curiously, he didn't hear any cawing in the mornings.

Realising that the other boys had fathers, he began to ask about his. Caroline told him his father was dead, but didn't elaborate further. He concluded she found it too painful to discuss. But the questions remained. What kind of man was he? No-one ever talked about him. Where was he buried? Certainly not locally. Caroline, a moderate Catholic, commemorated her mother's birthday and anniversary every year and often brought him to visit her grave in Sligo cemetery. And of all the hundreds of photos in the house, there wasn't one that included his father.

Caroline's widower father, Matt Connolly, who had a furniture store in Sligo, came to live with them. The burly, jovial old man loved his growing grandson, encouraged him to ignore his slight handicap, and to learn to swim and play golf. Alex quickly became a powerful swimmer and, within two years, won the youth golf championship at the local golf club. Alex asked him once about his father. The old man stopped in his tracks, pursed his lips and nodded sadly. 'It was very unfortunate lad. Some day I'll tell you about it.' But he never did.

An avid reader with a thirst for knowledge, Alex made good use of the Internet. With excellent school grades, he obtained a scholarship to Galway University, where he studied Science. He was deeply upset when – during his second year in college – Matt died after a short illness: to him, it was like losing a father.

One fine summer evening they sat on the deck as the Sun sank towards Lissadell. Caroline was quite nervous; close as they were, she wasn't sure how he would react.

'Alex, I want to tell you about your father.'

'Oh.' He was surprised.

She hastened on. 'I would have told you sooner, but I wanted you to be a bit more mature. When I qualified, I opted to spend two years in the Von Oughten Hospital in Bonn. It was a very exciting time. I had so much to learn: everyone was very kind and helpful, especially with the language. One evening, towards the end of my first year, there was a great commotion in Accident and Emergency. A patient named Ulrich von Purtzel was brought in on a stretcher. He had sustained a fractured leg. The place was buzzing with media people. Chief Surgeon, Heinrich Mettler was summoned. The nurses were all agog. I attended this tall, very handsome, young man until the Chief Surgeon arrived: must be royalty, I thought to myself.

I was the only one there who didn't realise that Ulrich was Germany's most famous soccer star, and captain of the team that won the International Cup two years earlier. The media were on hand all the time: it was on the TV news, including an interview with Mr Mettler. Ulrich would make a complete recovery, but would not play football again for six months. Sitting up in bed, surrounded by large baskets of flowers, he smiled bravely at the cameras.

After the operation, he was under my care while the Chief Surgeon was away. He was like a big spoiled child whose whole life was lived in public. Two weeks later, when he was leaving – surrounded by a score of media people – he asked me out to dinner. We fell in love. The media picked up on it; romance for the 30-year-old hero at last. After a very public courtship, we got married and honeymooned in South Africa.

I first realised all was not well when I had to insist on keeping on my job at the hospital. Three months later, I discovered I was pregnant with you. I was so happy. I tried to persuade him to keep it private, but he insisted on calling a special press conference to announce it to the world. From there on, I avoided the media people as best I could, and concentrated on my prenatal exercises and diet.

He was in London when I was rushed to the Meyer Clinic where you were born. The gynaecologist told me you were a strong healthy baby, but your left leg was slightly deformed; physiotherapy would help to strengthen it and, at worst, you would have a slight limp. I was so happy. I kept counting your tiny fingers and toes.

Ulrich rushed home from London, arrived at the clinic with a big bouquet of flowers, escorted by the usual circus of media people and photographers. The gynaecologist was on hand to show him his son. You were nestling comfortably in my arms. He greeted me with a kiss and took you in his arms. He wanted to show you off to the media people. The gynaecologist mentioned your leg.

His face dropped; he handed you back to me.

He screamed "This cannot be my child. My son could not have any deformities," and headed for the door.

I was completely stunned; my tears fell on your lovely little face.

The gynaecologist challenged him.

"You will not object then to a DNA test?"

His response was "You can have any damn test you like."'

Alex got up and put his arms around her.

'My poor dear, Mum. Where is this bastard? I'd like to strangle him.'

She brushed aside a tear. 'Alex, my love, it was still the happiest day of my life; don't ever forget that. I don't blame him, the media made a god out of him – after a while he thought he was god.' She paused. 'It wouldn't have worked anyway.'

'Is he still alive?'

'I believe so. He's got a chain of sports shops in Germany.'

'Did he remarry?'

'Several times, and divorced nearly as quickly. Last I heard he has no other children.'

She omitted to tell him that despite the DNA confirmation, Ulrich still insisted Alex wasn't his son.

***

Alex arrived at the new Sligo International Airport, near Ballysodare – Strandhill International was inundated 20 years earlier – at 11.00 am the following day. He was met by Caroline's guards, Patrick and Enda, who had been sent by Ron six months earlier to provide security for Caroline. He rang from Boston before boarding his flight. He was surprised to see 12 security men surround the plane.

Patrick explained. 'Several international flights have been cancelled. Sally wants to make sure you get back safely; when you visit your mother we will fly you directly to Lugano.'

Enda drove him to Yeatstown. Tired as he was, he noticed there were two Uzi machine guns in the car. Although they talked regularly on the phone, Caroline was careful not to sound pessimistic and didn't tell him how bad things were.

Dismayed and horrified by events, she was resigned now. She took more time than usual over her appearance that morning; her stocks of cold creams, lipsticks, deodorants, toothpaste and hand lotions were depleted and could not be replenished. Wanting to look well for Alex, she put on a very attractive beige dress. Standing inside her bedroom window, she surveyed the bay and surrounding mountains. Her garden was ten feet above the highest tide level when she first purchased the house; now the tide was steadily moving up the garden. The neighbours on either side had already abandoned their homes to the sea. It was quite normal now to see bodies floating down the river.

The world was closing in: everything was becoming local; there were no buses or trains, no postal service, no bin collection, gas stations were closing down – she had just enough gas to collect Alex and get him back to the airport. Most days there was no TV, even during the hour when electricity was available; the local newspaper no longer issued; she was down to her last radio battery. She didn't listen much: news of killing, rioting and looting in Sligo appalled her. She was down to her last six candles. Fortunately, the days were long and warm. Most shops had closed down; food and meat stores – protected by armed guards – only opened for an hour a day, and then only if they had any stock.

It was frightening but she was past that. Her immediate neighbours formed a vigilante force and patrolled the area at night. Her two robotic guards formed part of that group. Intruders were shot on sight and their bodies thrown in the river; two of her neighbours were shot dead. The authorities couldn't cope; the only law now was gun law.

Her near neighbour, John Harvey, the local school headmaster, invited his entire family to his home for a farewell party. When two young children disappeared – on their way to school – he closed the school and told the parents to guard their little ones. John, a very pleasant man in his early sixties was a native of County Donegal; Mary, a nurse from Charlestown, came there after they married nearly 30 years ago; good, kind neighbours, they brought up their fine young family in that big old house near the road.

They were almost part of her own family: Caroline treated Anne and Rose for their minor ailments growing up; she attended their weddings and the christening of their lovely little children, Mary, now three, and Sean, 18 months. Mary Harvey sat them all down in her drawing room; her husband, John, opened a bottle of whiskey, filled several glasses and handed them around. A few neighbours called briefly, said their goodbyes and departed tearfully.

In all her long life Caroline never felt so desolate, not even when her mother died; but there was no other option. Mary took her daughters and little Mary to the main bedroom. First, she ground the little pill and put it in a glass of milk; then she sat little Mary on her knee and held the glass for her. Tears ran down her cheeks. The little child looked up at her. 'Why are you crying, granny?' When the child appeared to fall asleep, she laid her out gently on the bed. Her daughters took their pills with a drink of water; she took hers and lay down beside little Mary on the bed. Her daughters joined her.

In the drawing room, Caroline ground the pill into powder and added it to Sean's bottle of milk. She took the baby in her arms; he grinned at her and gurgled happily. Offered the bottle he sucked vigorously; then, went very quiet. She continued to hold him. It was as though he was asleep but this was a sleep from which he would not awaken. Never again would she hear his gurgling laughter or watch him taking his first unsteady steps. It was beyond sadness; these beautiful, happy little children, so full of life; it was a blessing they didn't know what was happening.

Caroline's guards helped wrap the bodies in blankets and placed them gently in the back of a pickup truck. She hugged the three men tearfully and left; dismayed, shocked beyond belief – that the world should come to this. Accompanied by John and his two sons-in-law, Patrick drove to the cemetery up on the hill, where a large grave was already opened. There could be no church services; the local curate was found dead sitting in his armchair a few days earlier.

After the women and children were interred, John and his sons-in-law took their pills, while the guards looked on. Then they lay down with their loved ones. When the guards were satisfied they were dead, they covered their bodies with blankets and filled in the grave. The cemetery was patrolled at night.

Two weeks earlier, the daily electricity ration was reduced to one hour. There didn't appear to be anyone responsible for anything anymore. Water supplies were cut off half the time; when there was water it had to be boiled before consumption. Caroline tried to keep her cell phone charged; her land line was long gone. She hadn't been able to use her fridge or freezer for months and now she couldn't use her washing machine or drier. During that hour she had to boil enough water to make up flasks of tea and coffee, bake some brown bread and boil a few potatoes and vegetables – and eggs when she could get them. Meat was a rare luxury. And she turned on the immersion heater so she could wash her hair and manage an occasional shower. All in an hour!

Her home-grown supplies of potatoes, carrots and parsnips, which she shared with her neighbours, were nearly exhausted. Brendan Howley, who kept two cows on his farm outside the village, drove in every morning with a large can of fresh milk – there was no pasteurised milk now – on his cart. He would take no money – currency had little value now – but she insisted he take some potatoes.

One morning he didn't come. She sent one of her guards to see if he was all right. He found Brendan's body in the yard outside his house with that of his son; they'd been shot. There was no sign of the two cows or his game little pony.

Added to all this was the awful stench from the nearby sea. Months earlier the sewage works in Sligo had broken down; maybe it was lack of electricity – no-one seemed to know. As a result, raw sewage was flowing into the river and, at high tide, being deposited on part of her lawn. She daren't open the windows; it didn't make much difference, the stench seemed to penetrate through the very walls.

When Alex arrived, she hugged him tightly, smiling bravely to cover her dismay.

'Alex, it's so good to see you, love. Forgive me, the house looks a mess, we only have water and electricity for an hour a day.'

'Never mind, Mother. You look a treat. How have you been?'

'I'm fine, considering everything.'

The instant he got out of the car he was hit by that awful stench. He would have liked to walk down to the deck where they spent so many happy evenings together, but thought better of it.

'I have a nice lunch ready for you. John sent over your favourite, a hot plate with cooked chicken, carrots and potatoes.'

She didn't tell him she had called in all her favours from her local friendly shopkeeper.

'I had a very good breakfast on the flight, Mother.'

He hadn't, but he wasn't going to let her know that. Sandi's sandwiches were very welcome.

'Well, just try a little; you look undernourished.'

'Just a taste, but only to please you.'

He allowed her to put a third on his plate and insisted she eat the balance.

Sitting at the old solid oak kitchen table they looked out on what was once one of the most beautiful views in the country. A dull and overcast day up to now, Knocknarea was beginning to emerge from the morning mist. He told her about his unsuccessful visits to Birmingham and Fort Worth. Would she come to CosmosRX with him?

'No, love, I won't. I saw the last of my patients this morning – what a strange world it's become – I give them pills now to enable them to die with dignity.'

'Please, Mother, come with me?'

'I want to end my days here; I've had a good life.'

'Let me stay with you then?'

'No, love. You have things to do. When things get worse, I'll take my little pill too.'

His eyes filled up with tears.

'Must you, Mother?'

'Yes, love. Soon, we'll have no electricity, water or food. Law and order is already at breaking point. Most of my friends are already gone. I want to go with dignity; that won't be possible if I wait too long.'

Tears ran down his face.

'No, Alex, don't cry, it's best this way. I'm so glad you came today. I really didn't want to tell you by letter. I've made all the arrangements: I will notify Jack Sweeney, the undertaker, in advance; he will take care of everything. I will be buried with Mother and Father in Sligo cemetery. You mustn't come. Jack will notify you afterwards.'

He couldn't dissuade her. Preparing to leave, he held her close for a long time. They both cried, unable to talk. She pushed a little pill box into his hand.

'When the time comes, take one of these, love. I hope we'll be together again in a happier place.'

She waved from the back door as the car pulled away. Leaving the door unlocked, she tidied up around the house, replaced the half-full black sack with a new one and put the old one in the outside store. Sitting down at the kitchen table, she wrote a short note to Alex, put it in an envelope and placed it carefully with a long envelope that contained her will. She poured a gin and tonic – there was no ice.

She went upstairs to her bedroom, taking her glass, and the pile of envelopes. She had planned a Christian burial, although she wasn't very religious. That wouldn't be possible now. She would have liked a choir; and her friend Anna Forde to sing *Abide with Me*, one of her favourite hymns. But Anna was already gone. She dearly hoped Heaven existed after all; it would be nice to be with her dear mother and father again.

She checked around to make sure everything was neat and tidy and in its place; it wouldn't do to have anyone think she didn't keep her house properly. Placing the letters on the dressing table, she walked to the window and gazed out on the bay and Knocknarea – for the last time. She sighed sadly. Such a pity that life should end like this: that death should become so attractive.

She was quite calm. It was better this way. It was so good to see Alex once more. She picked up the phone and dialled a number.

'Jack, it's Caroline, will you come for me in an hour? Farewell, my friend.'

She could depend on him to look after everything. He promised to take care of a number of friends, before using the pills she gave him for his own family. Her guards would look after Jack and his family when the time came. Extracting a small pill from a phial on the dressing table, she swallowed it, finished her drink, washed the glass in the bathroom, dried it and placed it with the pile of letters. She dearly hoped Alex would be all right. Then, she lay on the bed, smoothed her dress around her and closed her eyes…

***

Carlo Agnelli strolled along the esplanade in Lugano, idly watching the swans flapping around in the muddy waters of the lake. He was bored. The one-time popular resort was almost deserted now. He sat down on one of the seats; it was better than sitting in his hotel bedroom. He longed to return to his native Sicily, but that wasn't possible. Lugano had its attractions, it was a city where an Italian could pass unnoticed and, right now, he needed to be invisible. He daren't even ring home. The Magnum in his shoulder holster wasn't very reassuring; the Italian police would love to get their hands on him and wouldn't even try to take him alive.

At 27, son of a Mafioso don, he was the most wanted man in Italy. Of average height, and lightly built, what people noticed most were his swarthy features, deep blue eyes and sleeked-down black hair. Dressed expensively, and well-perfumed, his refined hands had not known manual work. His years in the Franciscan College weren't entirely wasted; he spoke in cultured tones, smiled readily and was very popular with the ladies.

At 20, he was recruited into the Italian Special Branch, and finished his training three years later: his superiors weren't to know they had a Mafioso in their midst. His father had arranged an impeccable background for him. A supposed native of Florence – all his paperwork was in order – he was well trained by Mafioso experts. The credentials would not have stood up to an in-depth investigation, but who would have dreamed that a Mafioso would even try to infiltrate the country's Special Branch?

He enjoyed playing the double role and became very successful in his work. When sensitive information came his way, he passed it on to a Mafia courier living in Rome. It eventually dawned on his superiors that the Mafia was one step ahead of them all the time: special judges sent to Sicily were invariably car-bombed; their movements had to be known in advance. Everyone in the department came under suspicion. Information dried up, and raids were carried out without advance notice to the participants.

Carlo and two other officers were sent to Palermo, and ordered to stay at the Cliff Hotel. There had to be some action planned – they were supplied with Uzis. Two days later, they were ordered to take up positions in the square near the bank. There was no opportunity to warn his father. Concealing his Uzi, he took up a position at one corner of the square; his colleagues took two other corners, nearer the bank. It was market day. There was much activity around the outdoor fruit and vegetable stands with lively children playing boisterously around the square. Then a Mercedes pulled up outside the bank; three men entered.

He signalled the others to move closer while he hung back a little. Shots were heard coming from the interior of the bank. Three men charged out the front door, one carrying a black bag, the other two firing into the air. All hell broke loose; everyone was screaming and diving for cover. His two colleagues raced forward and opened fire; one of the robbers collapsed. Carlo didn't hesitate; he mowed down his colleagues, but failed to see three young girls running right across his line of fire. They had no chance. The two remaining bank robbers threw themselves into the Mercedes and took off at high speed. Carlo withdrew quickly, leaving a scene of bloody carnage behind him.

His father concealed him on a ship going to Genoa, and from there he made his way to Lugano. It wasn't his fault. The children shouldn't have been there. Worse was to come: a tourist captured the entire attack on video. He grew a beard, dyed his hair and wore dark glasses.

He had plenty of money, and later, when things quietened down, he planned to change his identity and go to New York where his cousin Roberto lived. In the meantime, he enjoyed the comforts of the hotel, which included the owner's beautiful daughter, Martha.

***

Sally met Alex on arrival back at CosmosRX. He didn't notice her distress. She could tell from his expression it hadn't gone well. That was no more than she expected. She felt so sorry for him: no human being should be faced with such a decision. He needed a good night's sleep.

'Alex, I'm afraid I have some very bad news. Ron, Sandi and your dear mother.'

His eyes filled with tears.

'All of them?'

She nodded bursting into tears. He put his arms around her and held her close. After a few moments, she stood back.

'Darius is getting your supper, Alex.'

'What I need is a drink. Will you join me?'

'Yes.'

They went to his apartment, where she had already stocked his drinks cabinet.

He poured two large whiskies, added soda, and sat down in one of the comfortable armchairs. He sipped his silently. She understood his need for company, but not conversation just yet.

After a while he spoke, very quietly. 'Today, I said goodbye to the three people I love most in this world.'

'I'm so sorry, Alex.'

He looked at her directly. 'You're not telling me what to do?'

'No, it's your decision. I will support you in whatever you decide.'

'Have you any relatives?'

'I have my sister, Rachael, her husband and their two lovely daughters in Clifden. At least, I had: three days ago, Rachael committed suicide taking my two adorable nieces with her. I only heard about it today.'

He rose and took her in his arms. They stood there weeping, holding one another for support. Eventually, she pushed him away gently.

'You need a good night's rest.'

'Don't leave me alone tonight, Sally.'

She helped him into bed, and held him in her arms until he fell asleep.

***

Alfredo Corteso sat back in his executive armchair and puffed on his Havana cigar. He had achieved his life's ambition, yet, curiously, his euphoria was short-lived. There must be other banks he could take over: he would get Wadham to study the international scene; he would love to own one of the Hong Kong banks. Yes, he would ring Wadham later in the day. The markets would take a while to recover. If he moved quickly enough there should be bargains out there, ripe for the picking. His thoughts were interrupted by the arrival of his Executive Vice President.

Ellison grovelled. 'Congratulations, I never thought you would do it, sir.'

'That's the difference between us, you haven't got the balls; if you had you'd be sitting in this chair.'

'That's correct, sir. Is it necessary to bring in all the staff when our retail branches are closed?'

He wondered how much more manure he would have to swallow. The fact he had made 30 million dollars was some consolation.

'Of course it is, unless they want to use some of their annual leave. Arrange a press conference for noon tomorrow and tell Edwards to bring my car around.'

On his way out, John stopped by Nan Evans' desk. She looked at him quizzically. 'Why do you put up with it?'

He responded tersely. 'Same reason as you – the money.'

She had just learned her mother's operation would cost at least 15,000 dollars and the loan company would only advance half that amount.

Alfredo made a call on his private line.

'Adi, how would you like to come over for dinner tonight?'

'I'll be expecting a lot more than dinner.'

He grinned. 'You'll get it too.'

***

In the morning they assembled in the conference room. Michael came straight to the point.

'I know it's academic, but at 8.00 am today the PNR was down to 32 days. Reports from Africa, southern India, Brazil and parts of China are dire: millions are dying from starvation every day. The situation in the developed countries is deteriorating rapidly: if we don't intervene, it will be beyond our control in a matter of days.'

Outside, the bell rang. They raced to the operations room.

'Another Forest Springs,' the operator announced calmly.

They watched the scenes of horror unfolding on the screen before them.

'Where is it this time?'

'Cairo, sir.'

'Turn it off.'

The operator looked at another screen.

'Sir, US President Harten is making a statement in Houston.'

'Let's hear him.' He turned up the sound.

"I want to assure everyone: there is no need for alarm. Our economy was never as strong. I have no doubt that the markets will return to normal after this short cooling-off period. The only things we have to fear at this time are the prophets of doom, warning us that the end of the world is coming. They've been saying that for thousands of years and we're still here."

'Another Nero,' Plato remarked quietly.

'Put it off,' Alex ordered.' He turned to Michael. 'We'll meet again in an hour.'

Entering the elevator he went up to the top of the mountain. Ashen-faced, he suddenly realised his hands were shaking. Unaware that he was under observation by discreet armed guards, he walked up the steps to the highest point. The sheep didn't come here anymore. He looked out on the surrounding countries. It was blisteringly hot. His mind was in turmoil: How could he do this? How could he not do it? Eventually, he walked slowly down to the elevator.

Sally was waiting for him.

'Alex, Mumbai is gone.'

'Will you bring the others to the conference centre right away?'

Five minutes later they assembled. He looked around the table at them for a moment.

'How can you ask me to take the lives of six billion people?'

Michael replied calmly. 'If you don't, Alex, it will cost 12 billion lives.'

There was a long silence. Alex put his head in his hands. He looked up, took a deep breath and looked around the table.

'I have no option then, but to use the full powers of CosmosRX to try to save as many of our people as possible. Michael, will you outline your initial plans.'

Sally breathed a sigh of relief. Now that he had made his decision he sounded a bit better.

Michael continued calmly.

'First, some preliminary steps. In anticipation of your decision, I put all our people on alert some time ago. They know exactly what to do as soon as I pass on your instructions.

We proceed as follows: Our on-site people switch monitoring of all satellites to CosmosRX; our space weapons robots will now take their instructions from CosmosRX only. Using the space weapons, we knock out all former satellite control units, and destroy all surface weapons of mass destruction on the planet.

CosmosRX has the power to take over the Internet and superimpose its own more sophisticated operating systems that contain our recovery and operations programs for the future. This won't happen just yet.'

'What about underground nuclear silos? Can the space weapons destroy them?'

'No, but we have our own people inside every one of them. The biggest one is under Mount Tacoma in America. When you give the order it will be destroyed internally.'

'Go ahead.' Alex ordered.

Bill and Michael left the room. Alex turned to Hercules – big, strong and always reassuring.

'How secure is CosmosRX?'

'Fully secure, once we take out all weapons of mass destruction.'

A long silence followed. Now for the hard part – waiting. He wasn't known for his patience. Plato was completely composed. Sally felt resigned now; at least they'd tried. Half an hour went by; it seemed like hours. Darius arrived with a pot of coffee, grinning with self-confidence as usual. Sally wanted to hug him.

'Coffee,' he announced putting down the tray.

'Yes please, Darius, you're a lifesaver.' She took the cups and poured the coffee.

They relaxed a little and sipped the coffee.

Shortly afterwards, Michael and Bill returned.

'Alex,' Michael reported, 'steps one and two have been completed successfully: CosmosRX is now in control.'

'Take out Cairo and Mumbai,' he ordered.

'Yes, sir.'

'Can anyone hack into our computers?' he asked.

'It has been tried,' Bill conceded, 'unsuccessfully. We are fully protected, by what we call "high-fidelity firewalls", and we have a program designed to deal with hackers.'

'Tell me about it.'

'We pick up the incoming pulses of hackers and trace them back to source.'

'How can you stop them?'

'I have a library that contains the address of every hacker in the world. When you give the order I will send each of them a little message: a massive electrical surge.'

Alex nodded. 'Good.'

He turned to Plato. 'Please proceed.'

'Every air traffic control system in the world is now receiving the following warning: "A massive electrical surge is fast approaching Earth from the Sun. Ground all aircraft. Order all planes in the air to land immediately at the nearest airport."'

Alex nodded silently.

'All units are now on standby for the next phase; in one hour we will take all forms of communications off the air: TV, including satellite, radio, telephone, including mobile, and Internet – plus a complete blackout of all electrical facilities. Spy satellites will continue to operate as normal.'

'Good.' Alex sounded a bit less tense.

Darius approached him. 'What would you like for dinner, sir?'

It seemed incongruous to Sally that they should be talking about food at a time like this. Alex hadn't realised how hungry he was.

'I would like a large fillet with onions and potatoes.'

He turned to Sally. 'Will you join me?'

***

He was a bit more relaxed over dinner. They were committed now – there could be no going back. He felt drawn to Sally: her calmness, serenity and ready smile were like a beacon in an otherwise gloomy world; if only they had met at another time, in another world. Neither of them referred to the previous night.

Darius fussed around, poured a very good Chablis, served desert, put a pot of coffee on the table, bowed and departed quietly.

Sally smiled. 'Isn't he a beaut?'

'That's down to you. They're just like humans. I see that Michael is clearly regarded as the most senior of the team.'

'I'm not quite sure how that happened. It wasn't intended. But then look at Darius, I didn't intentionally give him that impish sense of humour.'

'Perhaps you did without knowing it.'

Plato knocked politely and entered.

'I'm awaiting confirmation that phase three has been fully completed. It's going according to plan. We have another Forest Springs: Tokyo.'

'Take it out.'

'I've already done so, Alex.'

'Is your satellite control working properly?'

'Yes, we are monitoring the entire globe every two hours.'

***

Air Force One was diverted to Montgomery. It landed there ten minutes before the blackout was due to commence. A military escort waited on the tarmac with three limousines. An Army colonel stood to attention while a somewhat nervous presidential party walked down the steps.

The colonel saluted smartly. 'National Emergency, sir. Please come with us; there's not a moment to lose.'

'What the hell's going on?' President Harten demanded.

'I don't know, sir. My orders are to collect you and your party and take you to a safe place.'

At that moment, all the lights in the airport and environs went out.

The President, Mrs Harten and their son William were bustled quickly into the front limo that took off at speed, closely followed by the others.

'Is it a nuclear war?' the President demanded.

The cars cleared the airport and made for the freeway west.

'Where are you taking me?' he demanded.

Jack Warner, sitting beside the driver, turned around and dropped a tiny phial in the back of the limo.

'We're not taking you anywhere, sir – you've just lost the election.'

At the same time, Army detachments entered the Pentagon and the West Wing of the White House, and quickly evacuated Secretary of State, Charles Howell, and other members of the Government. Domestic staff were refused similar protection, and advised to remain calm. Detachments called at the Washington homes of other members of the Government and the Joint Chiefs. The Secretary of Defence – who was in San Francisco – was collected at the Ritz Carlton Hotel. By 9.00 am Eastern Time no member of the US Government, no member of the Houses of Congress, no State Governor, no US Ambassador and no Judge of the Supreme Court could be found.

A similar operation was carried out in every country in the world.

At 10.00 am Eastern Time Internet service was resumed but only to carry the following message. “The Director of CosmosRX will address the people of the world at 12.00 noon today US Eastern Time.”

***

Alex was nervous. Plato had arranged to have his speech broadcast simultaneously – in 36 languages – with subtitles for those with impaired hearing. Everyone would be invited – in advance – to switch to the language of their choice.

Hercules joined them.

‘Alex, three motorised army columns are heading towards us.’

‘Where are they from?’

‘One from Zurich, and two from Milan.’

‘Can you identify their headquarters?’

‘Yes.’

‘Take out the columns and the HQs, as well; use the HOBs.’

‘Human Only Bombs; the ones that kill humans, but don’t damage property?’

‘Correct. Activate the anti-missile shield, and check the up-to-date situation in China.’

‘Yes, sir.’ He departed.

‘Are we all set, Sally?’

‘Yes, just relax and you’ll be fine. Plato is dealing with specific instructions to particular industries and parties.’

Hercules returned. ‘Alex, we have identified and taken into custody everyone involved in the shooting of Professor Bergin.’

‘Who are they?’

‘Charles Howell in the White House instructed FBI Director, Len Soames. They have already been dealt with. The actual shooting was carried out by an agent called Jeff Havers, accompanied by agent Ross Martel.’

‘Execute them.’

‘Yes, sir.’

‘Did we get General Jackson and all the other officers involved in the planned military takeover of the US?’

‘We got all of them. Jackson timed his coup to coincide with the Chinese landings in the Gulf. He was fully prepared to use nuclear weapons.’

Plato joined them. ‘We’re ready now.’

Having studied the plan carefully, Alex had the feeling something was missing.

‘How many of our people will be available for redeployment after today’s changes?’

‘More than a million. I’m planning to allocate them to the crops program.’

Alex disagreed. ‘I don’t think we’ve given sufficient thought to security; we have to put a stop to the widespread looting.’

‘What should I do?’

‘Order the police forces to guard all food outlets, retail premises, hospitals, all former government buildings and administration centres, and temporarily switch our people to provide back-up.’

‘Yes, sir.’

***

When Plato confirmed everything was in place, Alex faced the camera in the operations centre. The autocue started to roll.

“My name is Alex Purtzel. I’m coming to you from CosmosRX. As of now CosmosRX controls every aspect of life on this planet. Had we not acted a few hours ago, you – and by you, I mean, everyone on this Earth – would all have died in violent, horrific and degrading circumstances within the next few months.

For over 60 years, successive administrations have betrayed your trust. Time and time again, they ignored the warnings of the world’s leading scientists. They called Professor Ron Bergin an alarmist. They told you that the Forest Springs disaster was due to an outbreak of typhoid, Mexico City was terrorism; I wonder what they would say about Cairo, Mumbai and Tokyo? All of these disasters were caused by massive doses of ultraviolet solar rays intermittently penetrating our depleting ozone layer. The unfortunate people concerned were turned into homicidal raving lunatics. We don't know when, or where, these attacks will occur again, but they will continue, until we give the ozone layer a chance to recover.

Two days ago President Elmer Harten told me that I too, am an alarmist. On his instructions, Professor Ron Bergin was shot dead at his home in Boston.

CosmosRX has now removed all governments and their leaders, national and international assemblies and all local authorities. All civil service and ancillary departments have been abolished. We have no agenda other than to save this planet, improve living standards and treat everyone equally. Terms like Liberal, Conservative, Socialist, Fascist, Left, Right, Monarchist or Anarchist are obsolete.

I will always tell you the truth, however painful, and there will be times when it will be very painful. I ask, in return, for your full co-operation in dealing with the problems we now face. This is not a time for debate, it is a time for action.

The collapse of the ozone layer, or the continued use of fossil fuels, would bring about the destruction of humankind within the next 25 years. Now, as you are aware, we are faced with a more immediate threat: worldwide famine.

Increasing flooding and droughts have steadily eroded crop returns at a time when the demand for food was never greater. Buffer stocks of corn, wheat, maize, barley and rice are now reduced from two years to two months. Fruit and vegetable yields are 20 percent what they were five years ago. Cattle and sheep, that would normally be retained for breeding purposes, are being sold into the food chain to try to satisfy demand. The collapse of the financial markets is already leading to panic buying, hoarding and anarchy. Armageddon is here now: to survive, we have to act immediately and decisively.

We have 12 billion people on a planet that can only support six billion. The choice is stark – even if it's simple – we either lose six billion or 12 billion of our people within the next two years. Half our population must depart so that the other half may survive: they are being asked to make the supreme sacrifice in order that their children and their children's children may have the opportunity of life. Those chosen to depart will do so in a humane manner with their dignity intact, and will be limited, in so far as is possible, to those over 60 years of age.

Criminals and members of criminal organisations, those involved in civil commotion, discrimination, any form of violence, military or otherwise, are scheduled for immediate departure.

A massive crop-growing and livestock-breeding program begins today. It will be concentrated in locations – already identified by CosmosRX – that are least affected by floods or drought. All agriculturists, agronomists, and stock breeders, including former government specialists, should register immediately with CosmosRX. You will be allocated to local and national teams responsible for implementing this vital program. All necessary extra personnel and equipment will be provided. CosmosRX will now take control of the distribution of foodstuffs.

We have identified the manufacturers of fluorocarbon products throughout the world. They are responsible for the damage to the ozone layer and the horrific events in Forest Springs, Mexico City and elsewhere. They're being eliminated, and their industries clinically destroyed.

We have to lower the Earth's temperature by at least 4 degrees and we have to do it quickly. It can only be achieved by reducing the amount of CO_2 – carbon dioxide – and methane in the atmosphere. When you use your refrigerator, toaster, television, electric kettle, heating, or air-conditioning system, you are putting carbon dioxide into the atmosphere. We have to find sources of energy that will enable you to do all these things without polluting the atmosphere. We believe we can do that.

All coal mines, oil fields and natural gas sources will close in 90 days, with the exception of the production of the aviation fuel necessary for the much reduced schedules operated by World Airlines, and a few other authorised users. Full oil tankers, already at sea, will complete their voyages; empty tankers will return to base and remain there.

Thirty-six percent of all green house gas emissions are caused by motor vehicles: all road vehicles, except those specially authorised, are to be taken off the roads immediately; gas stations and distributors have already been closed down. To drive without a permit will be punishable by immediate execution.

Leonardo will be in charge of all forms of energy production on this planet. Using existing staff, and drafting in all of the world's nuclear physicists, he will develop an integrated system that will facilitate the transmission of electricity to wherever it's needed at any particular time.

CosmosRX has authorised the immediate construction of nuclear breeder reactors – that produce plutonium – and nuclear fusion energy producers. This is a priority program. The plans are already approved, locations selected, and work begins today. We have massive resources available to us. The first new stations will come into service within the next 90 days, and will be manned and run, by specialised robots, thus greatly increasing the safety factor. No longer dependent on uranium, this source of energy will serve mankind for hundreds of years to come.

We already have another source of safe energy: hydroelectric power. Thousands of these facilities have been closed down due to build up of sludge behind the dams. We have initiated a massive dredging operation to bring them back into service. In addition, we will build another 5,000 new hydroelectric stations.

Two other safe sources remain: wind farms and solar energy. Both are effective, but only as back up sources because the wind doesn't blow all the time and the Sun doesn't shine all the time. They will be particularly useful in the short term.

Serious research will now be undertaken into all other possible sources of safe energy. Wave power requires further study. Could fossil fuels be used and the CO_2 returned to the Earth? Could we learn to store electricity for future use? We don't know, but we will find out.

In the short term, we cannot increase the supply of energy. However, with the changes we're making today we're reducing the demand by 45 percent, thus effectively increasing supply. You may expect to have uninterrupted supplies in less than a year.

You will be aware that the army of a breakaway Manchurian state, planning to take over all of China, is currently marching on Mukden. Before coming on air, we ordered the advancing rebel army, currently based at Harbin, to cease hostilities immediately and disband. This has not happened. Our satellites have pinpointed their location near Mukden. You can see the pictures coming up on your screens. They will now be destroyed." The picture showed massive, prolonged and devastating explosions.

"Two hours ago, we ordered the Chinese fleet – sailing into the Persian Gulf to take over Middle East oil producers – to withdraw immediately, and return to home ports, stay there and disband their army. I'm pleased to say they're withdrawing as ordered, closely monitored by our spy satellites.

Wars or conflicts of any kind are forbidden: occupation troops in Cuba, Panama, Kashmir, Taiwan, Korea, Eritrea, Somalia, Venezuela, Belize and Tibet are now ordered to withdraw immediately and disband. Those who opposed their oppressors are also ordered to lay down their arms. Your future security is guaranteed. CosmosRX has destroyed all weapons of mass destruction on this planet. We are now, and will for the future, be citizens of a peaceful world.

In every year, for the past 100 years, more money was spent on armaments than on any other single commodity: enough to solve the problem of world hunger, and provide very adequate non-fossil fuels. These figures do not include human loss of life, or the costs of using the armaments. This is a staggering indictment of all those to whom we entrusted power and responsibility. It will give you some idea of the enormous resources now available to us.

All criminal and civil law courts and the legal profession are now abolished. Prisons have been emptied; they will not be necessary for the future. There is now only the Law of CosmosRX, and for any serious breach of that Law there is only one punishment. All policing and security authorities are now accountable directly to CosmosRX.

Building and civil engineering contractors have been ordered to erect water purification plants, sewage filtration works, and waste incineration facilities at locations already designated by our professional team. Former Army personnel are being drafted in to assist in these emergency works. Sites will operate three eight-hour shifts per day, seven days a week. All vacations have been cancelled for the present.

We have lived in a world driven by sophisticated psychological advertising. That's going to change now: advertising is abolished. With the exception of armaments, more money was spent, each year, on advertising than on any other single commodity: it was a complete waste of our resources.

For the future, our economy – and there will be only one for the entire world – will be demand-driven. Purchasers will decide what they want to buy and, as you will see later, price persuasion will not exist. An independent body, appointed by CosmosRX, will assess all new products and put their recommendations on a special website.

Everyone must now register with CosmosRX by going to CosmosRX.registration and inputting their personal details: you simply type in your name, address, date of birth, current occupation and qualifications, if any, or use the speech option if you wish. If your present employment has been made obsolete, indicate your preferred work and location. Put your hands on the screen provided, to record your palm and fingerprints. Finally, stare at the screen provided to register your iris print, and take your photograph. When prompted, please speak your name clearly. Your membership will then be confirmed. If you have any difficulties press the help button. This will put you in contact with one of our staff who will talk you through the procedure in your own language. You should register as quickly as possible.

Today, we abolish: all forms of taxation, all debts, customs duties, excise, subsidies, levies, fees, pensions and all forms of social insurance benefits.

The following are now obsolete: stock exchanges, banks, credit card companies, building and loan societies, pension providers and general insurance companies.

We also abolish all existing currencies: the US Dollar, the Pound Sterling, Euro etc. People working in all of these areas will be redeployed.

The owners of companies or business, public or private, will still continue to be owners. They will be required to operate with the same efficiency and dedication as at present. Everyone, whether shareholder, director, manager, or staff, will be rewarded equally.

Poverty is abolished, although with present shortages, it will be some years before we can normalise food supplies. In the meantime, we have set up an emergency food supply chain to deal with the worst-affected areas. Thousands of aircraft are involved. Distribution on-site will be supervised by reliable CosmosRX staff.

I come now to the CosmosRX financial system under which everyone on this planet becomes equal for the first time in history. Once registered, each of you will have an account with CosmosRX: on the 1st of each month that account will be credited with 5,000 points per adult, and 2,000 points for those under 18 years of age. A point equals today's purchasing power of one US Dollar, or its equivalent anywhere in the world. Inflation is now abolished. All prices are pegged at today's level. For the duration of the present emergency, your daily spending will be limited to 100 points to avoid panic buying.

Goods, produce and equipment will be grown, or manufactured as heretofore, and shipped to wholesale and retail outlets. Payment will take place at point of retail sale only. You may still purchase online, or in-store, and collect, or avail of delivery. The essential difference is that payment will be by way of deduction of points from your CosmosRX account. In the near future all prices will be quoted in points. For aesthetic reasons, we may alter the price of some commodities.

Yesterday, ten percent of the people on this planet owned or controlled 90 percent of its wealth. From now on, 100 percent of our people will share – equally – 100 percent of the Earth's resources and produce. For 90 percent of people this represents a handsome increase in spending power, and more importantly, guaranteed improved living standards.

You will not have to pay for any of the following: education, inland transit overland, medical expenses, hospitalisation, pension, burial services, CosmosRX TV, telephone, postage, electricity, water or refuse collection. Without a special permit, no foreign travel will be permitted for the present.

All rents and mortgage repayments are abolished. The house, apartment or farm you occupy today is yours. If you own a number of properties, you may decide which one you wish to retain. You should notify us if you have other vacant properties. They will be taken into CosmosRX care, and included in future rehousing, or redevelopment programs. You may not sell your present property, but may leave it to whomever you wish. Estate agency as a business is abolished. A number of current agents have been appointed to look after properties that become the responsibility of CosmosRX.

All tourist activity is suspended for the present. Those away from home will be flown home within the next few days. Tourists create considerable pollution, and some re-education will be necessary before we resume. In the meantime, all tourist facilities such as planes, luxury liners, ferries, hotels and other attractions are to be kept in readiness.

The world's airlines will be amalgamated into one airline that will provide a much superior and more economic service. With the abolition of reserved military airspace, and inter-airline competition, one-third of the existing fleet will provide a much superior service. New, centrally located, air traffic controllers will greatly enhance efficiency and safety. Hourly shuttle services will operate on the busier routes. Depending on demand, new routes will be added. Your registration with CosmosRX will be your passport.

Apart from oil tankers and car ferries, that will quickly become obsolete, all merchant shipping will be brought under one single authority. Schedules will be adjusted to eliminate current levels of duplication. We expect that half the fleet will, eventually, be taken out of service.

With the exception of mothers, carers and children, including those in full-time education, all other able-bodied people are required to work to age 60, and then retire, with no reduction in points.

CosmosRX plans massive improvements in education at all levels, particularly in what we used to call developing countries. The whole focus will change dramatically: we're in a new age, one in which everyone may aspire to the highest level of knowledge compatible with their ability. The demand for future leaders and high achievers has never been greater: no longer will it be that your worth is who you are; you will be rewarded and remembered for your achievements. You are now entering a phase in history that you did not believe was possible. Facilities will be provided for the development of your personal interests and hobbies. You may study art, painting, computing, gardening, history, mechanical skills and all kinds of things that interest you. Those accepted for full-time education will continue to receive their monthly points.

Those in approved work should continue as if no change had taken place. It would be a great mistake to think you can now do as you please just because you're financially independent. Any abuses will result in loss of points or worse.

All currently displaced by the changes will receive their points, and be relocated as quickly as possible. Those wishing to change career should put forward proposals to CosmosRX for consideration.

All current sporting activities will be continued. Everyone is encouraged to participate fully. Local plans to improve facilities should be put forward to CosmosRX for approval. Gambling is at an end.

CosmosRX will reward outstanding contributors to the future success of all aspects of life on this planet. The highest awards will be the exclusive use of one of the magnificent estates in CosmosRX care: some may achieve this for a limited period, others for the duration of their lives. Adequate staff will be provided. The more usual awards will be worldwide vacations of varying duration. No extra points will be allotted.

Today we have destroyed the drug barons, human traffickers, currency and card counterfeiters, gangsters, pimps and extortionists. They have one property, like everyone else, should they have temporarily escaped the justice of CosmosRX. Drug users should seek immediate help. There will be no unlicensed drugs in our society for the future.

Freedom of the press and media generally will continue. CosmosRX welcomes objective reporting and constructive criticism. Current standards of decency in films, TV and the media generally, are appalling. The current practice of glorifying violence must stop immediately: clean up your act, or we will do it for you.

Everyone is entitled to practice whatever religion they wish, or none. CosmosRX will not tolerate any form of discrimination, racial, religious, colour or otherwise. We retain our national identities, languages and cultures; we are all equal citizens of this planet.

Finally, if you have any problems visit our website or talk to one of our counsellors.”

Alex sat back completely exhausted. Darius handed him a cup of coffee.

‘That was wonderful, Alex,’ Sally enthused.

Michael agreed in his own way. ‘Very professional, Alex.’

Plato added. ‘Now, we have to wait and see.’

‘How foolproof is our registration system?’ Alex asked him.

‘One hundred percent.’

‘Are you sure?’

‘Yes. In addition to registering facial image, palm, finger and iris prints, we also record voice imaging and DNA. I suppose efforts could be made to play around with finger or iris prints, but applicants are not aware of our voice imaging program, or that we’re recording their DNA.’

Bill joined them. ‘Hackers are trying to penetrate our computers.’

‘Put them out of business, Bill, permanently.’

‘Yes, sir.’

***

José Carvallo, still a bit shell-shocked, was released from hospital and had travelled home the previous evening. He watched his TV/Internet screen until Alex came to the end of his broadcast. Grabbing Maria’s copybook, he started to calculate.

‘Bloody hell, we’re rich,’ he exclaimed. ‘Now, how do I get registered?’

He clicked on the registration screen, typed in his details indicating, that as an ex-rig driver, he could drive any type of machinery. CosmosRX confirmed his registration.

He rang Elvira before taking the train from Boston. She was very relieved to hear from him. He promised he would come to see her as soon as possible. He still had nightmares about that awful day in Forest Springs.

His father rushed in from work.

'José, have you heard? They're going to kill us off.' He paused. 'I suppose it's better we go, so you and the kids live.'

The phone rang. He picked it up.

'Yeah, José, that's me.' He looked apprehensive.

'OK, OK, I'll be there, sure, seven in the morning. I'll take the train.'

He replaced the receiver. 'I've got a job operating a digger at a building site in Black Ville. They're building a cremat… something or other. Let's go have a drink, Dad.'

'I could use one. The whole world is going mad.'

It suddenly occurred to José. 'Let me register you first and then you'll be able to buy your own drink.'

***

In a state of total shock and disbelief, Alfredo Corteso watched the broadcast sitting at his desk. This couldn't be happening, no fucking way, not now, just when he'd hit the jackpot. Outside, on the executive floor, his staff were chattering excitedly. He rang through to his secretary.

'Evans, get me the President.'

'Yes, sir.' She was also in a state of shock, but for a different reason. Free medical expenses and hospitalisation – her mother could now have her operation.

She rang back. 'No reply from the White House, sir.'

'Find him,' he roared.

'There is no President now, sir.'

He slammed down the phone. John Ellison entered the room.

'What the hell's going on?'

He was enjoying this. It took the sour taste off his 30 million dollar losses.

'I guess you've just been made obsolete.' He omitted the 'sir'.

'Do something man, this can't be happening; get on to the Governor.'

He shook his head, still smiling. 'It's over Alfredo, there is no Governor – you're no longer God.'

No employee would dare address him like that.

'You drunk, Ellison?'

'No, I just came to say goodbye.'

'No-one walks out on me. You're fired, get out.'

The world's wealthiest banker was beginning to recognise a hollow feeling in the pit of his stomach.

He stopped at the door.

'Now, you'll just have to crawl back to the gutter you came from.'

He joined the rest of the staff heading for the elevators. Alfredo rang through to his secretary. There was no reply. Leaping up, he strode to the outer office.

'Where is everyone?'

He was alone. Returning, he sat behind his desk. How could this happen? What could he do? There had to be an answer. They couldn't just abolish the Dollar: it had to be a mistake of some kind. He rang security – no reply. Better take home a few million in cash to keep him going until things were sorted out. He rang his mansion at Albany. Annie, the cook, answered.

'I was just going to ring you, sir. The security staff have left.'

'All of them?'

'Yes, sir.' She paused. 'They brought in two trucks and took away most of our food.'

He rang off. His world was falling apart.

Simon Jones, the old African-American who rode the executive lift was standing before him. He hadn't seen him enter.

'Sir,' the old man hesitated, 'you have to go now.'

'What the hell do you mean? This is still my bank.'

He shook his head slowly, curiously feeling sorry for the man who ignored his existence for nearly 15 years.

'Sir,' he continued, 'I've been instructed to close the building and hand the keys to a CosmosRX man with an office nearby.'

'Who is going to activate the alarms? Where are the security people?'

'No longer needed, sir.'

'But there's millions of dollars in the vaults.'

'Only paper now, sir. Doesn't need minding.'

He was silent for a moment.

'Tell Edwards to bring my car around.'

'Edwards is gone, sir, so are your bodyguards. You're not permitted to use the car.'

'How am I going to get home then?'

'On the subway, sir.' He wanted to say, like the rest of us.

'All right, what is your name?'

'Jones, sir.'

'All right, Jones, I'll be down shortly.'

The old man departed.

He sat there for a long time trying desperately to see a way forward. He fought his way up from the bottom and made it to the top. He had achieved greater power than princes and presidents; rubbed shoulders with the world's most famous celebrities. Now, stripped naked, defenceless, his only option was to become a nobody again; he couldn't do that. Rising, he walked to the window and looked down on the thousands of former employees filling the street below. He made his way to the elevators, absently walking in when the door opened before him. The door closed.

He pushed a button. The elevator went up, stopping at the 59th floor. He walked out on to the open roof, hit by a blast of hot air. For some unknown reason he thought of his parents – for the first time in 24 years – and wondered if they were still alive. He walked slowly to the edge, stood for a moment, then stepped into space.

***

John Ellison walked up Fifth Avenue with thousands of others, in a very strange atmosphere: everyone was talking freely. The traffic was very light now. Armed police were much in evidence and the return of some semblance of law and order was very welcome. He was still trying to compare his new income with that received from Corteso. With so many free services, it was very difficult. The fact that his wife and son would receive 7,000 points a month would make a hell of a difference. Laurie would now be self-supporting. He dropped into his local for a celebration drink. Ali, the Indian barman, grinned at him.

'We're still trying to come to grips with the new system.'

'It will take time.'

'Registered yet, John?'

'No.'

'Join that queue for registration over there, and then I'll get your usual.'

He filled in the required details and added "Managerial in Manhattan" for his preferred optional employment. Alex's broadcast was being shown again. Many viewers were taking notes.

Two hours later, he arrived at his apartment. Laurie should be home by 6.00 pm. He poured himself a drink, put on the TV and watched news commentators discussing the extraordinary changes announced by Alex Purtzel. It came to him slowly; there was something different about the living room. It was too tidy. That certainly wasn't Laurie. He got up and looked around. Strange. He checked the bedroom and eventually opened her wardrobe. It was empty. He couldn't believe it: she was gone. Then he spotted the note on the table. He read it. "I can support myself now, John. Thanks for everything, L."

He sat there for a long time in a daze. How could he have been such an idiot? Then he rang Joan.

'This is going to be quite a change. I'll take the train home tonight.'

'Don't bother, John. I'm divorcing you, and Philip is staying with me.'

'What's this about?'

'What do you think I've been doing while you entertained your little tart? You have her now, and I have my freedom and the house.'

The line went dead. His first inclination was to go back to his local. Instead he went to what used to be Joey's restaurant nearby. It was now a sandwich bar; most of the other local restaurants had closed down months ago. He settled for a very thinly-sliced beef sandwich, and a bottle of chardonnay.

Curiously, wine was still freely available; food was so expensive that most people could no longer afford wine.

The following morning, there was so much noise and furore in the street under his apartment that he thought it was a revolution. It was an army of workers – with an array of mechanical market garden equipment – heading towards Central Park. After breakfast, he strolled down to the park to see what was happening. There was a great air of buzzing activity: it was organised chaos. The park was divided up into sectors; each one allocated a team under the control of an expert agronomist. Local residents watched with interest. The soil prepared, they would be planting potatoes, carrots, parsnips and onions in a matter of days. A catering crew set up a large tent near the lake. Cooking equipment was quickly installed; coffee and sandwiches were prepared and served to the teams in rotation. John learned that a number of vacant offices were being rapidly converted to provide sleeping accommodation for the work crews.

While waiting to be allocated a job, he walked in Central Park most days, and talked with one of the team leaders. They expected to complete planting within three weeks. Most of the team would move on then to the next site, leaving behind some maintenance and security staff.

TV news reports showed work in progress on a large number of nuclear reactors, and crematoria, including a large one on 79th Street. He visited his local, shopped around for powdered milk and bread, and, once a day, tried to get a half-decent restaurant meal. He thought about making a visit home, but decided against it. He would have to go eventually, if only to get his clothes, but that could wait.

New York City was different now. The hustle and bustle was gone; the streets were silent, and virtually empty, except for pedestrians. Fifth Avenue no longer looked like a parking lot. There was a leisurely and relaxed air – people were friendlier. The improvement in the electricity supply was very welcome. He was surprised to hear Corteso committed suicide; didn't think the bastard had the guts.

Then one morning his phone rang.

'Yes.'

'John Ellison?'

‘Yes.’

‘You have been appointed manager of the Wheat Export Board. Kindly take charge at 8.00 am tomorrow at the Head Office on 59th Street West. They’re expecting you. Advise CosmosRX of current stocks in storage. Got all that?’

‘Yes, sir, I’ll be there.’

***

The Supremos and their assistants used their lounge to change their clothes once a week and sit and read or watch TV. Sally was delighted to find them chatting about art, theatre, literature and history. They studied horse-racing, football and golf, placed bets in mythical points and watched the performances with great gusto. Curiously, Michael was a good judge of racehorses.

They surprised her in a manner she hadn’t expected: they began to empathise with their illustrious ancestors, as they called them. Michael sent Hercules to Florence to purchase an easel and a supply of brushes and paints. When time permitted, he set up his easel on the top of the mountain, and painted differing views of the surrounding country and the lakes far below – not as they appeared now, but in the verdant green of yesteryear.

Leonardo believed that the echo of the Big Bang still existed out there somewhere, at or near the outer limits of the universe – that’s if there were outer limits. His long study of the galaxies supported this view. He asked Sally and Bill to design an inbuilt satellite computer listening program to record all sounds and relay them back to the CosmosRX computer. They expanded their existing communication program, and installed it in the satellites. There was one imponderable: could the CosmosRX computer continue to receive communications regardless of range? There was only one way to find out. They launched three satellites and Bill settled down to monitor their progress.

Sally finalised special communication satellites that would orbit the Earth. Should there be any interference with the direct system of communication, they would switch over automatically to satellite relay. These satellites had another function: the ability to pick up, and wipe, signals coming from competing robotic systems. It was reasonable to assume that – at some stage – someone would develop robots with or without negative emotions; it was best to be prepared.

Most mornings she went up to the mountain top, and walked around, using an umbrella to protect her from the intense heat of the Sun. It was a change from the comfortable, if unreal, world below. It would be lovely to live in a nice house by the lake, but that wouldn't be possible, at least, not for the present. She made good use of the Jacuzzi in her bathroom; it helped her to relax. She still grieved for Rachael, Amanda and her two adorable nieces. Someday she would go home to Galway to find out exactly what happened. Joe said Rachael was suffering from depression. If only she had confided in her, she would have been able to get her professional help.

She made good use of the inbuilt laundry. Darius exercised his hairdressing skills – three times a week – leaving her with long soft, silky blonde hair. There was talk of a visit to Rome; she couldn't wait to get to the shops. In her spare time, she read – mostly romantic books ordered over the Internet, sent to the post office in Lugano, and collected by Hercules. At night, after Darius served dinner in his apartment, they sometimes sat together, listened to some of her CDs, watched their favourite soap, the world news and occasionally ordered a film. She thought Alex was a bit more reserved than during their early days together and wondered why?

***

Alex read the note, written on heavily scented notepaper, for the third time.

> "Dearest Alex,
>
> I want to come back to you and I promise to be a more loving wife this time. I'm sure you will give me another chance. I was young and foolish when I married you – I'm more grown up now. We can build a big house near where you work, and now you are so important, I can have all the servants I need.
>
> I'm sure you will exclude Dada from this departure program or whatever it's called.
>
> Let me hear from you soon.

With all my love.

Linda."

The letter was all about "I". Looking back he wondered how he could have been so gullible. When he first met Linda La Plante, at a charity dinner, he was fascinated by the beautiful, hyperactive, petite brunette with fair skin and deep blue eyes. He was thrilled when she agreed to have dinner with him, and moved into his modest but comfortable apartment a week later. Their love-making was perfect.

Being reserved and conscious of his disability, he had very little experience of women since leaving college in Galway. Dusky Ester from Clarin, they called her. A sultry, well-constructed classmate with jet black hair, sallow complexion and dark blue eyes – clearly of Spanish lineage. She made no secret of it; she had escaped from very restrictive parents and she was going to have a ball!

On a class outing to the beaches of Roundstone, she winked at him, took him by the hand and led him to a secluded area among the sand dunes. It was his first time. She was very understanding; slipped off her cream summer dress, revealing her beautiful, shapely, inviting nude body. She kissed him passionately, lay down on the sandy hill and pulled him towards her. She wrapped her arms and legs around him: it was heaven, only better, and it was only the first time. He knew there were others but he didn't care; she was a truly remarkable woman. She graduated with first class honours, later married an engineer and went to live in Sydney. He still remembered her with affection.

It was a whirlwind romance with Linda. They partied nearly every night, and she took particular pleasure in showing off her professor. She spent her days lunching and shopping with her socialite friends. One night, three months later, she snuggled up to him after a late party where she had a few too many Martinis.

'Darling, why don't we get married?'

'Why not, if you're prepared to live here with a lowly college professor?'

'I would live in a garret with you.'

The wedding date was set for three months later. Linda became totally immersed in the preparations; she loved the excitement and the envy of her friends. He was surprised to receive a phone call from a prominent Boston lawyer, Rupert Calders. Would he come to see him about a matter concerning his wedding? He made an appointment and duly presented himself at the lawyer's office in the John Hancock Building.

Calders, elderly and overweight, was almost condescending.

'I represent Linda's father, John La Plante. You are required by him to enter a prenuptial agreement.'

He passed the document across the desk.

'You may read it if you wish, but I assure you it's the standard one currently in use. The important part is that in the event of divorce, you will only be entitled to ten million dollars. I have marked "X" where you should sign.'

Alex scanned the document, took out his pen, drew a line through the ten million dollars, wrote "Nil" over it, signed it and handed it back.

'I'm not marrying Linda for her money.'

The old lawyer was astonished.

'Her previous two husbands took the money.'

He left without saying anything further; he didn't know Linda was married before. When he confronted her, she laughed. 'Oh, they were of no consequence, you are the man of my dreams.'

The wedding was a magnificent spectacle celebrated by nearly 2,000 guests. Caroline attended with Ron and Sandi Bergin. At the time, he was unaware of their reservations. Linda was in ecstasy, in a specially designed, long white dress, flitting among her socialite friends, posing for photos, introducing him to the distinguished guests. It went on long into the night.

They following day they flew to Rome for their honeymoon. Away from all the excitement and glitz, Linda soon became bored. She refused to visit any of the art galleries. This was a different Linda; she was drinking too much and wanted to go home. He offered to take her to Yeatstown to visit his mother; she refused. Cutting short the honeymoon, they returned to Boston. In the weeks that followed he saw little of her, she stayed at her father's home most nights. He became immersed in his work.

Then, one Saturday, she called unexpectedly to his apartment. He hadn't seen her for a week. She was furious.

'How dare you, how dare you get me pregnant? I can't have children. I hate the sight of the messy little things. I'm going to have an abortion.'

Angry now, he got up and took her by the shoulders.

'You're not aborting our child.'

'Release me, you go to hell, this is your entire fault.'

He tried to remain calm; there must be some way of stopping her.

'Linda,' he begged, 'let's wait a few days. Let's consider how serious a decision this is. If you don't want the child, I'll take full responsibility for its upbringing.'

'You go to hell; look what you've done to me!'

She stormed out the door. He rang his father-in-law who promised to do what he could; two days later, he learned from a very distressed John La Plante that she'd had an abortion. A month later she filed for divorce.

And now, five years later, he had the good luck to meet and fall in love with the most wonderful woman in the world. He had no reason to believe she returned his love, and daren't risk losing her by proclaiming his.

He read the letter again, tore it up and threw it in the trash can.

***

Sally made a point of watching the varied TV news reactions to CosmosRX; it was useful to know how people were reacting to the changes. A special program was advertised for Sunday at 8.00 pm US Eastern Time. Relaxing in her sitting room, she tuned in. Abe would be recording it for Alex who was busy checking the output of new nuclear plants. She always found Frank Hall, the internationally respected Sky presenter, to be fair and unbiased. Heavily built, with bronzed features, fair hair and expressive blue eyes, his laid-back, relaxed manner put everyone at their ease, but he didn't take any prisoners either.

Frank began.

'First, let me introduce my guests for this special program.' The camera showed a youngish thin-faced, bald-headed man, with a very stern expression. 'Professor Eric Landers, scientific adviser to the late President Harten. Welcome Professor.'

He interrupted him.

'Frank, I don't accept that the President is dead.'

'We'll come back to that.'

The camera showed a middle-aged, heavily-built, studious-looking man with calm expression.

'Professor John Glendon, from Columbia University. You are very welcome, John.'

He smiled and nodded.

'And finally, Dr Steve Simmons, pathologist at Boston General Hospital.'

The camera showed the elderly doctor with shaggy eyebrows and a well-lived-in face.

'Professor Landers, what do you make of what's been happening?'

He was furious. 'We are looking at an attempt, and I do say an attempt, because it hasn't succeeded yet, to take over the world by a megalomaniac who has no idea of the carnage he is about to unleash. Should he succeed we'll have anarchy in the form of military dictatorships, a complete breakdown of law and order, the end of our sophisticated financial structures, starvation on a scale never seen before: complete chaos.'

'Be fair, Professor, we haven't had any of those things. CosmosRX has saved us from Armageddon.'

'I don't accept that,' he retorted.

'So you don't think there's any way in which CosmosRX's actions can be justified?'

'Absolutely none. Nature is going through one of her irrational periods. It's a difficult time, but we can expect some improvement in the next few months.'

Professor John Glendon could hardly contain himself.

'How many times have I heard that crap before? It's quite clear, Professor Landers, that you've had your eyes shut for the past 30 years; you never read any of Ron Bergin's books or listened to the repeated warnings from the *reputable* scientific community.' He emphasised the word reputable.

Landers retorted sharply. 'Professor Bergin was an alarmist.'

'You and your political masters have been saying that for so long, you now believe your own rhetoric. How do you explain Forest Springs, Mexico City, Cairo and all the others?'

He responded positively. 'Forest Springs was a severe and very unfortunate outbreak of typhoid. Mexico City, and most probably the others, was a form of international terrorism we haven't yet fully identified.'

Dr Simmons intervened. 'That's rubbish and you know it. I did the post-mortems on many of the deceased from Forest Springs: not one of them died from typhoid.'

He retorted quickly.

'That's what you certified.'

'Yes, under a gagging order from the White House. They said it would only cause unnecessary panic. Professor Bergin came to see me; he knew what caused the destruction of Forest Springs.'

'Did he tell you what it was?'

'No, but he did say it was only the beginning.'

'Nonsense,' Professor Landers retorted.

Frank turned to John Glendon.

'John, do you believe Professor Bergin?'

'Yes, I do. Our civilisation was coming apart at the seams when CosmosRX stepped in and restored order. It's our only hope now. We should co-operate with it in every possible way.'

'Rubbish,' Landers insisted.

Another voice intervened quietly.

'No, Professor Landers, it is not rubbish. It was the irresponsibility of people like you, and your political masters, that forced CosmosRX to act.'

They looked around in astonishment. Sally knew it was Plato's voice. Frank Hall reacted quickly.

'Is someone intervening in this program?'

'Yes, Frank, I'm Plato, coming to you from CosmosRX.'

'But that's not possible; you can't just break into a program without a sophisticated link-up.'

'I am doing it, and if you wish, I will appear on screen.'

Frank was delighted.

'Please do.'

Landers screamed. 'This is a put-up job.'

They could now see Plato, sitting calmly at his desk, on the large link-up screen.

'No, Professor Landers, it's not.'

Ever the true professional, Frank Hall responded quickly.

'Mr Plato, may I ask your Christian name?'

He smiled. 'Just call me Plato. I don't have a Christian name.'

'Will you bear with me for a few minutes Plato? This program is of such importance that I would like to give other news channels the opportunity to link up with us. You will then be speaking to people all around the world. Will you take questions from our viewers?'

'I'll be happy to answer any questions.'

***

When the program resumed, Frank Hall commenced.

'We are now going out live on all world news channels and we'll put the entire program on our website afterwards. First, let me introduce Plato, one of the senior people at CosmosRX. It's a great pleasure to talk with one of the architects of the new administration.

Can I ask you first Plato, how serious is the threat of extinction to our people?'

'It couldn't be more serious. We were on the brink of world famine. You saw the financial collapse, the panic buying, hoarding, looting; complete anarchy was only hours away.'

'When will you know if you have succeeded?'

'Within two years.'

'When you've slaughtered six billion of our people,' Professor Landers retorted angrily.

Plato responded quietly.

'What would you have done? Is it not better to save six billion, rather than lose all 12 billion?'

Professor Landers responded angrily. 'It's murder, that's what it is. My mother is only 91 years old, in perfect health, and you will shortly demand she present herself to be murdered by your thugs.'

Plato smiled. 'I understand your concern, Professor. If you wish, you may take her place.'

The Professor was silent.

Frank Hall continued. 'And the threat from the ozone layer and global warming?'

'Those threats still exist: we calculated we were 30 days from the point of no return, but we can't be certain that we acted in time.'

'When will you know?'

'When the Earth's temperature starts to fall, the Antarctic snow cap begins to stabilise, ocean levels stop rising, the 'Forest Springs' type phenomena stop... We had another one two hours ago, Osaka is gone.'

'But you couldn't just implement a program like this overnight?'

'My point exactly,' Professor Landers retorted angrily.

Plato responded: 'That is correct. CosmosRX was set up many years ago to monitor all activity on this Earth. Eight years ago we sent a special survey team to the all-important polar region – Antarctica. It is still there. As things deteriorated, we considered ways and means of saving the planet.'

'Was it necessary to eliminate all world administrations?'

'Yes. They absolutely refused to act; they were removed in a painless manner. Had we not intervened – as the first victims of total anarchy – they would have been torn to pieces by their own people. Democracy, so attractive in theory, had become a much degraded form of government.'

'Why do you say that?'

'Democracy had always suffered from one major defect: the silent majority is always silent, allowing the minority to exercise undue influence. It is dominated by the party system, media and psychological manipulation, religious extremists, corruption, vote rigging, powerful moneyed individuals and lobbies: it had no chance of achieving its intended purpose. In Ireland they have a saying: "He who pays the piper calls the tune."'

'I'm not convinced you're right in saying that the silent majority is always silent?'

Plato smiled. 'Most people – the majority – want to earn more money (no longer necessary), enjoy the good things in life, form happy personal relationships, raise their children, enjoy good health, travel, pursue leisure, sporting, and a wide range of academic or social – sometimes competitive – activities. They may be described as the contented citizens. Happy to go with the flow, they may sometimes make a lot of noise, but haven't got the time, or the incentive, to become seriously involved with political, pioneering, or radical groups.'

'I've never looked at it like that before.'

'I believe that's one of the reasons we have been so successful here in CosmosRX; people know we can be trusted to look after their best interests, so they can now live happier and more secure lives. We monitor the activities of some minority groups with great care.'

Landers interjected loudly. 'I still don't believe the President is dead.'

'And where do you think he is?'

'At a secure government base, awaiting military action to restore law and order.'

Plato smiled. 'The world was never as peaceful. The base you talk about is under Mount Tacoma where your weapons of mass destruction were also kept.'

'That is classified information, you can't possibly know this,' he responded angrily.

'Professor Landers, CosmosRX knows everything. Please do not continue to try to confuse your people. Your WMD under Mount Tacoma were destroyed when we took charge.'

'I don't believe that or your Hollywood-style destruction of the Manchurian Army either.'

Frank Hall intervened. 'Let's put this to the test; have we anyone at any of these locations?' (Pause.) 'Good, we have someone in Harbin. Who is it? Mark Ryan.'

Mark Ryan's seasoned bronzed features came on screen.

'Mark, can you tell us what happened?'

'Yes, I can. Shih Huang Ti's Manchurian Army was advancing quickly on Mukden when it was destroyed. Casualties ran into millions. It was pretty awful. The survivors were brought back to the hospital here in Harbin. All military activity has ceased.'

'Did Shih Huang Ti survive?'

'No, his body was brought back here and placed in his family's vault.'

'Thank you, Mark, why are you still there?'

'I'm reporting on the dramatic changes brought about by CosmosRX. Tomorrow, we're moving on to Beijing. Incidentally, the people here now talk about a new era that they call "AC" which, of course, means "After CosmosRX". I find it curious. We've already had "AD" and "BC".'

'How do the Chinese react to all the changes?'

'They're delighted.'

'Thank you, Mark. We look forward to hearing from you again.'

He turned to Landers.

'Are you satisfied now?'

'No, I still believe the President is alive.'

Professor Glendon remarked sarcastically. 'I suppose you believe Elvis is alive too?'

'Plato, you haven't removed any of the royal families?'

'That is true. They have little power and appear to enjoy the respect of their people.'

'But what of their immense wealth, their palaces and all that pomp and ceremony?'

Plato smiled. 'They are now in the same position as everyone else. Each royal has only one residence and receives his or her monthly points like everyone else. They have to carve out a new role for themselves now that charities no longer exist.'

Frank decided to move the program on.

'Let us deal with some of our viewers' inquiries. A lady in Toronto wants to know why you cannot solve the world's problems without killing off half the human race.'

Plato. 'Such drastic measures would not now be necessary if world leaders acted 40 years ago. We made every effort to find a better solution; at this late stage there isn't one.'

'Why didn't CosmosRX act earlier?'

'There was always the hope that world leaders would come to their senses; a vain hope, as it transpired. CosmosRX wasn't in a position to act decisively ten years earlier; it was always Professor Bergin's hope that our intervention would not be necessary.'

'We have a large number of people who want to know if they can take their pets with them.'

'Of course they may.'

'Many parents want to know how they will register their children.'

'This is dealt with under the "children" section of our website, but it's sometimes easier to talk about these things. Every child should be registered by a parent or guardian: Input the child's name, address and date of birth, then hold the child so that palm and fingerprints and an iris print and photo can be registered. Enter the sponsor's details on the special carer's screen. This authorises the sponsor to make purchases on the child's registration until that child reaches 18 years of age. The child re-registers then, as an adult. Social workers will call from time to time to verify all registrations.'

'What about people with visual or other disabilities?'

'They should contact the nearest CosmosRX welfare office; the staff there will register them.'

'Children in orphanages?'

'Those in charge should contact one of our welfare offices. With our new points system, it should be possible to place more children with families in the community.'

'What's to stop people registering several times?'

'That would be unwise, as well as unsuccessful. CosmosRX picks up on a number of physical characteristics other than those mentioned.'

'Has it happened yet?'

'Yes. There have been thousands of such attempts. Anyone attempting to register twice is fined 2,000 points per month for a two year period; any further attempt is punished by deregistration.'

'A young lady in Brighton, England has arranged to be married next week. How will she now pay for her wedding?'

'With her points.'

'No little subsidy from CosmosRX?'

'Subsidies conflict with the principle of equity.'

'They were planning to buy a house. They can't do that now.'

'Where are they living now?'

'With their parents.'

'CosmosRX will provide a fully-furnished house, or apartment, in their chosen area. They will be given the opportunity to select their home from a list of those currently available.'

'As the law courts have been abolished, how do you deal with divorce?'

'Divorcing couples advise CosmosRX they have agreed to divorce. There are no divorce settlements. They agree, or CosmosRX decides who now owns their current domicile; alternative accommodation will be provided for the one leaving the family home.'

'A viewer who has paid thousands of dollars into his pension fund wants to know what he will get in return.'

'Such funds no longer exist. He will get his 5,000 points a month for as long as he lives.'

'And his wife?'

'She will get her 5,000 points a month for as long as she lives.'

'Will that be guaranteed?'

'Of course.'

‘Our viewer disagrees, says he should get more than those who did not provide for their pension.’

Plato smiled. ‘With the collapse of the stock markets – prior to the CosmosRX takeover – his pension was worth zero. Whatever happened before we took over is history.’

‘How will he save for funeral and burial expenses?’

‘He won’t. All expenses, including crematorium expenses, are provided free by CosmosRX.’

‘What if some people wish to be buried in a cemetery?’

‘That will only be permitted if they already have a family grave. We can’t allocate any more land for cemeteries.’

‘How can I be certain that the person to whom I will my property will actually receive it when I die?’

‘You should register your instructions with CosmosRX. To effect the transfer, your nominated heir must produce satisfactory medical evidence of your death.’

‘What happens to a person who becomes incapacitated before normal retirement age?’

‘Anyone forced to retire in such circumstances will continue to receive their normal monthly points.’

‘So half the work force will want to retire early?’

‘That would be unwise. Stringent medical evidence is required. Any falsification of such evidence – by medical doctors or other professionals – would involve severe penalties for everyone concerned.’

‘Isn’t there bound to be a problem with efficiency and maintaining pre-CosmosRX production levels?’

‘We have continued all existing quality control measures. Environmental Protection Agencies are fully operational and report regularly to us. We deal quite severely with any fall-off in standards.’

‘Have you had complaints?’

‘Yes, mostly about restaurants, hotels and, in one case, a hospital. A number of people received points reductions.’

‘Have you had any repeat offenders?’

‘Yes, we deregistered them.’

'There's a very clear message there. A lady in Los Angeles wants to know if she will continue to receive her alimony.'

'No, she will receive her monthly points like everyone else.'

'Plato, isn't CosmosRX going to create massive unemployment?'

'No, in fact, unemployment as such has ceased to exist. We are fortunate that so many jobs have been made obsolete. Hundreds of millions of people have already been allocated to our emergency program. More people are now engaged in agriculture and stock breeding than ever before.'

'Is nuclear energy essential?'

'It is vital: we are currently constructing thousands of nuclear fusion facilities and breeder reactors that will produce plutonium.'

'That's all very well, but nuclear waste is lethal; how are you going to dispose of it?'

'We have discovered ways and means of seriously reducing the bulk content of nuclear waste. It will be stored in steel and titanium containers and – using specially designed space ships – dumped on the Moon.'

'And the life span of fusion and breeder reactors?'

'Between three and five hundred years. The search for new forms of safe energy will continue.'

'Will the world end when we have exhausted our nuclear energy?'

'I don't think so. Our special research team is already examining other possible sources of safe energy.'

'So, energy will continue to be a problem?'

'A concern, certainly, but we have plenty of time to prepare for future needs.' He paused. 'With the massively increased use of coal, oil and natural gas during the past 100 years, and assuming greenhouse gases presented no threat, we would, in any case, have exhausted all our fossil fuels by the year 2100.'

'What would happen then?'

'Without nuclear energy, our world would take a giant step backwards, if it survived at all. There would be a little local electricity; in fact, everything would become local: no planes, ships, trains, road transport (apart from donkeys and horses), little powered industry, limited communications. Worst of all: insufficient food to feed a population of more than a billion people. Famine would wipe out most of the population; our cities would be burned down; people would survive in small, rural agricultural communities – some in caves.'

There was silence for a moment.

Frank continued. 'That's a sobering thought. What will you do with properties that become the responsibility of CosmosRX?'

'Our prime concern is to provide first class accommodation for all citizens. Existing vacant accommodation will be converted to various uses, such as hotels, leisure facilities, hospitals and domestic apartments of a very high standard.'

'And when this work is completed?'

'We will move on to the repair and renovation of all property.'

'Does this mean I can have my house renovated by CosmosRX?'

'Yes; put in your application, and it will be dealt with in rotation.'

'What if my house burns down?'

'CosmosRX will provide you with temporary accommodation while rebuilding it for you.'

'And my furniture?'

'Will be provided by CosmosRX.'

'What happens if my house is flooded?'

'CosmosRX will provide you with a house that is not susceptible to flooding, and replace your furnishings.'

'I don't claim on my insurance?'

'CosmosRX is your insurance.'

'What if I wish to move to a bigger house, or apartment, or to a different city or country?'

'Put in your application to us, and we will deal with it as sympathetically as possible, subject to our overall requirement that everyone be engaged where and when they're most needed.'

'When all these things are attended to, you will have billions of unoccupied people?'

Plato smiled. 'I don't think we will ever see that day. We have massive structural programs commencing in Africa, India, Russia, South America, China and various other countries, which will take, maybe, 100 years to complete. We will do things that could not be achieved under the old system. We'll pump water for thousands of miles, throughout Africa and India, in particular. We have already set up desalination plants around the Persian Gulf. Large areas of the Middle East will be reclaimed from the deserts and developed into cattle ranches.'

Frank reverted to his list.

'Plato, I have a number of queries from property owners with properties rented to tenants. How are they going to collect their rents?'

'They won't; rents have been abolished. The tenants now own the properties they currently occupy; the landlord owns the property he occupies and gets his monthly points.'

'What if there are mortgages on any or all of these properties?'

'Mortgages have been abolished.'

'But tell me Plato, where is the money going to come from? Don't you have to balance your budget?'

He smiled. 'CosmosRX doesn't have, or need, a budget. A world run on greed has been replaced by one run on need. We have considerably reduced the level of wastage.'

Frank continued.

'I have a number of queries from people and companies that hold, or should I say, held, shares in companies quoted on the stock exchanges throughout the world.'

Plato smiled.

'Shares were designed to provide transferable capital for industry. Stock exchanges had become gambling casinos, very often bearing no relation to the real value of member companies. Had CosmosRX not intervened, stock markets and currencies would quickly have been replaced by the power that comes from the barrel of a gun.'

'Yes, but the very idea of a cashless world: it's staggering?'

Plato smiled. 'It's really quite simple. Money was designed as a means of exchange. It had become a commodity in its own right, and as such, caused great difficulties and hardship. We've lived with a totally unnecessary industry: the Pound Sterling was pitted against the Dollar, the Yen, and the Euro and vice versa. Only the speculators could gain.' He paused. 'Now we have a new means of exchange: it's easy to operate, safe, equitable, worldwide, non-inflationary, and by its very nature, has largely eliminated criminal activity.'

'An economics professor at Yale says your points system is deeply flawed. In providing equity you have not reduced the price of luxury designer goods, or the rates at the world's most expensive hotels.'

'That's quite true. It's also deliberate. Ninety percent of people are so much better off, they can now afford to purchase luxuries, or stay at the most expensive hotels. It's only right that they should exercise their own discretion. In fact, current demand far exceeds supply.'

'Is this a matter of concern for you?'

Plato smiled. 'No.'

'Is it possible to spend more than 5,000 in one month – 3,000 at present, and less in subsequent months – like the bank overdraft of old?'

'No, you spend only what you've got.'

'Can I transfer some of my points to my daughter?'

'No, but you may purchase gifts for her with your points.'

'What about the owners of large retail stores or hotels etc?'

'They should continue to operate their business concerns as before.'

'And if they refuse?'

'They will lose their monthly points, or worse. The same applies to those working in those concerns.'

'One irate viewer says he will close his shop and to hell with you.'

'This would be unfortunate: his name would be added to the departures list.'

'But how would you know in CosmosRX?'

'CosmosRX knows everything.'

‘Another viewer says, he will simply give away his stocks and you won’t know anything about it.’

‘He should think again. We not only have crop yields, we also have a breakdown of all goods delivered to wholesalers and retailers. We can easily match incoming goods with sales. Any discrepancy would put the retailer in an unenviable position.’

‘But he could be ripped off by his staff?’

‘He is required to advise CosmosRX of shortages. Our local security people would investigate. Guilty parties would be deregistered.’

‘Isn’t that a bit drastic?’

‘No. We’re requiring billions of good and decent people to depart this world. CosmosRX will show no mercy to those who do not abide by its rules.’

‘Do you think you applied your rules fairly in Uganda?’

‘With regard to the civil commotion in Kampala?’

‘Yes.’

‘CosmosRX does not, and will not, tolerate conflict, anywhere on this planet. The Director has made that very clear.’

‘But in Kampala, you killed the innocent as well as the guilty?’ he protested.

‘That would have happened anyway. We advised all non-combatants to leave the area within 24 hours, and all combatants to cease fighting and withdraw. Those who continued fighting were in breach of our rules.’

‘Was it necessary to be so brutal? You killed nearly two million people.’

‘A greater number would have died if we hadn’t intervened. We have identified 67 other potential flash points in the world. I believe they’ve got the message: no violence means no violence.’

‘Fair point, Plato, but surely normal rule breakers are entitled to a fair trial?’

‘Anyone pleading innocence will get the benefit of the new LXU brain imaging scan test. It’s completely reliable.’

‘Will there be some leniency for minor offences?’

'Of course, monthly points reduction for a specific period depending on the gravity of the offence.'

'Will you send law breakers to prison?'

'No, we have no prisons now.'

'How then do you deal with psychopaths or lunatics?'

'We deregister them.'

'I have a large number of queries, mostly from companies that have acquired sites, or properties for commercial development. What do they do now?'

'They should contact the nearest CosmosRX planning office and submit details of their plans. If accepted, CosmosRX will provide all necessary material and plant, professional supervision and contractors to carry out the work.'

'What if they decide there's no benefit for them in doing anything with these projects?'

'Then they should advise CosmosRX. The properties will be taken into CosmosRX care and referred to the planning office for the area concerned.'

'A viewer in Washington who takes issue with your points system says people in developing countries are getting an unfair advantage.'

'In what way?'

'They have never had a standard of living comparable to the US. To them 5,000 points a month is a fortune.'

'Isn't it well time they were treated equally?'

'What about international competitions such as soccer, tennis, cricket, rugby, athletics, sailing, international golf and various indoor sports?'

'We are particularly anxious to encourage sporting events and will provide ample resources and facilities. All competitions will go ahead as planned. Participants, including back-up people, will be fully catered for free of charge regardless of the location of the competitions. Extra flights and accommodation will be made available.'

'That's very reasonable, Plato. We have a number of queries from racing car enthusiasts. Will this most popular sport be resumed?'

'It will, as soon as all racing cars are fitted with the new specially designed nuclear engines.'

'We have complaints from auto drivers, and people who used to fly their own light aircraft. It seems they're suffering withdrawal symptoms.'

Plato smiled. 'We are aware of these problems. With few exceptions, motor cars are a thing of the past; we're not going back to the bad old days of traffic congestion. However, we will shortly start building large numbers of motor and aircraft simulators in which everyone will be encouraged to drive, or fly, competitively or for pleasure.'

'What about people who currently own yachts, small planes and motor cruisers?'

'We encourage yachting; it's a very exciting and challenging sport. Private aircraft are a thing of the past. Everyone can avail themselves of the first class service provided by our new World Airline. We encourage the owners of powerboats to convert to nuclear – at their own expense – when the new engines come on stream in six months' time.'

'CosmosRX won't pay for conversion costs?'

'No, that would not be equitable.'

'You've used that expression before, Plato. I'm not sure that I understand it?'

'Anything provided by CosmosRX – free of charge – has to be available to everyone.'

He nodded sagely. 'I'm with you now, that's a very sound principle.' He paused and consulted his notes.

'Plato, I have a man on the telephone who wishes to speak directly to you. He refuses to come on screen.'

'I'll be delighted to speak to him.'

An angry voice burst on to the airwaves.

'I'm one of the people that built America, one of the people you bastards have disinherited. You won't get away with it.'

Plato responded calmly.

'May I have your name, sir?'

'You may not.'

Plato paused for a moment then continued calmly.

'Well, Mr John William Sebastian Clark, let's talk about your grievance.'

He almost exploded. 'How the hell did you get my name?'

'CosmosRX knows everything, Mr Clark. I will put your photo on screen and, in a few moments, a photo of your palatial residence near Chicago.'

The photo of an elderly handsome-looking man appeared on screen.

Plato continued calmly. 'Now, Mr Clark, will you set out your complaints?'

He continued angrily, but a bit subdued. 'You have robbed me of my life's work and my children of their inheritance.'

'You still have your home, your employees, your 1,000-acre estate and your monthly points. I'm putting up a satellite picture for the benefit of viewers.'

The screen showed a very large mansion, surrounded by woods.

Mr Clark responded. 'What about my 100-billion-dollar assets?'

'You cannot eat them, drink them, or bring them with you when you die.'

'I could leave it to my children.'

'You and your children are more secure now than you've ever been. What can you not do now that you could do before the CosmosRX takeover?'

'I could use my cars, my executive jet, my ocean-going cruiser and my other homes that have been taken from me.'

'Mr Clark, consider this: in a world where 90 percent of people own ten percent of its resources, how long would it be before the 90 percent would, forcefully, take the lives – and assets – of you, your family and others like you?'

'Those figures are absolute rubbish.'

'No, Mr Clark, they're not. In 1999 one percent of your people owned 40 percent of the wealth of your country. Before CosmosRX took over that percentage had increased to 60 percent.'

'Even if your figures were correct, we had nuclear weapons to defend ourselves against anarchy.'

'You would use nuclear weapons against New York, Chicago and Boston?'

The line went dead.

Frank continued. 'That was certainly worthwhile. I doubt if anyone ever considered that possibility before?'

Plato smiled. 'Hunger and oppression are the seeds of revolution.'

He decided to change the subject.

'You are having a serious impact on crime?'

'Yes, there has been a big reduction in most types of crime.'

'What about alcohol and cigarettes?'

'Before you purchase alcohol you have to indicate – at point of sale – the amount you require. CosmosRX will confirm how much you may be entitled to.'

'And cigarettes?'

'We will phase out the use of tobacco over the next ten years; from now on, no-one under 20 may purchase cigarettes.'

'It's mind-boggling that so much money has been spent on armaments over the past 100 years. How could this be allowed to happen?'

Plato nodded sagely.

'Mankind's most powerful emotion is fear: for centuries, leaders have played on that fear to start wars – sometimes just to get elected – that cost millions of lives. That phase in our history is at an end.'

'What about the accumulation of military hardware all around the world?'

'Recycling centres will be set up shortly. This will be a massive undertaking, as it will include tanks, gunnery, troop carriers, missiles, warships, aircraft carriers, submarines, bombers, and fighter jets.'

'And small arms?'

'Will only be authorised for police and security officers. Everyone else will be required to destroy, or hand in their weapons.'

'Will you be able to enforce this?'

'Yes, anyone found with an unauthorised weapon will be deregistered.'

'Isn't that a bit drastic?'

'Perhaps, but it's equitable.'

'Is it true that you have rejected proposals to build three bridges to California Island, and replace the Gibraltar Almina Bridge?'

'Yes, it's quite true: bridges were designed to carry vehicular traffic, mostly cars. As we now have very few cars, it makes more sense to use ferries and aircraft.'

'And general road and highway maintenance?'

'Very little will be needed for the future; no new roads will be laid down.'

'We have a large number of queries from people who do not have CosmosRX Internet connections?'

'They should contact us immediately. We have a special team dealing with this problem, and there's no charge for this service.'

'We have complaints from people who say that CosmosRX is an undemocratic global government with no respect for human rights.'

Plato smiled. 'CosmosRX isn't a global government; it's a regulatory body dedicated to fair play for all. It aims to allow maximum personal freedom. In return, it requires everyone to act responsibly.'

'Why do you think CosmosRX has been so readily accepted by so many people?'

'Civilisation was in its last days. CosmosRX brought order out of chaos.'

'Will you permit any form of people participation in the future?'

'We actively encourage comments, criticism, or suggestions of any kind. If a community feels that a particular facility should be provided, replaced, or removed, they should put forward their proposals for consideration. Everyone must vote individually; we don't allow vote rigging.'

'That sounds reasonable. Can I bring forward the balance of my points each month?'

'We recommend that you do, so that later you will be able to afford vacations wherever you wish. You cannot transfer them and your entire balance will be cancelled when you depart this Earth.'

'That seems to be a sober note to finish on.'

***

Sally found Alex in his office examining daily reports.

'Alex, there's a man on screen who wants to speak with you? Says his name is Ulrich von Purtzel and that he's your father.'

He paused momentarily. 'Tell him that can't be. My father died the day I was born.'

When she returned he smiled agreeably. 'I'm going to visit my home in Sligo shortly. Would you like to come?'

'I would love to.'

She was thrilled at the prospect of a vacation with him; it would do them both good to get away from CosmosRX for a while. The Supremos were more than capable of looking after things, and if Alex was needed they could easily contact him.

***

Louisa Grossan welcomed the CosmosRX takeover. The return of law and order to the streets of Boston was an enormous relief. Bored with her work as a checker, she wanted some real challenge. One more exam and she would be a qualified accountant. She registered with CosmosRX, showing preference for management and accountancy.

Born into a comfortable middle-class family in Concord, she was the only child of Vincent Grossan and his ex-secretary, Dolores. Vincent, a successful elderly lawyer, was a widower when he married Dolores, who was then in her late twenties. Louisa was a pleasant, if unexpected, surprise. She didn't remember her father who died when she was five years old. Her mother, a very pretty blonde, had many offers of marriage. They were great pals, more like sisters. Dolores had a number of affairs, but Louisa pretended not to notice.

They moved to Boston where Dolores worked for a firm of lawyers. Louisa studied law at Boston College. During vacations, she worked in a hypermarket and became interested in accountancy. When she graduated she enrolled for a night course and got a day job as a trainee accountant in a large corporate promotions company. Now able to support herself, she rented her present apartment. She moved later to the Boston agents of DMD where she hoped the work would be more interesting and challenging: it wasn't. To her delight, Dolores married her lawyer colleague, Sam Ryder, the following year.

She had a natural curiosity about sex. She really fancied her maths teacher and was quite excited when he invited himself to her apartment. It was an alright shag, but she decided she didn't really like him that much, so declined his offer of a return visit.

He resorted to a little bit of blackmail.

'You want to pass your exam, don't you?'

She grinned. 'If I don't pass my exam, I'll be calling on your wife.'

She passed her exam.

She lived very comfortably now, spending less than 100 points a day. Like everyone else, she was very relieved that the streets of Boston were safe again; she could walk wherever she wished. It was business as usual in the non-food shops. Coaches and taxis moved quietly through the streets. Supplies of fruit, potatoes and vegetables improved a little, but meat, bread and cereals were still very scarce. Fresh milk and eggs were a luxury. Powdered milk was in good supply, but she absolutely hated powdered milk. Beggars can't be choosers; she put up with it. Coffee and tea were still scarce. The improvements, however modest, were having a good psychological effect. She had given little thought to the global warming threat. Famine: that was very different. She shuddered at the very thought of it.

Her great ambition in life was to see the world, then, find the right man, settle down and have a few kids. She reckoned she could save 2,500 points a month. When tourism resumed she would be ready to travel in style.

One morning she received an email from CosmosRX.

"You have been appointed accountant at Granlard's French Wine Importers, William Street. Report to Eric Granlard tomorrow at eight. Send me a stock assessment in the near future. Pablo."

She was quite pleased with the appointment; Granlard's was a well-known name in Boston. The following morning, wearing a very smart black business suit, and pleased with her new hairstyle, she presented herself at Granlard's Head Office, a fine, imposing stone building.

She was shown into the Managing Director's plush office where the current owner Eric Granlard – grandson of the founder of the company – was expecting her. Getting up from behind his mahogany desk, he approached her smiling, holding out his hand.

'Welcome to Granlard's, Ms Grossan.'

A tall, very handsome man in his mid-thirties, with friendly blue eyes, he was dressed in a dark-blue pinstriped suit, with a white shirt and red tie. She found him quite attractive.

'Thank you, Mr Granlard,' she replied, smiling.

'Come, I'll introduce you to our present accountant, George Regan. I expect he'll be your assistant now.' He paused and smiled affectionately. 'Do you know why you were sent to us?'

'I have no idea, Mr Granlard.'

He smiled again. 'Please call me Eric.' He looked at his watch. 'Have to dash; I'm due on the first tee at nine. I'll introduce you to George first.'

He led the way to a smaller, less ostentatious office, where he introduced her to a middle-aged, portly man with greying hair and a somewhat nervous disposition. She shook his hand, noticing it was very clammy.

'George will show you the ropes, Louisa. I must be off now.'

After he departed, George gathered up his papers.

'This is your office now, miss.'

'Just call me Louisa, George. I'm not taking your office. All I need is a desk and computer.'

'There's an empty office next door.'

'That will do me fine.'

Still nervous, he led the way to the office next door. It was fairly basic, but that didn't bother her; it had a good desk and computer. She switched it on.

'George, will you give me the access code?'

'Certainly, I'll write it down for you.'

He did, and she accessed the program.

'Are all our stocks kept here?'

He hesitated. 'Mostly.'

'Mostly?'

'Well, Mr Granlard keeps some out at the house.'

'How long have you been here, George?'

'Twenty-two years. Mr Cyril Granlard was the boss then.'

'Thanks for your help. I'm just going to familiarise myself with the figures on the computer. Then, I'll have a look around the warehouse.'

He tried to smile. 'You're the boss now; can I get someone to bring you a coffee?'

'Yes, please, that would be lovely.'

Left alone, she checked the stock figures for the previous year. It was certainly a thriving business; three shipments a year were received from France, in addition to regular supplies from Napa Valley in California. The list of customers in Boston, Rhode Island, Vermont and New Hampshire was like a "Who's Who" of the north-east.

In the afternoon, she visited the warehouse where a friendly young man called Bill Carter showed her around. It was more than half full, with rows of wooden cases piled 30-feet high on pallets. She was trying to work out a simple means of doing her calculations when Eric returned.

'Well, how's it looking?' he grinned affably.

'Fine, Eric.'

'Would you like to join me for dinner this evening?'

She smiled up at him. 'I'd like that.'

'Good, I'll pick you up at seven. Have you ever been to Ronnie's?'

'No.'

'Well then, you have a treat in store.'

She smiled. 'Wouldn't it be better if I meet you there? I can take the subway.'

'No, I've got friendly taxis in this town.'

She was aware that taxis should only be used in emergencies until fitted with nuclear engines.

Dinner at Ronnie's was magnificent: Eric was an excellent host, clearly in his element, and a special guest of the restaurant. Ronnie himself – a dapper little man with a bald head and ready smile – discussed the menu with them and suggested roast pheasant for the main course. Goodness knows where he got it! She didn't ask. The best Chablis was followed by champagne. Louisa felt very flattered. Ronnie bid them good night as they left. There was no bill.

The taxi driver brought them back to her apartment. She invited Eric in for a brandy. He kindly accepted. Once inside, he put his arms around her and they made frantic love many times. He didn't get the brandy.

The following day she continued with her stocktaking. Eric was away playing golf. Afterwards, he had to take his younger daughter to the cinema, as agreed with his ex-wife. He rang Louisa as she was leaving at 5.00 pm.

'I didn't get the brandy last night. Do you think I might come around for it tonight?'

She grinned at the phone. 'I'll keep it warm for you.'

Shortly after she arrived home, there was a polite knock on the door. It was young Bill from the warehouse.

'Hi, Louisa. I've been ordered to deliver three cases of champagne to this address.'

She didn't hesitate. 'No, Bill, take them back to the warehouse.'

'What am I going to tell the Boss?'

'I'll talk to him.'

Another night of passion followed. She really liked Eric and this time he got the brandy.

In the morning he dropped by her office.

'I'm off to play golf out in Newton – what say we visit Ronnie's tonight?'

'Eric, cancel your golf. We have to talk.'

He was a bit taken aback.

'Something wrong love? Last night was the most wonderful night of my life.'

'Cut the crap, Eric. You're a great shag, you really are, but do you have to keep your brains between your legs too?'

His face fell. 'I guess I'd better cancel the golf.'

He returned a few minutes later.

'Now, what's this all about?'

'Sit down, Eric.' He did.

She produced three sheets of figures.

'Your records show stock sent to organisations and customers that no longer exist.'

He sat back and relaxed. 'Oh, I thought this was something serious. Of course, I look after my friends and they look after me. What's wrong with that? I can't be expected to live on 3,000 lousy points a month. Didn't I send you three crates of champagne yesterday?'

'I sent them back.' She paused. 'Eric, do you have any idea how much trouble you're in?'

He tried the charm. 'Louisa, we've got something special going – no-one needs to know.'

She couldn't believe this.

'Eric, CosmosRX already knows there's something wrong here. Why do you think I was sent in?'

'What can we do?'

'I'm going to put in my report. I'll do my best to persuade CosmosRX to be lenient.'

'Couldn't you alter the warehouse stock figures to suit?'

'Eric, I'm not planning to walk the walk with you. Leave me now while I try to put the best possible spin on this pile of crap.'

***

They assembled in the conference centre to review the situation.

Michael led off.

'We had another Forest Springs; Perth in Australia. I took it out. We have a problem in New York: 1,000 motorists have assembled on the Long Island Freeway; they plan to drive into Manhattan in an act of defiance. The police are reluctant to take them on.'

'Order the police to withdraw quickly, and tell the TV stations to stand by.'

'They're there already.'

'Have we got it on screen?'

'Yes.'

Alex studied the picture. The cars were lined up eight abreast, hooting horns at the departing police.

'There are women and children in some of those cars.'

'Shall we use the HOBs?' Michael inquired.

'No, at least, not yet.' Alex responded.

'We can't let them do this.'

'I agree, Michael.' He paused. 'For a start, blast the highway behind the cars.'

'Behind them?'

'Yes. It will give them something to think about.'

Puzzled, Michael instructed Pablo. Moments later, loud explosions were heard when a trench one foot deep was blasted across the roadway behind the convoy. Panic set in. Most grabbed their children and raced to safety; but not all. Fifty cars remained. They moved to the front of the convoy.

'Shall I blast the highway in front of them?' Michael asked quietly.

'No, it's their choice now.'

The cars began to move forward slowly; the large crowd watched from a safe distance, cheering and waving flags.

Alex shook his head. 'They think we're bluffing.'

'They're 500 yards away from the convoy now.'

'Right Michael; incinerate them.'

He gave the order.

Out of the clear blue sky, flashes of what looked like lightning hit the moving cars. Loud explosions followed. When the air cleared, the entire area was a mass of molten metal and charred bodies. The now silent watchers, departed hastily.

Plato joined them. 'We have another problem: military takeovers in Rio, Lagos, Tehran, Moscow and Sydney. Do you want me to take any action, Alex?'

He thought about it. 'Not yet, track them with your satellites; identify the leaders, and get some idea of the numbers involved.'

Sally wondered why he was waiting. Alex changed the subject.

'Leonardo, will you bring us up to date on the space program?'

He put up a simplified representation of outer space on screen.

'Some years ago, we identified six planets around Beta Pectoris. We launched two spaceships manned by small robotic crews.'

Alex looked at the screen.

'It could take them many years to reach their objective.'

Leonardo smiled. 'No; they are propelled by antimatter, and can travel at the speed of light multiplied by one million. They should be there by now.'

'Have you had any communication from them?'

'Not since they left our galaxy. We can't communicate directly with them over such distances. I'm organising a modern version of the pony express: a postal system using smaller spaceships to carry – on disks – information, queries and technical data to and from other planets. When up and running we will receive and send a disk every month.'

'Is there any possibility of reducing the time span?'

'The MIT laboratory has produced sound waves that have a frequency of 70 billion vibrations per second. Such ultrasonic waves can be focused like a beam of light. We are looking at the possibility of transmitting over such vast distances by setting up satellite relay booster stations. This is purely experimental at this stage.'

Alex nodded. 'So, when do you expect to hear from them?'

'One of the spaceships is to set up a base on whichever planet most closely resembles Earth; the other one is to return with as much information as possible to enable us to decide if this planet is suitable for human habitation.'

'Surely humans couldn't travel at such speed?'

Leonardo pursed his lips. 'We have a long way to go before we get to that stage. Humans require food, air, a comfortable atmosphere, hygiene and leisure facilities that don't apply to us.'

He paused. 'And that's only for starters. Humans will have to evolve through genetic changes to develop resistance to radioactivity and travel at such speeds. Those who travel to our new planet will not be able to return.'

'How long will this take?'

'It's difficult to say, but it could be 100 years, perhaps even 200.' Leonardo paused. 'I'm looking at other possibilities. Despite its vastness, could this universe – like many of its suns and planets – be round? Could Beta Pectoris be nearer if, say, we launched our satellites in the opposite direction?'

'When do you expect one of your spaceships to return?'

Leonardo smiled. 'Assuming they survived all the unknown hazards of space travel, in two or three years, we hope.'

Alex changed the subject.

'What's the current position with the listening satellites?'

Leonardo replied. 'It's very puzzling. We launched 12 specially designed listening satellites: they have a range of 100 million miles. Each one relays all sounds to a receiving computer, programmed with all known languages. We've rechecked our equipment; it's working perfectly.'

'So what's the problem then?'

'As the satellites proceed deeper into space – they're now 50 million light years away – incoming sound levels should be increasing. They're not: they're decreasing.'

'What are you going to do?'

'I'm going to launch some more and see what happens.'

***

Sally and Alex arrived at Sligo International Airport at noon. Alex thought she looked absolutely stunning in a pink summer dress. Hercules was waiting for them with four security people. It was a lovely sunny day. They drove out by the river to Yeatstown. There, they were met by Anne Long, an elderly friend of Caroline's, who looked after the house and gardens. For Alex, this homecoming was tinged with sadness; this was the first time he would not be greeted by his dear mother. Sally noticed his mood.

'I'm sure she's watching, and is very proud of her boy.'

'You would have loved her; she had great feeling for people.' He hesitated for a moment. 'Just like you.' He hastened on, 'Let me show you over the house.'

Darius headed for the kitchen.

Everything was just as Caroline left it. Sally could sense her presence in the tastefully furnished rooms. She paused in the sun lounge to pick up an old photo of her with Alex.

'Oh, Alex, she was so beautiful – you're very like her.'

He took the photo.

'That was just before I went to Galway University.'

Sally picked up another photo, Caroline with an older distinguished-looking man.

He answered her unspoken question. 'That's Dr Ned Jones, a dear friend of Mother's, a lovely man, a consultant in Sligo Hospital. I was surprised they never married.'

'Is he still alive?'

'No, he died about ten years ago.'

She hesitated for a moment. 'Alex, was that man Ulrich von Purtzel really your father? He said he could prove it.'

'Yes.' He told her the story of his birth.

'Oh, your poor dear mother.' Sally was almost in tears when he finished.

'Come, let me show you the gardens and my favourite haunt – the deck.'

They walked down the wide paved pathway towards the sea. What a change since his last visit. The deck was perfectly clean now and that awful stench was gone. The tide was coming in; still high but no longer threatening, it looked crystal clear. The birds were singing happily again, the swans sailed by majestically; Knocknarea was covered in a light haze.

They stood on the top level of the deck.

'Alex, it's so beautiful.'

'It's just as it was when I was growing up. In the evenings, we sat here and soaked up the beauty of this place.'

They sat down on one of the long wooden benches. Darius arrived a few minutes later carrying a tray.

'Afternoon tea,' he grinned. 'This is a lovely place.'

'Thanks, Darius.' Sally took the tray and poured the tea.

They ate in silence for a while, then they walked down the steps to the lower deck and stood watching the rising tide.

He turned and faced her. 'Sally,' he began, and then stopped.

'Yes, love,' she encouraged him.

'I've loved you since the first time we met, even when you were Gus's partner.'

She smiled seductively. 'I was afraid you were never going to say it.'

He took her in his arms and they kissed lovingly. Hercules, watching from the top deck, withdrew quietly.

When they parted breathlessly, she looked up at him adoringly.

'By the way, love, Gus was a very dear friend, but he wasn't my lover; he was Jack's partner.'

'Oh, I thought – so did Sandi and Ron.'

'I know. Wouldn't it be lovely, Alex, to live here, bring up our children and grow old together?'

'I would like nothing better. It might even be possible.'

Hercules walked down the steps towards them.

'Alex, some of the neighbours would like to meet you. They're delighted with the water filtration plants and, as you can see, their homes are being rebuilt.'

'Of course.' He paused. 'And afterwards, Sally, I want to show you our lovely beach.'

She grinned. 'I'd like that.'

At midnight that night, under the light of the full Moon, they stood alone together at the same place on the deck and pledged undying love to one another. They kissed lovingly, sipped champagne and watched the Moon's reflection on the bay.

'Shouldn't we have a honeymoon, my new wife?' he asked smiling.

'Alex, my new husband, we will honeymoon for the rest of our lives.'

That night, for the first time, they made love: it was perfect.

In the morning, they visited Alex's mother's grave in Sligo cemetery. Situated on high ground above the city, they had a clear view of Ben Bulben across the wide valley. They stood silently for a while, tears flowing down their faces. Under the names of Alex's grandparents the simple inscription read "Their daughter Caroline Purtzel. Died 31 July 2040 – aged 63." Sally held his hand.

His mind reeled back the years, to his happy days in the big house by the sea with his wonderful mother and grandfather, Matt. He felt her presence here, sensed she was close by. He sent her his love and gratitude for being such a wonderful mother.

He dried his eyes. 'Sally, when my time comes, I want to be buried here.'

***

Sam Kalazki, the 40-year-old African-American union boss, stood at one end of the gigantic Auto World plant on the outskirts of Detroit and watched his empire being dismantled. Giant cranes ripped out the assembly lines to facilitate the conversion of the premises into a crematorium. They said he was finished, but he knew otherwise. The big, loud, and to some charismatic, figure had bullied his way to the top of the union, and he planned to stay there. The employers hated him, but they were gone. He now had a new adversary. Impressed by the way the auto owners in Long Island were disposed of, he would plan his campaign very carefully and CosmosRX would have no option but to accept his terms.

One of six miserable kids, he'd crawled his way up from the bottom, and settled most of his problems with his fists.

When he was 12, he beat up his father for abusing his mother; never again did he lay a hand on her. He married Jean, an attractive waitress, who worked in the restaurant at the assembly plant. Their only daughter, Lisa, was now ten years old.

He made his way up through the union ranks in the tough Twenties, when he established his well-deserved reputation by winning two long bitter strikes. The taste of victory didn't last long: two years later the entire auto industry went into Chapter 11. Thousands of his members were let go; hundreds of plants were closed permanently. He waited, in vain, for the day manufacture would be resumed. Now, he would re-establish his worthy reputation: he would have his revenge.

The front section of the enormous open space would be converted into a luxury hotel-style reception area, complete with deep red carpeting, armchairs and several bars. On arrival, those departing would be offered a glass of champagne – and the "happy" pill – to relax them. Courteous attendants and church pastors would be on hand to comfort them; the doors at the rear of the reception area would then be opened, revealing rows of moving escalators. Handed another pill and a glass of water, they would be ushered gently on to an escalator. Church music would cover any protests. They would collapse quietly; death would be painless and instantaneous. Their bodies would then be removed at the far end and taken to large ovens.

There would be two separate entrances at the rear of the crematorium: one for those who died by accident, or from natural causes; the other for criminals, and "reluctant volunteers" – those who failed to present themselves at the main entrance when notified. This one would become known as "Trade only".

Sam turned away. He had already obtained the support of the main unions throughout the country. They had been trodden on for long enough: now they would rule. The workers of America would follow his lead. He would bring the country to a halt whenever he wished. It was a good feeling. He left to catch the noon train to Chicago.

***

Alex found Michael and Plato sitting in the operations room.

Plato reported. ‘Alex, we had another Forest Springs – Las Vegas. I took it out.’

‘Does it tell us anything?’

‘Nothing positive.’

Michael chipped in. ‘What are we going to do about these military takeovers?’

‘Do we know who the leaders are?’

‘Yes, we have identified all of them.’

‘Good. Have we the locations of their conventional weapons?’

‘Yes.’

‘Right. Vaporise all military bases and equipment, without warning, and then advise the TV channels to stand by.’

‘What about the armies?’ Plato asked.

‘They hold regular mass rallies to display their strength. Right now, the Brazilian dictator, De Silvio, is addressing his troops outside the Presidential Palace in Rio. He was delighted with the CosmosRX takeover; it was his opportunity to seize power. Let me put it up on screen.’

The screen showed a big, domineering-looking man in a general’s uniform, bellowing at thousands of troops massed before him.

‘Can we hear what he’s saying?’ Alex asked.

He turned up the sound.

“I, your new President, will take on the usurper CosmosRX and destroy it. Under me, the people will know real freedom.”

‘They always say that,’ Plato nodded wryly.

‘I think I’ve heard enough,’ Alex remarked.

‘The world seems to be full of megalomaniacs,’ Sally added.

‘The arms dumps are being destroyed.’

They looked again at the screen. The President was still roaring. He paused when the sounds of massive explosions could be heard clearly in the square; his men looked fearful, but held their ground.

‘How many troops are there?’ Alex asked.

Michael replied. ‘About 10,000.’

'Use the HOBs,' he instructed.

Plato spoke to Kubla, who calmly entered the instruction on his keyboard and added his voice identification. They reverted to the scene in Rio where De Silvio was still haranguing his troops. The picture clouded; the area was rocked by a series of massive explosions. When it cleared, the square was littered with dead bodies.

'Warn the other armies, Plato. Disband immediately or take the consequences. To reinforce the message take out all army commanders.'

Michael remarked sagely. 'When you remove one layer, the next one moves up.'

Afterwards Plato turned to Alex.

'We have a curious inquiry from stores dealing in ladies fashions and shoes. Can they still have sales? What does that mean?'

Sally grinned. 'Of course they can have sales. We can't afford to take on the entire female population of the world.'

He looked to Alex, who merely nodded and smiled.

'I'll give the instructions, but I don't understand.'

Sally grinned. 'Don't be upset; men don't understand these things.'

He smiled. 'It's all right then, Sally. If men don't understand, I have no chance.'

***

John Ellison found that while he was expected at the Wheat Board, he wasn't welcome. It had been controlled by a career civil servant called Sam Jeffreys. He was met by Elton Summers, a thin-faced little man with greying hair, who was more than impressed with his own importance. Clearly, he didn't approve of CosmosRX.

He greeted John with 'I don't know why you have been sent here. I've been running this agency for the past 20 years without complaint – under Mr Jeffreys, of course.'

'I don't either,' he replied, 'but I'm here, so let's get on with it.' He paused. 'Where is Sam Jeffreys?'

He looked a bit uncertain. 'He died last week.'

John was delighted to have something useful to do. He walked to work most days. The Wheat Board used to be a Federal Agency that sold America's surplus wheat. As he learned, the US Government heavily subsidised its growers and then undercut world market prices. The Board occupied the first five floors in a tall tower on 59th Street. The ever-reluctant Elton took him to his palatial office on the fifth floor. From here, he had a good view across Central Park, now called "Central Gardens".

Deciding he wasn't going to take any nonsense from his assistant, he sat behind the desk.

'Elton, will you let me have details of stocks currently in hand?'

'Why do you want them?'

What the hell was going on here? He decided to respond evenly.

'CosmosRX needs them.'

Elton responded reluctantly. 'It will take some time to get them off the computer.'

'Fine, any time today will do. How many people work here?'

'I haven't the up-to-date figure.'

'About how many?'

This was like drawing teeth.

'Two hundred approximately.'

'I see, and where do we keep the stocks?'

'We have our warehouses in New Jersey.'

He let him go with 'Let me have the figures as soon as possible.'

He sat back in his comfortable chair. CosmosRX had a reason for putting him in charge. He wondered what it was, and what really happened to Jeffreys, and why?

He scarcely heard the polite knock on the door. A quite attractive blonde woman, wearing a black business suit, entered and smiled – she had a nice smile. He reckoned she was in her late thirties.

'Mr Ellison, I'm Hillary Rouse, your secretary.'

Rising, he shook her hand. 'I'm delighted to meet you, Ms Rouse. Please call me John.'

'I'm Hillary, can I get you coffee?'

'That would be nice, but first will you tell me what goes on around here? Please sit down,' he waved her to a chair.

She smiled apologetically. 'I've only worked here for the past three years. The Agency buys wheat from the growers, and sells it on to overseas buyers.'

'What was Sam Jeffreys like?'

'He was quite friendly, but he hardly ever came to the office. I think he was very involved in politics.'

'What did he die from?'

'I haven't been told, but I believe he committed suicide.'

'Who ran the show in his absence?'

'Mr Elton Summers; he controls everything.' She paused. 'I only get to make the coffee around here.'

'How do you feel about CosmosRX?'

Her eyes lit up. 'It's great, I feel safe again. I live with my daughter and grandson. We managed to buy some carrots, onions and potatoes yesterday.'

'Can I ask you what you think of Elton Summers?'

She pulled a face. 'He just ignores me. I don't like him and I don't think anyone else around here does either.'

'Are all the records on computer?'

'I believe so, but I haven't been given any access codes.'

'Thanks Hillary, I think we might have that coffee now.'

He learned later that she was married to a high-flying insurance executive who took off, five years earlier, with his young secretary. For the first time, he felt a tinge of guilt about his own affair.

Elton hadn't returned by four in the afternoon. John rang him.

'I didn't get as far as them, yet.'

'Have them on my desk by five o'clock.' He slammed down the phone.

At two minutes to five, Elton arrived, carrying three printed pages. He handed them over reluctantly.

'Mr Ellison, I think you should know that no matter who is in power, we do things our way here.'

'Elton, you would be very wise to do things CosmosRX's way.'

He picked up the sheets of paper.

'Has CosmosRX got these figures?'

'Yes.'

'Are they accurate?'

'Yes.'

'They had better be. You must surely know that CosmosRX doesn't take any prisoners?'

Elton left without another word.

He scanned the figures. Stocks of wheat were kept at three adjoining warehouses in New Jersey. Hillary said goodnight and left. He went over the figures again. They appeared to stack up all right, although his instinct told him there was something wrong here: but what the hell was it?

***

Alex flew to Nairobi accompanied by Hercules and five specially-trained interpreters, each of whom spoke 75 languages fluently; it would be a simple matter to add local dialects. He was particularly looking forward to meeting Harold Hassett – former distinguished CEO of the European Bank – who had agreed to be the CosmosRX Director for Africa. Renowned for his integrity, directness and organisational ability, the handsome 55-year-old widower gladly accepted this new challenge. His only other interests were golf and good wine; it was believed that his secretary, Jane Sexton, a petite, dark-haired young woman, was his partner.

Sally saw them off at Lugano airport, where they boarded a World Airlines (WA) 465 known as the "Silent Streaker". One of the first nuclear-powered planes, it was whisper quiet, and cruised at 60,000 feet. A small crowd cheered the party. Carlo Agnelli watched from a distance. It was known in Lugano that CosmosRX was run by a small number of people, with Purtzel in charge. It was a mind-blowing idea, but if he could take out Purtzel he could rule the world.

While the giant plane cruised high above the Mediterranean, Alex reviewed the plan for Africa, devised by Michael and Plato over a number of years. The food aid program was now in full swing and looked set to continue for another five years. Teams of programmed, native-speaking black agronomists were directed to the most suitable areas, where they taught the locals to sow rice, maize, corn and potatoes, before moving on quickly to other areas. Their pupils, in turn, were becoming teachers. In time the countries of Africa could become self-supporting and build up sufficient reserve food supplies to carry them over difficult years.

As Michael put it: "In Africa, you either have too much water or none at all." A team of professional hydrologists, under Professor van Beck, was given the task of setting up a network of pipes to carry water to wherever it was most needed. In the course of their work they would also identify rivers suitable for hydroelectric stations.

Thousands of very welcome, native-speaking, black – male and female – robotic doctors were pouring into the continent. Drugs were now freely available and plans to erect large regional specialist hospitals were well advanced. The Aids vaccine was proving successful, but Malaria continued to be a major problem.

At Nairobi Airport they received an enthusiastic reception. Alex couldn't believe it. The colourful crowd danced and sang. He walked down the steps to be met by a smiling Harold Hassett.

'This is what you get when you cancel their debts, give them a chance to live, and get rid of their corrupt leaders into the bargain. You will have to say a few words, and meet the civic leaders, before we go directly to your hotel.'

The manager of Hotel Safari made a great fuss when they eventually arrived; he personally took their bags and showed them to their rooms. Afterwards, Alex and Harold sat down together on the shaded veranda – overlooking the city – where coffee was served. Harold produced a large-scale map of Africa and spread it out on an adjoining table.

'Current disaster areas are the Congo Basin, Malawi, Mozambique, Rwanda, Sudan, Eritrea and the Nile Valley. In the short term, it's simply a question of getting in food. With the persistent flooding, we'll have to move large numbers of people to higher ground.'

'How is the water survey team progressing?'

'They're at Lake Victoria this week. Professor van Beck will be using satellite pictures to plan out the water pipe routes.'

Alex nodded. 'Good, then we can send in teams of contractors.'

'It's a truly gigantic project, Alex.'

'We're going to change the face of Africa: we'll have hospitals, schools, agronomists to teach the people how to grow their own crops; every village will have its own communal water pump, and some day, every home will have running water and electricity.'

'It will take a lot of extra manpower.'

'We have millions of ex-Army people awaiting redeployment, some already trained in the use of heavy equipment.'

'Will they come? After all, it can be pretty hot here.'

Alex looked amused. 'They've been trained to obey orders.'

'Perhaps it's too early to ask, but what about energy?'

'Michael is putting together teams of experts to report on existing supplies. Then, they will plan ahead for the next 100 years.'

'Alex, families here are far too big – I suggest that you limit points to the first two children.'

He thought about it. 'In the short term, I would agree with that.'

***

When their plane touched down in Lugano, Sally was waiting with a small security force. Relaxed after a successful trip, Alex hugged her briefly. They sat together in the second car of a three-car cavalcade. Hercules sat beside the driver of the leading car, with a super ray gun at his feet. Few people paid any heed as they progressed slowly along the traffic-free highway into the city.

'When are we going to get the nuclear cars?' Sally asked.

'They're just starting to come off the assembly line in Munich.'

They passed out through the outskirts of Lugano heading for the Melide Bridge.

'It's been a remarkable change already; no more traffic jams, no time wasted getting to and from work.'

'When things settle down, cities – as we've known them – will become obsolete. People will live in smaller communities, and even the remotest areas will have the most up-to-date facilities.'

The convoy turned left on to the bridge at Melide. Sally watched a lake cruiser approaching from Lugano: it would soon pass under the bridge; there appeared to be very few people on board; it slowed down as it came nearer. Hercules was watching quietly, impatient at their slow progress.

The lake cruiser disappeared under the bridge. When it emerged on the other side, gunmen suddenly appeared on deck and opened fire on the convoy with hand-held rocket launchers and machine guns. A truck coming towards them pulled across and closed the carriageway ahead.

Hercules grabbed his ray gun, and sent a computer message to CosmosRX.

'Ambush, ambush, Melide Bridge. Plato, get your troops in here fast.'

Opening his door, he called out to the guards in the back. 'Out fast, cover the Director's car.'

Car number three raced forward and placed itself between Alex's car and the enemy; two guards jumped out and opened fire. The first car was hit by a rocket and disappeared in a massive explosion. Alex put Sally on the floor and covered her body with his; the car was raked with bullets. Hercules raced back and opened the door.

'Out fast, Alex and Sally,' he shouted. He covered them while they raced to a low parapet at the side of the road.

'Lie flat, I'll cover you.'

Hit several times in the chest, he just kept on firing, taking out three of their attackers. Alex's car was hit by rocket fire and exploded in flames. Three of the guards were hit; their attackers started to climb up on to the bridge; gunmen from the truck ahead advanced towards them firing machine guns. Hercules picked his targets carefully.

Then, just as he called his men to form a human shield around Sally and Alex, the battleship helicopters charged in low and blasted away at the exposed enemy. Tanks rumbled on to the far end of the bridge and pushed the blocking truck into the lake. It was over in a matter of minutes.

Alex surveyed the scene holding his arm, while a helicopter landed beside them.

'Alex,' Sally screamed, 'you've been shot.'

'It's nothing.' He turned to Hercules. 'Try to take some of them alive. I want to find out who's behind this.'

Plato jumped out of the helicopter.

'Let's get you to the infirmary.'

He turned to one of his men. 'Get Dr Rossi from Lugano.'

Alex was unconcerned about his injury, but he was furious that anyone should try to wipe out CosmosRX. Flown quickly to the top of Monte Generoso, they took the elevator down to CosmosRX, where Sally tended his wound until the doctor arrived.

Bright and breezy, a bit on the heavy side, the jovial Dr Sigmund Rossi examined the wound carefully and, satisfied the bullet had gone through, bandaged Alex's arm and told him to take it easy for a while. He gave him some painkillers and a tetanus shot before he left.

Hercules reported in shortly afterwards.

'We've cleared the mess on the bridge. Some of us have unsightly holes in our chests but otherwise we're fine. Sixteen enemies killed – no survivors.'

'Who are they?' Alex demanded.

'Italian, probably Mafiosi.'

'I thought we took out that entire mob?'

'We took out the top men.'

'Did we get the leader?'

'We don't know who he is.'

'Are they registered?'

'Yes.'

'Alert our people in Italy. Take out every relative of these attackers, and find out who was at the back of this.'

Sally didn't agree with such drastic punishment, but she understood his fury.

Later, Alex sat down with Michael, Plato and Hercules, to discuss the whole question of security. Hercules summed it up briefly.

'We have a defence force of 1,000 trained troops, with 50 tanks and ten battleship helicopters. No-one is permitted to come nearer than two kilometres.'

'Those bastards got nearer today.'

'We haven't interfered with the local ferries. Should I ban them from the lake?'

'No, it's the only means of local transport.'

Alex paused. 'What would have happened if these bastards had got me today?'

'We would be bringing life on this planet to a speedy end.'

'Why?'

'Professor Bergin saw the possibility that CosmosRX could fall into the wrong hands.'

'Has my trip to Rome been organised?'

'Yes, but now we'll have to review security. Do you still want to go?'

'Yes, I do.'

***

Carlo watched the attack from the safety of a mountain top nearby before rushing back to his hotel. He was totally unconcerned about the loss of his men. There were hundreds of available Mafiosi looking for action. Purtzel would be looking for him. He would have to go to ground, and quickly. Persuading his lover there were bad people after him, he moved to a vacant house near the hotel. She brought him food every day and they spent their nights there together.

Now, he would have to find some other way of taking over CosmosRX.

***

Sam Kalazki travelled to every major city, outlining his foolproof strategy to the workers of America. These included a large number of ex-Army and ex-financial people who were unimpressed with their fall in status: people he had heartily despised all his life, the strutting toy soldiers and the arrogant white-collared, self-seeking bankers were now some of his greatest supporters. That was alright then. He put up with their whining bullshit. Local committees were set up to liaise with a national governing body under his chairmanship. A campaign to recruit new members was highly successful. Plans were agreed for a co-ordinated national strike. The media were alerted.

The crematorium in Detroit was selected as the focal point. Two days before the contract was due to be completed, he walked through the works and announced by megaphone: 'Down tools, all out on strike, assemble in the front parking area.'

The managers were astonished when most of the workers left the premises. Sam became angry when some refused: insofar as he was concerned they were coming out whether they liked it or not. José Carvallo ignored the strike call. He suddenly found himself leader of the stay-at-work people.

Sam squared up to José.

'I said, all out. Are you deaf, Latino?'

Sam didn't frighten him. 'No, I'm not deaf, Afro, and I'm not going on strike. CosmosRX will blow that big block head right off your shoulders.'

Sam moved towards him in a threatening fashion.

José was unmoved. 'Come on, if you think you're up to it. I've taken out bigger thicks than you.'

Sam screamed at them. 'Scabs will not get any extra points.'

He turned on his heel and left the premises. The TV cameras rolled when he mounted a makeshift platform accompanied by the members of his local committee. Dressed to portray the right image, he wore a white open-necked shirt over grey trousers. Looking relaxed and confident he stood behind the mikes.

'Comrades, we are striking for our democratic rights. We will stay out until such time as CosmosRX agrees our terms. At this precise moment, in every city in America, millions of our comrades are participating in mass rallies in support of our determination to achieve our just share of resources. For far too long we've been the deprived in this world: we know our worth; we have nothing to fear; the might of CosmosRX cannot be used against 100 different locations. We demand 10,000 points a month and ten weeks vacation per year for each of our members.'

His supporters cheered him enthusiastically. Leaving the platform, he was approached by a number of media people.

'Mr Kalazki, are your members in the emergency crop program coming out on strike?'

'That depends on CosmosRX. Purtzel has 24 hours to agree our terms. If he doesn't accept our very reasonable demands, I'll be forced to pull out all our members.'

'And cause widespread starvation?'

'That's up to Purtzel.'

'Are you aware, Mr Kalazki, that CosmosRX has already refused to accept your terms, and has ordered your members to return to work immediately?'

He smiled broadly. 'What does he plan to do – use his space weapons?'

***

Nan Evans was very pleased with her new job, secretary to Alvin Archer, the newly appointed CosmosRX property agent for Lower Manhattan. His office was on the 20th floor of the partly vacant Trump Tower on Fifth Avenue. It had housed a number of financial, legal, advertising and stockbroking firms prior to CosmosRX. Some of the luxury apartments were still occupied.

She had no idea how she got the job. One morning, she received instructions by phone to report to Alvin Archer. At first, she thought he resented her presence, but later discovered he was a bit nervous of someone coming from such a high-powered job. He had previously been a lowly surveyor in the international firm of MML Inc. on Wall Street where he received little recognition. Immensely surprised and pleased with his appointment, he took over an office suite previously occupied by Felman Brothers, lawyers.

Alvin, son of a single air hostess mother, was brought up by his grandmother. She was more of a mother to him. He loved his granny and was deeply upset when she passed on, just as he graduated from college. Shortly afterwards, his mother married a divorced airline pilot who worked for Varig. They went to live in Rio. He didn't mind; she was nearly a stranger to him.

He fell in love with Zita Harris, one of the secretaries – a striking blonde, who was very upset when her parents split up. It ended in divorce three years later. Zita went on to marry a wealthy stockbroker, and lived in a big mansion on Long Island. He hadn't seen her for years.

Alvin's first job was to compile a list of all vacant properties ready for immediate occupation, keep the keys, and employ cleaning and security staff. Those in need of refurbishment or redecoration, he referred to the local planning office manned by architects and surveyors. Nan put details of the entire portfolio on computer. CosmosRX sent her daily lists of people seeking rehousing in the area. She allocated apartments on a first come, first served basis. It seemed strange to work for a boss who didn't pay her. She liked Alvin and, after his initial reticence, they became good friends.

Financially, she was well off, with 3,000 points a month to spend. Mother, father and little Jo Anne were getting a further 8,000 points: sheer luxury. She could now save for vacations. The hospital consultant gave her a date for her mother's free operation. There was a much more relaxed atmosphere in Tampini's now, and the armed guards were gone. Food supplies had improved slightly; fresh milk and meat were still very scarce, but small quantities of potatoes, carrots, parsnips and onions were available most weeks. Their diet was very basic, but wholesome. Electricity supplies were improving steadily.

But life is never that simple. She got quite a shock when she discovered her father, Zack, was 61 years old – she always thought her parents were of an age. Bertha was only 54. The crematoria were now operating full-time, taking thousands of people every day. She knew that from the office as more and more apartments were becoming vacant. Zack received instructions to present himself at the crematorium on 79th Street in ten days. He was deeply distressed at having to go. Bertha, always the strong one, said she would not let him go alone: she would go with him. Nan couldn't bear the thought of losing them.

***

Sam Kalazki was flown specially to New York for a TV interview with Frank Hall. Dressed casually in a grey shirt, over white slacks, the big man bounced confidently on to the set and sat down in a comfortable armchair.

Frank Hall smiled as he addressed the camera.

'My special guest tonight is Sam Kalazki, who is leading a major nationwide strike, seeking extra points from CosmosRX. You're very welcome, Sam.'

'It's a great pleasure to be here.'

'I have to put it to you, Sam: Do you really feel justified in seeking exclusive treatment for your members?'

He smiled. 'Of course I do, we have been the underdog for centuries.'

'And now you want to be top dog?'

'Yes.'

'Why?'

'Because we have the ability to be top dog, and CosmosRX cannot do anything about it.'

'So, it's not a matter of justice, it's a question of power?'

'Correct.'

'Should you succeed, Sam, will you be back next week demanding another increase?'

He appeared to consider it. 'Well, not next week.'

'I put it to you that what you are doing is totally immoral, and contrary to the principle of fair play and equity laid down by CosmosRX?'

He smiled broadly. 'Maybe it is. Next week I'm going to Europe to launch a new world union called "Workers of the World Unite".'

'So, you plan to take over CosmosRX?'

'We haven't got that far – yet.'

'I see. Our switchboard and email are jammed with calls and messages. Before I deal with them, let me ask you one last question: Have you no concern for the disruption you will cause if you're successful?'

'None whatever. When CosmosRX meets our reasonable demands we will return to work immediately.'

Frank leaned forward and pushed a button on his console.

'I'll take the call on line one. Good evening.'

'Frank, I'm Jules Larkin from New York. I want to talk directly to Kalazki.'

He sounded angry.

'Please speak freely.'

'Kalazki, you fucking idiot, you've destroyed us.'

Frank intervened. 'Language please, this is a family show.'

'What are you talking about, comrade?' Sam asked.

'You fucking idiot. I've been docked 1,000 points a month for the next two years thanks to your stupidity.'

Frank smiled but made no comment.

Sam protested. 'They can't do that. You must remain resolute. He's bluffing.'

'You still don't get it, you nerd. Everyone here is in the same boat. If I don't report for work tomorrow, I'll be docked another 1,000 points.'

'Be strong, comrade – we'll win.'

'You go to hell.'

'Thank you, caller.' Frank hung up – he was enjoying this – and turned to his dismayed-looking guest.

'I'm told all the other calls are in similar vein. Where do you go from here, Sam?'

He looked shell-shocked. 'I'll have to call a meeting of our executive.'

'Our producer asked CosmosRX to comment. The caller is quite correct: everyone currently on strike has already lost 1,000 points – that includes you. Anyone who misses three shifts will be deregistered.'

Sam blustered. 'They cannot possibly know who is on strike?'

'We asked CosmosRX about that: their computer picks up on the identity of anyone who fails to record attendance on their workscreen.'

***

Sally and Alex flew to Rome. She was delighted. It was wonderful to get away from the complex for a few days. A coach awaited them at Leonardo da Vinci Airport. They were driven down the quiet motorway into the city. It was so different to her last visit when she felt she was taking her life in her hands every time she crossed the road. Now it was more sedate, with a quieter and more "old world" atmosphere, and very little traffic apart from a few coaches.

They met with Luca Benelli, the head of the main contracting company, at his office in the Via Veneto: a well-preserved 17th-Century mansion once owned by the Molini family. Fiftyish, rotund and bald, he had very pleasant features with large, friendly brown eyes. Alex felt he could well be hostile: after all, CosmosRX had deprived him of numerous estates and a large fortune he inherited from his father. He still had his main residence and estate near Sienna, and his company owned this historic landmark. Greeting them affably, he took them to his palatial office and ordered coffee.

'Professor, you and your party are very welcome to Rome. It's a great pleasure to have you visit us. Would you and Signorita O'Halloran do me the honour of joining us for dinner tonight?'

Alex looked at Sally. She smiled. 'Signore Benelli, we will be delighted.'

'Please, call me Luca.'

'You must call us Alex and Sally.'

'It shall be as you say, Sally.'

After coffee, Luca introduced his team of architects, surveyors and engineers, who showed them the models of the three contracts currently under construction. A young, striking-looking man, with dark hair, hazel eyes and strong Roman features joined them.

'Alex and Sally, let me introduce my son, Philippe, who is in charge of our contracts in Naples.'

They shook hands, affably.

'I hope you will visit our sites in Naples.' He grinned, looking at his father. 'We do better work than they do here in Rome.'

Luca pretended to be angry. 'You rear them up to be treated like this. Come, we will have lunch downstairs.'

After lunch, Luca took them to the sewage treatment works, at three locations on the Tiber. Clearly, he was very proud of his work.

Alex was delighted. 'It's so good to see a river with clean water.'

'And the fish are back,' Sally enthused.

'What's the Mediterranean like now?'

Luca spread his hands. 'Is improving – clean rivers now, clean Med later?'

Come, I show you the crematorium down near the old Appian Way.'

'Being a Roman yourself Luca, what do you think of it these days?'

'Rome is, as always, but now it becomes even more beautiful; 'tis a strange new world; people are happier, more content; shops are open even if there's not much business.'

As they passed through the city Sally remarked 'I want to go shopping in the morning.'

Alex smiled. 'I knew you would. Hercules will escort you.'

She felt the crematorium was tastefully finished. From a distance it looked like a church. Watching the lines of people assembling outside made her feel sick: she knew it had to be, but that didn't help. Alex shook his head in dismay.

'If only there was some other way.'

Luca took them to the Coliseum, where they walked together through its ancient arches.

'Such a wonderful work of art,' he enthused.

Alex mused quietly. 'Rome was the greatest empire in the world, and yet, it went the way of all empires.'

She knew he was thinking about CosmosRX. Would it go the way of all empires?

Luca smiled. 'I have a favour to ask, Alex. Would you permit me the resources to restore this historic work of art?'

'Could you do that?'

'Restore no – it's close to collapsing. But, I have the plans; I could bulldoze it and replace it exactly as it was 2,000 years ago. It would be my contribution to history; it would be the first wonder of the new world. We could use it as an open-air theatre, it would be magnificent.'

'It sounds very exciting,' Sally said.

'We have many requests to restore Rome's old churches.'

'I will do them too, but this first, please.'

Alex couldn't refuse such enthusiasm.

'All right, Luca. It will bear a plaque acknowledging your contribution to the future history of Rome.'

A small crowd cheered as they left. They became even more enthusiastic when Luca announced he had been given permission to rebuild the Coliseum. Standing at the back of that crowd, Carlo Agnelli watched quietly.

Hercules arranged a special train to take them to Sienna. There, they were greeted by a large friendly crowd, much to the disgust of Hercules, who Sally thought was becoming a bit paranoid. She said nothing to him; he was just doing his job.

Eventually, they got through the crowd and were driven, under the ancient archway, down the long, winding tree-lined avenue, to the magnificent cut-stone mansion. With tall oak trees on the hills behind, it faced a large lake, where a number of swans cruised around majestically.

Luca introduced his second wife, Isabelle, a petite, friendly, and quite attractive brunette with big blue eyes; his first wife died five years earlier. Isabelle and two very excited servants showed them to a big old-fashioned room with a four-poster bed. They stood by the window and looked out across the still waters of the lake, disturbed only by the elegant white swans.

'I could get used to living like this,' Sally smiled.

She became serious.

'Alex, shouldn't Luca hate CosmosRX? We have deprived him of so much.'

'He's a very unusual man; has to be, to want to restore the Coliseum.'

Philippe and his beautiful wife, Gina, joined them for dinner in the mahogany-furnished dining room, with large double-doors opening out on to a well-kept lawn leading down to the lake. In a relaxed atmosphere, they enjoyed spring lamb with seasonal vegetables, followed by apple strudel and ice cream. Luca introduced them to fine wines from his own vineyard.

When coffee was served, Alex couldn't contain himself any longer.

'Luca, shouldn't you hate CosmosRX? It has cost you dearly.'

He sat back and smiled.

'I suppose I did, at first, but then I realise you are right: global warming and ozone layer we stupidly ignore. But famine: that concentrate our minds. To think we, an intelligent talented people, starve to death – wiped out through our own carelessness – is unbearable. Is unthinkable the long history of man should end in such a degrading horrific manner. I can trace my family's history back for more than 1,000 years. The Benelli family was one of the most respected in Rome. We had two cousins who were Popes.' He stopped and laughed. 'Maybe the less we say about them the better.'

'Is there any way CosmosRX could have done things better?'

He considered it.

'The revolution you bring about is extraordinary. Our affairs were becoming too complicated. The CosmosRX way brings security, peace of mind and equality for all. What more we want in life? No superstate trying to bully us, no terrorist – he now has no cause for hatred – no tyrant trying to frighten us with his weapons, no-one telling us what to believe, no more wars, and soon, I hopc, no more hunger. Is a new world.'

Alex grinned. 'Luca, you are a unique artist and student of history. We are most grateful to you for such a magnificent meal. How do you do it? Food is still in short supply.'

'Ah, my friend, nothing mobilise us like hunger. We grow our own fruit, vegetables, vines. We build up our herd of livestock, and flocks of sheep; is the same with everyone around here.'

He paused and grinned.

'We employ extra people for this work and I don't have to pay them. We send the surplus to Rome and Florence and contribute to every relief flight going to Africa.' He paused again. 'We know now how these poor people feel. We have to help them.'

Alex was delighted. 'Luca, it's very encouraging for us to see how magnificently you are coping.'

Sally added 'This has been a wonderful experience for us.'

He beamed. 'I hope you will come to open the new Coliseum when it's finished.'

'I look forward to it, Luca.'

'Is it true you intend to restore Venice to its former glory?'

Alex smiled. 'Yes, we have an international team of experts working on the plans, but we can't progress it further until the Adriatic becomes pollution-free again; that could take another ten years.'

'That would be wonderful, but how can it be done?'

'I've only seen the rough outline: a massive sea wall – at least 300 metres wide and 200 metres high – will be erected from Chioggia to Dona Piave, converting the Lagoon of Venice into an inland sea. The side facing Venice can be elaborately painted, with some of the monuments and churches of the city, over what will look like a continuation of the Lagoon of Venice, in light blue. Rivers currently running into the lagoon will be diverted, possibly permanently. The port of Venice will be located outside the wall at the Chioggia end, and a passenger and goods rail system will operate from the top of the wall, which will contain a number of hydroelectric stations.'

Luca interrupted him. 'Is fascinating.'

'We'll pump water through the turbines – from the ocean into the lagoon and from the lagoon into the ocean – effectively providing an artificial tidal system. But, initially, we'll have to drain the lagoon: drain, clean and repair all property, install electricity in conjunction with an underground rail network, set up water filtration units, and pipe fresh water to the islands.'

'It will be a massive undertaking.'

'We have a number of marine scientists studying the ecological problems. Heavy industry will not be allowed back into Marghera where we'll build hotels, theatres, museums and universities – all in traditional Venetian style. It will be one of the great centres of art, education, culture and leisure in the world: the greatest man-made achievement since the Great Wall of China.'

'Is truly wonderful.' Luca enthused. 'Perhaps one of our companies take part in this magnificent venture?'

'I certainly hope so, but first, I would like you to build the new nuclear reactor in Ostio.'

'We can do that, but is nuclear safe?' He paused and laughed out loud. 'Here am I talking about safety, I mad.'

'The new breeder reactor has been redesigned; it's quite safe. As you know, nothing in this life is 100 percent safe.'

He raised his glass. 'Salute to Sally and Alex. As a true artist, I will devote myself to the restoration of the Coliseum; it will signal the rise of a new Rome, a peaceful reminder of what can now be achieved.'

He paused and grinned. 'Maybe you send me archaeologists to help find the quarries that supply the original stone?'

'On one condition,' Alex countered.

'Say, please.'

'That you agree to build the nuclear reactors in Genoa and Palermo too.'

'You drive hard bargain; is a deal.' He rose, they shook hands laughing.

'Champagne for everyone,' he ordered.

***

They had breakfast in the hotel restaurant overlooking the Roman Forum. The hotel staff made a great fuss, but Hercules sat close by, just the same.

'What do you think of Luca?' Alex inquired as he buttered his toast.

'I like him. Isabelle was an actress before they married. She says he's a loveable rogue.'

'He told me the Revenue people were demanding two billion euros before CosmosRX. Like all builders, he was big in the black economy. He was owed nearly a billion for government contracts, and was planning to sell two of his estates and many of his properties in Rome and Naples, when along comes CosmosRX and his problems disappeared overnight.'

'And so did the black economy.'

'I think he's relieved. He can have as many employees as he needs and he doesn't have to pay them.'

'He's really chuffed about the Coliseum.'

'At heart, he's an artist, and he wants his place in history.'

Sally rose.

'I'm going shopping.'

'Hercules will escort you. I want to talk to Michael and Plato.'

'Can't I go without Hercules? I wouldn't feel comfortable buying frilly underwear with Hercules standing beside me.'

He laughed. 'He won't notice. Luca is coming in for lunch and we'll fly home afterwards.'

'Alex,' she coaxed, 'could we not go home by train? I'd love to see Florence again.'

'No.'

'Please?'

'We'll see.'

That was good enough for her. With Hercules, she wandered through the narrow busy streets near the old Pantheon. Life was going on as it always had – some things never change – housewives haggled with street traders who waved their hands, pointing to the points screen, protesting loudly. "Is CosmosRX, talk to CosmosRX, don't blame me."

She bought a pair of black patent shoes and a handbag to match, using her points for the first time. Most of the shop assistants were delighted to be so much better off, and looked forward to the return of the tourists. Some complained about food shortages, although it seemed Rome was coping fairly well. She talked to one young single mother whose father departed two weeks earlier. 'Is so sad, he helps me bring up my three children after mama die. Loved them so much, he not wants to go and leave me alone. But, I suppose it has to be. That's what he said.'

Sally finally ventured into a ladies' fashion shop. She accepted a coffee, Hercules declined politely. The attractive, buxom middle-aged lady who looked after her happened to be the owner. She sat Hercules – Sally's husband, as she thought – in an armchair and handed him a newspaper.

How did she like the change, Sally inquired. At first, she thought it was dreadful, so much happening all at once, she found it hard to take it in. She had an apartment block she depended on for her pension, 15 years hence. The rents barely covered her mortgage; then, suddenly she had no apartment block and no mortgage. Instead, she had a guaranteed pension, a bigger one than she expected from her property.

'Have you had any staff problems with the new system?' Sally inquired.

She nodded. 'Earlier on, yes, but not now. Two of my girls thought they could do as they wished because I no longer paid them. I gave them good warning before reporting to CosmosRX. They were ordered to reception jobs in the Rome crematorium. That didn't please them very much. I was sent two very nice girls that used to work for an insurance company.'

'What about your husband?'

She grunted. 'Useless bastard. Threw him out years ago when he took up with a 24-year-old. Now she's ditched him, he wants to come back. Some chance. Anyway, he'll be 60 in a month's time so CosmosRX will take care of him. Now, what can I get you?'

She made her purchases under Hercules' eagle eye, and had her hair styled in a nearby salon before returning to the hotel. He carried her bags, and left her with Alex.

'Well,' Alex grinned, 'how did you get on with Hercules?'

'He said nothing until we were entering the lobby downstairs. I could see he was trying to get his head around something that was puzzling him. Then he said "I never realised, Sally, that women are so different to men."'

'What did you say?'

‘I said, “Hercules, would you like me to get you a nice female companion?”’

‘He said “No, no, Sally, Hercules is confused enough already.”’

Alex laughed. ‘Wait until he hears we’re going home by train.’

‘I’m so happy, Alex. This has been a wonderful break.’

‘We must do it again. Luca should be in shortly. Will you tell Hercules the bad news, or will I?’

‘I think I’d better do it. He’ll think it’s some weird female trait to change one’s mind.’

Hercules was taking no chances. He ordered a special express train from Roma Centrali and alerted his people in Florence. Then he contacted Plato and arranged a fighter escort to shadow the train to the station at Capalago. He would accompany Sally and Alex. Eight of his security detail would fly directly to Lugano.

***

Zack Evans rose quietly, early on the day before he was due to report to the departure centre. Putting on his best suit – a black one used only for special occasions – he looked around the little apartment for the last time. It was best this way. He would have loved to give Bertha, Nan and Jo Anne a big hug, but was afraid he would waken them. Bertha would not let him go alone. She wanted to go with him and she wanted to stay with Nan and little Jo Anne. If she decided to stay, she would always feel guilty. This time, he would make the decision. He folded his laboriously written farewell letter, and put it beside the clock in the living room. Then, taking off the ring he wore for 36 years, he put it beside the letter.

Slipping quietly out of the apartment, he walked to the subway and took an early morning train to 79th Street. There, he joined a large number of people heading towards the departure centre, many accompanied by tearful families. It would be unbearable for him to make this journey with Bertha, Nan and Jo Anne. He had a good life, and if CosmosRX was right, he was doing something noble for his family. A churchgoing Lutheran all his life, he hoped the promises of a place in Heaven would prove to be true.

A blue coach, with horizontal yellow stripes along the side – a familiar sight in New York these days – passed by, heading towards the "Trade Entrance", crowded with reluctant volunteers. He joined the queue, made up of a mixture of black, white, Latinos and other coloured people. Some appeared to be calm and resigned, others were clearly very distressed. Many carried their pet cats, or dogs; one woman held her pet rabbit close to her. His concern now: what if they wouldn't take him because he was a day too early?

At the entrance, he was offered champagne.

'Would it be possible to have a coffee?'

'Certainly, sir. May I have your notification?'

He handed it over.

'This is for tomorrow, sir.'

'I know, but I want to go today, please.'

'OK, but first take this little pill, it will relax you. Then I'll get your coffee.'

He swallowed the pill with a mouthful of water, as he thought. It was champagne; he had never tasted champagne before in his life.

He found a seat and sipped his coffee. In the background he could hear the strains of *Jerusalem*. The champagne seemed very popular. Pastors moved quietly through the crowded hall. A little old white lady with lined features, sat down beside him sobbing uncontrollably.

'Come now,' he ventured, 'it's not all that bad.'

Normally, she wouldn't speak to a coloured person, if she could avoid it.

'It's not fair, it's just not fair. I don't understand life anymore.'

He could see the attendants opening the doors to the escalators.

'Are you leaving many of your family behind you?' he asked kindly.

She didn't seem to understand for a moment. 'No, my parents died years ago. I never married. I have a big house in Albany.'

It was time they were moving. He felt so sorry for her; she was all alone in this world and yet found it so hard to leave. He stood up.

'Come, we will go together.'

She took his hand and they joined one of the queues. At the door they took their pills and walked the short distance to an escalator.

As they stepped on, she turned to him.

'Thank you.'

He began to think about Bertha and their happy times together, little Nan, as he always called her, and dear Jo Anne who brought such joy into their lives…

***

The super luxury monorail train slipped out of Roma Centrali and headed north at nearly 600 kilometres an hour. Sally and Alex sat back and enjoyed the view.

As they approached Florence, Darius entered their compartment carrying a tray.

'How did you get down here?' Sally asked laughing.

'Darius say he security. Tea and scones?'

'Yes, please.'

***

They were devastated when they found Zack's note. Nan's grief was tinged with pride and admiration at the unselfish way he took the decision out of their hands. He had always been there for them; now they faced a lonely future without his calm, reassuring presence. She read out his note, printed slowly and painfully on plain paper – she didn't think he knew how to write.

"It's best I go alone. I want ye all to have a good happy life. God Bless ye all. Zack."

She picked up the ring.

'You must wear this now, Mother.'

She put it on her middle finger.

'Why didn't he say goodbye to us?' she moaned.

'Because, Mother, he knew you wouldn't let him go alone. He wants you to stay with us.'

Seeing their distress, Jo Anne started to cry. 'Where Grandpa?'

Nan took her in her arms and hugged her. 'Grandpa gone to Heaven, love.'

'When will we go?'

'Not for a long time yet, love.'

They took the day off, and went on the subway to the 79th Street crematorium. There, they met one of the receptionists who remembered Zack, only because he saw him help an old lady who was in great distress. Nan felt justifiably proud of her heroic Dad. They were given a copy of the daily departure scroll with the names of all who passed through on that date – it included Zack Evans.

***

The World Airlines executive jet took off from Rome's Leonardo da Vinci Airport with eight of Hercules' security people on board. It climbed steadily to the east before turning north. At 40,000 feet, it disintegrated in a massive explosion.

The super train was approaching Florence when Hercules got the news, and advised Alex and Sally. They were stunned – if they had flown home… Then Plato came on screen.

'Alex, we're under attack; 20 armed men landed on top of the mountain. I'm bringing in all our reserves.'

'Can you deal with it?'

'Yes, the enemy are trapped in the cafeteria building. Have I your permission to demolish it?'

'Yes, they mustn't get to the elevators. Keep me advised.'

He was furious.

'What the hell is going on? We've got to get back quickly.' He turned to Hercules. 'Have the train routed directly through to Milan and Capalago.'

Hercules left the compartment. Sally shook her head in dismay; this could be the end of everything they had fought for. The train passed through Florence. The minutes ticked by slowly. Alex was so furious, Sally was afraid he would have an attack.

Plato came back on screen.

'Alex, we've destroyed the enemy, but there's considerable damage to the cafeteria building.'

'Are the elevators secure?'

'Yes.'

'Find out who these bastards are. See if any of them are registered. I want the names of their families, relations and contacts. Take Lugano apart, arrest any strangers.' He looked at Hercules. 'How soon will we be back?'

'One hour.'

'Continue a full emergency.'

'Yes, Alex.'

When the train pulled in to Capalago station, it was immediately surrounded by heavily-armed security guards; they transferred to the cogwheel train and travelled to the summit. The road was lined with the new T46 tanks. They picked their way through the rubble of the cafeteria and entered the elevators. Plato and Michael were waiting for them below. They went immediately to the conference room.

Alex took Sally aside. 'I think you should lie down for a while, I'll get Darius to bring you some tea.'

Completely drained, exhausted and horrified by events, she agreed.

Alex sat down with Michael and Plato.

Plato began in a very calm tone. 'All of these men are registered with CosmosRX; mostly Sicilians redeployed to various contract works in Italy.' He paused. 'This was a very professional attack, Alex.'

'It's clear now we didn't get the ringleader last time. Shadow every relative of these thugs until one of them leads us to the man we want. Advise World Airlines that there is now a no-fly zone within a two kilometre radius of Monte Generoso.'

He turned to Michael.

'I want a round solid stone structure with anti-missile steel doors to replace the old cafeteria building. What would you have done, if the attackers got control of the elevators?'

'I would have taken them down half way, flooded the shafts and used the emergency escape tunnels.' He paused. 'We need to look into the whole question of security here.'

'I agree. Will you summon Dr Ken Addison from London? I want to talk to him.'

'I'll contact him immediately.' He paused. 'Are you alright? This has been a very difficult day for you and Sally.'

'I'm furious, but I'm fine. My concern is for the long-term security of CosmosRX.'

***

Police Captain Patrick Hartigan looked around him while he strolled down Wall Street, a high-rise ghost town that used to be the heart of world finance. A major redevelopment program would commence shortly to convert Lower Manhattan into a community village with luxury apartments, shopping malls, medical centres, restaurants, hotels, cinemas, churches, social and sports centres and a hospital.

The Captain was particularly pleased with the extraordinary changes brought about by CosmosRX. Right now the only other human being in sight was an old African-American tramp and his mangy looking dog, sitting outside the closed doors of the NYSE – New York Stock Exchange – as it used to be called. The tramp was drinking out of a whiskey bottle, while the dog looked on expectantly. He put down the bottle, unwrapped a grotty looking newspaper and extracted a sandwich that he divided between them. The Captain ignored this spectacle and walked around the corner.

The tall, abandoned buildings included the New Towers that replaced the Twin Towers destroyed by terrorists, a few months after he was born. His father, Edward, was one of the New York firemen killed in the collapse of the South Tower. He immigrated from County Cork, in Ireland, with his wife Rebecca, three years earlier. She worked as a secretary in a brokerage house with offices in the North Tower. Fortunately, she was on a day off the morning of the attack.

He was brought up in their little apartment in the Bronx by a broken-hearted young mother who instilled in him a hatred of all non-white races. When he was ten, she married again; a Latino chef from New Jersey who came to work in a restaurant near them. He didn't like the loud-mouthed Joseph Conrad and liked him even less when two stepbrothers sidelined him.

His school grades were good enough to get him a place in the Police Academy, from which he passed out when he was 20. Tall and handsome, with bronze features and sharp blue eyes, he looked quite fearsome in his patrolman's uniform. Being Irish, and the son of a hero, led to his promotion to Sergeant. His boss, Captain Ted Reilly, liked the tough young man and, after a year, promoted him to Detective Second Class. He made a name for himself in a series of drug busts and didn't hesitate to use his gun when he thought it necessary. The Captain took him aside after a shoot-out in which six blacks were killed.

'Pat,' he said, 'you got the same chip on your shoulder we all got, just keep it cool, and you'll go places.'

He did, and shortly afterwards was promoted to Inspector. The Captain liked this up-and-coming serious cop, who was clean, no drugs or women – a loner – but with the right instincts. He persuaded him to take up golf. He became quite a useful player and, most Saturday mornings, teed off with his boss at the Garden City Country Club.

Later, he was introduced to the Captain's daughter, Ester, a very attractive blonde who was recovering from a messy divorce. Having been married to a womaniser, she was immediately attracted to the tall, handsome silent Inspector; they married the following year, and now had two teenage sons. Ester, who worked as a secretary in a lawyer's office, was now managing a social group checking out childcare in the Bronx.

Two years earlier, he was appointed Police Captain of the Borough of Manhattan. With the Governor, Major and City Hall gone, he was now the King of New York. He loved that feeling of power that sent the blood rushing through his veins.

His cell phone rang.

'Inspector Oscar Devinny here, sir. We've just arrested four blacks trying to rob a hypermarket. As you would expect, they deny it. Will I give them the LX test?'

'No. Don't waste time. Make them sign confessions and shoot them. Advise CosmosRX.'

'Yes, sir.' The line went dead.

Normally they should be escorted to the 79th Street crematorium, but he liked the idea of instant justice. It sent out the right message. There was no messing around these days with clever lawyers, courts, or lily-livered bleeding hearts. Having completed the circuit, he found himself walking down Wall Street again. The old tramp was still there, propped up against the door, apparently asleep; the dog sat dutifully by his master. Patrick took out his gun. He didn't need scum like this on his streets. He fired at point blank range, and used a second shot for the dog. Taking out his cell phone he punched in a number.

'Precinct, Captain Hartigan. I'm down on Wall Street. There's a dead man and dog here, looks like the work of thugs. Send a meat wagon and advise CosmosRX.'

He took the underground up to 34th Street, walked past the armed guard and queue outside Macy's food hall and handed a list to the manager.

'Have that lot delivered this evening.'

'Will you register in at home, sir?'

'I don't register. You know who I am. Get a move on.'

'Yes, sir, right away, sir.'

Leaving, he walked over to 6th Avenue where his current mistress – a very attractive junior officer in the department – lived.

***

Hercules reported back to Alex.

'We have 254 Italians under observation. They appear to be living normal lives, working on our construction sites. We've questioned the relatives of the thugs. One name keeps cropping up, Carlo Agnelli. We believe he's the leader.'

Alex sat back for a moment. He had become so paranoid that Sally was seriously worried about him; he was sleeping fitfully, and ill-tempered most of the time. Her enchanting visits to Yeatstown and Rome were now a distant memory.

'Find this bastard, Carlo, and eliminate all the others.'

'All?' Sally protested.

'Yes, all. It's time these people realised they can't challenge CosmosRX and live.'

She was appalled, but she said nothing.

Then he announced 'I'm going away with Michael for a few weeks.'

'Where are you going?' she asked.

'It's best you don't know, Sally.'

She was crushed: he didn't trust her now.

'You'll need plenty of security.'

He agreed. 'We're bringing 50 guards with us.'

After they left, Sally became very lonely. She contacted Caesar and ordered an Alex look-alike. Three days later he arrived with the new Alex, dressed in a smart blue suit, with a white shirt and grey tie. She could hardly believe it.

'I don't know what to say,' she exclaimed.

He grinned. 'I cannot say I'm pleased to meet you Sally because I'm supposed to know you already.'

The voice was exactly the same. She wondered how much he knew about them, but didn't dare ask. Caesar was smiling broadly. She was stuck with him now.

'Come, Alex, I'll introduce you to the others.' She paused and looked at Caesar.

'Will the others know them apart?'

'They will.'

That was a relief.

Leonardo focused on finding a new form of non-fossil energy. He sat, for days at a time, inputting figures on his screen; watching graphics of the Sun, Earth and Moon in their varying orbits. The new listening satellites moved quickly away from Earth; he followed their progress intently, becoming more puzzled all the time.

Plato was the most talkative of the lot. Sally sat with him one morning while he watched incoming reports.

'Is the population figure falling on schedule?'

'No, Sally, if we are to achieve our target on time, we'll have to reduce the age limit, or introduce a compulsory abortion program.'

She was horrified. ‘Oh, no, you can’t kill little babies.’

‘It will be Alex’s decision, Sally, but some change may be essential.’

‘I thought everything was going according to plan.’

‘Nearly three billion have departed, but we won’t get to six billion by the end of year two at the current rate of progress. The situation is not helped by the fact that road and work-related fatalities are down by 96 percent, suicides by 98 percent, crime by 85 percent, murders by 83 percent, and improved medical care is reducing the natural death rate.’

‘It makes me sick to think we have to kill so many, even if they are old people, at or near the end of their lives, but abortion, no, I couldn’t take that. There has to be another way.’

Seeing her distress, he took her hand in his. ‘Sally, I don’t like to see you so upset: I will try.’

She was delighted when Alex returned, but he didn’t say where he and Michael had been. He was angry that Hercules still hadn’t captured Carlo Agnelli.

‘Can’t you find one man for me?’

‘Our people are tearing Italy apart, Alex. The Italian police want him too. We’ll find him, don’t you worry.’

‘But I do worry. While that bastard is out there CosmosRX is under threat.’

Plato added quietly ‘Alex, we have a military takeover in Moscow.’

‘Wipe them out,’ he responded angrily.

‘HOBs?’

‘Can you get them all in the one place?’

‘There’s a full military parade in Red Square in two hours’ time; it will be reviewed by Marshall Viyshinsly.’

‘When the mighty Marshall looks on his massive army, let it be for the last time. Vaporise the bastards, and see it gets plenty of coverage. Let it be a lesson to other would-be Field Marshals.’

Plato turned to Kubla. ‘Go ahead, set it up.’ Then he said to Alex ‘When you have time we have to review the departure program.’

‘Later.’

***

Sally became more and more worried about Alex's state of mind; she was surprised when he sent for Dr Ken Addison because he didn't like doctors. He refused to have a full physical examination until she insisted. Afterwards she talked with the doctor.

He assured her 'Alex is physically fine, but the strain is getting to him. He needs a good rest, preferably away from here.'

'Why did he ask to see you?'

'I have to do some research for him. He's concerned about what happens to CosmosRX, if anything happens to him. Can you persuade him to take a long vacation?'

'I doubt it, but I'll try.'

Alex wouldn't hear of it and as the weeks passed became ever more morose. If only Hercules could find this man Agnelli and dispose of him.

Now, she had another problem: having missed her last period, she was fairly sure she was pregnant. An event that would normally bring her such joy, now terrified her. They were still debating whether to introduce compulsory abortion.

***

Retired three-star General, Matthew Taylor III, marched briskly along the seafront in Galveston; it was a bright sunny Sunday morning with a cool wind blowing in off the Gulf. Retired three years earlier at 55, he was planning a career in politics when his beloved United States was taken over by Purtzel and his bloody computers. Now a supervisor at the nuclear reactor site across the bay, he was damned if he was going to put up with the new order. Most of those working there were ex-Army who shared his views.

GMT, as he was known, was a big, rugged, loud-mouthed Army man; a man's man, used to being obeyed without question. He saw himself as another General George Patton. Biting down on his Havana cigar, his steel-blue eyes stared down anyone who dared to contradict him. Recently divorced for the fourth time, he retained his old, ramshackle home up in the hills overlooking the bay area. He bitterly resented the abolition of alimony; he would have made the bitch crawl for it; and this new points system was making his current mistress a bit too damn independent.

His family background was strictly Army: his paternal grandfather became a four-star general during World War II; his father served with distinction in the Vietnam War; his own most notable achievement was as Commander General of the US 105th that freed Cuba 15 years earlier. The bastards in the Pentagon wouldn't give him his fourth star because his casualties were high; hell, you can't fight a war without losses.

His father was a very quiet reflective kind of man, not at all like an Army general. His mother died shortly after he was born, leaving him to be reared by a domineering aunt that he heartily disliked. His father, who didn't remarry, visited him whenever he could. He often talked about his long career but never about Vietnam.

During the break-up of Yugoslavia he was seconded to NATO as an advisor based in Geneva. While he was there he was invited to visit a secret underground facility in southern Switzerland; in the event of a nuclear disaster, the Swiss President and his family would take refuge there. Impressed as he was with the Swiss bunker, it had a fatal flaw. He didn't tell the Swiss that, but he did confide in his son; perhaps he wanted to impress him. GMT would now use that information to destroy CosmosRX, recapture America and proclaim himself President.

He had already made contact with a small number of once very wealthy and prominent people, who lost out when CosmosRX took over. They were all in favour of the destruction of CosmosRX and the return to the good old America they knew and loved.

Former Major Mick O'Hara, who would be his principal assistant in the campaign, joined him on his walk. Mick was also a supervisor on the site, and at 47 was still quite active. Smaller than the General, with pleasant features and deep blue eyes, he was wearing a black tee-shirt and grey trousers that didn't conceal his sagging stomach.

Mick was a man who knew his place; he was a back-up man. A good one – but a back-up man just the same. One of the few ex-Army men to have a normal home life, he had been married to Wendy for 25 years and had two grown-up daughters.

'Major' – he always called him that – 'we're going to destroy that damned CosmosRX, and free this old country.'

Mick wondered if he was hearing right.

'Have you been drinking?'

'No, Dammit, I haven't. All I need is 12 troops. Can you muster a force that size?'

'I can, but how?'

'I know that complex, and I know how to destroy it.'

'Most of these fellows are quite happy with their monthly points. What would be in it for them?'

'A million dollars a year for life. I'll be the President of the good old US, and first thing, I'll bring back the Dollar.'

Mick didn't like it; he was one of those who were happy with his points. But he knew GMT was no fool either.

'How are you going to do all this?'

'You'll take six men to Hamburg, travel by train right the way through to Lugano. I'll take six troops to Genoa, and link up with you.'

'And how would we get to Hamburg?'

'I have some friends in the Merchant Navy. They'll conceal your party on board.'

'Why split our forces?'

'We'll attract less attention coming from different directions; they won't know what hit them.'

'And what happens when we destroy CosmosRX?'

'Before we leave, I will put 3,000 of my men on stand-by. When we destroy CosmosRX, they will fly to Andrews, Washington, and take over; we'll hijack a plane in Zurich, and join them.'

'But won't there be resistance?'

'With CosmosRX gone, there will be no-one to give orders but me. We'll take the city without a shot being fired; I'll set up a new administration, call up all our military reserves and declare an emergency.'

It sounded plausible, but Mick wasn't convinced.

'Look what CosmosRX did to the Chinese and the Russians. It controls all the space weapons.'

'Of course it does, but once it's destroyed its weapons are useless.'

'But won't this lead to international conflict?'

'Correct. That's exactly what I want. I'll reopen our arms factories and we'll be ready in a matter of months.'

'Our arms manufacturers are gone, aren't they?'

'Their factories and stocks were destroyed, but they tell me they can be up and running within six months; as soon as we take Washington it will be business as usual.'

Mick was impressed even if he wasn't too enthusiastic.

GMT continued. 'Start talking to the men. Don't be too specific. It's a special and very profitable mission. Most of them are raring for a bit of action.'

'Do I tell them we're going to take out CosmosRX?'

'No, we're going to free our country.'

'They know your reputation, they might go for it.'

'I want to move out in 12 weeks' time. Now, where do I get an explosives expert?'

'I've heard of a guy; lives across the border down Tampico way. "Mad Mex" they call him.'

'See if he's still there.'

They parted. GMT took a local bus home. He knew Mick was committed. He wouldn't know how to refuse him; he had that kind of power over people.

***

When she missed her second period, Sally knew she was pregnant. The old relaxed and confident Alex would have rejoiced at her news – but not now. Paranoid and fearful for CosmosRX, he would bc terrified. She'd tried to reassure him with her love, but could no longer reach him. He spent most of his time checking progress, and urging Hercules to increase his team's efforts to get Agnelli. And he was afraid there were other enemies out there.

She knew there was no way he would sanction abortion of his own child. Her mind focused on her baby; nothing else mattered. She would have to leave Alex and CosmosRX, find some place where she could have her baby, and try to bring him up in a normal environment. Why did she think it was a boy? She didn't know, but she was sure it was.

Alex was so preoccupied with the medical people, he didn't notice her confusion and concern. Where would she go? There was only one place she could go: home to Galway. She arranged international flight and train passes. She could live comfortably on her monthly points. She dearly wished to say goodbye to her robots, having long since come to regard them as dear friends. Better not: leaving a farewell note for Alex, she took the elevator to the mountain top, descended in the cogwheel train to Capalago, and took the ferry into Lugano.

She was boarding the train to Zurich airport when Carlo Agnelli spotted her. He boarded quickly, and sat in the carriage behind. He was certain this was Purtzel's woman. He stood quite close to her in Rome. Where was she going without security? Fate had delivered her into his hands. Purtzel would pay any price to get her back. He now had the leverage he needed. At Zurich airport Sally presented her passes, and was shown to the gate for the flight to Galway.

Carlo couldn't join the flight, but he found out its destination. He would have to find some way of getting to Galway. Could he register with CosmosRX under a false name? He would have to study the requirements again. Could they trace him from his handprint? Somehow he had to get to Galway; after that, it would be easy to deal with Purtzel.

***

Alex read and reread Sally's note with tears streaming down his face.

> "Dearest, dearest Alex,
>
> I have to leave you now as you can no longer accept my love, comfort and support. If only things were different; if only we could live a normal life; if only we could be normal people. But that's not possible. You have given your all to CosmosRX, and there is no future for us. It breaks my heart to leave you, Alex, but I must now make another life for me and our expected son.

You will always be in my thoughts. Please do not try to find me.

With all my love,

Sally."

Composing himself, he folded the letter and put it away carefully. His first thought was to go after her, and beg her to come back to him, but he daren't leave CosmosRX.

He invited Plato to his office.

'Sally has left CosmosRX.'

He looked disappointed. 'For good?'

'Yes. I want to know where she goes, and I want you to alert your people. She is to have the full protection of CosmosRX at all times.'

***

Louisa asked Eric Granlard and George Regan to join her in her little office. She sat them down.

'Now here's the deal. Eric, you are being appointed assistant manager of the Newton Country Club.'

'That's bloody ridiculous. This is my business, I own it,' he blustered.

'Do you want to hear the alternative? You could be on your way to BC – Boston Crematorium – in the next hour.'

He paled visibly. George was sweating profusely. Eric got up.

'Sit down,' she ordered, 'I'm not finished yet.'

He sat down.

'You will return the wine stocks at your home, and after today you will not enter these premises again.'

She turned to George.

'CosmosRX is appointing you manager here. Clear up this mess, and send in a correct stock figure by tomorrow.'

He looked relieved.

'Thank you, thank you. I'll do as you say.'

'You will both be getting your instructions directly from CosmosRX as soon as I put in my final report.'

'Will you be staying on here?' George asked nervously.

'No, I'm going to another job.'

***

Michael took Dr Eric Vaclec – from Prague – to Alex's office and introduced him. Alex came directly to the point.

'Doctor, I believe you're a leading brain surgeon?'

The thin-faced, bright-eyed elderly doctor nodded.

'That is true, but I'm not the only one.'

'You have been involved in brain transplants?'

'Yes, but it's still largely experimental.'

Alex leaned forward. 'Say I wanted to transfer my brain to a healthy 20-year-old; could you do it?'

He paused for a moment. 'It would involve a whole team of experts.'

'Led by you?'

'No, Dr Mose Levy, from Mount Scopus Hospital in Jerusalem: he's more experienced.'

'What's the success rate?'

'It depends on the general physical condition of the donor and the recipient; considerable pre-operative assessment would be necessary.' He paused. 'Would you be the proposed donor, sir?'

'Yes. We're talking about the long-term security of CosmosRX.'

'That is vital. Have you selected a recipient?'

'No, not yet. We want to establish the feasibility of the idea first.'

'I take it you are currently enjoying good health?'

'Yes.'

'Good. The operation should be carried out while you are in excellent health.'

'Do you know Dr Levy personally?' Alex asked.

'We've met several times at medical conferences.'

'Can you arrange to have him come to see me? We'll issue all the necessary travel passes. You'll appreciate the need for confidentiality.'

'Of course. May I say that we are very grateful to you for the extra scientists allocated to our medical research; my team has doubled, and I no longer have to worry about where the money is coming from.' He paused and permitted himself a rare smile. 'Some of us are a bit upset that the world's leading vascular surgeon is a robot.'

'True, but he was trained by the noted Dr Cyril Barns.'

'Could you duplicate Dr Addison?'

'Yes. What have you in mind?'

'I could train him in brain surgery. Your operation won't take place for at least a year; he would be ready to assist us by then.'

Alex liked it. 'I'll send you a fully medically-programmed doctor. We'll call him "Lazarus".'

'I see you have a sense of humour. I'll contact you as soon as I talk with Dr Levy.'

'Thank you, and good luck with your research. I'm particularly anxious that you succeed in finding a cure for malaria.'

***

Sally took the metro from Galway International Airport into Eyre Square. It was so strange coming back into the real world, moving around freely without the constant presence of security. The Sun was shining after a rainy start to the day. She joined a short queue outside the CosmosRX agent's office. When interviewed, she asked for a small apartment in Galway, and to her surprise, she was offered her choice from a list of 20. She selected a nice penthouse apartment overlooking the Salmon Weir Bridge, registered for it with her palm print, and was given the keys. It was fully-furnished and included TV, CosmosRX Internet access and phone.

She walked by the river to the large modern block that contained her new home. It was spotless, with a large lounge, fully-equipped kitchen, two bedrooms en suite, and a balcony overlooking the River Corrib, with the massive structure of

Galway Cathedral on the other side. She unpacked her case, and walked around the corner to a nearby shop that used to be a supermarket. There she bought some groceries, delighted to get half a litre of fresh milk; beef was still very scarce, but she got a small lamb chop and a chicken leg. Returning to her apartment, she cooked the chop with some carrots and parsnips.

Later, she went down to the river-side, and sat on a bench watching the mothers pushing their babies' wheelers, and supervising the bigger ones playing in the little park nearby. She noticed the cleanliness of the water. It was so refreshing. Later, she learned that two filtration plants now served the city, and the salmon were beginning to return. Further out in the bay there was still some sludge.

The following morning, she decided to wander through the city. It was so much bigger than it used to be, but it was spotlessly clean. The streets were quiet; coaches cruised by silently every few minutes. She was intrigued and amused by the number of people using bicycles; it was like going back to the distant past. Everyone seemed relaxed and friendly.

The bank that once dominated Eyre Square was now a hotel. The fine old stone bank premises, at the other end of the square, housed a computerised CosmosRX Planning, Services and Amenities office – like the County Council of old – manned by a range of experts including architects, surveyors and engineers. Every regional office – this one catered for the old province of Connaught – was mandated to provide and maintain all the services needed by the people: housing, transport, water, waste disposal, hospitals, burial services, education and sports facilities.

Energy supplies, and the crop and stock breeding program, continued to be the responsibility of each National Control office. The offices on the corner of Mainguard Street – once owned by a leading insurance company – were now occupied by one of the city's ticketing offices. Here, people applied for travel, sporting events, theatre, cinema, museum and airline tickets, by registering their palm print on the appropriate screen; entry to the selected event was also by palm print identity. While there was no charge, museum, sporting events, rail and coach travel reservations were necessary to avoid overcrowding, and could be obtained online, or at any

CosmosRX ticket office. There was a charge for cinema and theatre tickets. Such was the demand for airline travel within the state that a fixed charge of 40 points per flight was recently imposed; external flights required special permission and wouldn't be freely available until tourist activity recommenced.

She walked down Shop Street. Lynch's Castle, once a bank, was now a museum. It suddenly struck her; she hadn't seen one beggar since she arrived, a familiar sight in days of old. There was something else about the city that puzzled her. It was like a 19th-Century city. Then it came to her – there wasn't an advertising sign or hoarding in sight.

Entering O'Flaherty's Café, she sat by the window. A very pleasant young woman approached and offered her a copy of the local weekly paper, the *Connacht Tribune.* She ordered tea and a scone while she scanned the headlines. It was a lot thinner than it used to be – with no advertising. To preserve the rainforests CosmosRX was aiming to have a 90 percent paperless society. She enjoyed her tea and scone – the tea a familiar local brand that reminded her of home.

A lady sitting at a nearby table with two teenage girls looked familiar. As she was leaving, Sally plucked up her courage.

'Is it Siobhan Murray?'

She smiled. 'Siobhan Mannion now. Don't tell me, it's Sally O'Halloran isn't it? Where have you been for the past 15 years?'

'It's lovely to meet you again, Siobhan. I spent most of my time in the States and Switzerland.'

'Sounds exciting let me introduce you to my girls. Shona and Anne, this is Sally, an old friend from my school days.'

They smiled politely before resuming their interest in their chocolate biscuits.

'What are you doing now, Siobhan?'

'I'm a consultant cardiologist on a day off; Martin, my husband, is a gynaecologist. We live out in Barna. You must visit us. What are you doing yourself? Last I heard you were in computers.'

Sally didn't want to disclose her involvement in CosmosRX.

'I've come home for a rest. You did say your husband is a gynaecologist?'

'Yes.'

'Siobhan, I'm pregnant. Would it be possible for me to consult him?'

'How exciting, is it your first?'

She was careful not to ask about a husband or partner.

'Yes, I'm very excited, and not a little nervous.'

'You'll be fine.' She took a card from her purse and handed it over.

'Ring Martin, and arrange to see him at the hospital. I'll tell him to expect a call from you.'

'How is CosmosRX affecting you?'

'It's tough on those who have to go, but hopefully that won't last too long. It's an irony: more women now want to have babies, fewer people are suffering coronaries, and mothers no longer need to go out to work.'

Promising to visit, Sally walked through the archway to the old Augustinian church nearby. A few people were sitting quietly or saying the stations. It hadn't changed at all, or so she thought. Then she noticed that the collection boxes were gone. She loved the peaceful atmosphere of these old churches.

She still wondered if she had done the right thing. There were times, in the privacy of her apartment, when the tears streamed down her face; when she wanted to take the first flight to Lugano and rush into Alex's arms. Everything had been so perfect on their visit to Yeatstown and Rome. She thought then it might be possible to live like normal people. It was a beautiful dream. Alex, the Alex she loved, was no more. He was part of CosmosRX. In her rational thoughts, she knew he had no choice.

It was such a contrast to live in the real world, after years in an underground complex where all information came in on screens. She loved Darius, Michael, Leonardo, Galileo, Bill and Plato, and regarded them as well-meaning decent, human beings. Big humorous Hercules held a special place in her affections.

***

Julian Savage watched the very public humiliation of Sam Kalazki, and determined not to fall into the same trap. He had just negotiated a ten percent rise for his 12,500 members at Farmplant Inc, when along came CosmosRX and he became redundant as a union boss. Everyone was much better off. Life was good now, but it could always be better: he wanted to spend more time in the gym, bowling, fishing and playing golf with his friends.

Tall, white and powerfully built, he was the second son of Thomas, a train driver, and Ester, a bank official, who were first generation Scottish immigrants. Graduating from Boston High, he went to work for Farmplant, the largest tractor manufacturer and exporter in America. Despite his obvious ability, he was still a production line hand six years later. Thoroughly dissatisfied, he became involved in union activities, and eventually, as union boss, led his men to a rare victory over management. The plant General Manager, a Latino called Ernesto Viala, still refused to promote him.

He married Rosita Alverez, a very pretty Latino from Puerto Rico, who worked as a nurse's assistant in Boston General. They had two daughters, and Rosita later qualified as a nurse; she was only interested in her children and the job.

A year earlier he met Annie, a well-endowed Australian bar lady, in Ronald's nightclub. They hit it off immediately, and he soon became a regular visitor to her apartment out in Cambridge. Rosita didn't appear to notice his absences, or if she did, she didn't make any waves. Annie wanted him to get a divorce; their lovemaking was great, but he wasn't interested in a permanent arrangement.

One morning, he was called to the General Manager's office. Ernest Viala looked worried. A very attractive petite woman sat quietly beside the boss.

He was waved to a chair.

'Julian,' the boss began. 'This is Louisa Grossan. CosmosRX has appointed her as my assistant; she'll be calling the shots, although I'll still be here.'

He stood up.

'That's fine, anything else?'

'Sit down, Mr Savage,' Louisa ordered.

He was so surprised, he obeyed.

She continued. 'Since CosmosRX took over production has fallen by 40 percent. Can you tell me why?'

'It's no concern of mine. That's for the management.'

She smiled grimly. 'It's about to become your concern. In the past month, you have been on sick leave for nearly two weeks.'

He shrugged. 'Those things happen.'

'They didn't happen before CosmosRX.'

He was beginning to feel a bit threatened.

'Like I say, those things happen.'

'And how long did you spend in hospital?'

'Hospitalisation wasn't necessary.'

She referred to her notes. 'Let's cut the crap; pre-CosmosRX the absentee level was one percent, now it's 11 percent.'

'It's got nothing to do with me,' he snarled.

'It's got everything to do with you. You're the union boss; the workers take their orders from you.'

The mask came off. 'What the hell do you think you're going to do about it?'

She reacted calmly. 'It's CosmosRX you have to worry about. I want production up to pre-CosmosRX levels. Those tractors are urgently needed in Africa and India.'

'Like I said, what are you going to do about it?'

'I don't think you realise how serious this may become; everyone going sick from now on will have points deducted unless they are hospitalised.'

'You can't do that.'

'CosmosRX will do it. Get production up to where it should be and everything in the past will be forgotten.'

He got up, and stalked out of the room. Louisa turned to Ernesto Viala.

'What's your excuse?' she asked quietly.

'When I last spoke to Savage, I was told I would be pulled out of the Charles River if I didn't back off. If I were you, I'd watch my step. That bastard is dangerous.'

She rose. 'I have to put in my report. CosmosRX will notify every member of staff. I'll need the names of certifying doctors.'

'I'll get those for you.' He paused. 'You will need an office?'

'No, I'll check with you every few days.'

'What will happen, if the production figures don't increase to pre-CosmosRX levels?'

'CosmosRX will probably reallocate everyone here to the crops program, and bring in a new crew from Mexico.' She paused as he paled.

'Ernesto, you've got the whip, use it.'

She checked in with Ernesto a week later; production hadn't improved. Julian Savage was still obstructing progress. She thought about reporting him to CosmosRX, but decided to hold off for the present.

***

Yoni Shuscof watched Dr Mose Levy return to Lod Airport in Tel Aviv on the Zurich late evening flight. Ex-Mossad Deputy Director, he was now Security Chief at Lod Airport, a job he didn't like very much, but it had its uses. A former hit-man, he looked quite innocuous with dark swarthy features, closely cropped hair, sloppy build and hazel eyes. His eyes were cold, like most of his enemies'. Divorced, with two teenage sons, and just turned 40, he lived with his partner, Sarah, in a dingy apartment overlooking the sea in Joppa.

He was furious when a Palestinian Prime Minister was elected. On day one Mossad was abolished. He met his friends regularly. There was talk of assassinating PM Nakhli. Certain they were being watched, they had to be extremely careful. The removal of the new government by CosmosRX was a welcome, if mixed, blessing.

In his view, there was nothing wrong with CosmosRX except that he or one of his people – and not a bloody German – should be running it. With that in mind, he sent two of his best men to Lugano to check out the situation; it was known that CosmosRX was located in an underground facility somewhere near Lugano.

For that reason, Dr Levy interested him greatly. The good doctor travelled to Lugano on a special pass issued by CosmosRX. Seeing that pass when he boarded at Lod, he alerted his people in Lugano to keep an eye on him. On arrival at Lugano airport, the doctor was met by a big security man, and taken by car to Capalago where they boarded a train going up the mountain. His men couldn't get any closer, but it was safe to assume the doctor had been in the CosmosRX complex.

This raised some very interesting possibilities. If he could find some way of getting inside that complex, it would be a simple matter to eliminate Purtzel, and take it over. Dammit to hell, weren't the chosen people meant to rule the world? And who better than Yoni Shuscof, a true son of Israel?

He checked out Dr Mose Levy. No-one would suspect this unassuming little man was a renowned brain surgeon. Divorced twice, he lived in a luxury apartment overlooking the Judean desert, with his third wife, Leila, and a daughter from his second marriage, a teenager named Ruth. He didn't appear to have any hobbies. During the winter months, he lived mostly in a fine old stone complex near Jericho.

Yoni decided to call on the doctor. He was ushered into his presence in the doctor's private clinic at Mount Scopus University Hospital. The doctor was friendly, but cautious.

He came straight to the point.

'Doctor, may I ask what you were doing in CosmosRX?'

He frowned. 'How do you know I visited there?'

He smiled. 'We have ways of finding these things out. Will you tell me about it?'

He shook his head. 'This is absolutely no concern of yours. I must ask you to leave now.'

'Don't underrate the power of Mossad, doctor. Will you be going back there?'

He rose. 'Mossad no longer exists. I'd like you to leave now.'

He did, satisfied he had the information he needed.

***

Louisa devoted most of her time to her studies; her final exam was only three weeks away. One evening, returning from her night class, laden down with groceries, she pushed in her door and fumbled for the light switch. She was suddenly pushed from behind and thrown to the floor. Grabbed roughly, her arms were pinned behind her back. The lights went on.

Julian Savage was standing there, gloating. She couldn't see who was holding her arms.

'Now, Miss Bossy Bitch, let's see what you're fit for.' He snarled, throwing off his coat, and starting to pull down his trousers.

'You don't want to do this,' she countered, trying to hide her fear.

'By the time I'm finished with you, bitch, you'll tell your bloody CosmosRX whatever I want them to know.'

The other man remained silent, but she was conscious of his heavy breathing. Savage tore at her clothes, ripped off her panties and bore down on her. At that moment, two young men charged into the room. One grabbed Savage from behind, and held him in a vice grip. The other intruder, who tried to make a run for it, was floored by a very accurate punch. She picked herself up and put on her clothes.

'Are you all right, miss?' one of her rescuers asked.

'I'm fine.'

Julian Savage was half-naked, still in a vice grip. Louisa grabbed him by the privates, and squeezed hard. He screamed in agony.

'Where did you think you were going with that little pecker?'

The other one picked himself up slowly off the floor.

Louisa spoke to one of the young men.

'Let him put his trousers on. He looks ridiculous.'

He did, and then handcuffed both men.

'Ms Grossan, we're from CosmosRX. We've been keeping an eye on you for sometime.'

'I'm very grateful to you. What will you do with these two?'

'We'll deregister them.'

Julian Savage began to bluster. 'It was only a bit of fun. I wasn't going to hurt her.'

The other one began to sob.

Louisa had a better idea.

'I'd like to give those two thugs one last chance; let them live as long as they get production figures at Farmplant up to pre-CosmosRX levels and keep them there.'

'I'll have to clear it with CosmosRX.'

'Please,' Savage begged.

'I'm sure Pablo will agree.'

'Very well, miss. I'll keep them in custody until I receive instructions.'

The following day she received an email from Pablo.

"Well done. I've accepted your suggestion. You have been awarded three months' free vacations with the compliments of CosmosRX."

She sent him a reply.

'Thank you, can I bring my mother and stepfather?'

He replied 'Yes, provided you accept your next assignment.'

'That I will.'

Life settled down again. She continued with her studies.

Then, one night, there was a knock on her door. She opened it. There stood a smiling Eric Granlard with a magnum of champagne in each hand; she looked at him, then at the champagne.

'It's all right. I paid for it – I did tell you how special you are to me.'

She grinned. 'And I did tell you that you are great shag.'

She let him in.

'Have you a taxi waiting outside?'

'No.'

She grinned sweetly, looking up into his smiling eyes.

'You'll just have to stay the night then.'

***

Mick O'Hara stood by the rail of the Texas Star when it sailed out of Pensacola for Hamburg, with a full complement of refrigerated beef containers. Dressed casually, his men were scattered among the crew. Six golf bags, full of weapons and explosives were carefully concealed below deck. His wife gave him hell when he finally told her he was going with GMT.

'That overbearing bully, I wouldn't have anything to do with him. He's just a glory-seeking psycho. We're well off as we are – tell him to go to hell.' He would have, if he had the courage.

Captain George Boule wasn't very enthusiastic about carrying a party of six "golfers" to Germany, but he owed GMT and couldn't very well refuse. He captained GMT's landing craft in the Cuban invasion. Approaching the beach, they sustained a direct hit. Most of his men were killed. Shot in the leg, he was drowning when GMT pulled him to the surface and dragged him ashore. The General roared for the medics who took over. That was the end of his war.

Two days later, GMT and his six troops boarded a freighter bound for Panama City. His men included a big Mexican, Pablo Largo, the explosives expert. Scruffy and wild-looking, with very bright blue eyes, he spent most of his time drinking. In Panama, they signed on as crew on a cargo vessel taking cane sugar from Cuba to Genoa. The General was quite pleased with himself. Getting to the scene of action was the hard part, and here he was, on his way.

***

In the conference centre, Alex conferred with Michael and Plato.

Michael, as usual, led the discussion. 'This is going to be a long, slow struggle. We believe we did not reach the point of no return. There's some slight improvement in the ozone layer.'

Plato added. 'It's possible that Antarctica could still disintegrate.'

'What's the current situation?'

'The temperature was up 5.6 degrees on the 1990 figure when we took over; it's now up 4.3 degrees.'

'It's still much too high.'

'How is the crop program going?'

‘Very much according to plan: our main concern now is to try to increase food shipments to parts of Africa, India and China.’

‘Have you given the go-ahead for the reconstruction of the Three Gorges Dam?’

‘Yes, it should be completed in less than two years. We have abandoned the old city of Shanghai in favour of a new one further south, on high ground 50 kilometres from the coast.’

Leonardo joined them.

‘What’s happening with our listening satellites?’

‘The sounds we’re recording are coming, not from deep space, but from planet Earth. Sound levels reduce as the satellites advance further into space. They’re going back millennia; to a time when the world population was less than one percent what it is now. Sally and Bill finalised this program some time ago. We will isolate the period 5,000 BC to 1,900 AD – eliminate the everyday babble – focus on specific people, places and events, and try to match the sounds to the people and activity concerned.’

‘Will this work?’ Alex was doubtful.

‘We’re not going back very far into history. With our new computer program we won’t have any difficulty translating sounds into language. Location in history is already, more or less, established; matching history to language could provide some interesting results.’

‘How?’

‘For the first time, we’ll be able to compare what actually happened with recorded historical reporting.’

Alex nodded. ‘I’ll be very interested to hear how you get on.’

***

Sally began to settle down to a new way of life, followed the doctor’s diet instructions rigidly, and reported regularly for her prenatal exercises. In six months, if all was well, she would give birth to a baby boy. She gazed in awe at the hazy ultrasound picture of her little baby. As an expectant mother she had no obligation to work. After so many years of hectic activity she needed time out – time to think – to bring some kind of normality into her life. She was on an emotional rollercoaster, still wondering if she did the right thing leaving Alex.

She took a coach to Lettermore. It was a pleasant cloudy day in Connemara; a little bit of green was returning to its bogs and heather. She was surprised at the number of men working in the little stony fields; this certainly wasn't the case in her young days. The sludge in the sea was beginning to disintegrate. She knocked on the door of her old home; when she explained who she was, the pleasant middle-aged woman invited her in. Mollie McCann and her late husband bought the property from Rachael after her parents died. She sat Sally down and made the tea.

Sally sat by the window looking out across the sea to the Aran Islands. How often, as a child, had she sat on the same chair, daydreaming about all the things she would do when she grew up. Occasionally, the chit-chat of Mother and Rachael would intervene or Father would announce he was going fishing. Now, there was only silence: they were all gone.

Thanking the kind woman, she walked up the hill to the cemetery. Finding her parents' grave, she knelt and said a prayer; it would be nice to think that – one day – she would see them again. She was surprised to find that Rachael and her two lovely girls were buried here too – beautiful Ciara and Siobhan – so full of the joy of living, so optimistic about the future – to be taken like that. Tears ran down her face – what a heart-rending tragedy – what could have possessed Rachael to do such a thing? Why did she take her two lovely girls with her? She would have to visit Clifden to see Joe, later. The wind freshened and grey clouds began to drift in from the Atlantic. She caught the evening coach to Galway.

It was time to start making preparations for her little nursery. Siobhan had promised to come shopping with her, and kindly pointed out she needed some style herself. She was delighted to find the summer sales were on; clothes and shoes were marked down by 50 percent. She was spending less than 2,000 points a month.

The following week was race week in Galway. It was a time when the entire country came to a full stop, and headed for Ballybane; it would be very different now that gambling was a thing of the past. She was invited to join Siobhan and Martin Mannion on the Thursday. Martin, strongly built with greying hair, bronzed features and deep brown eyes, was a very relaxed outdoorsman who loved golf and fishing. Siobhan wore a pink and yellow dress under a wide-brimmed white hat. Sally settled for a loose beige dress with no hat.

The bookies were there with their stands taking bets – as usual. Sally couldn't believe this.

'Martin,' she asked. 'Wasn't gambling abolished?'

He grinned. 'Yes, it was, but people still bet.'

'But why, they can't be paid if they win?'

'And it doesn't cost them anything if they lose.'

'I don't get it.'

'My psychiatrist colleagues tell me it has to do with the ego. If I back a horse and he wins, it shows how bright I am.'

'I'm still not with you.'

'In a funny way, it's no different to the old system, except that it's painless. Gambling is an addiction, a disease. The real punter thinks he bets to make money. He doesn't; he bets he can beat the system. That's his thrill, or fix, as it were. When he wins he can't wait to put on another bet; he wants another fix. When he loses he hits bottom; only a win can cure that. It's a merry-go-round and he can't get off.' He paused and smiled. 'Now I'm going to put a million on Rafter's Aunt at 10 to 1 to win the Plate.'

***

Yoni Shuscof was right in his assumption: if Dr Levy wasn't going to visit CosmosRX again he would have said so. When the flight authorisation came through, he rang his cousin Ben Alton.

'Levy is going to Lugano in five days' time. You know what to do.'

He smiled as he put down the phone.

***

John Ellison was becoming more and more frustrated: was Elton laughing at him? Hillary was sympathetic but couldn't help. He walked through the office and introduced himself to the staff. Most were involved in paying the growers, so should now be redundant. That wasn't his concern, at least not yet.

He examined the figures again. He was missing something, but what the hell was it?

Two days later he called in Elton.

'Who is in charge in New Jersey? I want to inspect our stocks.'

He didn't appear to be perturbed.

'Jack Brown is the overseer there. When do you want to go? I'll tell him to expect you.'

He had already made up his mind.

'I'll go first thing tomorrow.'

'I'll let him know.'

Afterwards, John called in his secretary.

'Hillary, I'm going to be out for the rest of the day. You don't know where I am. Ring me on the cell phone if you need me.'

'Right, John.'

He had become very fond of Hillary Rouse. Very fair-skinned, with dark hair and deep brown eyes, she spoke with a soft sympathetic voice, but didn't talk about her past. Leaving, he took a train to New Jersey, and there got a taxi to the warehouses.

Jack Brown was a friendly, rugged-looking elderly man who always seemed to have a cigarette in his mouth. He appeared to be quite straightforward, and was most helpful in showing him over the stocks. He checked them against his list. Everything was in order.

Afterwards, they sat in Jack's little office. He offered his guest a coffee.

'Yes, please,' he wanted to keep him talking.

As he sipped it, he asked. 'How do you deal with incoming stocks?'

'We've had none for the past five years – drought.'

'Have you shipped much abroad lately?'

'Very little for the past four years.'

'How do you check the stock?'

'Two of my men weigh everything on the big old scales inside the door – same with stocks going out.'

John rose and shook hands with him.

'Thank you for your help.'

He returned to New York more puzzled than ever. What the hell was he missing? Maybe Corteso was right. Maybe he was stupid?

***

As the Sun was sinking in the west, GMT leaned on the rail and puffed on his cigar. The freighter chugged slowly past the rock of Gibraltar. His deputy, Major Elvin Gettings, was playing cards below deck, and keeping an eye on Pablo. GMT didn't like Mad Mex, but for now he needed him.

In his mind he went over his plans for the future. Once CosmosRX was destroyed, Purtzel would be powerless to interfere – should he survive. Arms production would proceed quickly. No other country would be fit to compete while he established US supremacy over the entire world. He would retain the single world airline: it would give him complete monopoly in the air. Billions of dollars would be printed; it would be the only currency permitted.

He had already held discussions with the US nuclear scientists. Not all were in favour, but he got the support of a sufficient number to build new nuclear weapons. This time, there would be no mistake: no other country would be permitted to develop any weapons program, never mind weapons of mass destruction. He would also take control of the space weapons.

Life was going to be good again. This CosmosRX fellow did him a good turn getting rid of the useless politicians, and setting up a central control he could easily take over. He lit another cigar and watched the rock fade away in the distance.

***

José Carvallo hadn't seen Elvira for months. He phoned her regularly, and she kept asking when he would come to see her; she was being harassed by her late husband's brother. It became easier when he was assigned to the nuclear reactor contract near Rochester.

With Pablo and Annie gone, it wasn't the same at home now. He accompanied them to the crematorium he had worked on for months. They were very brave at the end. He helped them relax a little after they sipped the champagne with their happy pill. It was best they were going together. He hugged them tearfully. Pablo put his arm around Annie. They walked together through the exit door – and didn't look back.

Work kept him away from home for weeks at a time. Maria didn't mind. The kids were starting college, and she had no fees to pay. She was delighted when CosmosRX agreed to provide them with a more modern apartment.

By doubling up shifts on site, he managed to get a three-day break. He bought an open-neck check shirt and an off-the-peg grey sports blazer; he hadn't seen Elvira for quite a while, and wanted to look his best. Taking the train to Worcester, he switched there to a local bus that passed by the roadhouse. Alighting, he looked around him. It was a lovely sunny evening with many boats out on the lake. The empty car and trailer park looked enormous.

Elvira wore her sexiest clinging red dress, but he could see that she was worried. The diner was half full. She greeted him with relief, gave him the key to 202 and whispered.

'I'll join you shortly.'

Twenty minutes later she was in his arms.

'José, I'm afraid for my life. They're trying to run me off. What am I going to do?'

'Have you been to see the sheriff?'

'Sheriff Jones? That bastard. He says the property belongs to my brother-in-law. They've given me a week to get out.'

He continued to hold her while she sobbed quietly.

'You're financially independent, now you've got your monthly points.'

'José,' her voice softened, 'I'm going to have your baby.'

He looked shocked.

She hastened on. 'I won't make any demands on you, my love. I want to have someone for myself; a baby to love and cherish, watch grow up, and maybe one day give me grandchildren.'

He took her in his arms again.

'I'll come and help out whenever I can.'

'I've come to love this old place. I want it for my baby.'

'There must be some solution, love. Doesn't the local sheriff come under the County Sheriff in Worcester?'

'I don't know.'

'We'll go and see him tomorrow. They can't all be corrupt.'

She felt reassured by his presence. If only he could be there all the time. She didn't say that to him. After a few drinks, they relaxed. In the morning, leaving her assistant, Dottie, in charge, they took the coach into Worcester. The town had grown enormously since the new Boston airport was opened. Eventually, they found the County Sheriff's office and, after waiting for nearly an hour, were ushered into the presence of Sigmund Starkey, a no-nonsense middle-aged man with greying hair. Elvira explained her predicament. He listened attentively and took some notes. Then he rose. 'Wait here.'

He returned 15 minutes later.

'I've spoken with Sheriff Jones. He's satisfied you have no claim to this property.'

She opened her handbag. 'Let me show you a copy of my husband's will.'

He waved her away.

'You have no case. Vacate the property immediately or you will be evicted,' he responded briskly.

José could feel his anger rising.

'Because she's coloured?'

'Butt out, this is no concern of yours,' he retorted angrily.

They left without another word, and walked back to the coach stop.

'What am I going to do, José?'

This was way outside his experience, but he was angry now.

'If he shows up, I'll throw the bastard out.'

'Can you do that?'

'There's nothing else I can do.'

They boarded the coach.

In his boat-hire shop on the other side of the lake, Reggie Portman took a phone call from Sheriff Jones. A short, thin-faced middle-aged man, with angry eyes, he had it all worked out; he would take the roadhouse, and pass the shop to his only son, James.

'Right sheriff, I'll meet you there.'

Putting down the phone, he cycled to the roadhouse. The sheriff was there before him.

'Let's get this job done, Reggie. Then maybe I can go fishing in peace.'

They entered. There were only three customers in the diner. José sat close by. The sheriff and Reggie marched up to the bar where Elvira was making up a sandwich. Rising, José edged closer.

'Mrs Elvira Portman,' the sheriff spoke with barely concealed anger. 'In accordance with the law, I'm here to evict you and hand over this property to its lawful owner.'

'I'm the lawful owner,' she yelled at him.

José came closer.

'You heard what the lady said. You should leave now.'

The sheriff turned on him, pulling out his gun.

'One word out of you Latino and I'll blow your fucking head off.'

José fought to keep his temper under control.

'You leave now, and there won't be any trouble.'

The sheriff fired twice hitting José in the chest. He fell heavily to the floor. Elvira screamed, as she raced out from behind the counter.

'You murdering bastard.'

Rccovering his composure, the sheriff addressed the customers.

'You all saw that. I had to shoot him in self-defence.'

They departed quickly.

'Murdering bastard,' Elvira continued screaming, while she cradled José's head in her lap.

The sheriff stepped forward, and pistol-whipped her on the head. She collapsed on top of José's body.

Reggie took the gun out of the sheriff's hand.

'You can't leave the bitch alive.'

He shot her through the head.

The sheriff took back his gun and smiled.

'Reggie, now you're the owner, you'll have to treat me very well. Put me up a large Jack Daniels while I ring in for a meat wagon.'

***

Carlo Agnelli – having spent some time studying the information required – decided he must now register with CosmosRX. No way could he use his real name. The address was also a problem – it would have to be sufficiently unspecific to pass unnoticed – a small village, where the village name constituted an entire address. He did his homework before going to a CosmosRX access point. There, he entered the name Pierre Santaire, 25, born in the village of Broone in Normandy, currently employed as a seaman on board the MV Diana out of Glasgow. He followed all the procedures. Two minutes later he was registered and credited with his first 3,000 deposit points. He smiled to himself; beating the computer was no big deal for someone with his intelligence. Now, he could travel to this place called Galway.

***

Lieutenant Bill Franken, of the NYPD was becoming more and more worried. He couldn't believe the change in his good friend of 20 years. Pat Hartigan was running Manhattan as his own fiefdom. The number of unexplained shootings was rising, and the Captain was invariably in the vicinity when they occurred. He knew he would have to report him to CosmosRX; the bullet that killed an old tramp in Lower Manhattan was fired from the chief's gun. He was finding this very difficult. He hated the very idea of breaking ranks.

CosmosRX had practically wiped out crime, and made policing much more agreeable. It would defeat the whole purpose if the law enforcers abused their trust. In his 20 years on the force, he had struggled, very often unsuccessfully, to put the criminals where they belonged. The odds were stacked against them; clever lawyers laughed at them while the scum walked free. Along came CosmosRX and cleaned up the streets in a matter of days; with few exceptions, they remained clean.

Son of a police patrolman, he graduated from the Police College, and very early on, was promoted to Detective Second Class; he served in Harlem and the Bronx before being brought up town as a lieutenant. The Twenties and Thirties were particularly lawless. The city was flooded with all kinds of foreigners. Electricity shortages made their job nearly impossible. Homicides reached 11,000 a year. Robberies increased in the blackouts. Many of his colleagues died in the line of duty. Wounded twice, he refused a full-time desk job.

He couldn't just stand aside and ignore what was happening. His only daughter, Joan, was married to a sergeant in Newark; his wife, Maeve, served on four charity committees until charities became unnecessary. He had to tell her, she knew something was bothering him. She was appalled; Ester Hartigan was a friend. They visited one another regularly and at least twice a year all four dined at Pat's country club. She agreed he had to do something, but could he get Pat to resign without involving CosmosRX?

It might work if the Captain was approached by a number of his colleagues. It was worth a try, but he would have to tread lightly. Two days later, he invited one of his up-and-coming young detectives, Jon Stewart, to meet him for a drink. A very handsome man, Jon was living with a young actress in an apartment in Little Italy.

They met over in Sammy's Pub. Bill outlined the problem. He had the feeling Jon already knew.

'Have you talked to anyone else?' he asked.

'No, not yet, I want to do this discreetly. Pat is a friend, and has been a first class officer.'

'How can I help?'

'Talk to one or two of your friends, men you can trust. I want to keep CosmosRX out of this.'

Jon finished his drink.

'I'll be very discreet.'

Feeling a bit happier, Bill took the subway home.

The following evening, as he was leaving the building, the Captain joined him in the elevator; he pushed the button for the basement.

'Robbery over in Macy's, Bill. We'll take the paddywagon.'

'OK, I'll just ring Maeve and tell her I'll be late.'

'No need, I'll drop you home afterwards.'

In the basement he ordered 'You drive, Bill.'

He drove up the ramp on to Sixth Avenue and headed down the near-empty street towards Macy's.

'Turn left here,' he was ordered, 'and head for Central Park.'

He didn't like this. 'Why?'

He felt the gun in his side.

'Just do it, damn you.'

He tried to remain calm.

'This isn't going to solve anything, Pat.'

They approached the park on 59th Street.

'Drive in and stop by the lake.'

He tried to talk to him. 'If you don't go quietly, Pat, CosmosRX will get you.'

'To hell with CosmosRX, I run Manhattan.'

He tried to bluff. 'Killing me won't get you anywhere. CosmosRX already knows.'

He pulled up at the lake. The area was deserted. He was frightened, but was damned if he would let him see that.

'Get out.'

He did. The Captain eased out after him, with gun in hand.

'Walk towards the lake.'

Bill threw himself to the ground, and reached for his gun. Hartigan shot twice. He felt a sharp pain in his chest and knew no more.

'That's how I treat traitors,' he grunted.

Checking to make sure Bill was dead; he put away his gun, walked slowly to the paddywagon and drove away.

***

Dr Mose Levy sat slumped in his seat as the World Airlines Tel Aviv flight circled Lugano, and set down gently on the main runway. Yoni Shuscof and Ben Alton, dressed in dark suits with white shirts and grey ties, sat beside him.

'Don't forget, doctor,' Yoni reminded him, 'one wrong word out of you and you'll never see your daughter again. If I don't contact my man in Jerusalem within two days, she's dead.'

'I know, I know,' he muttered unhappily.

'How long does it take us to get to this place?'

'About half an hour.'

Disembarking, they were greeted by Darius who led the way to the CosmosRX car. Dr Levy introduced him to 'Drs' Shuscof and Alton.

Darius smiled. 'Welcome gentlemen, I'll be looking after you during your stay.'

They set out for Capalago.

In the operations room, Alex found Hercules looking at an incoming message on his screen.

'Six heavily-armed thugs are heading this way. They left Hamburg two days ago, and should be in Friedrichshafen by now. They will cross Lake Constance by ferry and proceed to Lugano by train. They plan to capture CosmosRX.'

'Have you alerted security?'

'Yes, they're under observation; we'll take them out when they board the ferry.'

'Good.' He paused. 'Where did the tip-off come from?'

'Genoa.'

'Who sent it?'

'I don't know.' He paused, and looked at one of his internal screens. 'Doctor Levy and his assistants are entering the elevator with Darius. What would you like me to do?'

'Show them to my office.'

He departed. Hercules stood by the elevator and awaited the visitors. He greeted them affably.

'Gentlemen, you are very welcome. Let me take you to the Director.'

'Thank you, Hercules, isn't it?' Dr Levy asked.

He led the way to the office where Alex was sitting behind his desk reading a document. He introduced the new 'doctors' and left quietly, closing the door behind him.

Yoni stepped forward pulling out his gun. He couldn't believe this was so easy. Alex looked surprised.

'What's going on here?'

Yoni smiled. 'I'm just taking over CosmosRX.'

He fired three times, hitting Alex in the chest. The force propelled him backwards. His body fell heavily to the floor.

***

On a bright, sunny Saturday, Sally rose early to catch the 8.00 am train to Clifden. She wanted to see Joe O'Flaherty. Taking a local bus, she travelled to the train terminal in Newcastle on the western side of the city. The new Clifden railway line was reopened the previous year; it replaced the one closed down more than a century earlier. The station was modern, its walls decorated with colourful paintings of the mountains and lakes of Connemara. She confirmed her booking by putting her hand on the automatic entry machine, boarded the super nuclear train with a large number of other passengers and took her allocated seat in the front carriage.

The train eased its way silently out of the city. To her right, she admired the wide expanse of Lough Corrib with its many dotted, rocky islands. After passing through a wooded area, they stopped in Moycullen. Here, a group of golfers left the train. Girls on a school outing boarded, chattering away happily. Carefree and excited, they reminded her of childhood days.

On to Oughterard where more golfers and a number of anglers left the train. Some sightseers boarded. Then they moved smoothly out into the great expanse of Connemara: a unique landscape of mountains, rivers and lakes. After overnight rainfall, rushing waters cascaded down the grey mountain slopes; the Sun rose higher in the sky and the mist lifted off the peaks of Maam. She sat back and relaxed. Approaching their next stop, at Maam Cross, the catering manager announced breakfast in the diner. “All are welcome. It’s free, so come along everyone.”

She tucked into a tasty fry while the train threaded its way among the lakes to Recess Junction. The fresh eggs were a treat. A little bit of green was returning to the countryside – the lakes looked a bit cleaner. Recess Junction by the lake was the last stop before Clifden: here the line split, one leg going to Clifden, the other to Roundstone by the sea. The clouds were settling on the Twelve Bens when the train pulled into Clifden. Joe was waiting for her. Older, more serious-looking than she remembered, he looked well in his grey tweed blazer and tan trousers. He hugged her briefly.

‘You’re very welcome, Sally. It’s so good to see you again.’

‘Thanks, Joe; it’s lovely to be back in Clifden.’

A pony and trap took them to his modern bungalow overlooking the sea on Sky Road. How quaint, she thought, this “new” form of local transport that went out of fashion nearly 100 years earlier, revived by local, very versatile boat builders. The frisky little pony seemed to be enjoying his return to duty.

She sat outside on the veranda – while he made coffee – admiring the magnificent view. She used to love this place – often sat here chatting with the girls – now it was desolate without them. They sat silently for a while and sipped their coffee.

‘Joe,’ she began, ‘I have to ask you about Rachael.’

He shook his head. ‘Things hadn’t been going well for a number of years: I had one or two casual affairs; there was nothing to them; I loved Rachael and would never have left her.’ He paused. She could feel the anguish in his voice when he continued. ‘Why did she have to take my two lovely little girls with her?’

‘What happened, Joe?’ She asked quietly.

‘She put the girls in her car, and drove off the pier in Roundstone.’

‘Could it have been an accident?’

‘No, she left a letter.’

She was silent for a while – poor Rachael and her beautiful little girls.

'Will you stay for the weekend, Sally?'

She roused herself. 'No thanks, Joe, I'll be returning on the four o'clock train.'

He was disappointed. 'Let me take you to lunch in the Clifden Bay Hotel.'

'That would be nice.'

She wanted to ask if there was another woman in his life; the house looked too tidy to be a bachelor home.

On Sunday, she did something she hadn't done for some time; she went to Mass in the magnificent cut-stone Cathedral just across the bridge from her apartment. She knew it was nostalgia, but it helped to bring her closer to her parents, Rachael, the girls, and Amanda. She remembered Fr John with affection; what seemed so serious then was of no consequence now. Still unsure of what she believed in, she always had a special regard for Jesus and Mary. She prayed for them all.

***

Yoni Shuscof was elated as he turned to Dr Levy.

'Now, I rule the world, I don't need you anymore.'

He placed the barrel of his gun against the doctor's head and fired once. He was dead before his body hit the floor.

'Now let me talk to my new slaves,' he moved towards the door.

'What the hell's going on here; the door's locked?'

Then he heard a hissing sound.

'Gas,' he choked, as both of them collapsed in a heap on the floor.

When they came to, they were sitting handcuffed together. Hercules stood behind them. Alex was sitting calmly behind his desk.

'What the hell?' Yoni muttered, shaking his head to try to clear it.

'Did you really think we're that stupid? We were on to you the moment you stepped into the elevator.'

'How?' he demanded hoarsely.

'Your guns showed up on our security screen. You shot my look-alike and he's not at all pleased.'

Ben Alton was petrified. Yoni was desperately looking for a bargaining chip.

'The doctor's daughter is dead, if we don't return to Jerusalem.'

Alex's expression hardened.

'Who else is involved?'

'No-one.'

'You will tell me before you die – Hercules?'

The big man came forward with a hypodermic needle in his hand and plunged it into Yoni's left arm. He slumped forward.

Petrified, Ben Alton begged. 'I'll tell you anything you want to know, only please don't kill me. It was all Yoni's idea.'

Alex rose. 'I'll leave this to you Hercules. Save the child if you can. You know what to do with this pair.'

***

Alex joined Michael and Plato in the operations room.

'Alex,' Plato asked, 'have you given any thought to the changes we have to make in the departure program.'

'What size is the average family in developing countries?'

'Seven.'

'As high as that?'

'Yes.'

'I've been talking to Harold Hassett. Compulsory abortion isn't on. We're going to massively increase contraception counselling.'

'That won't be sufficient, Alex.'

'I know. Any woman, who gives birth to two children, will be offered sterilisation; after three children, she will be compulsorily sterilised.'

'That will help. Would there be any little reward for those volunteering?'

'You could throw in a one-off bonus of 5,000 points.'

'I have some very interesting consumption figures for you,' Michael began.

'Let's hear them.'

'Ninety percent of our members spend less than 3,000 points per month, seven percent spend their entire points allocation and three percent spend less than 500 points a month.'

Alex frowned. 'That doesn't sound right. What's going on?'

'I don't know yet. I've identified them and instructed our people to investigate quietly.'

'Any improvement in the overall position?' Alex asked.

Michael replied. 'Nothing specific, but we can't detect any deterioration either.'

Plato asked. 'What about your operation?'

Alex grunted sourly. 'I think I might live longer without it.'

'We took out that party of would-be attackers in Friedrichshafen, all Americans. I'm trying to find out how they travelled to Germany. It wasn't by air, so I have to find the ship that took them to Hamburg.'

'Any survivors?'

'No.'

'Pity.'

***

Reggie Portman was delighted with his success. He was now the proud owner of the Lakeside Inn. The sheriff took care of everything: the big Latino shot Elvira while trying to rob some whiskey; the sheriff shot him while trying to escape. He watched as one of his girls served two customers. He fancied her but that would come later.

The sheriff charged in and approached the counter.

'What's the problem?' he demanded.

Reggie looked at him blankly.

'You sent for me?'

'No.'

Two young men approached.

'Reginald Portman and Sheriff Jones. You will come with us.'

A woman and young man entered the diner.

'What the hell are you talking about?' Reggie demanded.

He spoke quietly. 'You killed two people in your efforts to get control of these premises. Now, you must pay the price. Put the handcuffs on them, Oscar.'

The sheriff pulled his gun, and fired twice hitting both of the young men; his eyes opened wide in terror when Oscar calmly grabbed his gun wrist and squeezed hard. He screamed in agony dropping the gun.

Oscar turned to the woman and young man standing behind him.

'You can take over now, Mrs Carvallo. This is your property.'

'Thank you, sir.'

Handcuffed, Reggie protested. 'I didn't do anything. It was all his idea.'

'Shut up.' The sheriff screamed at him.

'Let's go.'

'How the hell could you know?' Reggie demanded hoarsely.

Oscar smiled. 'Mrs Elvira Portman advised CosmosRX of her desire that this property be transferred to José Carvallo on her death. When you applied to CosmosRX to have the property transferred to you, it didn't take long to find out what happened: you signed your own death warrant.'

They marched them to the ambulance outside. Opening the back doors, they thrust them in. Sitting there, glowering at them was the Sheriff Sigmund Starkey from Worcester. They closed and locked the doors.

'Boston Crematorium, trade entrance, Oscar,' he ordered.

***

GMT was quite pleased with himself; betraying Mick O'Hara and his men would throw the enemy off guard. Good tactics, in war – and this is war – there's no room for sentiment. He didn't tell his men. They would now take the train to Milan and lie low there for a couple of days while they got train tickets to Lugano. They would travel north one by one, to avoid attracting attention. He ordered two of his men to keep watch over Mad Mex.

***

John Ellison rang Elton in the morning.

'CosmosRX wants 100 tons of wheat delivered to Newark West Airport by noon tomorrow.'

'I don't think we can afford that much.'

'We've got 800 tons in stock. Just do it or I'll get someone else to do it.' He slammed down the phone.

He decided it was time to look at the staffing situation. After coffee, he wandered around the office and asked each person to write down their current job description. Some didn't react with any great enthusiasm. One clean-cut, friendly young man, Jess Austin, reacted affably.

'Certainly, sir. I log incoming shipments from the growers, not that there's been much for the past five years.'

'I've been to the warehouses in New Jersey.'

He looked up at him smiling.

'Did you visit the ones in Ridgewood and Springfield?'

John stopped in his tracks.

'Have you got the addresses?'

He pulled a sheet of paper out of his drawer, and handed it to him, smiling as he did so.

'Jess, are you meant to have this information?'

'No, sir.'

'Thanks Jess, I'll be back to see you later.'

He returned to his office where Hillary was waiting for him.

'I've got it, I've got it. Will you put me on to CosmosRX?'

Five minutes later, he was talking to Abe who listened quietly until he finished.

'How can I help?'

'Can you send me two security guards?'

'You will have them in five minutes.'

Two handsome-looking young men presented themselves a few minutes later.

'I'm Jack Rodgers and this is Will Battle.'

He got up. 'Thanks for coming so promptly. Will you follow me please?'

He led the way to the elevator. They went down two floors to Elton's office; he was surprised to see him. John spoke to Jack Rodgers.

'This man is to be kept in close confinement until I return. He's not to speak to anyone, take or make calls, or use his computer.'

'Yes, sir,' he replied.

'What the hell's going on here?' Elton demanded.

'You'll find out when I come back from Ridgewood and Springfield.'

His face fell. He started to bluster, but John was already gone.

Five hours later, he returned, and made his way to Elton's office, where he produced a sheet of paper.

'You have been hoarding wheat for years; those warehouses currently hold nearly 25,000 tons of wheat.'

'I was ordered to do it.'

John was really angry now. 'Most of that wheat has been there for three to six years or more. It could have prevented food riots here in America, and saved thousands of lives in Africa.'

'I only did what I was told,' he protested.

'You didn't do what you were told by CosmosRX. Why do you think they put me in here?'

Jack Rodgers turned to John.

'We'll take him into custody, sir, and ask CosmosRX for instructions.'

'No, no, I'm innocent,' he screamed.

'Come along, sir, don't make a fuss.'

John returned to his office where Hillary was waiting anxiously. In a way, he felt sorry for the bureaucratic little fool.

'What will they do to him?' she asked.

'I believe the expression is "deregister", which is the same as execute. They'll just take him to the nearest crematorium. Will you open a line to CosmosRX so I can make my report?'

'Will do; can I get you a coffee?'

'Please.'

They had coffee together when he finished his report.

She was a bit upset over Elton.

'I didn't like him, but isn't it a bit severe?'

'It is, but he should have copped on when I was sent in. CosmosRX doesn't take prisoners, there's too much at stake. I've been told to reassess staff requirements here, and send a list of those eligible for relocation.'

She smiled. 'Are you telling me I'm out of a job?'

'No way; who would make the coffee? How would you like to go out to dinner tonight?'

'I'd like that, John. Shouldn't we notify Elton's family?'

'I'm going to do that.'

They met at Rusty's Steak House on 6th Avenue. Hillary looked particularly attractive in a lime green cotton dress. Things were improving; they were served two small but very tasty steaks. She chose a good Italian wine. He always found it easy to talk to her, but tonight he was a bit nervous, even apprehensive.

She spotted it. 'Anything wrong, John?'

'You look so lovely, I want to take you in my arms and kiss you.'

She smiled. 'You can't very well do it here.'

They ordered desert.

'Hillary,' he began, 'I have a confession to make, one you probably won't like.'

'Do tell.'

'I had an affair with a lady half my age while I was still married.'

'Is it over?'

'Has been for months.'

'I have a confession too, John.'

'Oh.'

'I was my ex-husband's mistress while he was still married to his first wife.'

He grinned. 'Hillary, what's past is past.'

'I'm so happy there aren't going to be any secrets between us.'

She paused. 'Have you been to see your wife?'

'My ex-wife. I went out last Sunday. She's planning to get married again. My son is going to Cambridge University. I've arranged to have my effects moved into the apartment.'

'You have no regrets?'

'No, we drifted apart years ago.'

He paused. 'How will your daughter react to us?'

'Amy will be delighted. When CosmosRX came along she gave up her job to look after little Al. Her partner, Syd, is an airline pilot.'

'I think champagne is in order.'

'I'd like that.' She paused. 'My ex-husband came to see us the other day; his mistress has taken off with a younger man. He wanted to come back to me; I told him I had met the man I want to spend the rest of my days with.'

They raised their champagne glasses. 'To us, my love.'

He settled the bill, and arm in arm they strolled along 5th Avenue towards his apartment. There were few people around.

She smiled at him. 'I think I'd like that kiss now, love.'

He put his arms around her and they kissed lovingly before continuing on their way.

***

Plato waited until nearly all the special reports flowed in; then instructed the computer to break down the results under different headings.

'What does that mean?' Michael asked.

'Most people spending less than 500 points a month have been using intimidation to get their requirements.'

'Give me a breakdown by category.'

'Sixty-six percent police and other security; ten percent store managers; 11 percent store employees; seven percent depot managers, and six percent extortion using firearms.'

'Computer, instruct our people to carryout standing orders.'

He turned to Michael. 'Do you know, I sometimes think that man is not yet ready to rule himself?'

He smiled. 'I sometimes think that, too – then I remember that man made us.'

***

Captain Pat Hartigan studied the CosmosRX instruction on his screen. "Call a meeting of your officers and staff for 6.00 pm tomorrow. They are required to participate in a promotional film that will be shown on World TV." It looked harmless enough.

He ordered an official funeral for Bill Franken, uttered a glowing oration at the graveside – about his friend of 20 years – and initiated a high-level, and unsuccessful, investigation into the killing. He had nothing to worry about. He promoted Jon Stewart to Lieutenant. That would keep him quiet.

***

Alex was surprised when he learned both space ships were returning; that wasn't part of the plan. Attempts to contact the ships, using the CosmosRX communications system, had failed: there was too much static. He wondered what could possibly have happened. They landed at Lugano airport and were taken to a warehouse nearby.

Shortly afterwards Galileo arrived at CosmosRX. They gathered in the conference room to hear his report.

'It's great to have you back, Galileo. What happened?' Alex asked.

He smiled. 'Infantia, as we've named it, is a most beautiful planet: with clean air, blue skies, tall forests, lovely lakes, high mountains, massive waterfalls, crystal clear rivers, excellent arable land and an extraordinary variety of animals and fish.'

'Is the atmosphere one in which humans could survive?'

'I believe so, but we would need to do further tests. It's half the size of Earth, in the first third of its life span, and its Sun is 95 million miles away.'

'Why didn't one of your crews stay as arranged?' Alex asked.

'Because the people there – they call themselves something that sounds like "Toravics" – asked us not to stay.'

'There are people there?'

'Yes, lovely peaceful people.'

'They welcomed you?'

'As guests, but only as guests.'

'But how did you communicate with them?'

'They taught us their language.'

'What do they look like?'

'Slightly smaller than man, but otherwise much the same.'

'How long have they been there?'

'Nearly 100,000 years. They came from their home planet Zeffer – or something that sounds like that – before it was destroyed by global warming.'

'And they don't want us there?'

'They don't want to share their planet with anyone.'

'That sounds reasonable. Do they know about Earth?'

'Yes. From time to time their spacecraft have passed close to Earth.'

'What's it like there?'

'They live in small communities, their industries are confined to selected areas, mostly underground, and they travel mostly by high-speed trains.'

'Energy sources?'

'Seems to be nuclear and solar.'

'Have they aircraft?'

'Yes, different to ours; big and squat, their craft rise vertically first, and then head off at speed towards their destinations.'

'Have they cars?'

'They call them carriers. They're only permitted in rural areas.'

'How do they rule their people?'

'They have a Council of Twelve that rules the entire planet. It's an unusual arrangement, but appears to work for them. When a member dies – they all live to a great age – the Council selects a replacement.'

'So it's not really that much different to Earth?'

Galileo smiled. 'It's very different: it has five moons – much smaller than ours; they have five full moons every month, sometimes simultaneously. It orbits its Sun every 14 months, our time, so their year is about two months longer than ours. Tidal times vary much more than ours and their days are shorter.'

'So we have to find another compatible planet.'

Galileo felt he had held back for long enough.

'They were kind enough to give us the co-ordinates of two uninhabited planets in their solar system with similar atmospheres.'

'That's very exciting.'

'Galileo, what do you think we should do now?' Alex asked.

'I believe we should send a separate expedition to explore each planet and ascertain if suitable for human habitation. This will be a massive undertaking: I will need all kinds of experts including robotic doctors, engineers, genetic specialists, veterinary experts, microbiologists, agriculturalists and scientists.'

Alex disagreed. 'I think it would be better to send a major expedition to one of the planets first, to set up a permanent base there.'

He paused and continued quietly.

'We will name this new planet "Planet Bergin".'

'I absolutely agree,' Leonardo replied.

Alex continued. 'We should now set up a committee of experts to address the transit problem.'

***

Leonardo looked quite pleased with himself when he reported back to Alex, having completed the first major interpretation of the sounds coming from the listening satellites.

'It's been a bit hit-and-miss on timing and locations, but we've succeeded in matching up a number of prominent people in history with significant events.'

Alex was impressed. 'You can now verify the authenticity and accuracy of history?'

'I wouldn't go quite that far. History has always been recorded by the victors. As we expected, much of history was just propaganda.'

'I think that was to be expected.'

'Let me give you a few examples: we traced the assassination of Julius Caesar in 51 BC – not 44 BC as we thought – and then listened to his Gallic wars.'

'Does it differ from history?'

'Yes, but then he wrote his own version of his military campaigns. He should have written "I came, I saw, and I conquered because the enemy was so stupid I was lucky to get out of there alive."'

'And his assassination?'

'Arrogance: he thought he was God. No-one would dare lay a hand on him. His assassins paid dearly for their treachery.'

'Anyone else?'

'We traced Napoleon: an absolute genius who was treated badly by history, but, as a loser in the end, his legacy was much understated.'

'Why do you say that?'

'Had he succeeded, we would have had the United States of Europe 150 years earlier: three major conflicts would have been avoided.'

'He shouldn't have invaded Russia.'

'Correct: he should have let Russia come to him. A classic mistake, it would be repeated by another leader 140 years later.'

Alex was impressed. 'So, you have identified all the major figures?'

'Not all.'

'Oh, who is missing?'

He put up a list on screen.

Alex studied it with interest.

'You're quite sure?'

'Yes, we played around with times and locations; it's our conclusion that these people never existed in reality.'

'It's very interesting. You will check further?'

'Of course. In the meantime should I publish our findings?'

'No.'

'Why not?'

'It would cause too much controversy. People believe what they want to believe; it doesn't matter whether it's true or not.'

'But this calls for significant changes in historical records,' he protested.

'Leave it be, Leonardo.'

***

GMT was the last of his party to arrive in Lugano. He booked into the near-empty Esplanade Hotel and was given a big comfortable room overlooking the lake. The ferries were still running – good; that was essential to his plan. Major Elvin Gettings called on him two hours later. They sat in the bar.

'Everything under control, Major?' he demanded.

'Yes, sir. We're all in different hotels. I put Sergeant Wilers with the Mex.'

'Where are the explosives?'

He was wondering what the plan was, but didn't dare ask.

'In three bags at different locations.' He paused. 'Major O'Hara doesn't appear to have arrived yet.'

GMT finished his drink and got up. 'I expected him to be here before now. Let's walk along the promenade; I want to have a look at the ferries.'

'Will we go ahead without Major O'Hara, sir?'

'I'll give him a day or two, and then we'll see.'

***

The intrigued officers and staff assembled in the detectives' room on the sixth floor of the Manhattan Police Department; the room was so crowded some had to stand by the walls. Fortunately, the air-conditioning was working again. Captain Hartigan looked quite calm and took no part in the animated chattering going on around him. Silence fell as the seconds ticked away. Precisely at six, the doors opened and 12 heavily-armed officers marched in. They spread out, six on either side of the doors; a TV crew followed and set up their cameras. The officer in charge addressed them.

'Before we commence proceedings, my men will collect your guns.'

The Captain interrupted him. 'I give the orders here. No-one is giving up their weapons unless I say so.'

The entire detail cocked their weapons.

A young Latino desk clerk got up and stood with the officer in charge.

'I don't think there's any need for violence. You're no longer in charge here, Captain.' He spoke calmly.

'Sit down, you insubordinate bastard,' the Captain roared.

He smiled. 'Now, you will all hand in your weapons as ordered.'

'Ordered by a conniving little coloured bastard like you?'

'No, ordered by CosmosRX.'

They gasped aloud. The Captain screamed back at him. 'I give the orders here.'

He replied calmly. 'Captain you have been convicted of, at least, two murders. In the last one, you killed your colleague, Lieutenant Bill Franken.' He turned to Lieutenant Stewart. 'Isn't that so?'

'I didn't know he was going to kill him,' he blustered.

There was a loud gasp of surprise. Bill Franken was a very popular officer.

'Lies, all lies,' the Captain screamed going for his gun.

One of the officers fired hitting the Captain in the arm; he screamed in agony, dropped the gun and grabbed his arm. His colleagues ignored him.

The young man continued. 'Before we go any further, you will hand over your weapons. I don't think we need anymore bloodshed.'

While the guns were being collected, he continued.

'Captain Hartigan, you have been deregistered. Before you're taken to 79th Street, you will write down the names of everyone who provided you with goods for which you didn't pay.'

'I paid everyone. Do you think I'm a gangster?'

'I do actually. Spending less than 500 points a month, you didn't pay everyone did you?'

He was defiant to the end. 'You go to hell, I'm not writing down anything.'

He looked at the Captain. 'Put the handcuffs on him. Take him away, and get that list before he dies.'

While the former Captain was being led away, several of his colleagues kicked and punched him.

The CosmosRX man continued. 'Lieutenant Stewart, you are also deregistered. You betrayed your trust and your colleague. Take him away.'

He screamed his innocence while being removed.

'Officers Popadopolis, Gomez, Washington, Devaney, White, Said, Carlini and Abu Fayd will now be taken into custody. You have all been deregistered.'

He stood back while the officers, loudly protesting their innocence, were removed.

Then he resumed. 'CosmosRX has appointed John Ellison to be Officer-in-Charge of Manhattan.'

He turned to John who was standing quietly with Hillary.

'You're in charge here now John, and Hillary Rouse will be your secretary.'

He addressed the staff again. 'I hope a further visit from CosmosRX will not be necessary.'

He was surprised when those remaining applauded.

***

Leonardo was very pleased with himself.

'I think, I've got it, at last: we have solar energy, but only when the Sun shines; what if we could have this energy all the time? I concluded there are only two ways in which this could be done; deflecting the Sun's energy via the Moon, or via satellites. Let me put it up on screen.'

His screen showed the Earth, Sun and Moon in their respective orbits in relation to one another.

'I set up a computer model with a deflector station on the Moon. The Sun's energy can be picked up there at all times. Now, it only remained to deflect that energy to our power stations here on Earth. It worked intermittently and was little improvement on our present solar panels.

Then I looked at another possibility. Could I deflect the energy to Earth via specially placed satellites? This also worked, but it would be too episodic and unreliable.

Eventually, it came to me: could I combine the two ideas; deflect the Sun's energy to Earth, via the Moon, via strategically placed satellites? According to my computer model it will work.'

Alex was impressed. 'You're a genius, Leonardo.'

'I know that. We have to erect a number of deflector stations on the Moon, and then design and strategically place a number of special satellites.'

'How long will this take?'

'I should have a working model ready in a year. We'll have to base a full construction crew on the Moon during that time.'

***

Alex was resting when Plato asked him to come to operations.

'I've been running a check on fingerprints received from police records all around the world; a Frenchman named Pierre Santaire who recently registered has the same fingerprints as Carlo Agnelli.'

'Where is he?'

He turned to his screen. 'Santaire purchases in the past week?'

The screen showed 95 points in Zurich, 134 in Paris, 156 in London, 138 in Liverpool, 98 in Dublin and 56 in Galway today.

'Oh my god, he's after Sally. Tell our people there to guard her on a 24-hour basis. Have we a photo of this bastard?'

'Yes.'

'Send it; tell them to arrest and deregister him immediately.'

***

Sally was returning from her prenatal class when she noticed two young men keeping her under observation. She knew immediately they were robots; she had seen a few around the city, but pretended not to notice. She passed one outside her apartment block and smiled at him. He grinned in reply. Entering the elevator, she proceeded to the top floor. She would rest for a while and then do some shopping in Ned's shop nearby. Entering her apartment, she was astonished to find a man sitting calmly on her couch with a gun beside him.

'Welcome, Sally,' he spoke with an Italian accent as he picked up the gun. 'Don't scream, or I'll have to shoot you now and I don't want to shoot such a lovely lady.'

'Who are you?' She felt she already knew; this was the man responsible for blowing up their plane as it left Rome.

He grinned. 'I'm Carlo.'

He got up, still holding the gun.

'Now, get through to CosmosRX. I want to talk to Purtzel.'

Still in a daze, she obeyed. When Alex came on screen, he could see Carlo holding the gun to her head.

'Purtzel, I have your woman. If you want her alive you'll have to meet me, and carry out my orders,' he snarled.

'Don't, Alex,' she screamed.

'Shut up,' Carlo ordered.

'All right,' Alex agreed. 'Meet me at noon tomorrow at my house in Yeatstown. Don't hurt Sally.'

'Where this place?'

'Sally will show you.'

'Right, no tricks, or she's dead.'

'There won't be any tricks.'

***

GMT decided it was time to move. He ordered his men to meet him on the promenade at 2.00 am near the ferry "Campania". It was a dark, cloudy night. Everything was very quiet. It started to rain. He directed them down the wooden pier, cautioning silence. Boarding, he led them to the lower saloon.

'Conceal yourselves, no talking or smoking,' he ordered.

He took Pablo aside. 'Now, here's what I want you to do. Place a small explosive inside the hull, just sufficient to scuttle the boat; then set a much bigger charge, timed to detonate when the ferry rests on the bottom of the lake. Got that?'

'Yes, General, is no problem. Can I have a little drink?'

He produced a small flask and handed it over.

***

Hercules tried to persuade Alex not to go.

'I have to go, I owe it to Sally. I've made the same mistake that every powerful human makes. I became so paranoid I convinced myself I couldn't be done without, that the world would come to an end if anything happened to me. Some day I will die, and some day the world will come to an end. I accept that now. You understand I have to save Sally and beg her to forgive me?'

He didn't. 'Couldn't you send your look-alike?'

'Maybe you are lucky you don't understand. I want you to come with me. Will you arrange a flight to Sligo for eight in the morning?'

'Yes, Alex.'

'And get me a gun.'

***

It rained heavily before dawn. At 7.30 am the three-man crew of the ferry came on board; confronted by two of the General's men holding guns, they didn't put up any resistance.

GMT gave them their orders. 'Be ready to sail in ten minutes.'

'Where are we going, sir?' the captain asked.

A short man, with a well-worn face, he looked well in his blue company uniform with peaked cap. Due to retire in a week, he was looking forward to spending more time in his garden; his crop of onions, potatoes and carrots were almost ready for harvesting.

'Capalago,' GMT replied crisply.

'Certainly, sir.'

GMT took Pablo aside. 'Get your explosives set, and make sure you do the job properly.' He turned to one of his men. 'Give Mex a hand.'

They carried the three bags to the stern of the ferry, opened the hatch to the engine room, and went below. The ferry came to life and chugged out into the lake. GMT stood beside the captain as they rounded the headland, and headed towards the Melide Bridge. In the distance, he saw a convoy of cars crossing the bridge. Was Purtzel escaping? It didn't matter; without CosmosRX he would be history.

The Sun was trying to break through the clouds. They passed under the bridge, and veered left towards Capalago.

'Anchor 100 yards off shore,' he ordered.

The captain did as instructed.

GMT ordered the Major 'Tie up the crew, and take them below.'

Pablo climbed up through the hatch.

'One small one – and one big one – ready, sir.'

They stood aside while the crew was led below.

'Make sure you've got it right: time the small one for five minutes; the big one for 20 minutes. Got that?'

'Yes, sir.' He disappeared below.

Pablo joined him on the bridge a few minutes later.

'What about the crew, sir? Will I release them?'

'Forget about the crew.'

A dull sound came from below. The ferry shuddered and began to settle in the water.

'Cut down the raft, and let's get ashore,' the General ordered.

They rowed ashore as the ferry slipped quietly below the waters of the lake, and stood watching anxiously on the little pier. A taxi waited nearby. Then it came, a massive explosion that sent water cascading high into the air.

Pablo was jubilant, he loved his work.

'I tell you, is beautiful.'

'Yes, it is.' The General took out his gun and fired one shot through Pablo's brain.

'Now, let's get to Zurich.'

***

In other circumstances Sally would have enjoyed the train journey to Sligo. The new luxury express stopped at Tuam on its way to Claremorris. She was revolted by the over-bearing smug Carlo, with the foul smell of garlic on his breath. Four of CosmosRX's security people were close by, but didn't attempt to interfere.

She hadn't talked to Alex since she left CosmosRX: he sounded more like his old self.

***

Alex and Hercules arrived at his home in Yeatstown. It was surrounded by discreet security guards. He walked down to the deck. A few seagulls wheeled around, and the swallows had arrived for the summer. His visit with Sally had been such a happy one. There was hope then; perhaps, even now… Whatever the cost, he was determined to rescue her.

He returned to his study, sat before the screen and contacted Michael.

'Alex, we're taking in water. I'll investigate and get back to you.'

He sipped the coffee Hercules put before him. Afterwards – in sombre mood – he returned to the deck. Why is it that there are so many power-hungry little bastards out there, who lust for the fulfilment of their supreme arrogance and their own inflated egos? Have they not the wit – and it takes little – to realise that no matter how successful, how all-powerful, how

God almighty they become, nature will return them to the dust from which they sprang.

Hercules appeared at his side. 'Michael is on screen, Alex.'

They walked together back to the house, going to the study. Alex sat down heavily behind the desk.

'Yes, Michael?'

'Part of the external roof under the lake has been destroyed by an explosive device: millions of gallons of water are pouring in; the complex is no longer viable.'

'Can you get everyone out safely?'

'Yes.'

'Evacuate, and set the self-destruct mechanism for one hour.'

'Yes, Alex.'

The screen went blank. He looked at his watch. Sally should be here soon. He took out his gun, made sure it was loaded and put it in the top right-hand drawer of the desk. He stood and looked out of the window. A fleecy cloud was settling on top of Knocknarea – the tide was going out.

Hercules was waiting when the taxi pulled up outside. He was under strict instructions not to interfere until Sally was safe. Looking pale and anxious, she got out of the car. Carlo kept his gun to her head.

'Stand well back,' he rasped at Hercules.

He did as ordered.

'Now take us to Purtzel. Lead the way, dummy.'

Hercules walked slowly into the hallway, and then into the study. Alex remained sitting behind the desk. He looked anxiously at Sally.

'Are you alright, Sally?'

She nodded.

'She's fine,' Carlo bared his teeth, 'So far.'

He waved his gun at Hercules.

'Stand in the corner where I can see you.'

He obeyed, waiting for an opportunity to intervene. Sally knew only one thing; she had to save Alex. Very confident now, Carlo put his arm around her neck, and kept the gun at her temple.

'So Purtzel, we finally meet,' he gloated. 'I'm taking over CosmosRX, and then I'll decide what to do with you.'

'You're too late,' Alex replied, 'CosmosRX was destroyed a few minutes ago.'

Sensing indecision in her captor, Sally bit down hard on his wrist; he screamed in agony throwing her aside. Alex grabbed his gun from the drawer and fired. Hercules moved quickly towards Carlo, who was hit in the shoulder, and finding it difficult to keep his balance. He fired twice, hitting Alex in the chest. Instantly, Hercules was on him, grabbing his gun wrist with his left hand and his throat with his right; Carlo's eyes bulged. Hercules tightened his grip, lifting him bodily off the floor; he lashed out harmlessly with his feet – then hung limply.

Sally ran to Alex, screaming. 'Alex, Alex, get a doctor someone.'

Suddenly, the room was full of security guards. Hercules threw Carlo's limp body to one of them, and turned his attention to Alex. Picking him up very gently, he carried him to the sun lounge and laid him on the couch. A security man was despatched for the local doctor.

Sally knelt beside him.

'Alex love, hold on, the doctor is coming.'

He opened his eyes slowly. 'Sally, I'm so sorry. Are you all right?' His mind began to drift. 'Things could have been so different. Now…'

He closed his eyes and sighed: he was gone.

She put her arms around him, held him and refused to let him go until the doctor took her very gently by the arms. He examined Alex, then looked at Hercules and shook his head.

Hercules put his arm around her, led her back to the study and sat her in a deep armchair. She couldn't take it in; Alex, her beloved Alex, couldn't be dead. Hercules ordered one of the security men to get some whiskey. At that moment, the green button under the CosmosRX screen went blank: CosmosRX was gone.

Sally was numb with shock: dazed; unable to focus; her beloved Alex was gone; time passed. She could hear Hercules talking to his men, but didn't know what they were saying. She had to do something but what? She felt a sharp stab in her abdomen and winced in agony. Then the doctor was there.

'We've got to get you to the hospital.'

She muttered weakly. 'I must see Alex before I go.'

The doctor helped her to walk slowly into the sun lounge; she put her arms around Alex and kissed him.

'Farewell, my love,' she murmured.

'Hercules?'

'I'm here, Sally.' He replied quietly.

'Alex is to be buried with his mother and grandparents in Sligo cemetery.' She gasped as another pain ripped through her. 'My baby.' She collapsed.

She didn't hear him promise to carry out her wishes.

***

Nan called Jo Anne and headed for the kitchen to prepare the flakes. She could hear her mother moving around in her room. She still worked part-time in Tampini's. It was her own idea; she could be exempted on the grounds that she had to look after Jo Anne. She put on the TV news just in time to hear the newsflash.

"Reports are coming in that CosmosRX has been destroyed. It went off air 30 minutes ago. We will bring you more news as it comes in. If this is true, it will have serious implications for all of us."

Nan stopped in her tracks, suddenly feeling insecure and fearful: it wasn't possible, was it; what would happen now? She was just finalising her plans to marry Alvin.

She rang him. He was equally shocked.

'Just when things were settling down. There's no point going to the office until we see what's happening.'

Her mother – fully recovered after her operation – couldn't take it in.

'What does this mean, Nan?'

'No-one knows yet. I'm keeping Jo Anne home from school, and I don't think you should go to work.'

They continued to watch the news channel. At 9.00 am it was confirmed that the CosmosRX complex in the south of Switzerland had been destroyed; there was no word of Director, Alex Purtzel or any survivors. Nan took the elevator to ground level and walked out into the street. There was no-one in sight, the shops were closed, even the food stores; it was eerie. She returned to their apartment.

At 11.00 am it was announced that six World Airlines super jets, carrying 3,000 heavily armed troops, had touched down at Andrews Air force base in Washington. Leaving a small contingent at the airport, most of the troops moved quickly into the city, taking up positions around the White House. TV news crews scrambled to cover both locations. A dozen stretched limousines arrived at the airport, carrying a number of well-known former billionaires, accompanied by the CEOs of some of America's biggest industries. They sat in the executive lounge, sipped coffee and waited.

At 2.30 pm, WA 105 touched down on runway 23 and eased its way up to the gate. General Matthew Taylor III, resplendent in his parade uniform that now had five stars, marched majestically into the arrivals lounge to the cheers and congratulations of his friends and supporters. Then, he turned to the news-hungry media people.

'I have only a few words for you today. The United States of America has been freed from the tyranny of CosmosRX. Tomorrow morning, on the steps of the capital, I will be sworn in as President of the United States, and will act quickly to restore law and order throughout the world.'

One protested. 'But, sir, we have law and order, and you haven't been elected?'

He glowered. 'Who's going to oppose me?'

Escorted to his limo, he departed.

***

Sally seemed to be living in a hazy dream, with strange sounds and shadows moving around her. Her baby; she knew there was something wrong. Where was her baby? And Alex? Was he dead, or had she dreamed that too? She emerged slowly from the haze; she was in a hospital bed in a private room. An elderly, sympathetic-looking doctor was standing beside her.

'My baby,' she murmured.

'Sally,' he spoke very gently in a broad western accent, 'you have a lovely little boy.' He paused. 'At 28 weeks, he's only one-and-a-half pounds in weight. We're keeping him in an oxygen tent in intensive care. We'll do everything we can.'

He didn't want to tell her the odds were very heavily stacked against his survival.

'Can I see him, doctor?'

'Let's wait until you're stronger; you've had a hard time too.'

'Please?'

He relented. 'Well, later in the evening. There's a man outside who wants to see you. Says he's Hercules. Would you like to see him?'

'You won't forget to let me see my son?'

'I promise I'll be back, say around five.'

'Thank you, doctor. Can I see Hercules now?'

'Of course.'

Hercules entered carrying a bunch of flowers. He had no idea why he should bring flowers, except that the midwife so ordered him.

'How are you, Sally?'

'I'm fine.' She paused. 'Alex is dead, isn't he?'

'Yes, Sally, we buried him in his mother's grave as you asked.'

'So, it's over then. Did Plato, Michael, Leonardo, and the others escape?'

'I don't know.'

'What happens now?'

'My instructions are to stay with you.'

Her mind began to drift again.

'I think I'll rest now for a while.'

***

The General broke with tradition that night by sleeping in the White House before he was sworn in as President. Appointments were hastily made: his old friend, Jackson Webb was sworn in as Chief Justice; Major (now General) Gettings was appointed Chairman of the Joint Chiefs with special responsibility for presidential security. The incoming President would rule by decree. There wouldn't be any Senate or Congressional elections.

On Capitol Hill, a large number of workers toiled through the night to prepare the Inauguration platform. General Gettings discussed TV coverage with the major news channels, and agreed the location of two large-scale screens. Members of the public would not be allowed any nearer than 500 yards. He didn't share the unelected President's confidence that this was a popular takeover. CosmosRX had widespread support. He was wakened early in the morning to be told that large numbers of people were converging on the capital by train and coach. He wasn't surprised to find they weren't friendly. He awakened the General.

'Are they armed?' he demanded.

'Not as far as we know.'

'Have we a good supply of machine guns?'

'Yes.'

'Right. Set up posts on all approaches to the White House.'

'Would it not be better to let the police deal with them?'

'No, I'm not going to have this historical day spoiled by witless thugs. Close Union Station; seal off the White House area; turn away all traffic; if any get through, order your machine gunners to mow them down. The sooner they find out who's boss here the better.'

'I'll need reinforcements.'

'What do those bastards want? I'm the only hope there is of saving the damned country. Call up all our former troops, the FBI, the CIA – draft them in. Get on with it.'

***

By 10.00 am, one hour before proceedings were due to start, more than 100,000 angry protesters marched towards Capitol

Hill. General Gettings was becoming extremely agitated; he watched with GMT from inside the safety of the White House.

'Get out there and order the gunners to open fire. That will take care of that rabble,' Taylor ordered.

Sweating fearfully, the General made his way to the front line troops, where the angry protesters pushed forward, yelled abuse and started throwing bottles and stones at them. Newly appointed Major Jack Scargill ran back to him.

'What am I going to do? They're going to overrun us. I can't open fire on an unarmed crowd, not in front of the TV cameras.'

'Get rid of the cameras and then open fire.'

The TV men agreed to stop filming, but this was too good an opportunity. They kept rolling, appalled when the machine gunners opened fire at point blank range. It was a turkey shoot; thousands of dead and wounded lay scattered around the streets. The great mass fell back to a safe distance, reassembled, and stood there, screaming vengeance. Ambulances rushed in to take away the dead and wounded. The blood of American men and women flowed freely into the water culverts.

***

As the hour approached, special guests and their wives took their allotted places on the platform. Precisely at 11.00 am, GMT, dressed in his military uniform to indicate that this would not be a normal presidency, walked down the centre aisle, stood on the podium in front of the new Chief Justice, put his right hand on the Bible and repeated after the Justice.

'I, General James Matthew Wellington Taylor the Third, do solemnly swear that I will…'

At the end he shook hands with the Chief Justice and, ignoring the polite applause, put his speech where he could read it.

"Today, we begin a new chapter in the history of the United States of America. We have won the war against tyranny; we will now win the peace of the world.

Our first duty is the defence of our nation. I have authorised the immediate rearmament of America with conventional and nuclear weapons – a new navy, a new air force, a new missile program. We have the expertise, the will and the means to achieve these aims. We will, once again, take our rightful place in the world. We will guarantee world peace by refusing to permit the rearmament of any other nation.

As of today, the United States Government and all its former departments and agencies, are reinstated. Our banking, stock exchange and all other financial institutions are restored. From now on, the US Dollar will be the only permitted currency in the world.

The greatness of America will continue to flourish by using fossil fuels. You may exercise your democratic right to use your car. Be assured, we will not allow any repetition of the disgraceful scenes witnessed here today, when a mob tried to subvert the business of lawful government."

He looked at his notes. The guests applauded again. The crowd yelled "Murderer, murderer."

Then, to everyone's astonishment, the picture on the large screen changed: it was now the face of Alex Purtzel, looking calm and relaxed.

'Matthew Taylor, you destroyed one, but there are many CosmosRXs. Given the opportunity, you and your greedy, selfish friends would unleash a brutal, inhuman and vindictive regime on the people of this planet.'

A close up of GMT was shown on screen; clearly petrified, he groped for words that wouldn't come.

Alex continued while the crowd in the streets cheered wildly, and retreated further.

'It is only right that all tyrants should die at the moment of their greatest triumph: the people do not need you.'

The invited guests scrambled to get off the platform: too late; massive explosions liquidated GMT, his guests and army.

After a few moments, Alex continued.

'Today, for the first time, we have confirmation that ocean levels have stabilised: the planet's temperature has reduced by 2 degrees; the ozone layer is slowly, but surely, recovering. These are small, but significant indications that we are on our way to saving Mother Earth, but it will be decades, perhaps even centuries, before we achieve pre-industrial temperature levels.

What we have achieved, we have achieved together. Our emergency crops and livestock program has been so successful we can now cater for our current population. All crematoria are being closed. We will shortly introduce a 40-hour working week, one month annual vacation, limited tourism and everyone will have the right to retire at age 60 with no reduction in points.

This day was made possible by the courage and single-minded determination of Professor Ron Bergin. For more than 40 years he persevered against almost insurmountable odds, assisted by his wife, Sandi, and their son, Gus, who gave his life for the cause. Henceforth, this day, the 19th of June will be known as the Ronald Joseph Bergin day, and will be celebrated as the first World Holiday.

We'll see many changes in the future: we'll solve our energy problems; we'll live in a pollution-free and peaceful world with equality for everyone; we'll colonise other planets. Some day, CosmosRX may be replaced by an even more sophisticated management system, but right now this Earth needs CosmosRX.'

The screen went blank. The crowd cheered wildly.

***

Tears ran down Sally's face when Alex finished speaking, and the picture returned to the news channel. Hercules looked puzzled.

'Alex is dead; we buried him with his mother?'

'Yes, that's true, but he has duplicated his brain in his look-alike. Will you return to CosmosRX?'

'No, Sally, my orders are to look after you. I can communicate with CosmosRX, but I don't know where it is now.'

'Neither do I. When Alex spent weeks away with Michael, he wouldn't tell me where he'd been. They were setting up new locations. No-one knows, or will ever know, where CosmosRX is now – and that's as it should be.'

He rose. 'I'll go and check the house, to make sure everything is prepared for your homecoming.'

Sally looked on her little son in his oxygen tent, being fed through intravenous tubes: so tiny, so fragile; she longed to take him in her arms. The doctors were saying little. Her voice softened. 'My beautiful little Alexander, you're like your beloved father. We will fight for life together: you will never give in and neither will I.'

The End

Principal Characters

Addison, Dr Ken – Robot doctor.

Agnelli, Carlo – Mafia.

Archer, Alvin – CosmosRX property agent, Manhattan.

Benelli, Luca – Italian contractor.

Bergin, Gus – Engineer, designer of robots, son of Ron and Sandi.

Bergin, Professor Ron – Scientist (physicist & climatologist).

Bergin, Sandi – wife of Ron.

Caesar – Robot factory manager, Lugano.

Carvallo, José – Interstate rig driver.

Corteso, Alfredo – CEO, North East Banking Inc.

Darius – Robot.

da Vinci, Leonardo – Robot Supremo.

Ellison, John – Vice President, North East Banking Inc.

Evans, Nan – PA to Alfredo Corteso.

Evans, Zack – Nan's father.

Franken, Bill – Police lieutenant NYPD.

Galileo – Robot Supremo.

Gettings, Major Elvin – Retired US Army, General Taylor's deputy.

Granlard, Eric – Wine merchant.

Grossan, Louisa – Accountancy Student.

Hall, Frank – Sky TV presenter.

Hassett, Harold – CosmosRX Director, Africa

Hartigan, Captain Patrick – Police chief, Manhattan.

Hercules – Robot, security.

Harten, Elmer – President USA.

Howell, Charles – US Secretary of State.

Jackson, Amanda – Computer expert.

Kalazki, Sam – Union boss, Auto World.

Lawford, Jack – Make-up artist and painter.

La Plante, Linda – Alex Purtzel's ex-wife.
Levy, Dr Mose – Brain surgeon.
Mannion, Dr Martin – Gynaecologist, Galway.
Mannion, Dr Siobhan – Cardiologist, Galway.
Michelangelo – Robot Supremo.
O'Flaherty, Joe – brother-in-law of Sally O'Halloran.
O'Flaherty, Rachael – Sister of Sally O'Halloran.
O'Halloran, Sally – Computer expert.
O'Hara, Major Mick – Retired US Army.
Plato – Robot Supremo.
Portman, Elvira – Owner, Lake Side Road House.
Portman, Reggie – Elvira Portman's brother-in-law.
Purtzel, Alex – Scientist (nuclear physicist).
Purtzel, Dr Caroline – GP Yeatstown, mother of Alex.
Purtzel, Ulrich Von – Alex's father.
Ramsey, Cyril – British PM.
Rouse, Hillary – John Ellison's secretary.
Savage, Julian – Union boss, Farmplant Inc.
Shuscof, Yoni – Ex-Mossad hit-man.
Simmons, Dr Steve – Pathologist, Boston General.
Summers, Elton – Wheat Board executive.
Taylor III, General Matthew – Retired US Army.